The Roots That Clutch

The Roots That Clutch

By Joseph Kerwin

Writers Club Press
San Jose New York Lincoln Shanghai

The Roots That Clutch

Writers Club Press
an imprint of iUniverse, Inc.

For information address:
iUniverse, Inc.
5220 S. 16th St., Suite 200
Lincoln, NE 68512
www.iuniverse.com

ISBN: 0-595-25248-6 (pbk)
ISBN: 0-595-65053-8 (cloth)

Printed in the United States of America

for Regan

my ideal reader

"What are the roots that clutch, what branches grow Out of this stony rubbish?"

—T. S. Eliot, *The Waste Land*, 1922

CHAPTER 1

Henry died on a Thursday. I didn't know he was dead until halfway through the following week, though. That's how long it took for the news to reach me. So there was a whole weekend when my brother was alive in my mind, but he was really dead already. When I did find out, the news was a shock, of course, and the first chance I had, I allowed myself to get completely drunk.

It was Christmas Eve night, 1918, in a little beer bar beneath a ten-room hotel. The cold was everywhere, and it didn't help that someone kept opening the door. The wind that was circling outside would jump up and thrust its way in every time, blowing our cards all over the table. The boys at my table would yell at the others to keep the damn door closed, but they kept opening it. They had to stumble out into the cold and do their business in the little alleyway, after all.

The only deck of cards we had was a Belgian deck. It had thirty-two cards, with everything below the seven spot missing. We played some creative versions of poker and gin with that deck, sitting at a round table in the center of the room. A fair amount of currency changed hands, even if it was usually chocolate or cigarettes. We drank as we played, waving at the plump girl behind the bar to keep bringing the beer.

She didn't speak English, but I think her father owned the place. He was the severe man in the corner whose black, beady eyes stared out from behind a mass of gray hair and smoke. He never stopped smoking the whole time we were there. The tendrils of smoke floating in front of his face were the exact same dirty grayish color as his beard. He would nod at her whenever we waved, agitating the swirling smoke, and she would bring us more. I imagine they lived in the room behind the bar.

She had served us our black bread and sausage that night. That had been one of the best dinners I had during my time overseas, despite the fact that it was a very German meal. I wondered if perhaps the last soldiers this taverne had entertained were German. Laon had supposedly been occupied by them. We'd washed the food down with a burgundy, had shelled almonds and chocolate cake for dessert, and then resumed our drinking with a brandy from the bar. It was Christmas Eve, after all.

The officers had eaten with us, but they left after dinner to sleep at a nicer hotel down the road. I guess they figured that nothing could happen now, with everything over with and all of us just waiting to go home. They probably weren't supposed to leave us alone, but I'm sure the captain wanted to sleep in a better place. Another couple of squads who were coming through town were over there, and he and the sergeant knew a few of those officers from training.

They were only allowing us to let loose because it was a holiday, but it was our first real chance to celebrate the end of the fighting. I planned to drink as much as I could that night.

I hadn't had a real conversation about Henry's death with anyone, including my Mother. She had written me a letter a few weeks before, and I had written her back a postcard. Neither of us said anything about it, though. We just talked about when we thought I would be coming home.

The booze swirled around in my head. Someone was speaking to me.

"You gonna deal?" asked Lovejoy.

"Yeah, quit your soldierin' over there," said O'Malley from across the table. I smiled and dealt the cards. Soldiering was a slang term for being lazy that had been used a lot before the war. Everyone knew that the only thing soldiers did back then was dig the canal down south of Mexico. We were probably the only people who kept using the term for each other during the war, though.

"You're the one who's goin' home to more unemployment, soldier O'Malley," said Bill Jarret through his crooked teeth. "You should at least've put some money on the fighting...they bet at Lloyd's on how long it would go."

"Yeah, I'll bet the winners were all English blokes who were already rich as hell," I said, trying to show that I'd rejoined the conversation.

"I'll make all the money I need right here offa you, Billy boy," O'Malley said to Jarret. He took a drink and threw a few coins on the table. "I don't need a job...who knows when we're goin' home anyway."

"Hey, maybe you could be secretary of war after this," said Delgrew. A few of us looked at him. "Anyone could do better than Baker."

"Willie, what are you talkin' about?" Bridges asked without looking up from his cards. A cigarette hung from the side of his mouth. Tommy Bridges was proud of his mustache, which was really nothing more than a few straggly dark hairs. I guess he thought a mustache would distract people from the steadily increasing distance between his eyebrows and his hairline.

"I'm just saying we could've been here sooner, and maybe seen some action," Willie said. I knew they were going to make fun of him for saying it.

"Well, we can't all be jingoes like you, Willie," said Jarret. "We can't all just charge right in. Some of us've got to be the conscientious objectors." A jingo was an overzealous soldier, someone who really wanted to fight. Everyone laughed, because Willie Delgrew was the last guy you'd call a jingo. He was used to a little ribbing, though. Willie was a smart guy, and things like that normally didn't bother him. He was probably the smartest of all of us.

"Yeah, jingo..." said O'Malley, whose eyes looked like they were already having trouble focusing. "Have a drink with me to celebrate all our kills." Willie smiled. We all knew that he considered himself a devout Christian, and he never drank.

"You know I can't do that," said Willie. He was a small guy, with curling brown hair and a nose with a round tip. His eyebrows were thin and arched high. His face made him look years younger than he was. Back at camp, one officer was convinced that he was just a kid, trying to sneak into the service.

"God don't mind if you have a little drink," said O'Malley, turning his round, reddish face toward Willie. "I'm a Christian, too."

"When was the last time you saw the inside of a church?" asked Bridges, setting his cards down and collecting the pot.

"I went to church when I was a kid," answered O'Malley. "More times than you've ever been in your life. And I go to confession. I just don't know why a guy's gotta set hisself up to be better'n his neighbors by not drinkin' or smokin' or swearin'."

"Willie's not like that," I said quickly. "He's gonna be the new secretary of war or secretary of state or something while us drunks are cleanin' up his office."

"Why are you talkin'? Why can't he stick up for hisself?" O'Malley was having trouble not falling out of his chair now. His eyes couldn't even find me as he spoke. They were just sort of darting around. The rosy splotches were spreading on his cheeks.

"Oh shut it, O'Malley," said Bridges. "If he wants to wait 'till he's older to do his drinkin' and have his first woman, well, let 'im. It'll probably be your little sister by that time." They guffawed.

Willie was really only accepted by them because I stood up for him. We were both from the same town, and I had known Willie when we were just kids. We had also gone to the same high school, although we weren't as close during that time. But when we met up again at training camp back home, we started talking and remembering things from when we were little. We stuck together after that.

"You know what the Germans said about us?" asked Jarret after a moment's silence. "Their saying was *God punish our enemies.* That's what they would say. I seen it on a sign, and a guy told me what it said. He heard it from a captured Fritzie...used to give the guy cigarettes and the guy would tell him what things said."

"So what?" asked Lovejoy.

"And they went to church all the time too, I'll bet," Jarret answered. "But God didn't punish us, even though they asked him to."

"Maybe he just hasn't done it yet," I said, thinking I was clever.

"No...I'm just sayin'," he shrugged toward Willie, "you think you know what God wants you to do, but you don't really know."

"Leave 'im alone," said Lovejoy.

"I guess God punished the fella hanging in that barn," said Bridges with a laugh.

"I think that boy punished himself 'cause he didn't want to go through what we'd do to him," said O'Malley.

There was a story going around that a German soldier was hanging in a barn nearby. Sarge had told us about it at dinner, but he'd warned us not to go looking for the barn. I think he was afraid that we would try to go get some souvenirs from the German uniform. The soldier probably had a lot of stuff with him, since they always gathered up everything after an engagement. They had heavy knapsacks, too, that were bound with straps and covered on the back with undressed red bull's hide. At least that's what I'd heard at a little store where a Frenchman was trying to sell me one. I think that's what he said. I'd like to get my hands on one of those for free, I thought. And I knew that any German pins or decorations would really impress a gal back home.

The story went that the dead soldier had been left over from the occupation of Laon. Rather than be killed, he'd hanged himself in the barn when the American boys got there. For some reason the owner of the barn decided he'd rather lock it up than have to touch the body, so it was still there. I wondered how decayed it was.

"We would've made him string himself up, if we'd got there first," I said loudly, echoing O'Malley. I was angry now. I wanted to laugh and joke about the soldier's suicide. I wanted to make sure that there was nothing somber or serious about the thought of him killing himself. I hoped the rope breaking his neck had been painful for him. Maybe he was the one that had killed Henry, after all. They all deserved to be dead. That was why we were there, wasn't it?

"You think Sarge would really mind, if we just went to take a look?" asked Jarret.

"Not if he didn't know," said Lovejoy with a smile, waving the French girl over again.

"Hey…here comes Willie's best girl now," laughed Bridges, knocking the ash from his cigarette onto the floor.

"He wants a beer," O'Malley shouted at her, waving his floppy arm toward Willie. The poor girl looked around in confusion. She had the same dark eyes as her father.

"This is our greatest soldier," said Jarret. He seemed to think that the louder he spoke, the easier it would be for her to understand. "Single-handedly won the war for the AEF. Say *Jingo*. *Jingo*…can you say it?"

"Jingo?" she finally said quietly, looking at Willie. This brought forth endless laughter from everyone. Willie looked at me.

"The war's over, buddy," I said. "God looked out for you. Have one on me."

She brought his beer, giggling a little as she set it down in front of him. Her pudgy hand had little, round nails. Her fingers were a little like the sausages we'd eaten, I thought. I almost said so, but then I realized that only a drunk person would say something like that.

Willie thanked her quietly, and she left, still giggling to herself. He looked at the beer for a while. I thought he was going to say something to me, but he didn't.

I lost a hand of the game doing something stupid. If I'd been paying better attention and not worrying about him I wouldn't have lost. It made me mad, so I ignored him, talking loudly with the guys while playing the next round. After all, it wasn't my job to babysit him. He could do whatever he wanted. It was a little snobby, anyway, to refuse to drink with people who wanted to be your friends. We had lived through a war, and I got him a drink, and now he was looking at it like he didn't know what to do with it.

No one talked to him as the game went on. I couldn't worry about him all the time, I knew, or they'd start making fun of me along with him.

The next time I looked at him out of the corner of my eye he was drinking. After a few more games, some of the guys started to notice that he'd drank the beer and they got the brandy back out. They all wanted to drink liquor with him. We'd never seen him let loose before, after all.

I remember him smiling a lot, and laughing. The guys even dealt him into a game or two, even though by then the games were beginning to disintegrate. I clapped him on the back a few times. Everyone there had set out to get drunk. It was a celebration that the war was over and we'd all lived. But at the same time I think we were depressed because we weren't spending Christmas at home. We were kids, really. But none of us said anything about that, of course.

We were up for a long while, drinking and singing. I remember O'Malley sitting in a wet puddle on the floor for a while at the end of the night. I think he spilled beer and then fell in it, somehow. I remember him sitting there, with a few playing cards scattered in the beer as well, slowly sliding around him. He giggled at the queen of spades as she stared up at him.

I stamped up the creaky wooden stairs and collapsed on the bed. The mattress was flat and hard, and smelled like mold and beer. The frame was covered with bright, blood-colored rust. There were a few thin, ratty blankets that did very little against the cold in the room. I was too drunk to complain, though. Ted Lovejoy was in the other bed across the room.

I don't know what time it was when I awakened, or what it was exactly that snapped me back to reality. The room was dark and silent. The silence and the cold seemed to go together, somehow. The only light in the room came from a few stars that were visible through the tiny window.

I heard a loud noise then. It sounded like someone stumbling down the stairs, or running down the hall or something. I shot up off the bed like a flash. Then a weight in my head tipped over and jerked me back toward the mattress. I wanted to ask Ted if he'd heard the noise, so I said his name loudly. He growled and turned over.

"What the hell..." His voice was raspy, and he coughed. Even in the dim light I could see that his yellow hair was standing at attention in an unruly spike on top of his head.

"You didn't hear that?" I jerked my thumb toward the hall. He blinked at me, rubbing his eyes. Both of us were still so drunk we could barely tell what was going on.

"It's probably O'Malley fell over tryin' to get outta his trousers," he said. But then we heard voices in the hallway, and we looked at each other.

Immediately we thought of the officers' prank. We lived in constant fear of it. We'd heard all sorts of stories about what they would do to us on a night like this.

"Who's there?" I whispered loudly.

Someone knocked at the door. I pulled it open, and Bridges and O'Malley came barging into the room, laughing.

"What the hell?" asked Lovejoy.

"What time is it?" I asked.

"Oh, shut up, girls," said Bridges.

"Don't you want to meet a real German?" asked O'Malley. His speech was very slurred, and he was having a lot more trouble standing than I was.

We both knew what they meant right away. It wasn't a great idea, of course. But I wasn't going to be the one to say so.

"How far is it to the barn?" asked Lovejoy, trying to push down his cowlick. No one answered, though.

We went out into the hall, and I saw the shapes of several of the boys standing around. They were knocking on all the other doors.

"Go get Willie," Bridges said to me. He pointed toward a room at the end of the hall, near the stairs.

I knocked on the door and pushed it open. I heard someone cry out in the darkness in front of me. This room didn't have a window, so it was completely black. I had startled Willie, and I heard him fumbling with something.

The lamp was illuminated, and the light crawled toward me slowly from the center of the room. It was one of the oil lamps that they had everywhere in France back then. They lit slowly, casting a feeble light. The rich, oily scent was the strongest thing about the lamps. They put off more smell than light.

Willie didn't look so well. His hair was damp, and he was shaking a little. He had put on his glasses in a hurry, and they sat on his nose crookedly. There was no one else in the room.

"Come on," I said. I'm sure he could hear the movement in the hall. He just sort of looked at me.

"Should…should I bring my pack?" he asked, motioning toward it. Should he bring it? I hadn't thought of that. All of our packs held the same things: wool stockings, undershirts, underdrawers, shoes, flannel shirts, blanket, wool breeches, wool coat, overcoat.

"Get your coat," I said. "Let's go." I could tell that he didn't want to be a part of it. But he trusted me. We turned off the lamp and went out into the hall. The boys were trying to be quiet. I guess they were worried about waking up our hosts downstairs. They'd have to be pretty heavy sleepers not to have already heard the commotion in the hall, though.

"You got 'im?" someone asked me as I entered the dark hall. Whoever it was had been right next to me, and I hadn't even seen him.

"Yeah," I said. I ducked back into my room and grabbed my own overcoat.

We filed down the stairs and through the taverne. The smell of beer and sweet liquor was nauseating. The wood floor was sticky, and the tables were a mess of bottles, playing cards, and even some food. A lot of the chairs were overturned. I saw a hairy, black shape scurry away under the bar.

We went out the front door and into the cold night, and my breath steamed around me immediately. Tommy and Ted were in front now, and Willie was looking around, confused. I hadn't even told him where we were going. A lot of the guys probably didn't know. No one said anything, though. They just followed whoever wanted to lead, as usual.

All I knew about the little town of Laon was that it was somewhere between Verdun and Brest, on a railroad line that most of the American Expeditionary Forces hadn't had much use for. Across the street from our hotel was the little shop that we had explored the evening before. It didn't look like a real shop, though. There were no proper shops there, just cottages that had something to sell. Willie had bought some post cards there, Lovejoy and I split some cheeses, and O'Malley even got some underwear. There were also big round disks of bread, fresh butter, milk, eggs, coffee, weak beer, and even cognac. I longed for some of that bread and butter now.

We passed the quiet cottages on the street. The bicycles and dog carts and horses that had been here yesterday were all gone. The night was silent and still. We made our way down the cobbled street, past the tall, narrow stone houses and the crooked little side streets. It was strange, the way the houses were all the same gray color. The roofs came to high peaks, making each one look as if it were reaching as far up as it could, grasping for air.

I wondered if any of us really knew where this barn was. An outsider observing us would have thought we did. We were soldiers, and we took a mission such as this one seriously, even if it was an assignment we'd given ourselves. Rather than an unruly, drunken crowd, we probably looked like a squad on a nighttime exercise.

"How do we know where it is?" I asked Jarret, who was beside me now. He shrugged. He and several others had lit cigarettes.

"Bridges knows," he said. As I heard it later, Bridges and O'Malley had actually asked the French girl about the hanging German soldier, and she had told them where the barn was. I have no idea how they could have communicated with her, though, so I'm not sure if I believe that story. They were leading us somewhere, though. If they didn't know where it was, they certainly thought they did.

We passed more modern homes now, made of burnt red brick, with flower gardens and plum and pear trees in little square patches of grass. Beyond them, the town mill hung out over one side of the little river, and I could hear the sound of the water as we got closer to it. There was a railroad bridge nearby, and we crossed it.

I wondered what sort of buttons, pins, or patches I could take from the German uniform. I thought about where I could hang them on my wall at home. I could probably even convince some people that they came from a soldier I'd killed.

We turned left after the bridge and out into a field. A dark shape loomed ahead of us, just near a stand of gently blowing trees. It was shrouded in shadow, but it gradually grew sharp edges as we approached, and I saw that it was an old barn.

It didn't look as if it had been used by anyone for a long time. The wood itself was rotted black. It was completely boarded up.

I was in the front of the group now, near Bridges and O'Malley. We were almost to the barn.

"How're we gonna get in?" someone asked.

"We'll get in," said Tommy. O'Malley was busy laughing hysterically.

"Someone's gettin' in," he said, trying to control his explosions of laughter.

"It's initiation time," said Bridges, with a wide smile. He turned the smile toward me, and then let out a little laugh. He always had the stupidest sounding laugh. It was more like a yelp, just one quick noise each time.

"What are you talking about?" I asked. He leaned in toward me. Our feet crunched in the grass. Had there been a freeze during the night?

"We're puttin' Willie in," he said.

I just looked at him.

"He's gonna spend the night with our friend," he said. O'Malley laughed so hard he stumbled.

All I had planned on doing was stealing things from the uniform. I had no idea that they'd been planning this. I didn't do anything to stop them, though. I didn't say anything about it at all. It was important to me that the German in there was nothing but a joke. He had to be the punch line of a joke, in one way or the other. He wasn't even a man, decayed or not. He was an animal who had killed Henry. My head swam a little. I wished I hadn't had so much to drink.

News of the plan gradually got to everyone. Willie had no idea, of course. He had been drinking that night, after all, for the first time in his life. The beer had really affected him. That had to be the reason why he had come along with us without protest. He was smiling happily at the scenery now.

There were two boards nailed in front of the barn door, holding it closed. They were a much lighter color than the rest of the structure. Jarret shoved his shoulder against the creaking door several times, shaking the entire barn. He was the type of really skinny guy who thinks he's indestructible. Then, as he stood to one side and rubbed his bruised arm, Lovejoy produced a large knife and started prying the nails out, one by one. Someone else had a knife, too, and they joined in.

When the boards were pulled free and the door opened at last, O'Malley and Bridges stumbled inside. A few seconds later they came back out, somber expressions on their faces. They nodded to the rest of us. A few of the other guys crowded forward, just to see in. No one really wanted to go all the way inside.

When it was my turn, I moved up toward the door. It was dark inside, and only a little starlight came through slats in the roof. It looked completely empty at first. But then I saw something. My vision was still a bit blurred, so I'm not sure what it was.

I saw something hanging there, swinging, in the center. A dark, long shape. Ted must have started it swinging when he hit the barn with his shoulder. I couldn't really make out what it was. I wasn't going to get any closer, though. I knew that if someone decided that I was a good enough victim, I could easily be shoved inside and made to spend the night. That's probably why most of us didn't go in very far. We didn't trust each other when there was a prank in the air.

When it was Willie's turn, though, everything went according to plan. I remember the way his face looked when he stepped up. He looked like a little kid, curious and trusting. They crowded up behind him and shoved him inside. I stayed at the back so I wouldn't have to do it. They pushed the door shut after him as quickly as they could, and shoved the boards back across it, pushing the nails in with the meat of their palms.

I don't think Willie even struggled against the door, though. I didn't hear a sound come from in there. It would have been difficult to hear, of course, since everyone was laughing and shouting. But I think he just sort of gave up as soon as it happened. After the laughter and whoops had died down, there was just silence from the barn.

"Just a little initiation, Delgrew," shouted Bridges. "No hard feelin's. If you want to drink with us, you gotta let us have our fun, too."

"It'll make you a man," called Jarret.

I smiled and laughed along with the rest of them. I only felt badly when I thought of his face in the moonlight, just before he stepped up to look. But it was no big deal, really. Just a silly prank. I tried not to think of his face.

We stood around in the field for a while, smoking and talking, lying around and looking up at the stars. I was wrapped tightly in my coat, watching the steam float up from my mouth and nostrils like smoke from a flame. I'm not sure how long Willie was in there. Someone asked if we should go back to the hotel and go to bed, and come get him in the morning. But there was too much chance of getting caught if we went all the way back there. So we decided to stay. We made sure we gave him plenty of time, though. I think I even nodded off right there in the field. We had slept outside before, so it didn't bother me.

"Whadda ya think he's doin' in there?" asked a voice nearby, startling me. The silence of the barn was making everyone uneasy. We were all wishing that he would at least yell a little so we could have a good laugh. But he never made a sound.

"Maybe he's made a new friend in there."

"You think it smells?"

"Depends on how long it's been there."

"Whadda ya think?" It was Ted now. "Should we let him out?"

I sat up and looked around at them. They were all lying around in the grass, looking at me.

"I guess," I said.

"Let 'im out, O'Malley," said Tommy.

"You do it."

"I'll do it," said Jarret. He got up and walked over to the barn. I could see a soft light gently sitting on the horizon now. It would be dawn soon. It was becoming Christmas morning. I tried not to think about what Christmas was like back home. It would never be the same now that Henry was gone. My head hurt from the beer now, and I was already feeling the effects of not having gotten much sleep.

Jarret pulled the boards off the door and threw it open. From where I was sitting, I couldn't see inside.

"Okay, Willie," he said. "Wake up time." Then he just stood there for a while, looking in.

"What's he doing?" I called.

"He's just sittin' there." Jarret squinted into the barn. "Come on, Willie."

Jarret came back with Willie, and we all got up. Willie looked fine. He wasn't happy, clearly, but he looked normal. Tired, perhaps. Everyone was looking at him.

"Just a little joke," Bridges clapped him on the back. "No hard feelings, pal."

"Did you boys have a talk?" asked O'Malley. "You and the German?" He laughed.

Willie looked at me, his face blank. I couldn't tell if he was just very tired or if he had become immune to all of them. It was painful, though, for him to look at me like that.

"We were just having some fun," I said, trying to convince myself as much as him. "It was just a joke."

He nodded then, mustering a little smile. There was something different in his eyes, though. He certainly wasn't happy.

"I'm fine," he said. He coughed a little, then a little more. Then he bent over and vomited into the grass. We all stepped back to give him room, and looked at each other. He raised his head, and a strand of saliva hung from his mouth. He wiped it with the back of his hand and spit again. He tried to smile a little, to show us that he was all right.

"Just had too much to drink," said Jarret, patting Willie's back as he stood back up.

"It's gonna be light soon," said Ted.

We walked back to the hotel at a brisk pace, intent on getting there and into bed before the officers woke up and discovered that we were gone. I told myself that Willie was being a spoilsport. He should have at least laughed along with us to show that there were no hard feelings. It was just a barn, after all.

But he never laughed. He was quiet throughout the walk back. I wanted to ask him about the hanging German, but I just couldn't. Either it had really affected him, or he was just being sore about it. Maybe he was just sulking to make me feel bad, I thought.

When we got back to the hotel and got our packs together, I decided to go down the hall and into his room. Perhaps when no one else was around, I thought, he would talk to me.

He looked up when I entered. He was packing his things quietly. The lamp was burning, giving out its low light.

"Hi," I said. He just kept packing. "Listen, it was just a joke. I just…I just wanted to make sure you were all right. That there're no hard feelings about it or anything." I pulled the door shut. I didn't want anyone to hear us. I knew they would make fun of me for apologizing.

He stopped what he was doing and just looked at me now, a strange expression on his face. He looked as if he had been through quite an ordeal. I could see shadows around his eyes beneath the glasses now, and they had that reddish, puffy look. Perhaps he'd been crying.

"I'm really sorry," I said. I had to say it. He looked so worn out.

He started to nod a little, then. It relieved me somewhat. At least he was acknowledging my presence.

"It wasn't my idea," I said quietly.

And then suddenly, he smiled a little. He laughed.

"You should've seen your face," I said, encouraged now, "when they pushed you in there."

But then his laughter died away. He shook his head, still smiling a little.

"I'm sure it was funny," he said then, looking at the floor.

"So what was in there?" I asked. "I couldn't really see."

He started stuffing things into his pack again, faster now.

"Just what they said," he answered.

"A German?"

"I don't know. It was someone, though."

"Hmm," I nodded. He finished packing and just looked up at me expectantly now.

I just nodded again, not sure what to say. I turned then, starting to leave.

"You know what's funny?" he said. "About the whole thing? Do you wanna know?" He was speaking loudly now.

I turned back again.

"Sure."

The shadows cast by the oil lamp made his face look even more drawn and haggard than it probably was.

"This is nobody's business," he said. "You understand?"

"Yes."

"So I don't want you to tell them about this, because nobody really knows this, all right?"

"Sure."

"Well," he said with a strange little chuckle, "the funny thing is, my…my father…just a few years ago. He hanged himself."

I just looked at him.

"So you see, it's even funnier than they think it is."

I thought about everything I knew about his family. I had never heard anything about this. I knew that his father was dead, and this was something we had in common. I'd never heard how it happened, though.

"I…I'm sorry," I said. "We didn't know."

"I know. That's what I just said. It's not anyone's business. But now you know. I don't want you telling any of them, though."

"I won't."

"Thanks."

Merry Christmas, I thought.

CHAPTER 2

❦

There was a rowboat that had been leaning up against the back of our house for as long as I could remember. I think it had belonged to my Aunt's husband when he was alive. There weren't many fish in the little lake nearby, but every once in a while on a Sunday afternoon I would row out to the center and just sit there with my fishing pole. I never caught anything, but it gave me time to think.

In fact, the last time I caught a fish was a few months before I went through the registration. The water was almost entirely clear then in several places, especially where the creek emptied into the lake, and I could see its brown spots against the white pebbles on the bottom. It darted around on the bottom and then started nibbling on my line, and I reeled it right in. Henry was out there with me that day, and I remember him laughing at how small it was. I thought about cooking it up and eating it, but there wouldn't have been much meat. So Henry pulled it off the hook and held onto it. I kept asking him to hurry up and let it go, because it was going to die soon. He kept fidgeting and dawdling, though, taking his time, knowing that it was bugging me. I could see the sharp-edged gills struggling against the air. I was about to jump at him and knock the fish out of his hand when he finally dropped it back in. It swam away as if nothing had happened.

I hadn't been fishing much since I got back from Europe, though. But I remember I was planning to go on one Sunday during the fall of 1920. It was right after church, and my Mother and my Aunt were straightening up the house.

"I thought you were going fishing," My Mother said as I entered the kitchen.

"I might. What are you doing?"

"We're having some guests…just some young lady friends."

The word *young* sparked my interest. Sometimes they had women from church over for cards, but they certainly weren't young.

"Who are they?" I asked.

I could tell that she didn't want to answer.

"Just women," she said. "Just to talk."

"What are you going to talk about?"

"About our Henry," she finally said quietly, staring out the window above the sink. It took me by surprise, to say the least. The clock ticked loudly.

"Have I met them?" I asked.

"No, they've only been over once before," said my Mother.

"When?" I asked, following her from the kitchen into the dining room.

"It was last week…you were at work," she answered, pulling the tablecloth from the table.

"Why would you talk about him?"

"They help us, honey," she said. "They help us…we're not young like you. This has been very hard on your Aunt and me."

"How can they help you?" I asked. She sat down in one of the chairs. She looked tired.

"Colbert, please," she said. "I won't make you leave. Your Aunt would probably want you to go. But I won't make you. Just let us have this…let us do this, two old ladies."

"What do they know about Henry? How can they talk to you about Henry?" I was angry now.

"They're good people," she said. "They're good people. They just want to help us. I don't know...I don't really know if they can help us...help us find him, but it's good to try. It feels good to try."

"What do you mean, find him?"

My Aunt entered now, carrying a dark red quilt. It was made of many panels stitched together. I had seen it on her bed before.

"Now you let her alone," my Aunt said, spreading the quilt across the table. "You let your Mother find some peace. Just some peace. If the Pilford sisters make her feel better, then that's just fine. Those girls have a gift. They're called spiritualists. I don't know if you've ever heard of that. They lived at the camp in Lily Dale...there's a whole lot of them there." She straightened the quilt, and put her hands on my Mother's shoulders. "If you ever lose a child someday you'll know. You'll know what the most terrible thing in the world is."

"Why don't you go fish, honey?" My Mother asked, pleading. She sounded like she wanted to avoid an argument more than anything else. I felt like being stubborn now, though.

"I don't think I'm going to today," I said, standing. "What are you doing with that?" I asked, pointing at the quilt that now covered the table. It draped all the way to the floor, covering the table completely on all sides.

"That's a quilt made by your grandmother," said my Mother.

"Why are we putting it here?" I asked.

"Now Colbert," my Aunt said, suddenly louder. "You can let us have this and let us do this because it makes us feel better just like fishing makes you feel better. This is something a lot of women do, a lot of mothers do it nowadays. In England they all do it. It's part of the bereavement...all of them are doing it over there. When people lose someone they love in a war they need to say goodbye. If they didn't get to say it."

I left the room, angered by something I didn't understand. They had barely ever spoken about him in front of me, aside from asking me about his grave. I was jealous that they were confiding in these women instead of me. Who were these women? What kind of a camp was there at Lily Dale?

I wandered around the house a little bit, thinking about whether or not it might be better if I did go fishing. I looked out the back door. It was going to be a nice afternoon. I went to get my fishing pole, but something pulled me back. I was too curious to go anywhere. I waited, delaying my decision until I heard a quiet, pronounced tapping on the front door.

I heard my Aunt get up and answer the door. The voices were low and quiet, but they were definitely female. I decided that I'd just walk through the living room, to see who these women were. They had already moved into the dining room by the time I got there, though. I could hear my Aunt speaking.

"It says so right in Munsey's," she was saying. "Here it is, it says: 'If our world is ever to be destroyed, its destruction will come from outside of our own solar system. Accordingly, we should probably have plenty of time to await such a possible disaster.' I thought I'd ask you about that. What do you think about that?"

She was answered by a low voice that was much too quiet for me to hear. There was a sprinkle of women's laughter, too.

"I really felt like we came close last time," my Mother was saying. "And I think things feel right today."

"Is there someone else home?" asked a new voice. It was louder now, but calm and somewhat breathy. It sounded bored, really.

"My other son is here," said my Mother. I listened closely for what came next. I was standing in the living room, around the corner. Someone spoke, but the sound was drowned out by the whooshing of the drapes being pulled. I walked around the corner.

"Here he is," said my Aunt.

My Mother was sitting at the dining room table, her chair pulled up and her legs underneath the heavy quilt. A single candle was burning in the center of the table. Hardened pieces of wax decorated the quilt around the candle, sitting there like pebbles.

One of the women was standing near my Aunt with her hands on the back of a chair. I was immediately struck by how young she was. She was younger than me, I thought. Her hair was straw-colored, and fell straight to her shoulders. Her eyes were light, and she had a sharp, pointed little nose and angular, dark eyebrows. She wore a dark brown coat and a black skirt that began at her hip and went to just above her ankle. Instead of black stockings, she wore skin colored hose. She had nice ankles. She stared directly at me. Our eyes met for a second, and I quickly continued looking around the room.

The other woman was drawing the drapery on the two windows, shrouding the room in darkness. She turned toward me now. Her hair was dark brown and her eyes were darker than the other girl's. She was much taller, too. She had on a Sunday dress and held a matching hat with a large feather. Her hair was shorter, and bobbed. The eyebrows and the nose and even the tight-lipped mouth were exactly the same, though.

"Colbert," my Aunt was saying. "This is Eleanor Pilford," she waved toward the woman pulling the drapes, "and her sister Beth. Ladies, this is my nephew, Colbert." Eleanor smiled and nodded. Beth just stared at me with those eyes. I became aware of the strong scent of perfume in the room. It didn't smell flowery, though, like most women. It was deeper, more musky.

"Pleased to meet you," I said to them.

"It's delightful to meet you, Mister Whittier," said Eleanor. With a tug of her hand, the last shade was drawn. The room was now lit only by candlelight. Some sunlight seeped in around the drapes and from the hall, but it was still very dark. Their faces were a lot harder to see.

"We didn't expect you to be here, but you are the man of the house," Eleanor said. I smiled and nodded, not really knowing how to respond to that. My Mother was sitting quietly. She wouldn't look up at me. I followed her gaze across the table, and was given a start.

There was Henry's face, looking back at her. It was a large, framed picture that had been taken of him a few years before we left for training. He looked young. My Aunt had commissioned a photographer to take pictures of us shortly after we left school. I had seen this picture many times. Henry wore a suit and sat on a velvet chair in a room of the photographer's house. I had sat in that chair just before him and had my picture taken as well.

The sight of the picture made me angry. The flickering candle danced in a reflection on the glass. They all looked at it together now, following my own gaze.

"Will he stay?" asked the quiet, breathy voice again. It was Beth, who looked at her sister now.

"Should he?" my Aunt asked them.

"I sense a negative and critical energy," said Eleanor, moving toward the table. "I don't think he should be in the circle. If he is to be passive, he should stand outside the circle. We made progress last time, and we need the sitters to be in the same places."

Her voice was the same as before, but it didn't sound like anything a girl my age would say.

"Do you want to stay, Colbert?" My Mother looked at me now.

"Well...what are you doing?" I asked. The women all sat down now.

"Please stop the clock," Beth whispered toward me. I watched her intense little face, eyebrows arched, illuminated by the candle. She looked at me as if her very life depended on my obeying her.

"Oh yes," said my Aunt. "Colbert, please take the clock out so it's not distracting." I went over and took the heavy old clock off the top of the china cabinet.

"Do you know anything about spiritualism, Colbert?" Eleanor asked. I carried the clock into the living room and placed it on the end table. She started talking again when I stepped back into the room.

"Spiritualism is about faith, and belief." She spoke slowly, as if she were lecturing a child. I watched her mouth while she talked. Shadows bounced around it as the light of the candle dipped and sputtered. "Your Mother and your Aunt believe that death is not the end of life. You believe that, don't you?"

I nodded. I knew what was going on by now, but I had never seen anything like this in person.

"I think you should be here," Eleanor continued. "You were close to Henry, weren't you?" It didn't sound as if she really wanted me to answer. When she said his name, I felt my anger rising again, though. She had never known him.

"He is angry," Beth said to her sister quietly. They were sitting next to each other, with my Aunt and my Mother on either side. I just stood there in silence, looking at the picture of him.

"What happens here may seem strange to you," Eleanor said. Her dark eyes bore into mine. "But remember that we see this everyday. Nothing at all may happen here. But you deserve to be present...you should be here. You must decide if you share the faith of your Mother and your Aunt. If you do, perhaps you may join the circle itself during our next session. It's not a good idea this time, though. Those with critical energy or a self-centered nature should not sit with us." A few moments passed. No one else reacted to her insult. I didn't allow myself to get angry at what she said. Maybe I was scared that Beth would be able to tell somehow. "Are we ready to begin?" Eleanor asked then, smiling around the table. My Mother and my Aunt both nodded, looking very serious.

Despite the strangeness of the situation, I felt a familiar stirring that held me there. Both of the Pilford sisters were attractive women. The way they stared at me so completely was unusual, but I won't pretend it wasn't exciting as well. I had to stay to keep watching them.

All four women placed their hands on the table now. The room was bathed in silence for a number of minutes. They all seemed to know what to do. I remained standing there, leaning against the doorframe, not daring to move. Now that the clock was gone I realized just how much its ticking sound had been an inherent part of this room. Slowly, I moved toward a chair in the corner and sat in it.

"I am the leader of this session," Eleanor said finally, ignoring my movement. "My sister Beth will attempt to be our medium once again. Beth is an experienced medium for the spirit world. Many spirits have used her to communicate with the living. I will tell you when she has entered her trance." My Mother and my Aunt both had their eyes closed and their heads bent toward the table. It almost looked as if they were praying. In fact, I had seen them in almost the same position in church only a few hours earlier.

"It may take some time for our medium to enter her trance," said Eleanor. Her head was bowed so low that I couldn't tell if her eyes were closed or not. Beth was staring at the candle and the picture. "She may achieve it, and she may not. But I have no doubt that we will be successful, eventually. Spirits who die suddenly, in a violent way...through murder or battle...often have messages to bring. This is what we must remember to be successful...we have a reason for being here, but spirits also must have a reason to come to this room. We must respect their motive as well." She was an eloquent speaker. I wasn't used to hearing young girls talk like this. I wondered how long she had gone to school.

"There are a few other things we must remember," she continued. "All spirits can communicate with the living, but they do not all choose to." Beth's eyes were now closed, and she was slowly slumping down toward the table. Was she falling asleep? "A spirit who has departed violently will often cling to what has been left behind," Eleanor went on. "Someday we may be able to travel to the battlefield where Henry was killed. This area would be highly charged with his energy. But this is the house where Henry grew up, and these are the people who love him. He will communicate with these people through us if he chooses to, but we must also remember that his personality and level of knowledge about the universe will have stayed the same...these things will be the same as when he lived. He may not be able to answer all of the questions we have, or even choose to."

Beth's forehead made contact with the table. Eleanor's eyes were closed now. In fact, everyone's eyes were closed but mine. I studied the shadows on Eleanor's face. She was flawless. I watched her dark red lips come to rest. Her hands were still spread out on the table before her. They were smooth and white.

Suddenly, Beth's shoulders began to twitch violently. It startled me a little. Her head jerked upwards, and she sat up straight in her chair. Her eyes were open wide, and she was staring across the table at nothing.

"Beth is now completely under," said Eleanor, her own eyes still closed. "She is ready to be contacted. She will call out to a spirit guide that we have used before, and this guide will find Henry for us if he can be found."

More time passed. Beth shuddered and her upper body jerked.

"He is here," Beth said at last. Her voice sounded hoarse and strained. "He is with us, but he does not wish to manifest himself through me." All of the women had opened their eyes now, and were staring at Beth.

"Can he answer us through raps or tilts?" asked Eleanor. She spoke much louder now, as if she was calling to her sister across a great distance.

"He will answer...one rap for no, two raps for yes," Beth said. My eyes went to the picture at the center of the table. Eleanor spoke softly again.

"Is the spirit in this room Henry Whittier?" The question hung in the air. The candle flickered, casting shadows across all four of the women's faces. Eleanor and Beth stared at the picture. My Mother and my Aunt looked at the sisters. They were all waiting for something.

And then, a loud bang erupted from the center of the table. It was so forceful that the candle and the picture both jumped. It was immediately followed by a second loud knock. The picture danced sideways, so that it was now facing me. The table had been struck twice dead in the center. Had it come from beneath the table? Could either of their legs have possibly reached that far? They hadn't moved at all, though. They were both completely still.

A shiver ran from the base of my spine all the way up to the back of my neck, where the hairs stood erect and tingling. I couldn't look at the picture. I couldn't move my head. I was absolutely terrified. Had that really happened? Something had knocked twice on the surface of the table quite forcefully, and it couldn't have been any of us.

I finally glanced at my Mother. I could see that she was breathing heavily, and her face was flushed. She kept looking back and forth between the sisters. My Aunt was now holding my Mother's hand tightly, and her own eyes were squeezed shut again, as if she were deep in concentration.

"Do you have a message for us?" asked Eleanor, looking around the room slowly. There was no response. I realized that I'd been gripping the arms of the chair with all of my strength, my fingers digging into the cushions. Even in the dim light, I could see that my knuckles had gone white with the effort.

"Do you have a message for us?" she asked again. There was no answer, though. A few moments passed. "Should we dim the light in the room more?" she now asked.

One loud rap was heard, emanating from the same spot on the table. Now I knew this was really happening.

"Should we change places at the table?"

Another single knock, and this time it came more quickly after her question. Eleanor looked around, confused. Beth's eyes were closed now, and I saw her shiver.

"Do you have a message for someone who is not at the table?" Eleanor asked. Two loud knocks. My spine crawled again.

"Do you have a message for a family member who is not at the table?" Two knocks. The blood rushed to my head. I could hear my own heart pounding. I was holding my breath, without even realizing it.

"Do you wish to communicate with your brother?" A few moments of silence, and then two knocks. My Mother and my Aunt turned and looked at me now. I looked back and forth between them, at a loss. I can't imagine what expression they saw on my face, but on theirs I read both surprise and fear. Eleanor and Beth remained focused, and didn't look my way at all.

"Do you feel your brother here?" Eleanor asked. Only one knock came. I had become so agitated that I had momentarily forgotten the code of knocks. Was that yes or no? My Aunt and my Mother looked at me strangely now, as if I had done something wrong. One knock meant no, I remembered.

"Are you Henry Whittier?" she asked again. Two knocks. "Can you see your brother?" One knock.

Beth's hand shot out, and she grabbed her sister's arm.

"He wants to say something," Beth said. "He wants us to go through the alphabet."

They immediately began speaking letters of the alphabet aloud. Eleanor started with "A" and then Beth said "B." Aunt Edna followed with "C" and my Mother said "D." It continued like this, around the table. My Mother and my Aunt had jumped right into it, so they must have done this before.

Right after Eleanor said "M" two knocks were heard. She nodded and started again with "A." They went around and around, until Eleanor said "Y" and the two knocks were heard again. She started over. They were spelling something out.

The next time, as soon as Beth said "B" the knocks came. Beth started again with "A." When my Aunt got to "R" we heard the knocks. It must have been a slow process, but I don't remember being aware of the normal passage of time at all. I thought I could really feel a presence now. The back of my entire head was tingling.

I struggled to remain clear-headed, stringing the letters together in my mind as they circled around and around the table. M, Y, B, R, O, T, H, E, R. Silence. Would there be more? And then, it came. R, A, L, P, H.

My Mother was silent, but my Aunt gasped loudly and dramatically. At the same time, Beth shuddered and slumped over in her chair all the way, her head hitting the table again. Eleanor placed her own elbows on the table, smoothing her hair with her hands. She was breathing heavily. She looked around at everyone. She looked exhausted.

"He's gone," she said. The flame flickered. My Mother was now trembling visibly. "He's gone," Eleanor repeated. She put her hand on Beth's shoulder. "Beth, are you all right? Are you back with us, Beth?" Beth raised her head and nodded. Her forehead was drenched with sweat, and I could see it glowing in the candlelight. Dark circles surrounded her eyes. She swallowed and looked around slowly, confused, her severe eyebrows turned downward.

My Mother covered her face with her hands. My Aunt was looking at the picture, and then she turned and looked at me. I got up and threw the curtains open, and the sun poured in. I really wanted the light in there all of a sudden. I leaned over the table and cupped the candle's flame with my hand and blew it out.

The long tendril of smoke climbed from the charred wick toward the ceiling. My Mother rose and left the room, and then the rest of the women left as well. I followed them into the entryway. My Mother had disappeared back into the hallway that led to her bedroom. Eleanor had her arm around Beth, supporting her. She spoke quietly to my Aunt.

"Did the spirit's message have any meaning to you?" she asked. My Aunt stared back at her. "Sometimes they play jokes," she continued. "Did Henry mislead you or joke with you when he was living?"

"No, no," my Aunt answered, looking back and forth between them. "We understand. We understand. Thank you." She grasped both of Eleanor's hands in hers now. "Thank you…this is just very difficult." Beth's eyes locked with mine.

"I understand," said Eleanor. "What your nephew communicates with you is a message that is meant for you only. We can help him speak to you, but the message is not for us."

"Yes," my Aunt was mumbling, nodding her head. "Thank you." She sat down on the couch slowly.

"He may have more to say," Beth whispered suddenly. "He has more to say."

"We will come back when you want us," said Eleanor. "We made progress today, and he knows now that you are ready to listen."

"But was he troubled?" asked my Aunt. "Was he happy?"

"We don't know. I didn't sense great trouble. But he will say more when he is ready," Eleanor answered, looking back and forth between us.

My Mother came from the hallway. Her face was pale, and I could see the streaks of tears.

"Jean," my Aunt stood and went to her. My Mother walked over to the sisters. I saw her press some money into Eleanor's hand.

"Thank you," Eleanor said quietly, smiling. She put her hat on and turned to me.

"It was a pleasure to meet you, Mister Whittier," she said. "I think your presence was helpful. It's up to you whether you wish to join the circle next time."

"It was nice to meet you," I stammered as they left. My Mother and my Aunt were quiet for the rest of the day. I left them alone and went fishing. My heart wasn't in it, though, and I didn't catch anything.

CHAPTER 3

❦

When I had been home for almost a year, I started to think about how quickly my life had returned to normal. I was living in the same house with my Mother and my Aunt once again. I had even returned to my old job.

I had found myself naturally going back there when I'd been home for a few weeks, and the foreman, who was glad to see me, told me that he still had my job for me. The peace economy was terrible compared to what it had been during the war, and we actually had a bit of a depression that spring. But he just seemed happy to see me there alive. I don't know why, really, since everyone in town knew who had come back and who hadn't.

So I went back to cleaning out the trains. I'd wrestle the big hose all day, blasting every piece of dirt from the inside of the freight cars. I had worked this job since I was seventeen years old. Most of the guys who were working there now were about that young, or even younger. A lot of them were kids who had left school to work like I had. The guys that I'd worked with there before the war weren't around any more, though. I didn't really get to be close friends with any of the new kids. I could've been more friendly to them, but I didn't really have the energy. I felt old around them. At first they had been all over me for war stories, but they figured out soon enough that I didn't really have any good ones. The only other guys that worked there were a few Negroes, some of which had even been there before I left, and would probably be there forever. We left each other alone, just as we always had.

Sometimes while I cleaned the cars I thought about our slow rail trip across France to the front. My life felt kind of like that now. I knew that I would eventually get somewhere, but it was taking forever. I wondered what the dirty little French children that ran after our train were doing now. It was hard to imagine that people still existed over there now that we'd left. Sometimes I'd look at the grime-covered faces of my fellow car cleaners and I'd realize that they looked just like those kids. I half expected them to open their mouths and ask me for a biscuit.

I remember one spring evening when I trudged out of the yard, covered with dirt and grime, hitting the road home. I shouted goodbyes to a few guys. They usually went out on the town together at the end of the day. I wasn't really up for it, most nights. Walking home that night, I thought about Willie Delgrew. I knew that he was still living in Greenwood, but I hadn't kept up with him or even tried to reach him since we got back. I took on a lot of hours at the yard, and I was busy working. I had to work even harder to bring money in now that Henry was gone and I was the only man left in my family.

That Saturday afternoon, I decided to go see Willie. I walked into town and toward the Delgrew house. I hadn't known exactly where he lived, but all I had to do was give my Aunt a last name, and she could tell me the street. She had lived there forever, it seemed. Willie had no warning that I was coming, so I was prepared for the chance that he wouldn't even be there.

It was one of the main streets in town, lined with houses and little yards. Once I reached the street I saw two young kids throwing a medicine ball in one of the yards. They looked like they were probably still in school. They were brothers, I saw. They had the same buck teeth and sunken eyes. They were throwing the ball back and forth. I asked them where the Delgrews lived and one of them told me which house it was, grunting as he bent over to pick up the ball again. It seemed like everybody was interested in physical vitality back then. It was a real trend after the war. Everywhere you looked, people were studying their caloric consumption or maintaining the nutrition in their diets. I thought about what would make a couple of young kids like that want to start throwing the medicine ball so early. If they had just been born a few years earlier, I thought, they would have gotten their exercise overseas like us.

The Delgrew home was just another house on the street, crowded between two others, taller than it was wide. There was an older man in the front yard, pulling weeds along the little white wooden fence. I wasn't sure if this was the right house now, since I had no idea who this man could be.

I walked up to the gate, past the little mailbox. The old man looked up. He stood, wiping sweat from his forehead, where the thin white hair had stuck. He must have been working hard to be sweating like that, because it wasn't particularly hot outside.

"Hello there," he said.

"I'm looking for the Delgrew house," I answered.

"This is it," he said. He wiped his hand on his trousers and extended it. "I'm Jonathan Crowe…the neighbor." His voice was very loud, and I would learn later that he was one of those people who speak loudly all the time.

"Nice to meet you," I said. He held open the gate and I stepped through it, shaking his hand. His grip was tight. I could feel the creases in the tight skin of his hand, like a thin cloth drawn over the bones.

"You're one of…" he cleared his throat. "You're Edna Smith's nephew, aren't you?" he asked.

"Yes," I said. Everyone knew my Aunt, and they all knew her by her late husband's name. "And I'm a friend of Willie's." He looked at me strangely then.

"Well, I just do a few odd jobs for the women of the family nowadays," he said. "Helping them out, you know. They sure need it."

I didn't know what he meant by that, although it was clear that he'd assumed I did.

"Do you know if Willie's here?" I asked.

"Why don't you go on in?" he asked, motioning toward the little porch and the front door. I thanked him and he turned his attention back to the weeds. I stepped onto the porch and knocked on the door.

A woman in an apron pulled the door open. Her dark hair was flecked with gray and tied in a bun. She squinted at me through her glasses.

"Yes?" she asked, frowning.

"Misses Delgrew? I'm Colbert. Whittier." She said nothing. "Cobb Whittier." There was no recognition in her face at all. I had assumed that Willie would have said something about me. "I'm Edna Smith's nephew," I tried. She squinted a bit more.

"Oh," she said quietly. Her features were large and coarse, and I saw no resemblance to Willie whatsoever.

"I…actually, I'm a…I was a friend of Willie's. We were together in Europe." I smiled.

"Mmmm," she nodded her head slowly. "Well come in, come in." I entered a small, cramped kitchen. The greenish paint was peeling around the windows and the door. The only decoration in the whole room was a heavy-looking wooden crucifix hanging on one wall. The house was very quiet. "Would you like something?" she asked. I declined. I felt strange being here inside the cramped kitchen. "Please sit down," she said, waving at a chair that was pushed back from the table.

"Thank you," I said. The house smelled vaguely spicy, as if she'd been cooking. A stream of sunlight came through the window and landed on the sink, and I watched a mass of dust swimming in the stream.

"William's not here," she said simply, tidying up the sink.

"Oh," I answered. "Well…he wasn't expecting me. I hadn't seen him in a while, actually, so I was just dropping by."

I felt someone watching me, and turned to see a girl standing in the doorway. She must have come from the back of the house, but I didn't know how long she had been there. I stood up when I saw her and smiled politely.

"This is Gertrude, William's sister," Mrs. Delgrew said. The girl came forward.

"Pleased to meet you," I said. Her smile was as slight as her mother's, but at least she gave a nod of the head. She had the same rounded nose as Willie, and I could see that her hair had the same tight curl. In those days, of course, it was fashionable for women to have waved hair, but she didn't seem to mind. I also noticed that her skirt was cut to the ankle, instead of above it like a lot of the gals in town. She was what my Mother might call a plain-looking girl. She must have been a few years younger than Willie.

"You were with William in the war?" Gertrude asked, sitting at the table.

"Yes…we trained together at Devens and we were in the same squad in France," I answered. I sat back down as well. "I feel bad that I haven't really kept up with him since we got back."

"Have you talked to him at all?" she asked.

"No," I said, confused by her tone. "He still lives here, doesn't he?" I turned my head to see what Mrs. Delgrew was doing. She had her back to us and was working at the sink.

"Yes," Gertrude finally said. She smiled now. "He hasn't told us many stories about the war. He's been…quiet, mostly."

The front door opened and Jonathan Crowe stuck his head inside.

"You ladies need anything from the store?" he asked.

"Flour, please, Doctor Crowe," answered Mrs. Delgrew sweetly. She almost sang it. Her voice had changed entirely.

"All right," he said. "I fixed the fence out here for you, too. We had a weak board out there…just needed to be nailed back in. I think this weather's dried it out."

"Thank you so much," Mrs. Delgrew said quietly. "I'd like to have a look, I think." She followed him outside without looking back at us. The door banged shut.

I listened to a clock ticking, and looked down at my hands. I could feel her watching me. Neither of us spoke for a few seconds. I thought about how unusual it was for a girl's mother to leave her alone with a strange man.

"Well…uh," I finally stammered, "I guess if you could just tell…tell Willie that I came by." Our eyes met, and I smiled and started to rise from the table.

"Could you go get him for us, Colbert?" She asked suddenly. I stopped moving. Her eyes slid toward the front door and then back. I could hear Dr. Crowe talking loudly outside, and his round, nearly hairless head was visible through the small window near the door. She fixed her eyes on me and lowered her voice to a whisper. "I can tell you one or two places he might be. Just tell him his Mama needs him. I don't know what else to do…he won't listen to me. Even if I could go there."

"You want me to go find Willie now?" I asked.

"I know just where he is," she whispered, eyes wide. Her round nostrils were slightly flared. "It's a place at twenty-two Rose Street. Just a brown door…you have to knock." She turned toward the front door again as it opened with a loud creak.

"What would we do without Doctor Crowe?" Mrs. Delgrew asked as she made her way back to the sink. I couldn't tell if she was talking to herself or to us. Neither of us answered. Gertrude looked at me, and then stood up. I stood as well.

"Well, I'll be going now," I said. "It sure was nice to meet both of you." They thanked me for coming over, and I excused myself and left. Dr. Crowe wasn't around when I went out through the gate. It was the middle of the afternoon and the sun was high overhead.

I thought about what had just happened. She had asked out of desperation, and as far as I knew no one else could help. I had no real choice. I knew the address she gave me wouldn't be difficult to find, since Rose Street was directly in the center of town.

CHAPTER 4

❁

That same spring I finally quit my old job and started out a new one. A man my Mother knew from church was looking for someone to help him out at his practice, and all I knew was that he was in insurance. I was happy enough working at the train yard, since it was pretty easy, and the pay was fair. But I don't think my Mother had ever really liked it. She'd probably been waiting until I was old enough to convince me to try something else.

I was often the topic of conversation at our dinners in those days. There was an empty spot at our table, of course. It was just the three of us now, and we didn't really talk about Henry. The only conversations we ever had about him were about his grave. Every once in a while they would ask me to describe it again, and then they'd talk about how they were going to go over there someday to see it. If anything, I made it sound nicer than it was, because I knew that's what they'd want to hear. I didn't think they'd ever be able to see it, since we'd never have the money for a trip like that. My Aunt said that she would write to her brother Stephen who still lived over in France and ask him to bring flowers to the grave and take care of it. I don't know if she ever did that, though.

My Aunt and my father were from France originally, and had been raised in the countryside there. She liked for me to talk about the places I'd seen over there. She hadn't been there since she was eighteen years old, but her memories were very vivid. She recalled them happily, most of the time. But sometimes when I would talk about marching through certain places she would cry. She cried when I gave her the etching of the church with the statue I'd bought over there. That etching hung in our living room for as long as I can remember after I returned. I think the picture of that church became a symbol for them. In a way, it was more a memorial to my brother than anything else, simply because it was a monument that they could look at.

"Mister Durham and I talked about you again today...I saw him at the market," my Mother said over dinner one night.

"That Mister Durham is a fine man, Jean," said my Aunt.

"He is...he's a very sad man, really, and I think you could help him, Colbert. Jobs aren't easy to find these days...I think you're lucky this has come along."

"What would I be doing?" I asked, cutting into a pork chop.

"He just needs help in his office," she answered. "It must be a good job...he told me he would have given it to his son if he hadn't lost him in the war."

We moved on as if we hadn't lost anyone in the war.

"It has to be better for you than the train yard," said my Aunt. "That's just not a good element for him." She was speaking to my Mother as if I wasn't there now. "I've heard from quite a lot of people that those men drink away their pay."

The Volstead Act was a godsend for my Aunt. She felt that the abolition of liquor was her lifelong goal, and now that our country had finally made the decision, my generation would have a fighting chance to make something of ourselves. "The Noble Experiment" was what she called it. The greatest war in the history of mankind had just been fought and won, but to my Aunt, the battle against alcohol was a much more important issue.

"Edna, Colbert's not like that," my Mother said.

"Oh, I know, I know," she said, turning back to me now. "But it's just the element…you see? I'm sure many of the men are probably Catholics, and they have to go to church on Sundays and listen to that terrible priest speak out against the Eighteenth Amendment. Can you imagine a man of the cloth taking such a stand?"

It was a rhetorical question, and we knew it. It was best just to let her go when she got onto this subject.

She had been a heavy woman for almost as long as I could remember. In her day, though, she had supposedly been thin and very beautiful. You could tell, really. She had the type of face that looked as if it could have been pretty years ago, and her hair was still a soft reddish color.

"You know," said my Mother, trying to change the subject, "Mister Barnes at the drug store was telling me today that since the Volstead Act, he's sold twice as much coffee and tea and even ice cream sodas. So I know he's very happy about that."

"I'm sure he is," said my Aunt. "You know Mister Barnes is always complaining about the cost of living and the inflation and all. But when I was in there the other day I saw that he's got himself a new Victrola…the kind we saw for one hundred and fifty dollars in the Sears Roebuck catalog, Jean. Have you seen it, Colbert?"

"No," I answered.

"He's playing music in there all the time now. Well, I even talked to him about it. Those popular songs are having quite an influence on our young people, and the Women's Club has been trying to stop it. I don't know why they can't play good music like 'Keep the Home Fires Burning' and 'The Long, Long Trail'…good American music."

My Mother nodded slowly, a far-off look in her eyes. My Mother and my Aunt got along quite well. There was only a difference of three or four years in age between them.

My Mother was a small woman, with dark eyes and dark grayish hair. Her nose was large, and her lips had always been drawn tight and thin. No one had ever said she was a looker like my Aunt when she was young.

A few moments of silence passed, and she smiled faintly.

"You know, Colbert," she said, "I think you could work your way up to good money if you stay with Mister Durham for a while."

"I know," I said.

"Well," said my Aunt. "We'll let you decide what's best for yourself. You've certainly been pulling your fair share around here. I hope you know that we're very proud of you." Sometimes my Aunt said things like that, all of a sudden. She stood up and took my empty plate.

As we left the table I told them I would go to Mr. Durham's office that week and talk to him. They were both happy to hear it.

CHAPTER 5

I strolled down Rose Street, which was near the little park that sat in the center of town. There were stores along the road, but most of them didn't have numbered addresses. Then, down toward the corner, I saw a plain brown door wedged between a general store and an office. As I approached, I noticed a brass "22" on the door.

I looked around and saw that a few people were walking in the park. It was a nice Saturday afternoon. A woman was pushing a baby carriage, and two young boys were rolling an old bicycle wheel and chasing it around the carts that rolled by on the street. The traffic in those days was still mostly drawn by horses.

I knocked quietly on the door and cleared my throat. A minute or two passed, and I knocked again, a bit louder. I was ready to leave, convinced that Delgrew's sister was crazy. Just then, a little panel slid open next to the door. I hadn't even noticed that it was there. It had been moved aside to reveal a pair of eyes, squinting at the bright daylight. The eyebrows were heavy, sprinkled with gray, and connected in the middle. This definitely wasn't Willie.

"Yeah?" a gruff voice asked.

"Um...I'm looking for...uh, Willie Delgrew, actually," I said. The single brow furrowed itself like a lazy caterpillar stretching and relaxing. The eyes jumped up and down, looking over me.

"Who're you?"

"Tell…tell him it's Cobb," I said. The panel slid shut.

I turned back to the street and watched a kid selling newspapers on the corner, shouting at everyone to "read all about it." I heard the wood panel move aside again and I turned.

"I need a word," the voice said.

"What?" I answered. I should have known what was going on.

"Ya need to know the word," the voice said, more quietly now. The eyes shifted back and forth, making sure that there was no one else with me.

I suddenly realized that I was trying to enter a speakeasy. The Volstead Act had just gone into effect a few months before. This Act was what really made the Eighteenth Amendment something the government enforced. You could now get arrested for making liquor, selling it, or even transporting it. Of course, in a little town like Greenwood people got away with a whole lot. We weren't exactly known for having an overzealous police force. But the guys running this place had a sense of drama, and they covered their illegal activities in the same way as it was done in the big cities.

We didn't have real saloons for a whole decade, after the Eighteenth Amendment. Places like this were everywhere, though, and they started up right away. They were called speakeasies because you had to speak a password to get in, to make sure that you weren't with the cops.

I think a lot of guys my age thought it was unfair that just when we should have been celebrating our victory, somebody decided that people should quit drinking for good. I'd never been to a proper speakeasy like this one, but I had been to a place outside town where the workers would go after a day at the train yard or the steel mill. It was really just a barn where a few farmers operated stills of their own, selling the homemade stuff. You didn't need a password there.

The door in front of me was in the middle of everything, though, and there must have been people inside, even though it was afternoon. Of course, I had no idea what the password was. I just stood there.

"You fight in the war?" The pair of eyes looked at me expectantly. I had been standing there in silence for a little while. Maybe he thought I was trying to remember the password.

"Yes," I said. "I fought with…I served with Delgrew. Can you just let me know if he's in there?"

The panel slid shut, and a few seconds later the door opened. It was so dark inside that I couldn't see a thing as I entered. I hit a wall of smells right away, though, and tobacco and beer were definitely among them. As my eyes adjusted I saw that the owner of the single eyebrow had a sloping forehead and that his hair was both black and gray. It was as if every other hair alternated colors. He was much shorter than I was.

In front of us was a set of stairs, leading down. He motioned for me to descend. I could hear loud voices from below.

"What kinda name's Cobb?" he asked from behind me as we went down the stairs.

"My real name is Colbert," I said over the squeak of the wooden stairs.

"What kinda name's that?"

"I don't know." He passed me on a landing at the bottom of the stairs and opened a door. The voices suddenly grew louder.

It was a basement with rock walls and no windows. There was carpet on the floor and a wood paneled bar in the corner, and tables and chairs stretched out in front of me. The room was so full of smoke that I could barely make out the ceiling. The smoke hung like a fog above everyone. There were men everywhere, all of them drinking. I didn't know who any of these people were. I'd never seen them in town before. Where did they come from? They ignored my entrance, continuing their loud card games and slurred arguments.

The man who let me in walked toward the bar without saying anything. I stood there for a moment, confused, and then decided to follow him. I saw the bartender now, stroking his mustache and laughing at some men sitting at the bar. His hair was slicked back and an unlit cigar protruded from his mouth. He was almost doubled over with laughter now.

The doorman started talking to someone who was sitting alone at the bar, a short distance from the conversation that had the bartender in stitches. The guy turned around, and I saw that it was Delgrew. I never could have picked him out. He looked like everyone else in the place.

He had a glass of whiskey in front of him. He looked different, somehow. I know it hadn't been that long, but he did. I couldn't really put my finger on it.

He was dressed as if he had just come from church or something. I guess a few of the men in there were dressed up, too. His collar was mussed, though, and his jacket was unbuttoned. It looked as if he had slept in what he was wearing.

"Cobb Whittier," he said, pointing at me. The way he said it didn't sound like Willie. The man from the door still stood there, watching both of us. It made me uncomfortable. I realized that I hadn't thought of what I would say to Willie when I found him.

Ever since I'd figured out what this place was, of course, I knew what condition I'd find him in. Still, it was unbelievable that Willie Delgrew could be in a place like this. I thought about the desperate plea of his sister. She had known exactly where I'd find him. How much time had he been spending here?

"Willie," I said, too quietly. I cleared my throat and said it again, loud enough to be heard over the uproar of drunken men.

"Thanks, Louie," Willie said. The doorman finally turned away. "Pull up a chair, Cobb. What are you doing here?"

"What are you doing here?" I asked instead of answering.

"Relaxing," he waved a hand around. "Relaxing my mind. You want a drink?"

"I'm fine."

"Have one…have one on me. Joe!" he shouted at the bartender, who ignored him and continued laughing. "Joe! Hey, Joe!" The bartender's smile faded slowly, and he waved him off, annoyed. "Hey, I got a friend here…from the war. This guy's from the war!" He put his arm around me, and the bartender looked at me. The other men who had been laughing with him looked at me too.

"If 'e saw as much action as you, Will, we can hear all 'is stories in ten seconds," said Joe. They all laughed. Willie shook his head.

"See…we don't get respect," he said to me. "These people spend their whole lives in this little place." He took a drink. "They don't know what's out there. We protected them from it all, right?" The bartender slid another glass of whiskey toward us, barely looking up. Willie pushed it in front of me, the ice clinking. "To the boys over there," he said, raising his glass. The person in front of me looked like Willie all right, but he sounded like someone else. I reluctantly toasted and took a sip. The bitter taste hit my tongue, and a fire flared up behind my eyes. The stuff was terrible. "Good, huh?" he asked.

"What've you been doing?" I asked.

"This is it…recovering," he said. "From…from everything over there."

"No, I mean, where are you working?"

"Work's for boys who haven't fought for their country." He laughed, a bit too loudly. "I'm just kidding. Boy, it's good to see you again, Cobb. I've never seen you come in here. I didn't know you were around."

"Sure, Willie. I work at the train yard."

"Oh."

"I could probably get you something there."

"What, do you mean…a job? I could get one if I wanted one. I'll do it soon. I just need a little time, you understand." He downed a large portion of the drink. His eyes swam as he turned back to me. "You ever hear from any of the guys?"

"What?"

"The guys?"

"No. No, I don't."

"Hmmm," was all he said. There was a moment of silence. I raised the glass, letting the liquid touch my upper lip, pretending to drink. The smell alone was overpowering, and my eyes watered. I put it down.

"You look like you just came from church," I said.

"What?"

"I said you look like you just came from church."

"Church?" he looked at me. "This is my church, pal." He laughed hysterically for a few minutes, holding his side. Then, he leapt off the chair and bent over, coughing.

"You upchuck in here again and you're on the street, Will!" yelled the bartender, red faced.

"Aw, shut up," said Willie quietly, waving at him. He stood back up. "Nobody's upchuckin' here."

"You okay, little Willie?" a woman was standing by him now. I hadn't noticed her before at all. There was makeup smudged around her mouth and eyes. She looked like she had slept in the clothes she was wearing, too. Her corset was mostly undone. Her voice was high but gravelly, and she held a cigarette. She put her arm on Willie.

"I'm okay," he said. "Hey, Mary…this is Cobb. My friend. My good friend," his words were slow.

"Okay, honey," she said, coughing a little. She gave me a wink. I looked at her arm, the way it was draped on him. That was just about the last straw, as far as I was concerned.

"Look, Willie, we need to talk. How about we go outside."

"He's not usually like this, Mary," Willie said. "He's a good guy." Now that he was standing, it was obvious how drunk he was.

"You oughta have one of these," she said to me, slurring her words just like him. She was waving the drink in her hand. "It's one of Joe's specialties…it's called a 'between the sheets'" she giggled. "It really is."

"Come on, Willie, let's go," I said. Mary moved away, draping herself on the next guy at the bar.

"There's a game I want to get in on here, Cobb," he drawled, turning all the way around and looking at the tables. "I need to win some dough back." A few of the men at the card game nearest to us looked up and snickered.

I grabbed his arm and pulled him away from the bar. As I dragged him away, I heard yelling. Someone was yelling at me.

"Hey! You!" It was the bartender. I turned around. "You gonna pay for that?" he motioned toward my glass on the bar. It was still full. "And he owes me," he pointed at Willie. "Your friend there owes me."

"I'm winning it back, Joe," Willie said, looking in the general direction of the bartender.

"Yeah, well, you ain't winnin' anything back by sleeping on my floor at night. It's a good thing I like your friend there," he was talking to me now. "Because there're some guys I know who collect their debts a lot quicker than I do…and I don't wanna see 'im in here again until he settles 'em, cause he's gettin' hisself into some trouble. I don't need trouble, you unnerstand?"

Willie muttered something. He was still leaning on me and his weight was starting to pull me down. I took out my wallet and put some money on the bar. I didn't even stay to see anyone's reaction. We made our way up the stairs and back into the light of the world.

I squinted for a while, waiting for my eyes to adjust to the daylight. People passed by on the street, not even noticing the two men coming out of the door marked "22." The taste of the homemade whiskey sat in the back of my mouth like a squatter. I needed water badly.

Willie's body crumpled on the side of the street. I helped him sit up. I don't know if he was listening to me or not, but I told him that

I'd seen his mother and his sister, and that they had sent me after him. I told him that an old man was doing his jobs around the house. I told him that his family wanted him. And then I sat down next to him on the ground.

He sniffled a bit, and spit on the ground. He was a mess. I thought about the kid I'd known, back in camp. I couldn't help but picture his face on the night when we pushed him into the barn. I wondered how long this had been going on.

"Have you had a job since you came back?" I asked.

"Gimme a hand," he said. I stood and helped him to his feet. He was wobbly, and he smelled of strong, sour liquor. There was another smell, too. As he turned toward me I saw a large wet spot that had spread across the front of his pants. He followed my eyes and grinned sheepishly. "I had an accident, I guess," he said. "Boy, I'm sure glad about Volstead…the homemade hooch really packs more of a wallop."

It was difficult for him to stand, and I watched as he tried to keep his eyes focused on me. I was aware of a few people looking at us.

"Hey," he said. "Come to this other place with me…it's not far. It's nicer than that place. I'm sorry about that place, Cobb," he said.

"No thanks, Willie," I said. "I need to get home, and so do you. Your family's worried about you," it sounded silly, I know. But I had to say it. It was true. He walked toward the window ledge of the general store and sat down on it to get his balance. A few people walked in and out of the store. I hoped they didn't notice the front of his pants.

"My family doesn't understand," he said. "How can they understand what we went through? You talk to your family about it over there?"

"Not really," I said. I hadn't thought that there was much to say. In my family, I was just the one who came back, and that was all.

"You know what my Papa used to say," he said suddenly. "He would tell me to be a righteous man. That was the only thing that was important to him…to be righteous. I didn't even know what it meant back then. Always go to church, so you can grow up and be a righteous man…no mistakes, no stumbles along the path to righteousness. I know he wasn't that smart, or that rich, and I know he and Mama didn't get along great. So that's all he had. That's all he taught me."

He looked down, and then back out at the street. He squinted into the sun. He seemed to have sobered up quickly.

"Sometimes he'd come home from work, and he'd see me reading a book, and he'd ask why I was reading that and not the Bible. He used to sing the loudest of anyone in church. That's what he loved. That's all he loved."

He looked at me now, and I felt sorry for him. I sighed, not really knowing what to say.

We sat there for a while.

"Look," I said finally. "I'll help you get home. You don't need to go out today any more. I could talk to someone at the train yard about getting you work maybe…you just need to work…to get your mind off things," I kept talking, wanting to get it all out before he had a chance to react. "Your mom and your sister need your help…they've got to run a house."

"Sure," he said quietly. "You're right. You're right, pal." He didn't ask how I knew about his family. "You'd get a job for me?"

"Yeah," I said. "You're a dependable guy…it won't be hard. I'll talk to 'em on Monday. I used to work there. Maybe they haven't even replaced me yet."

He nodded. I had only seen my old foreman once since I left my old job, in the post office in town one day. He had made a big deal out of the tie I was wearing, as if I had suddenly become a rich man or something. You would've thought he hadn't seen me in years. He would probably give a job to someone that I recommended, I thought.

Willie stood suddenly.

"I'm goin'. I'm goin'. I'm goin' home, Cobb," he said. "Thanks, Cobb. I'm goin' home." He started to walk away.

"Are you okay?"

He waved me off.

"Be careful," I said. I turned slowly to go toward my own home.

"I'll see you around, right Cobb?" he asked.

"Yes, def'nitely," I said. I watched him walk away down the street. I vowed then and there to keep checking on him, to make sure he was all right.

As I walked home I noticed that the smell of cigarette smoke and whiskey from the speakeasy had clung to my clothes. I wondered if his family would know that he'd been drinking. It would be difficult for them not to, I thought. I felt bad that I hadn't gone to see him before. I felt bad about everything, especially whenever I imagined his sister sitting there, asking me, someone she'd never met, for help. She had waited until her mother couldn't hear. There was just something in her voice. I kept seeing her nose and her hair. They were just like Willie's. She wasn't a very pretty girl, and I guess I felt sorry for her. I had lost a brother over there, after all. Maybe she was thinking that she had, too.

CHAPTER 6

Mr. Durham worked in a small room above a new clothing store in the middle of town. I climbed the stairs to his office and knocked on the door.

"Come in, come in," he said with a broad smile. He was dressed in a black suit and his hair was pure white, like snow. It was quite a contrast.

"Hello, Mister Durham," I said. "I'm Colbert Whittier."

"Of course," he said with a smile. "How is your mother?"

"She's fine," I said.

"Sit down, Colbert," he waved toward a stuffed armchair. The office was crammed with papers. There were only a few chairs, two small desks, and a large filing cabinet. A lone window overlooked the street. There was a fireplace on the back wall as well, but it looked as if it hadn't been used in a long time. He sat down in another chair.

"Yes," he said, gazing out the window. "I'm sure it's been difficult for your mother, losing a son over there," he didn't look to me for a response, so I was silent. "When I first got the news about Robert, I thought it couldn't be true." He was still staring out the window. "I thought it must have been a mix-up. Maybe it was someone else that just looked like him. That's what I told them. But it was him." He looked at me now. "You probably knew Robert...he went through Camp Devens."

"There were a lot of us," I said. "And different registrations. I don't think I knew him."

"He was a good boy," he said, ignoring me. "My only son. But he fought well over there. All you boys did. You put an end to it. Robert would have taken this place over from me some day. He wanted to do it, too. He was good with people already...ready to be an insurance man."

I saw a picture behind him on the desk. It was a young man in uniform, with a trim mustache and broad nose. He stared out from the brown and white picture, a serious expression on his face. He looked ready to go to war for his country. I wondered if Henry or I had looked like that before we left.

My eyes moved back to Mr. Durham, who had the same broad nose. He was talking to me about the job now.

"As field employees, we're charged with upholding the standards of the company out here...we've got the same way of keeping records and doing things as the boys at the headquarters in New York. This field office was set up around the turn of the century...there was a fantastic fire in Greenwood, and it destroyed a lot of the town. I'll bet your Aunt would remember it. Has she ever told you about it?"

"I don't think so."

"A lot of farmland was destroyed. Some of the property was insured, and some wasn't. We set up a field office here to handle the claims, and it's been running ever since." He leaned forward in his chair. "You see, the uninsured properties were all bought up by companies that built factories...that's when the textile factory and the steel mill came in. Normally, the field employees would have been let go after a while, but we kept this office open, because the factories brought with them just as many claims as the fire had."

I nodded. He had certainly changed a great deal from the man who was mourning a son only moments before.

"In fact, a lot of the policies sold out of here in the last five years have been life policies for workers in those factories. That can be hazardous work." I thought about the idea of representing whole lives with pieces of paper. How did he calculate how much money someone's life was worth? I wondered how he would have appraised Robert.

"You'll be helping me out with paperwork mostly," he said now. "I just need an office clerk. Organizing policies, maintaining accounts, arithmetic...how much schooling have you had?"

"I went until I turned seventeen," I said. I was quite proud of that. In those days most people I knew had far less schooling than I did. My brother had left at fifteen. Mr. Durham seemed impressed.

"You ever think about going to college?" he asked.

"Not really," I said. More school didn't sound like the thing for me. I was glad to get out when I did. "I'm just wanting to work to help out my Mother and my Aunt." I knew it was a good answer.

"Good," he said. "That's good." He looked me square in the eye. "I like a man with responsibility. You're the man in your family, and you know it. I think you have a lot in common with my boy."

He talked to me about the pay, which was a lot more than I made at the train yard. He said he wouldn't make me wear a jacket unless I started following him into the field, but I would need to wear a tie and shirtsleeves each day. He told me to use his credit to buy those downstairs. I could start the following Monday and then pay him back gradually.

I went down into the clothing shop right away. I was surprised by my excitement to be leaving the train yard for good. He'd said that I wouldn't need a full suit, but I ended up buying one anyway. In those days they had just started selling suits with two pairs of pants, so I figured that I could get more wear out of it even if I didn't use the jacket.

I looked at a tweed coat as well, thinking about the cooler days. Thirty-seven dollars and fifty cents. It was more money than I'd ever spent before. I decided that it could wait. I looked around on my way out, and found a Waltham wristwatch for five dollars that I planned to buy as soon as I saved some money from my paychecks.

The man at the register managed to sell me a pack of Miloviolet scented, gold-tipped cigarettes for ten cents. I only bought them because I was celebrating a new job. I hadn't smoked since the war, but I was thinking about taking it up again. Of course, there wasn't anywhere good to smoke now that I was living at home again.

CHAPTER 7

❦

My brother Ralph died as an infant right after my parents first came to America and got married. I was born about ten years after that, in 1895, so I think Ralph probably lived in the mid-1880s. I had never seen Ralph because nothing existed in this world proving that he had ever been here. There were no pictures of him, or belongings he'd left behind. My parents hadn't even been able to afford a marker for his grave. So to me he was nothing more than a story of my Mother's. It wasn't a story she liked to tell, either.

My father and Henry knew about him, and my Aunt knew about him, but that was about it. No one in Greenwood certainly, since that had been long before any of us had come here. I'm sure it had been very painful for my Mother, coming over here and leaving her entire family behind, with a man she couldn't have known that well. They had nothing. And then the baby died. I can't imagine what happened during the ten years between Ralph and me.

I thought about Ralph every once in a while, trying to imagine what he would look like, and who he might be. When I was little, I used to picture us as great friends. He was an older kid who would spend all sorts of time with me. I could never really imagine his face, though. His face was always blurred in my daydreams. I used to picture him in very old-fashioned clothes. I would pray for him in church when I was younger, too. My Aunt had told me to pray for the deceased once. So I used to pray that he was happy, and that he would like me if he looked down from heaven.

I asked my Mother once if she had kept anything of Ralph's, but she said no. Henry hadn't really been as interested in him as I had. I guess he already knew what it was like to have an older brother.

When the Pilford sisters brought Ralph's name back into our home, it changed things immediately. My Mother and my Aunt were convinced that we had contacted Henry, since no one else could have possibly known about Ralph. I can't blame them really.

My Mother cried a lot more after that day, and we even talked about Henry more. Sometimes she would even smile when we talked about him. That was mostly when I would tell stories of things that happened when we were young kids.

My Aunt continued to be worried, though. She was worried about everything now. She fretted over my Mother's state, my own happiness, and most of all, the well being of Henry in the afterlife.

"There are three levels of spirits, you see," my Aunt told us one evening just before we went to bed. "The highest are closest to our perfect Lord. And then there are middle ones, and the newest to die are the lowest ones." My Mother and I both listened intently, sitting in the little parlor on the couch. "Sometimes the lower ones are lost and confused. Sometimes they don't want to leave their life behind. Now I'm just hoping that that's not Henry. We all need to pray that he's not like that.

"But I can't help wondering why he asked about Ralph," she continued. "Did he say he had a message for Ralph? Do you remember? Because I think we ought to be concerned if he's not with Ralph. They should be together."

"I never thought of that," my Mother said.

"How do you know about this...about the levels?" I asked her.

"The Pilford sisters showed it to me in one of their books," my Aunt answered. "I've always been a reader. I was the first one in my family to really read in English."

My Mother was looking more and more distressed. Her hands guided the knitting needles as they pulled and wove a mass of rust-colored yarn. I had always liked to watch her hands do this when I was little. Sometimes the rhythm of the clacking needles would even put me to sleep.

"Well if there are different levels," I said, "then Ralph should already be on a higher level, because he's been there for…for longer." It felt strange saying his name aloud. I could probably count the number of times I'd spoken his name during my life on one hand. "So Henry's probably looking for him. That's what I'd do. But he won't be able to be with him until he gets to a higher level."

"That's true, Colbert," my Aunt said. "That might be true, and I didn't think of that." My Mother seemed satisfied as well, and we didn't say any more about it. She went back to concentrating on her knitting.

"Mister Marshall down at the dry goods store tells me they've been absolutely selling out of silk stockings lately," Aunt Edna was speaking again. "Can you imagine? I remember when that was a real luxury item. Now everybody can get them for two or three dollars. Of course, they all complain about the cost of living, but they must have their stockings. Can you believe that sign in the front window of the store now? Have you seen it, Jean?"

My Mother shook her head.

"The Fleischmann Company is telling women to buy bread instead of baking it. Well isn't that something? As if everyone can afford to just buy all their bread. I asked Mister Marshall about it but he wouldn't take it down. And they wonder why the cost of living is where it is. You know, Mister Marshall also told me that they've been seeing more of you down at the store lately, Colbert."

"Yes," I said, surprised that the topic of conversation had abruptly turned to me. "I've been doing some shopping for Misses Delgrew there."

"Does she pay you for all the work you do for her?"

"No."

"Well I think that's very nice of you to help her out like that. That poor woman."

"Colbert's been helping out around her house...haven't you?" asked my Mother.

"Yes," I said. "A little."

"I don't know why Doctor Crowe can't just help her out himself. He lives right next door, doesn't he?" my Aunt asked.

"Yes," I said. "He lives next door. He used to help with things, but I...I do a lot now, so he doesn't have to."

"It's a shame a retired man with nothing to do but spy on the neighbors can't help out Misses Delgrew. You have to give up your time when you're working all week and helping us out here," my Aunt said.

"Edna, Doctor Crowe's getting on in years now, I think," said my Mother.

"Have you ever spoken to him?" my Aunt asked me. She suddenly sounded accusatory.

"Doctor Crowe? Yes, a few times," I said.

"You should probably just stay away from him," she said in return.

"Why?" I asked. My Mother didn't raise her eyes from her knitting. One needle passed over and then under the other in tempo.

"Doctor Crowe is not a good man," my Aunt said. She seemed surprised that I'd even had to ask. "A lot of people in town stopped going to him at around the same time that I did and I think they all knew what was going on. That's when I started seeing Doctor Morris. But there were a lot of people who just wouldn't listen to me, and they kept going to him. We could have run that man out of town if more people had been willing to listen to me."

"What happened?" I asked.

"You don't need to hear it all, a young man like you," she said. She shook her head dramatically and looked around at the corners of the room, one by one, as if it was something she just couldn't face. My

Mother remained quiet. I could hear the clock from the dining room.

"Doctor Crowe came to this town as a young man," my Aunt said. "I believe he came from out west somewhere...probably California, which explains a lot. And he's been here for a long time. Sometimes when men have been somewhere for long enough they think they can get away with anything. They think they can do whatever they want to do, no matter how bad, and that nothing will ever come back to them." She turned toward me now, focusing me in her gaze. "And you just remember...and I know that you know this already...but you just remember that in the life after this one it all comes back to you. And people who maybe aren't punished here...well, that's all right because they'll have it coming when they answer to the Lord. And the men with dignity who treat women with respect, they'll get their rewards."

She sat back, smiling, suddenly very happy. She exhaled loudly, satisfied with herself.

"Well," she said, leaning forward and picking up a newspaper from the table. "I certainly hope Mister Harding wins the election." Whenever my Aunt wanted to change the subject entirely she would bring up politics. "I can't stand that Cox. And Franklin Roosevelt as vice president? Just imagine, a secretary of the navy. How does that qualify him? This country is much too interested in war these days. That's what's wrong with it, don't you think?"

"Well, the war's still fresh in everyone's minds," said my Mother.

Aunt Edna let the paper drop again. "I suppose you're right. If you ask me though, the sooner we stop thinking about it, the better off we'll be. Oh, well. I will see you both in the morning. Don't stay up too late, Jean."

"I won't," my Mother answered. "Good night."

"Good night, Aunt Edna," I said.

She lifted herself from the couch and left the room. I watched my Mother knit for a few minutes. Then, without looking up, she spoke.

"She thinks that Doctor Crowe was a bit too free with his hands during one of her visits," she said. "That's why we all had to stop going to him."

"Really?" I asked. I pictured the old man next door to the Delgrews. I found it hard to believe.

"Yes," my Mother said. She looked up at me with a very serious look on her face. And then, a little chuckle escaped from her. She glanced toward the hallway that led to my Aunt's bedroom. We both smiled.

Lying in bed that night in complete darkness, I thought about Henry. I imagined what kind of things we might have done around town if he had come home from Europe with me. He would have liked *The Mark of Zorro* with Douglas Fairbanks at the movie house. He would have liked how Douglas Fairbanks married Mary Pickford, too. We could have gone fishing again and talked about it.

When we were very young, before my father died, we lived in a tiny apartment in what was a very poor section of New York City. Our neighbors there always called us the twins, even though we knew we weren't twins and my parents didn't think we looked that much alike. My Mother used to say that Henry looked like our father, and that I looked just like her brother in Boston had when he was a small boy.

We both slept in the main room in a small bed that was barely big enough for the two of us. My parents' bedroom was really just one end of the same room with a curtain in front of it. I can remember how we would approach that curtain slowly in the middle of the night if we were cold or had a nightmare. If I wanted to go in and sleep with my parents, then Henry would come too, and if he wanted to go in there, I had to accompany him. This was our unspoken rule, mostly because we were scared. We were frightened of the loud, low snoring that would suddenly erupt from my father. I can remember more than one occasion when all at once this guttural growling would descend on us and send us running back into our own bed.

Awake or asleep, I remember my father as an intimidating man. I can still see his thick, black beard. I remember the way it scratched our faces and hands when we climbed on him in his chair. He worked at the docks loading and unloading ships back then, so he was a strong man. He used to bring home a fishy smell with him every night, and we loved it. It was the smell of the ocean. He never did lose his accent, and my Mother told me once that he had few friends in this country because he had such trouble with the language. And yet, neither Henry nor I grew up with any trace of an accent at all. He was proud of that, my Mother said.

I pictured Henry's face, and the way he moved and talked. Then I thought about those knocks on our dining room table. The shivers ran through my spine right there in bed again. Could it really have been him?

The truth was, this kind of thing scared me a little. I remember back during the war when guys used to talk about seeing angels a lot. When something bad was happening in the war, like friends dying around you, they used to say that you could see the Angel of Mons right there. It was just a story, really, but a lot of different guys used to claim that they'd seen the Angel.

I had looked for it myself. That day when the Germans were hitting our dug-out over and over again, I glanced up and around just a little bit, just to see if I could see the Angel myself. I didn't see anything, though. But maybe that's because none of us got killed.

I wouldn't call myself an extremely religious person. I went to church with my Mother and my Aunt every Sunday, and I had gone to a religious school. But I hadn't really liked it as a kid, and I was glad when my Aunt allowed me to go on to secondary school at the public town school. She said she wasn't going to pay for our religious education anymore if we weren't going to listen anyway.

Most of the guys I knew who were my age weren't really religious, though. That was the difference between old people and young people. All the old people complained about how nobody cared about religion and morals anymore, and the young people weren't going to church on Sundays, and things like that. The truth is that religion was something that I never really thought about.

I knew some guys who took it very seriously. I remember O'Malley really throwing a fit when the pope died during the war. He said that was probably why the president was ill, and that now that the pope had died this war was probably going to end the whole world. I had never really known too much about the pope, though, so I just sort of shook my head along with him. O'Malley always wore a crucifix around his neck, too. Willie and I thought it was strange how he was so proud of his crucifix, and yet he'd drink and cuss and chase women all over the place.

I finally fell asleep thinking about Henry and the guys I knew over there, and I went right into a dream. I didn't know it was a dream at first, because I was lying in bed in the dream itself. There was something or someone in the room, though, and I felt it, somehow. There was a presence in the room, looking at me. I stayed still, holding my breath. I was scared to look around, because I didn't want to see it, whatever it was. And then it was sitting on top of me, holding me down. I tried to get out of bed, but I couldn't move. My arms and legs were pinned tightly against my body. I was helpless. Whatever it was was sitting on top of me, pushing me down.

I woke up and saw that it was still dark. It was a long time before I fell back to sleep again.

CHAPTER 8

One Saturday soon after I'd started my new job I decided to stop by the Delgrew house. I assumed they'd be happy to see me, since I had convinced Willie to come home. The air was heavy and humid, and I could feel summer coming. I went up the walk and knocked on the door, but no one answered. The sound of someone coughing came from behind the house. I walked through the narrow alleyway between homes and into the small, square back yard.

Dr. Crowe was coughing and sneezing into a large handkerchief. He was kneeling by the fence, and when he put the handkerchief away he resumed pulling large weeds out of the ground with both hands. Sweat stained the front of his shirt. He stopped to wipe his forehead with the back of his hand. Then he went back to lifting and tugging at the stalks, fighting them in the small space of the yard. There were a lot of weeds there. He was concentrating so hard that he didn't see me.

Beyond him, in one corner of the little yard, Mrs. Delgrew was squatting and staring intently at the ground. She wore yellow gardening gloves and an apron. I watched as she lifted a small clump of dirt from beside her and placed it into a small hole in the ground. I could just barely see a tiny, twisted green shoot protruding from the top of the clump.

I stood there for a little while, watching her. I felt as if I was seeing something private and personal. I guess I was just surprised by how gently she moved the dirt and the sprouts, placing them in the best locations to live and grow. I couldn't help being sad for her then. I wondered what it had been like when she first learned what Willie's father had done to himself. Had she seen it coming? Did she blame herself at all? I wondered if she was the one who found him after it happened. Or maybe it was Willie.

I walked over to Dr. Crowe, rolled up my sleeves and stood there, waiting for him to notice me. His chest was heaving. He was an old man, after all.

"Doctor Crowe," I said quietly, slowing placing my hand on his shoulder. I didn't want to alarm him.

"Hello," he said, loudly, looking up at me and sneezing again. I could tell that I'd startled him. His nostrils were wide and filled with gray hairs.

"Let me," I said.

"Oh, I'm…I'm fine," he answered. A bead of sweat clung to the end of his prominent nose. I could feel Mrs. Delgrew's eyes on us. "It's just my allergies." He pulled out the huge handkerchief again and pressed it to his forehead.

"Please," I said. "You…you're almost done," I looked around the yard. Actually, it was difficult to tell which areas he'd passed over already.

Reluctantly, he let me help him to his feet. Without looking over at Mrs. Delgrew at all, I knelt down and started pulling a large weed back and forth along the fence, gradually working it free.

I concentrated on the work, staring at the ground. When I did look up I saw that Mrs. Delgrew had gone back to hers as well. Dr. Crowe had left the yard, and I hadn't even noticed.

After I had pulled just about everything, I looked at the pile of weeds I'd created in the center of the yard. Then I took them to the ash can and dumped the cans in the alley behind the yard. Mrs. Delgrew had gone inside without a word.

I put everything away as best as I could, and crossed back into the front yard. Mrs. Delgrew and I had exchanged no words at all. And yet, I felt as if there was an understanding between us. I wanted to ask her if there was anything else I could do now.

I only made it a short distance toward the front door when I saw Gertrude approaching from the street, carrying a large suitcase.

"Hello," I said as she approached.

"Hello," she answered. She looked confused.

"I…I was just, in the yard, in back," I said.

"Oh," she answered.

"Let me get that," I took the dark red case from her. It was chipped and scratched, and one of the latches looked ready to spring. It wasn't as heavy as it looked, though.

"Did you bring him back again?" she asked.

"No, actually…no. I was just helping out. I haven't seen him."

"Thank you for bringing him back before. It was nice for a few days."

I didn't know what to say. The silence seemed to go on forever.

"What's in the case?" I asked.

"It's my sewing," she smiled.

"Where do you do that?"

"I do it for ladies all over town," she answered. "I'm making a little money for Mama. And…so I can go to college."

"Really?" I said. "You shouldn't be walking home alone."

"I always walk home alone," she said. "You think I can't find my own way just because I'm not a man?" She looked just like Willie for a second. Her tone surprised me. I didn't know her very well, after all. I decided not to argue.

"I'm sure you can take care of yourself," I said.

She opened her mouth and closed it again.

"William is a good person," finally came out. She still seemed angry about something.

"I know," I said. "I know that."

"This is about Mama," she eyed the front door and her voice dropped and became calmer. "I don't know what happens in places like that…in wars. Something must have happened to him over there, though. He's not the same." She was quiet for a while. "She needs him," she said. "If there's anything you can do…"

The front door opened, then, and Mrs. Delgrew stood on the porch.

"Hi Mama," said Gertrude, walking up the steps. I followed, placing her suitcase on the porch.

"Hello, dear. Hello, Colbert," she said. Hearing her say my name surprised me, somehow. She even smiled a little. They were both looking at me now.

"I was wondering if…you needed anything else," I said.

"Thank you," she said suddenly. "For helping out in back."

"You're welcome," I said.

"Poor Jonathan is really getting on," she said, looking toward the house next door. "He was going to paint the fence today. And the shutters. They haven't been painted for so many years." This was the most I'd ever heard her speak. "He's already bought the paint and everything. It's on the side of the house."

"I can do it," I said.

"Thank you," she answered. "I'll go tell Jonathan we won't be needing him." She walked past me. Gertrude picked up the suitcase and went inside.

I went and got the buckets and brushes. I carried them back around to the front, swinging the cans so the paint would slosh back and forth inside. I picked a spot to begin and knelt down. Mrs. Delgrew passed me on her way back from Dr. Crowe's.

"I have lemonade, when you're thirsty," she said as she walked by. It sounded more like a statement of fact than an invitation.

I painted all afternoon. The wood was chipped and rotting in places, and the fence really did need a good coat of paint. I had done a little painting once at the train yard when we had to completely restore a car. That hadn't been so bad, since we were all working on it and talking. This time I was completely alone, but it was easier on the mind than my usual job. There were no figures or policies or complex coverages here.

An hour or two passed, and I thought about my father and my brother. I suppose I missed male company in general. Here I was in another household of women. I didn't remember all that much about my father, really, since I was only nine years old when he died. As for my brother, though, I had no memories of life without him there. He had been born a year and a half after me, and I remembered nothing before him.

When I reached the end of the fence, I stepped back to survey my work, and decided it looked all right. I touched up a few spots and put the paint away, careful to avoid the drying fence. I thought some lemonade sounded good, and I told myself I'd earned a little break before tackling the shutters.

To my surprise, Mrs. Delgrew had lunch ready for me. She had made bread and butter and a piece of baked chicken. She insisted that I wash up and then sit and eat. Then she just stood there, watching me chew.

"I'm going to go ahead and work on the shutters after lunch," I said, just to say something.

"You can do those some other time," she said. "Gertrude needs to go pick up some bolts of fabric for her sewing today. You know that store in the factory?" I nodded. She sat down. "I don't like her going over there alone. I don't like the men working in that store."

My brother had worked at the textile factory after he quit school. She didn't know that, of course. He never worked in the store, anyway. But a lot of the factory workers did do double time at the little store that was in front of the warehouse. If I had a daughter I probably wouldn't want her to go there alone, either.

"I'll go with her," I said. "And I'll come back next week to do the shutters. Maybe even during the week if I can." I wanted to assure her that I wouldn't quit on her.

After I finished my lunch, Gertrude and I set off across town. She had brought the big suitcase along for me to carry. I noticed that she looked more dressed up than usual, in her black stockings and high-laced shoes. The way she dressed was always sort of old-fashioned.

"Thank you…for helping us out like this," she said.

"It's my pleasure," I answered.

"William was back for a few days…the time you got him to come back. He talked about you then."

"Where is he now?" I asked.

"He went away again, after a while. Days ago. Doctor Crowe has been a big help…it's important to Mama that people don't know about our troubles."

"Hmmm," I said.

"Can you tell me?" she asked. "I mean…Mama doesn't have to know. What happened to my brother?"

"I'm not sure. People change, I guess," was all I could muster. We walked in silence. I wondered if she could tell that there was something I wasn't telling her. "So you want to go to college?" I asked.

"Yes," she said quietly. "William was helping me. He was tutoring me in the subjects I have trouble with. He was…he is very smart."

"I know," I said. "He was always much smarter than me."

"You knew him in school, didn't you. That's what he said when he came back."

"Yes, I did," I answered. "We were there at the same time."

"Where did you go to grammar school?" she asked.

"Magnus Martyr," I answered. "That's where my Aunt made me go." I thought back to the musty old school building, full of one hundred and fifty boys in uniform every single day. The Anglican mass was the most important subject in school to my Aunt.

"Does your Aunt live with you?" she asked.

"Yes...well, we live with her. My Mother and I. My father died when I was nine."

"I see," she said quietly. I wondered how old she had been when her father passed away.

"I didn't like school very much," I said. "I think the only reason I went on to secondary school was that we got to go with the girls." She smiled a little. I couldn't tell if she found that humorous or not.

I felt very awkward around her from the start. I had never been great around girls. I just hadn't had that much experience. I wasn't that young, I know, but in those days things were different. I hadn't had a sister, and I hadn't even really known a girl until after grammar school. I was a pretty shy kid for a while.

The first girl I ever kissed was named Sue. It happened because my friend Carl's dad had a Pierce-Arrow back before the war. Carl wasn't from Greenwood, but his family had a summer home here, and we used to take that car out on picnics by the river during the summer. One year Carl had a girl in town, too. A couple of times Carl's girl brought her friend Sue with us on the picnics. She had red hair and freckled skin and her eyes were close together. We kissed once, just because Carl and the other girl were kissing. That was my first kiss, even though Sue didn't know it. I couldn't tell anyone, because I felt like I was much too old to be having my first kiss then. I always had the feeling that Sue was just killing time while her friend was with Carl.

There was another gal at church just before I was picked in the registration. We used to look at each other every once in a while. I used to think about her in certain ways and it made me feel guilty. I was in church, after all. I was looking at this girl and thinking about things, and there were her parents and her little sister right there next to her. Her dad had the exact same face, too, and they all had the same black hair. I met her at a church picnic one time, and we talked in the woods, and we did a few things. She seemed a lot younger than me, though. And then we didn't talk any more. When our eyes met in church after that I felt really bad. Going off to war kind of saved me that time. When I got back she'd gone away to a school somewhere else.

But Gertrude made me feel different, and I wasn't even sweet on her or anything. She wasn't like most gals. I don't think she really had that many friends. I guess I thought of her just like I thought of Willie. I could tell that she was smart like him, too.

We passed the hardware store on our right. There was a shiny vacuum cleaner in the window that attracted Gertrude's attention. It looked very modern. The sign told us that it cost forty dollars, but it could be ours for two dollars down and four dollars monthly.

"We sure could use something like that," she said.

"You know what else they sell in there?" I asked, showing off.

"What?"

"Little portable stills," I said. It was true. "They're right in there...they don't even try to hide them. For six dollars." She smiled but didn't seem so amused. I thought about Willie and realized it was probably a stupid thing to say.

A stocky man carrying several pieces of wood left the store and crossed the sidewalk in front of us. A cigar hung from his mouth. He looked familiar to me. It was a pretty small town, and I almost always recognized someone, even if I didn't know their name. This man had hair like salt and pepper. It was very dark and then light gray, in intermittent patches. His brow was heavy and dark.

He stood to the side as we passed, looking at Gertrude and then at me. His big, wide hands were hairy and dark where they held the boards over his shoulder. When I got a closer look at his single eyebrow, I recognized him.

"Hey," I said. He nodded, as if I was just giving a friendly greeting on passing. "Have you seen Willie?" I asked, stopping. I'm sure Gertrude was surprised, but she was behind me so I couldn't see her expression.

He looked at me strangely.

"I think you're mistaken," he said, gruffly. The door with the "22" on it was right across the street and down a little ways, so I shot a glance toward it. He followed my eyes and immediately understood. I don't think he recognized me personally, but he knew what I was talking about now.

He looked around, shifting his eyes this way and that. He gave Gertrude an uneasy glance.

"That place got shut down," he said quietly. "I don't see nobody from there." Maybe he thought that I didn't believe him. "Okay…I see some guys every once in a while. A lot of 'em go further outta town now…there're some farmers out there." He brought his voice to a whisper. "You can go checking 'round out there," he said. "But I'd watch out, because things get rough with the law so far away. I'm willin' to sell you a password, though."

"No thanks," I said. He looked Gertrude up and down again as we walked away. I didn't like it. I wondered if he even remembered who Willie was. He didn't seem very trustworthy, and for all I knew the place across the street could still be open.

"Who was that?" she asked, when we were a safe distance away.

"Just a friend," I said.

"He's from that saloon, isn't he?" she asked.

"Yes," I said. She didn't say anything else. We walked on in silence. I suppose she was probably thinking about Willie. We crossed through the park and walked south, out of the center of town and toward the factory.

Henry had worked at the textile factory since he left school. It was massive, and there were a lot of men employed there, most of them younger guys. When it was new, almost all the guys I knew had ended up there as soon as they left school. I thought about him working there. I imagined him coming in the morning and heading out at lunch and at the end of the day. I had a strange, empty feeling. I forced it down and away when I remembered that I was with Gertrude.

Henry hadn't talked much about what it was like to work there. I remember him telling us about skilled and unskilled workers one time, though. I think he was proud to be considered skilled. I'm sure he did his job well.

A few of the offices in front had been converted into a little store where merchants and certain families could buy cheap cloth. In those days, only the very rich bought their clothes at a store. Almost everyone made what they wore, so fabrics and raw materials were very important to the average family. Gertrude must have been good at what she did, since she was getting paid to make clothing for people outside of her family.

We went through the gate and into the front entrance. She seemed to know where she was going. We passed through a door and into a fairly nondescript room. There were no signs on the windows or doors. The store sure didn't advertise much. I guess the only people who came there already knew about it, though. Layer after layer of fabrics were draped everywhere, and she began looking at them. I could see the entrance to a vast warehouse through a door behind the counter, and the sounds of machinery reached us even in the front of the store.

"Anything I can help you find?" a voice asked. A young man had stepped from the back and was standing behind the counter. He looked younger than me, and he was dressed very well, especially for a factory worker. I was surprised that I'd never seen him in town before. His shiny hair was parted neatly, and he had an angular nose and jaw. His face was smooth and youthful. He smiled, showing his straight, white teeth. Even I knew this was a handsome fellow. He was much better looking than me, I was sure.

Gertrude seemed unaffected, though. She told him what she was looking for, and he came out from behind the counter to help her. I wandered over to the wall near the cash register. There was a calendar hanging there, advertising Firestone Tires. It had a picture of a truck in front of an American flag. The caption read:

> *When the French stood at the line at the Marne, people realized all at once that the motor truck was essential. Please, ship by truck.*

There were a few pieces of paper pinned to a bulletin board next to the calendar. I wasn't really interested in Gertrude's conversation with the clerk, and I had nothing else to do, so I glanced over the papers. One looked like it had been up there for a while. The small, typewritten print said:

> *There are agitators, prowling about the mills, spreading German propaganda for the conversion of foreigners especially. These IWW and Socialist vermin, working under the guise of AF of L organizers, teach that war is bad. These strangers are Liars and German propagandists, some of them probably in the Kaiser's pay.*

That's all it said. It seemed like a strange thing to be hanging in a store. Gertrude and the man discussed rayon behind me. Another piece of paper hung next to the first. This one appeared to have been cut from a magazine of some kind. It had a poem on it:

> *Said Dan McGann to a foreign man who worked at the selfsame bench.*
>
> *"Let me tell you this," and for emphasis, he flourished a monkey wrench,*
>
> *"Don't talk to me of this bourjoissee, don't open your mouth to speak*
>
> *"Of your socialists or your anarchists, don't mention the bolshevik,*

> *"For I've had enough of this foreign stuff, I'm sick as*
> *a man can be*
> *"Of the speech of hate, and I'm telling you straight,*
> *that this is the land for me.*
>
> *—Edgar Guest*

"Don't pay any mind to those," the clerk was saying. He folded Gertrude's purchases over the counter and moved around to the register.

"Oh, I was just looking," I said, turning around.

He didn't say anything else, so I looked back. The last piece of paper appeared to be a clipping from a newspaper:

> *"The Department of Justice has undertaken to tear out the radical seeds that have entangled American ideas," says Attorney General A. Mitchell Palmer, defending the arrest of 6,000 Communists on New Year's Day. He promises to target "the IWW's, the most radical socialists, the misguided anarchists, the moral perverts and the hysterical neurasthenic women who abound in communism."*

"The old man's a bit of an isolationist," the clerk said now, smiling at me. "He owns the place. Don't let that stuff go to your head. I haven't seen you two in here before."

"I come in all the time," said Gertrude.

"Well, I suppose I'm not usually working up front," he said with a smile. "My name is Jack," he nodded at Gertrude, and extended his hand toward me.

Gertrude introduced herself and then me. She didn't sound terribly friendly.

"Whittier, huh?" he asked, pushing the register buttons.

"Yes…my brother used to work here." I hadn't told Gertrude about Henry working here. As usual, though, her expression betrayed nothing.

"I remember," he said. "I didn't know him well myself, really, but we were all sorry to hear about what happened. Did the boss ever come by with his condolences?"

"I…I'm not sure," I said. "I don't think so."

"Hmm," he said. "We lost a few good guys over there. I lost some friends. Did you serve too?"

"Yes," I said. "I went in through the first registration."

"I was in the second, myself…never made it over there though. You boys finished the work early." He smiled. I just nodded. So I was right about his being a few years younger than I was. He looked as if he wanted to say more, but I guess he thought I probably didn't want to talk about it. He turned back toward Gertrude.

"You're getting some good stuff," he said as they finished the transaction. I started folding the fabric as best as I could and cramming it into the case. "See this jacket I'm wearing?" he was talking to me again.

"Sure." It was a nice three-button sports coat.

"This is cartridge cloth…did you know that?" He turned toward Gertrude. "It's the fabric they used to hold powder charges during the war." He said it to her as if he was letting her in on a secret. I didn't tell him that I hadn't known what cartridge cloth was either.

I managed to shut the case and we thanked him and made our way toward the door.

"Hey, Whittier," he called as we were going out. "Don't believe everything you read." He stabbed the papers on the bulletin board with a finger, smiled broadly, and winked. I smiled back, having no idea what he was talking about. He seemed like a guy who tried too hard to me.

"He seemed like a nice gentleman," Gertrude said as soon as we got outside.

"Hmm," I said. We walked on for a while.

"You don't have to walk me all the way home," she said.

"Oh, it's my pleasure," I said.

"It's probably easier for you to just go home," she said. "Where do you live?"

I told her where it was.

"See, you'd have to walk me all the way back and then come across town," she said. "It'll be dark by the time you get home. I'll be all right."

"Are you sure?" I asked.

"Mama just worries about the factory," she said. "I'm fine now."

"All right," I felt bad leaving her, but she obviously wanted me to. I went as far as I could, and then I handed her the case.

"Well…" I said.

"Are you coming over again this week?" she asked.

"Sure," I said, a bit surprised.

"Good." She nodded and walked off.

CHAPTER 9

The usual plan was six months of training at home, then two overseas. After those two, we were to enter what was called a "quiet sector" of the battle line. This was an area where it wasn't likely that we were going to come up against the enemy, men the Brits called the "baby killers." After a month in the quiet zone, though, it would be off to what was called an "active sector."

We had been in the quiet zone through the middle of September. It was quiet, all right. We kept up our training, and our discipline, and we never saw any fighting. It was really just another training camp, like the ones we'd already been through back home. The fight that history would call the battle of the Meuse-Argonne had been raging for a while to the east of us. We were playing catch up, and it was starting to look like we were going to miss the whole thing. Meanwhile, the rest of our boys kept pushing further and further away from where we were.

This was the biggest, bloodiest battle of the European war. There was a definite feeling in the air that this was the battle to end all battles in the war to end all wars. The ides of war itself was coming to an end, and everyone knew it. There would be nothing left to fight for after this. The whole world was there, and the destructive power made it the perfect final conflict. The Meuse-Argonne was, quite simply, the greatest battle Americans had ever fought, and probably would ever fight. And I missed it entirely.

Whenever they do counts of how many men fought and died there, they always have a category for "troops not in divisions." These were men who got tired of sticking it out in the quiet zone and deserted their own squad to head to the front. They were listed as AWOL but they were in the battle, because they wanted to be. These guys were true jingoes, but I understood them. Our time in the quiet zone was very frustrating. We knew what was going on to the east, and we were all worried that it might end before we could officially enter an active zone. None of the guys wanted to go home and tell their girls and their parents that we'd missed it. Going in AWOL was never a realistic option for me, though, since that would mean leaving my friends behind. If I went in alone I wouldn't have anyone to back up my stories later, and that would be almost as bad as missing it together.

The only difference between our time in the quiet zone and the rest of our training was our proximity to the battle itself. Everyone was involved in this one. The French were attacking near the great salient of the front, the English were up north driving eastward, and the Belgians were resuming the offensive south of the coast. It was the greatest offensive in the history of the world, and America got to hit the most vital spot of the enemy's lines. We saw tommies from just about everywhere in the world heading in through and around our zone.

Almost all the movement was at night. I used to talk to a few of the truck drivers when they came through our camp. I remember one kid, I think has name was Tim or Tom. We started talking because he was originally from a town not far from Greenwood. One time he told me that we had about a thousand trucks bringing foot soldiers in night after night. I tried to imagine that many guys, each one just like me, with a family and friends and a town back home. It was incredible.

One sight that always excited us was when the really big guns came through. The noise was unmistakable. We would always find some excuse to be hanging around by the road when we heard them coming. They would use caterpillar tractors to haul the huge guns. I remember watching them slide by, wide cannons pointed at the sky, wondering if anyone in Austria or Servia would have ever imagined facing these things down in their back yards. Of course, in the next war they stopped dragging the guns with the tractors and just put the tractor wheels on the guns themselves, and drove them around. But that's getting way ahead of myself. Back then, there weren't going to be any more wars after this one.

The day finally came when the captain told us we were moving into the active sector. I'll never forget that day. It began rainy, dreary, and gray, but then cleared up quickly, the sun peeking through the clouds. The weather was like that a lot there. It was quite cold, though, since it was already the first of November by then.

We were on the move early, leaving the camp behind. There was definitely an air of both anticipation and anxiety. Lovejoy finally broke the silence.

"Hey Bridges," he said. Bridges turned. We all turned, glad that someone was going to say something cocksmart. "If you go west today, don't worry…I'll be right there to comfort Sarah when I get home." Sarah was Tommy's gal back in Pittsburgh, as we all knew. "Go west" was what we used to say instead of get killed.

Bridges smirked. "Lovejoy, if I go west out there, I'm takin' you boys with me. Along with the whole front line of Prussia." We laughed, concentrating on not showing any fear. Sarge had just told us the night before that the enemy had no words in their language for panic or fear.

While we were laughing I heard a new sound. It was a whining that had started out low and moved higher in pitch. It seemed to be all around us. Our laughter died away.

No one else looked worried, though, and at first I thought the ringing was in my head.

"Monoplane," Sergeant Clark called back to us. "They're up north...tryin' to fly in supplies. Look over the trees." I followed his finger but saw nothing.

"There it is," someone shouted.

And then I caught sight of the little plane. It was amazing that it could make such a sound. Planes in the sky weren't such a common sight back then. From the ground it looked like a foreign toy that a young German boy might play with. The wings curved downward, and the rudder hung low. As it turned away over the trees, I could just make out a black cross painted on its belly.

Two massive objects appeared to be following the monoplane at a short distance. They were big yellow German balloons, quite garish even at that distance. I had heard about sightings of these things before. They looked like zeppelins, but they were about seventy-five feet in length and probably about twenty around. They moved jerkily, and I soon realized that the tiny monoplane was actually dragging them away from the fighting on tethers.

We stood and watched as the whole procession slid by in the sky, moving even further north. The gangly design of the Imperial Eagle stretched out in black across the bottom of one of the giant balloons, its tendrils trying to hug the whole thing. I imagined what a nice target that would make for one of our caterpillar guns. The whining grew higher in pitch, and then faded away. This was my first experience of the enemy. I had been given a glimpse of the presence that awaited us. Everything was suddenly rendered sharp and real by those silly yellow shapes. They signified what was perhaps the greatest fear of my young life. I could never admit this to anyone, of course. A few of the guys cracked some jokes, and we kept moving. I think Lovejoy may have even compared one of the balloons to poor Sarah back in Pittsburgh.

We met up with a small division just before the Argonne forest, and the captain spoke with a few of the officers. I recognized them from the quiet zone. There was one severely pockmarked lieutenant whose eyes were so light blue in color that they were almost clear. The captain talked with him at length. They were moving in almost the same direction that we were, cutting across our path.

This lieutenant looked around at all of us. He turned back to the captain, and spoke in a low voice. I could have sworn that I heard my name. This man didn't know me, though. Sergeant Clark joined them and after a few moments he and the captain glanced up at me at the same time. A strange feeling came over me. They moved toward me slowly.

"Whittier," Sarge said. "Lieutenant Stanson." He waved toward the lieutenant. The captain stared at the woods in the distance quietly. Then he and Clark turned and walked away. The sergeant eyed everyone else, and they slowly followed, looking as confused as I was.

"Son." The lieutenant's voice startled me. He was probably only a few years older than I was, so it seemed like a strange thing to call me. His mouth opened a few times, as if he was speaking sentences that I couldn't hear. A bird chirped in the distance.

"It's about your brother…I'm sorry to have to tell you," he shook his head quietly. He seemed legitimately sorry. I saw it coming before he even said it, though. A tight knot grew in the center of my stomach. I was already going over the different ways Henry could've died in my mind.

The influenza epidemic hadn't been that long ago, and that killed a huge number of ours. For a while we'd even thought it was germ warfare. There was a theory that the enemy was putting something in Bayer aspirin, which was German. And there was lockjaw, too. We had to make sure to clean every little cut on our feet or hands or lockjaw could kill us, they said. Henry had never really been the heroic type, but I hoped desperately that he'd been killed fighting rather than by some disease.

I looked at the lieutenant. I wasn't going to say anything until I heard it all.

"He was killed in action," he said. "I wasn't there, but I met his command back at camp. A few of his boys came in just after you left. Some of the officers asked me to maybe let you know if I caught up with you. They said he was in the thick of it and there was a bullet with his name on it. Simple as that. He went down a hero, along with most of his division. It was a few days ago, I think. I've lost a brother myself, and it's a tough thing."

He apologized again quietly, and that was all he said. He gave me a little pat on the shoulder, and slowly walked away. I saw the rest of the guys milling about near the trees. They must have known that something was in the air, because they were respectfully quiet.

The first thing I felt was relief that he had been shot rather than blown apart by a shell. I don't know why this was important, but it was. I hoped that he was conscious of his own death, and that maybe he bled to death slowly and got to think back on his life and our family. Nothing could be worse, I decided, then getting blown up without even knowing it. There was something truly scary about the idea that you could be here one minute, and then just not exist the next.

I stood there alone for a while. I can't really describe what I was feeling. I suppose some people would say that the truth hadn't sunk in yet. But it sure felt real to me as soon as I heard it. Probably even before I heard it. I wondered if the telegram from the U.S. Army had reached my Mother yet.

I thought about the last time I had spoken to him. It was when we said goodbye at camp Devens. I knew I probably wasn't going to run into him over here. We had shook hands and wished each other luck. I don't know if I'd ever shaken his hand before then.

I imagined him now in one of those thin, yellow pine boxes. I'd seen them on our way in through the countryside. They were always being brought out by train or automobile, or waiting to be loaded. Everyone got a box, and they were all the same. There was one for each of us, somewhere. I couldn't really see him in one of those. It made me think of a birdhouse I'd tried to build when I was a kid. It was the same type of wood, I think.

I don't remember anything else about that day. When I think back, the two things that stick out in my mind are the yellow pine box and the tiny monoplane pulling those balloons through the sky. Those are the two things I really remember. I read somewhere later that the Germans called those planes "Taube," which means "Dove."

CHAPTER 10

"Well, Jean, when do you suppose we should tell Colbert?" asked my Aunt Edna. They'd both been a bit quieter than usual during the first part of dinner. My Mother smiled weakly and finished her spoonful of soup. "He's certainly going to have a lot of the responsibility around here," my Aunt went on. "I know he can handle it, but we'd better prepare him, don't you think?"

"For what?" I asked, putting my own fork down. Aunt Edna had never been good at keeping secrets for very long.

"You remember my brother Edwin who lived in Boston?" my Mother asked.

For as far back as I can remember I'd heard her talk about our relatives the Boston Benthams. They were our only relations in America, and I had always wondered if I would ever get to meet them.

I'm not sure if my Aunt had ever even met my Mother's brother, but she definitely knew that he was "no good." Long before I would have had any idea of what this phrase meant, I knew that it characterized my uncle in Boston. Henry and I used to call each other "no good" from time to time when we were little, especially when we were angry at each other. The only other thing we'd ever heard about this uncle was the news of his death a few years before the war.

"Yes," I answered my Mother.

"Well," she said slowly, "His son Ambrose is going to be staying with us for a little while. Here."

"How old is he?"

"I'm not sure...he's a few years older than you are. You're finally going to meet your cousin," she looked pleased.

"How long will he be here?" I asked.

"Well," she shot a glance at my Aunt. "I'm not exactly sure. But I know you'll have a good time showing him around."

"Why is he coming?" I asked. "What does he do? Doesn't he have a job?"

"His mother wanted him to have a little vacation away from Boston," she said. "She's asked us to take him in here for a little while, to give him a change of scenery. She also thought it would be nice for him to meet some of his relatives on our side of the family."

"His mother is from a very influential family in Boston," said my Aunt as she leaned forward, placing her heavy elbows on the table. "A very old family with old money. So I'm sure she's used to getting what she wants."

I wasn't very happy at the prospect of having a relative I'd never met follow me around town for a while.

"When is he coming?" I asked.

"He'll be arriving next week," my Mother said.

"Is he planning to find work here?" I asked.

"I'm not sure," my Mother said. "I...I don't really know any more than that. We'll just have to see."

"Misses Elizabeth Goodwin Bentham just contacts us all of a sudden," said my Aunt, who was much more eager to discuss the subject. "Imagine, ignoring your husband's relations during his life and even after his passing, and then suddenly sending a telegram asking them to bring your son into their home for as long as he wants to stay there? Can you imagine? She's lucky that Jean is too nice to give her a piece of her mind."

My Mother sighed quietly. My Aunt continued, focusing on me now.

"Colbert, I wanted to have this talk with you just because I have a feeling that this boy is not like you. He is a rich, spoiled child who was raised wealthy, and he's probably not a very nice boy."

"Edna," my Mother said, "we don't know that. We don't know."

"Oh, I know, Jean, I know we don't know. I just want to warn Colbert just in case. Listen to me. I've had a lot more experience with people of this class…with old money who think they can do whatever they want. When I got married I stepped into this world of old money, and it can be very harsh. Of course, we didn't have as much as everyone else, but William was a member of those circles. I was twenty-two years old when we got married, and I had to learn quickly. Did you know that, Colbert? I was younger than you. You can't imagine those other accountants' wives. Of course, William's investments hadn't been doing that well, but we still had to be around all of those people. We went to all of the dinners and the parties before William's death, and I can tell you that those women would look down their noses at you just as soon as they laid eyes on you. A lot of their children grew up wild and spoiled, and I wouldn't be surprised at all if this boy is just like that."

"He probably just needs to see the countryside," offered my Mother. "I know he's traveled around Boston and New York when he was working with his father, but I don't know if he's ever been anywhere like here. You can take him around with you, right Colbert?"

"I'm busy a lot of the time," I started, picking up my fork again. "But I guess I can do it when I have time."

"That's fine," my Mother said.

"That's all we ask of you," chimed in my Aunt. "We know you're busy, because you're a responsible person. And if this boy tries to get you to be like him, well, we know you'll resist him. And you just let us know, and I'll tell his mother that we're packing him right off again. I know Jean would never do that, and I would never make you do that, dear. But I'll be happy to talk to that woman, if it needs to be done."

My Mother didn't talk about her family very much. I had never really asked her about them, either. As a kid growing up, I had other things on my mind, of course. But now I realized that she might want to talk about them. So I tried to start a conversation. Maybe I just wanted more hints as to what Ambrose was going to be like.

"Edwin was your oldest brother?" I asked.

"Yes, Edwin was six years older than I was, and Robert was…" she cocked her head toward the ceiling in thought. "Robert was three years older, he was born in eighteen sixty-one. And my sisters were both younger. Agnes is two years younger than I am, and Elizabeth was the youngest…she was four years younger than I am."

"When did Edwin come to America?" I asked. My Aunt looked at her curiously also.

"Edwin was the oldest. He was supposed to become a professor at Oxford, and follow in our father's footsteps. But I think he took more after our mother's side of the family. Our uncles on that side were said to be a bit wild. I don't think Edwin really wanted to be a professor. He left for America when he was only about fifteen."

"Can you imagine?" asked my Aunt.

"My father was so angry," my Mother continued. "I'll never forget the day when we found out he had run away. My father went down to the docks and looked for him all day. But Edwin was gone. We were all devastated. He was the first born son, after all."

My Aunt stood and began clearing plates. My Mother started to rise too.

"No, no, Jean," said my Aunt. "Go ahead. I'll take care of this." My Mother sat back down.

"Did you know anything about America?" I asked.

"America?" she said with a smile. "We thought it was a crazy, horrible place. My father had always told us that it was uninhabitable. We never heard from Edwin once he went there, either. In fact, I didn't speak to him again until I was in America too. Robert did well, though. He concentrated on his studies, and he was a lot more like my father."

"And you went to finishing school," said my Aunt as she gathered our silverware and headed back toward the kitchen.

"Oh, yes," my Mother said with a broad smile. "I started at finishing school when I was sixteen years old. I got to go to Paris for that." Her eyes lit up. "It was the best place to go. But I had to get an education there, too. My father was not like a lot of those professors...he wanted his daughters to be educated too. I'm very glad of that. And I'm sure a lot of people didn't like that about him.

"And that's where I met Gerard, too," she said. "We met at the marketplace in Paris. It must have been when I'd been there for about a year or so. And he would visit me at school from time to time then." I'd never heard this story before. Or at least I didn't remember ever hearing it. I pictured my Mother as a young woman. It was odd to think about her that way.

"And we went to America together and got married when I was eighteen years old," she was saying. "I knew my father would be so angry that he'd lost another child. So I wrote back to him from Paris and I just left right from there, with the few things I had with me at school. They never would have let us get married, we knew. But I wrote again from New York...I wrote them all the time. My sisters and my mother would write back. They asked me to find Edwin, and I did that, too. We went and visited him there in Boston."

"You know, Gerard didn't like him one bit," my Aunt said, hovering overhead now.

"He was always nice to him, though," my Mother said.

"Oh yes, of course he was always nice. But Gerard didn't like some people. He never did."

"That's true," my Mother said. "That's true. I probably should have known that he wouldn't like Edwin, though."

"So did he seem different to you," I asked, "after so much time?"

"No…that was the funny thing. He was married to a very wealthy girl and her father had got him a job as a banker, but he was really the same to me. He seemed exactly the same."

"He married a Goodwin in Boston," added my Aunt. "That's one way to work your way up."

"That's true," said my Mother. "That's true."

"You never saw your father again, did you?" I asked.

"No," she said quietly. "No, I didn't." My Aunt's hand rested on her shoulder. "He wrote to me though. He forgave me for going and all. He wasn't angry. I wanted him to come over and visit so badly. But he was always busy, right up until he died. And then Robert took over the house and became a professor, too."

"Really?" asked Aunt Edna.

"Yes, Robert was a professor at Oxford. But my mother did come over here to visit. That was when I was pregnant with Henry." It was strange to hear her say his name. "You were about one, Colbert. I'm sure you don't remember."

"I remember the horses," I said. She laughed.

"That's right, she brought those wooden horses for both of you. Those had belonged to my father. They were bookends, really. He had carved them. But you boys didn't know that. You thought they were toys."

"Where are those?" I asked.

"We still have them, somewhere, I'm sure. But you know, my mother didn't visit Edwin while she was here. I told him about it ahead of time and tried to get him to come down, but he was busy, and she didn't want to go anywhere but New York. So they didn't see each other."

"He still wasn't forgiven for what he did," said my Aunt with a wagging finger. She sat down again.

"No, that's true. He wasn't. Maybe it wasn't fair. I left too. But it was different with the first born of the household. And my mother passed away back in England a few years later, and then Robert went not too long after that. So really it's just the sisters left. Agnes got married and Elizabeth was a governess for a long time. But they're still living over there. Agnes writes to me from time to time." She turned to my Aunt. "You remember when my mother visited, don't you?"

"Oh, yes," she said. "Of course I do. I'll never forget how nervous Gerard was." She looked at me now. "Imagine running away with a girl and bringing her across the ocean and getting married, and then having to finally meet her mother years later."

The thought of my father nervous about anything was funny to me. I tried to picture him pacing back and forth in his huge boots, his broad hands stroking his beard.

"But I don't think your mother liked me very much," said my Aunt.

"You don't?" my Mother asked.

"Oh no. I can tell that sort of thing."

"She knew you were one of my only friends over here, though. She knew that."

"Yes," my Aunt nodded her head for a long while. "Yes…" she trailed off, looking into the distance.

"What year did Edwin die?" I asked.

She thought for a while.

"You had been out of school for a few years…It must have been about nineteen fifteen," she said at last. "Yes, that's right. I went up for the funeral. That's the last time I saw Ambrose."

I remembered when my Mother took that trip. I had waved good-bye to her as she stood on the train. That was the first time she was away from me for any period of time. It was only two days. She hadn't had much to say about the hospitality of Edwin's widow when she got back.

"Well, he was probably already over twenty years old then," said my Aunt, still talking about my cousin. "But he probably seemed young to you because that type of child is immature. A wealthy child, who grew up in those kind of surroundings."

"You'll be nice to him, won't you, Colbert?" my Mother asked as she rose from the table, a far off look still in her eyes. I thought about her losing her brothers, her parents, her husband. I thought about her losing her son.

"Of course I will," I said. I couldn't have said anything else.

CHAPTER 11

During my lunch break one day I was sitting by myself in Myrtle's Restaurant. It used to be called Greenwood Restaurant, but then the Myrtle family bought it. Mr. Myrtle was a New York stockbroker who had a summer home in Greenwood, and at the end of one summer he decided not to go back to New York. He needed something to do with all his money, though, so he bought the Greenwood Restaurant and put his whole family to work there. His two sons were notorious troublemakers. "The Myrtle boys" is what everyone called them, since they were always together.

The Myrtles had fixed the restaurant up quite a bit. I liked it because there were a lot of small tables there, so I didn't feel silly eating my lunch alone. Whenever it was too cold to walk all the way home, I would go there for lunch and sit with the newspaper and enjoy the lemon chicken or the spaghetti and meatballs.

It was just another storefront, really, but you'd never know it from the inside. The door had a small stained glass window in it, and the front windows were stained as well, so it wasn't too bright in there. The walls were dark wood, and the little lamps on the tables were turned on all day long. There were pictures on the wall of different parts of the United States that had been there since before the Myrtles. Niagara Falls, the Grand Canyon, San Francisco Bay, The Alamo.

I'd never been to a single one of these places. I was sure that if I ever went to them they would be a lot different than I imagined, and they probably wouldn't look much like the pictures. That was what had happened when I went to Europe, after all.

On this particular day I was ignoring the pictures and reading my paper. An empty bowl stained with bright spaghetti sauce was pushed to the side of my small table. I had been peeling my orange and drinking black coffee. I usually ended my lunch with an orange and a cup of coffee. I was hoping that they would be good for my throat, which had been growing sore lately. Every winter, it seemed, I had a sore throat for at least a month. I didn't mention it to my Mother or my Aunt anymore, because I wanted to avoid the endless parade of household oils and ointments that they would inflict on me.

I was sitting against the wall, as I usually did. The paper was open to a page about the economic troubles of American farmers, and my hands were getting messy from peeling the orange. I kept reaching down and wiping them on the napkin on my lap.

The place wasn't usually very crowded at lunchtime, especially during the week. It was more of less the same people every time I went in there.

"Cobb?" I looked up. There was Jim Garrison.

I knew little Jimmie Garrison in my school days. He was a wide kid who took up a lot of space when we were little. He thought he was a bully of some kind, and he even tried to beat Henry up a few times. We always stopped him together, though. And after a few years, as is often the case with young boys, we went from being sworn enemies to fairly close friends. I even remember him coming over to our house a few times.

But he ended up going to a different high school than I did. He stayed in the religious schools when I left. We barely knew each other by the time we were teenagers.

From what I heard, he had gone off to the war at about the same time that I had, like a lot of guys in town. I imagine he probably went to Devens, although I never saw him there. He could have gone to Alfred Vail in New Jersey, though.

Now, here he was, standing over me at lunch. His black hair was slicked back on his scalp. He was wearing a heavy coat that was tight around the hips, and a red scarf was draped around his large neck.

"Hey, Jim," I said, trying to sound friendly. I started to stand, but he sat down in the other chair instead.

"You mind?" he asked.

"No, no," I said. I folded the paper again and put it aside. His sharp eyes stared directly into mine, and he smiled slightly. "So how've you been?" I asked.

"Good, good," he said. A few moments passed. "It's been a while."

"It sure has."

"Yeah, I was just sitting over there," he said, leaning back in the chair.

"Really? I didn't see you."

"I didn't see you either. I was just on my way out, in fact." He loosened the scarf, and it hung down onto the table. It was dangerously close to the sauce-covered bowl, but he didn't notice.

"I just come here at lunch sometimes with the paper," I said.

"You working around here?"

"Mmm hmm," I nodded, taking a sip of the coffee. The hot liquid poured down the back of my raw throat and warmed me up considerably. "I work for Mister Durham," I said. "He's in insurance."

"Sure, sure," he said. "Sounds good."

"It's not too bad. What are you doing these days?"

"Oh, I work for my father. He still hasn't retired from running the mill. But he's training me to take the whole place over any day now."

"Wow…that's great. That sure sounds great." I popped a piece of orange into my mouth. There wasn't much juice.

"Well, it's a lot to do," he smiled, folding his arms in front of the scarf. "A lotta men working there. I can handle the men, though…the numbers is the hardest part, you know. I don't think I learned any arithmetic from school. The figures really make my head ache." I laughed with him.

"Where are you living now?" he asked.

"At my Aunt's. Same place."

"Right, right." The waiter came and took the empty spaghetti bowl away, and the distraction gave me a second to think about how strange this conversation was. Jim was someone who I hadn't talked to for years. All we had in common, really, was that we happened to be the same age. But that was enough for a conversation.

"Where are you living?" I asked. The waiter backed away with the bowl.

"I've got a place on the north end of town…a flat up there." A lot of nice apartments had been built up north just before the war. "I got married, you know," he said.

"That's what I heard," I said, eating another piece of orange.

"Did you ever know Kate Sherwood?" he asked.

"Yes," I said. "I remember Kate." Her family had gone to our church when I was little. She went to a different school, though. She and her sisters had always looked so blonde and pretty in church. When we were older, I had gone to school with her for a few years at the town school. At school she was one of the wealthy girls who always acted a little uppity. There was a whole flock of them, all slim with blond hair and freckles. She used to play croquet with the rest of them on the school lawn.

"Well, she's Kate Garrison now. We got married a little while before the war." I knew this already, of course. The town wasn't that big.

"Well, I know it's late, but congratulations," I said.

"Thanks," he smiled. A moment of silence passed, and I took a few gulps of the coffee, which had cooled down a little. The burning in my throat subsided and returned again.

"So did you see any action over there?" he asked quietly, sitting up and leaning in toward me.

"Not a whole lot," I shook my head slowly with a smile, putting the cup down. "They tried to hit us a few times, but we were really just backing everyone up. We got to the big fight a little late."

"Mmmm," he said. He looked down at himself and adjusted his scarf.

"What about you? Where were you over there?"

"All over, really," he said, looking up. "I got to see most of Europe once I got injured."

"How bad was it?"

"Oh, it's not bad now…not now," he said, his face flushing a little. "I'm fine now…really. But it was bad then," he said, smiling up at me. He turned and looked toward the stained glass window, and I followed his gaze. Shards of red and yellow shone out from behind a large brown and white sailboat made of the colored glass. It had always looked like a pirate's boat to me. The bottom of the window was blue and white, like the sea. I could never quite figure out what the yellow and red streaks were. The best I could imagine was that they were supposed to be rays from the sun setting behind the ship. "You know anyone who got hurt bad over there?" he asked, turning back.

"No," I answered truthfully. "Not really."

"Well, you're lucky. Most of my time over there was recovery. I was on the front, and the next thing I knew I'm on an ambulance, and they're cranking the damned thing. They're cranking it over and over again and it won't turn over. And I'm lying there…that's where I woke up. And I start thinking that I'm gonna die because this ambulance won't start." His voice had grown a bit louder. I just nodded, encouraging him to continue.

"That's all those dressing stations were...just ambulances coming and going day and night."

"So yours finally started."

"I suppose so," he laughed. "Though I don't remember that part. I was sort of in and out after I got hit, you know. They'd just let you lie there for a while, and take a look at you, and then move you somewhere else. That's all I remember for a while. Waking up and being moved. They moved me down to the casualty clearing station, which was the first hospital behind the line, and then they moved me to a base hospital farther away...back from the fighting, you know."

"Where was that?"

"Somewhere in the middle of France...that's all I know. You know, it was just like that," he clapped his hands loudly. "I didn't see any of my buddies over there ever again. All I remember is that damn ambulance cranking. And I never got to say goodbye to any of them, or see how the fight turned out or anything."

"So how long were you there?" I asked. "At the base hospital?"

"About three months, probably," he said. "You don't get to leave on the hospital train until they say you're good and ready. I got to know those little French nuns pretty well, I guess. They took good care of us. I had septic poisoning set in to one of my wounds. That's why I had to stay for so long." It sounded very painful to me. I didn't ask about it, though, because he seemed to be in his own world now. He reminded me of a teacher giving a lecture. He had become quite animated.

"I got to know a lotta the British fellows then," he said. "There were a whole lotta them there. All you'd hear, all day long, was the swinging door in the ward when the nuns came and went, and the bath water running, and the gramophone. That's probably what helped so many of those boys keep their sanity. We loved that gramophone. When they weren't listening, the British guys used to sing songs of their own. They taught me one, and I used to sing it with them all the time."

I took the opportunity to glance at the grandfather clock that was snug against the opposite wall. I still had a few minutes of my traditional break time left. The next thing I knew he had leaned in toward me and was singing quietly.

"We'll have a little cottage in a little town
And we'll have a little mistress in a dainty gown,
A little doggie, a little cat,
A little doorstep with Welcome on the mat;
And we'll have a little trouble and a little strife,
But none of these things matter when you've got a little wife.
We shall be as happy as the angels up above
With a little patience and a lot of love."

He sat back again and smiled broadly. I didn't quite know how to react, so I just smiled back at him and nodded.

"That's nice," I finally said.

"I'll tell you, though," he said, suddenly shaking his head sadly and looking at the tabletop. "I saw some men there without much hope. I got to go eventually...I got to leave. I was one of the lucky ones. I woke up one morning with a tag tied right around the top button of my pajamas," he showed me on his chest where the tag had been. "This tag has the whole history of your injury on it. They come and put it on you, while you're sleeping. That's how you know you're going to get to leave on the hospital train that day. They come do it at night...they sneak in and do it so the others won't feel bad or something."

"Hmm," I said.

"I got to go. But there were one or two boys there that weren't going anywhere...some of the Brits. There was one fellow, his whole face was just bandages...you can't even imagine. And as bad as my pain ever got, I'd just look across the ward at him and I'd know it could be worse. He could speak too...just a little bit, and really quiet. These low, sort of whistling noises would come from him when he talked. His whole nose and jaw had been taken off by a shell.

"And he was a British guy. You know what he used to tell me? He used to whisper that he dreaded going home, because he didn't know what his girl would think of him now. And this guy'd been there for two years. They never discharged him. He would stand there every day, watching that train come and leave. They told me he'd been doing that for two whole years. He used to wear his uniform all the time, too. He thought he was gonna be called back home at any time. Those British Sam Browns were polished, and the buttons were shining, and he was in full uniform, just watching that train come and go and listening to the gramophone."

We both sat there in silence for a few minutes. He lit a short cigar, and offered me one as well. I declined, still in horror over the idea of this man. I was thankful that Henry had gone quickly and simply.

"And then, that was it," he said. "By the time I took my ride on the hospital train the war was over, and I went home," Jim said. "You ever hear a story like that?"

"No," I said. "No, I haven't."

"You're lucky you came back in one piece and never had to go through that."

"I know," I said.

"So that's why I can deal with managing all those men at the mill. When you've seen something like that, and been through that, and seen some real problems, everything else doesn't look so bad."

"You're right," I answered.

"Well, I'll let you get back to the job," he said. "Thanks for letting me tell my war stories, Cobb," he stood and threw one end of the scarf over a shoulder. He extended his hand and smiled.

"Sure," I said. "I appreciate it."

"I thought you would," we shook hands again.

"Good luck with the mill, anyway."

"Thanks," he hurried off. The rest of the orange and the coffee sat there in front of me. I dropped seventy-five cents onto the table and went back to work.

CHAPTER 12

The hardest thing about my new job was sitting at a desk all day long. It reminded me of school, and it had been a long time since I'd been in school. Besides the four "Rs," which were reading, 'riting, 'rithmetic, and religion, all I remembered about school was staring out the window. Now here I was, seated at a desk staring out a window again. I looked forward to my lunch break everyday just so I could be on the other side of that window.

The job itself wasn't bad. It was just writing out policies and figuring out how much money people owed Mr. Durham. There were a lot of strange legal terms that had confused me at first, but I got it after a little while. Mr. Durham helped me a lot when he was there, but some days he would be gone for hours.

I knew how to charge people and figure out coverages based on what type of insurance plans they had. Some of it went back a long way, to things that happened years ago. I was just a kid when a lot of the accidents or catastrophes happened. The oldest papers even went back to the big fire.

We got communications from the head office in New York almost daily, and most days I took the short walk to the post office to get the mail.

Sometimes I would get distracted by the picture on Mr. Durham's desk. His son was a guy just like Henry, who went off and fought and didn't come back. And we never even knew him, and he didn't know us. It made me think about all of the people that came and went that I never knew or saw. I thought about the guys I'd served with over there, and how we had all been from different places. It was just chance that we'd ever met. If there hadn't been a war, I would have lived my whole life without knowing any of them. I wondered what they were all doing now. Did they have jobs like this one back where they came from?

I wondered if they ever thought about the yellow balloons or the bombs dropping in our dug-out or anything else. I wondered what they remembered about the day the lieutenant told me about Henry. To them it was probably just another day. I was bored at the job a lot I guess, and my mind wandered.

One day Mr. Durham had been out "in the field," and he came back just as I was straightening things up and getting ready to leave for the day. I had been working for him for a number of months now, and he had never mentioned whether he was pleased with me or not. I had been keeping busy, and I felt as if I got a lot done. Still, I wondered if he thought I was doing a good job.

I sat up quickly when he entered, trying to look busy. His snow-white hair stood up in large strands where the hat had been.

"Mister Durham," I nodded at him as he hung up his jacket and hat.

"Any mail today?" He looked around his desk.

"None," I said. "But I sent the new policies off to New York."

"Good," he sat, smoothing his hair down. "They may take a while with those. Some of our boys up there are going to have a hell of a time with what just happened in front of the J.P. Morgan offices." Just a few days before, a bomb had exploded on Wall Street, killing a whole lot of people. "Too bad about that," he shook his head. "It's better living out here, I'll tell you that much. You ever been to New York City?"

"I was born there. But I haven't been there in a while."

"Good for you."

"How's the weather outside?"

"It's getting cold…too cold. It's still early. It shouldn't be this cold yet."

We sat there in silence for a few moments. It was almost time to go. I wasn't sure if I should shuffle some papers and get busy again for the last few minutes of the day or not. He just sat there.

"I think about Robert a lot this time of year," he said suddenly. "He used to chop the wood and pile it up for my fireplace over there. He was a strong boy. Strong and smart, too though," he pointed to his head. "He was a sharp one. Could have been a lawyer…that's what I used to tell him. But I'll bet he was a good guy to have around in a jam, too. You know, right Colbert?"

"Hmm?" I raised my eyebrows slightly.

"You knew him over there. I'll bet serving with him was something else. He was probably a leader over there. I'll bet people listened to him. He was in top physical shape when he went through camp, wasn't he?"

"I…I'm sure he was," I answered.

"Tell me something, Colbert. Did you ever see him take down a German? Over there? Before they got him, I mean…I'll bet he took a few of them down. His officer wouldn't tell me about it. They wouldn't answer me about it. I wrote to them and everything, even. I gave them postage to answer back. But they didn't. They didn't let me know. Did you ever see him in a fight?"

I had no idea what to say.

"I didn't really see much fighting myself," I finally stammered.

"I'll bet you got along well, though…You and Robert. You did, didn't you?" A silence hung in the room.

"Yes."

"I thought so. He was the type of guy that could help you out of a jam, wasn't he?"

"Yes," I nodded.

"I'll bet he took some of them down with him," he chuckled. He stared at the fireplace now, at the dead ashes from last year's flames. "He was a strong fella...good at sports. He took a few down, didn't he?"

"Yes, he did."

"You kids changed things over there," he said. "I'm proud of you. You and Robert. I can see you both over there." The light from the lamps in the room was reflected in his eyes. "You made this country what it is now, you know. Now we're running things. Who knows how long it'll last. I'll tell you one thing, though...there's no more wars." He looked back at me now. "There won't be any more. The weapons...they're just too big now. Man isn't meant to have them. He's not meant to kill each other like that. Too many boys died. That's how I know there won't ever be another one."

We all knew it at the time. There was no more reason for war, and it was only fitting for this one to be the final war of the history of the world. Everyone really believed that the manufacture of guns would stop any day. They were going to stop making any ships of war or weapons. This was a very common sense solution, and we were all just waiting for it to happen. I could only imagine what the world would be like in the future, once war was gone. I liked to think about futuristic-sounding years like 1934, when no one's brother or son would be killed.

His hair still stuck up a little bit, and the redness in his cheeks from the outside air was still there. I glanced at the picture on his desk and then back at him. I saw Robert's face there in his own.

"I guess you'll be running on," he said.

I stood and put on my jacket.

"Thank you," I said. And then, on my way out the door, "I can probably start bringing some wood from home. For the fire. I chop it there anyway."

He nodded some more, without looking at me. I don't even know if he heard me.

When I got to the street outside I was surprised to see Gertrude. She wore a heavy gray overcoat and a matching hat with a wide black ribbon.

"Hello there," I said.

"Hello," she answered.

"Are you waiting for me?"

"Yes."

"Do you need help with something tonight?" It had been a week or two since I'd gone by their house, and I felt a bit guilty.

"No," she said. "Mama's fine."

I nodded, waiting.

"I think I know where he is tonight," she said finally, looking around. She was avoiding eye contact with me. "I'm going," she said. "But you can come with me if you'd like."

"You're going where?" I asked.

"To that speakeasy where he goes sometimes. I know he's there. I went down to the train yard myself."

"Your mother wouldn't like that."

"They told me he went there. The man who was at the train yard told me he had to fire William because he caught him drinking on the job."

"He hasn't worked there in a while," I said. I thought she knew that Willie had been let go a while back. They said he'd missed a lot of work, and was unreliable. With the kind of equipment they had around there they couldn't keep a man like that on without putting the rest in danger. "Why would they know where he is?" I asked.

"Because he still runs around with the men who work there. The man who talked to me was angry because Willie has them all going to some tavern all the time now."

"I don't think your mother would like you going to a place like that," I said, holding my jacket closed as a breeze blew up.

"It doesn't even matter to me if he comes home now. Or ever. It doesn't matter, because he doesn't want to stay there. But I know he got paid before they made him leave. Mama's too proud to ask for it, but we need that money. We're entitled to it. He's just going to spend it all on liquor, anyway."

I had no choice. She needed my help, and she would probably try to go without me if I said no.

"All right," I said. "Don't ever tell your mother that I'm letting you near a place like this." We made our way down the street.

"She thinks I'm finishing up a sweater for Misses Langston," she said.

"Do you lie to your mother a lot?" I asked.

"No," she said. "I never lied to her until William came back. Now he's got me lying just like him." She scowled under her hat.

As often happened around her, I had no idea what to say.

"It doesn't really bother me much…lying," she said after a few moments. "You know Mister Scott Fitzgerald calls us a generation 'grown up to find all gods dead, all wars fought, all faiths in man shaken.' What do you think of that?"

"I don't know," I said. I was wondering why she would've memorized something like that. "Who was it that said that?"

"F. Scott Fitzgerald," she said. "It's in a book called *This Side of Paradise*. Haven't you ever heard of him?"

"I don't think so," I answered.

"He's a real wild partygoer in New York," she said. "They say he rides on the top of taxicabs all over town, and he and his new wife jump into the fountains on Fifth Avenue and swim around when they've had a bit to drink."

"Sounds like quite a guy."

"Have you heard of a new book called *Flappers and Philosophers*?"

"Did he write that too?"

"Yes, he did."

"I haven't heard of anything by him. What's the title?"

"*Flappers and Philosophers*."

"What does that mean?"

"The British call a woman whose fiancé was killed in the war a flapper. Did you know any British men in the war?"

"No," I said. "I don't think so." We walked on quietly. "So do you know who Mister Babe Ruth is?"

"I've heard of him."

"Well, did you know that he hit fifty-four home runs this year, and the previous record was only twenty-nine?"

"No," she said with a slight smile. "I didn't know that."

"Did you know that the Boston Red Sox sold Ruth to the Yankees for one hundred thousand dollars, plus a three hundred and eighty-five thousand dollar loan? I'll bet Fitzgerald isn't worth that much money."

"How do you know if you won't read his books?"

We were silent for a few moments. Her boots made loud clacking sounds on the sidewalk.

"Do you like your job?" she asked after a while. She seemed more talkative than usual. She was probably excited about going to the speakeasy.

"It's fine," I said. "It's interesting, sometimes."

"I really don't see how insurance could be interesting."

It was almost entirely dark by the time we reached the door with the "22" on it.

"You can wait out here," I said. "I won't be long." She was silent for a few seconds. I raised my hand to knock.

"Can I come in with you?" she asked. I stopped my fist in mid-air.

"You're his sister," I said. "I can't go in here with you to get him. No way." I couldn't walk in there with Willie's sister and ask him for money or to come home. I wasn't his mother or anything.

"I want to," she said quietly. She was staring at the number on the door. "You can't leave me out here alone anyway," she said, looking at me again. "It's getting dark."

She was right, I couldn't leave her out there. As I knocked on the door, I hoped that the place would really scare her and she'd learn her lesson.

"I'm just escorting you in," I told her. "You can talk to him." She looked at me as if she hadn't really thought about that. Then she nodded.

The panel slid open, just like the last time. I thought it was the same pair of eyes, but it was darker now, so I couldn't be sure.

"Yeah?" The voice gave it away. It was definitely the same doorman.

"I don't have the password," I said. "My friend's in there, though. I just need to talk with him."

The eyes moved over to Gertrude, looking her up and down.

"We don't want nobody's wife comin' in here," he said. "No trouble."

"She's with me...she's nobody's wife." I answered. Gertrude was silent now, looking down at the ground. "I just wanna talk to my friend," I said. "There's nobody out here that's going to break up your party." I realized I was still wearing my tie from work. I probably didn't look very tough.

"Yeah, well, you can't come in tonight," the disembodied voice said. "There's kind of a meetin' goin' on."

The eyes faded back into the darkness, and I heard the sounds of men shouting. Gertrude and I looked at each other. The sound of the voices had probably intimidated her a little. I hoped she was realizing that this wasn't such a good idea.

"What's your name?" The eyes were back.

"Cobb Whittier," I answered. They went away again. The panel closed.

And then, the door opened.

"The war hero, huh?" asked the voice as he stepped from behind the door. His eyes were bloodshot, but it was definitely the same guy. I wondered if he remembered running into us on the street.

His huge hairy hand held the door open. I thought about being polite and letting Gertrude go before me. I was worried about her safety, though, so I went in first and she followed close behind. He went down the steps in front of me just like last time. I couldn't hear any voices at all now. There was only the sound of our shoes on the stairs.

The smell was immediate and familiar. It was a heavy mixture of smoke, liquor, and old sawdust. A blast of stagnant heat came up the stairs to greet us as well. The light of the lamps burning in the tavern filled the doorway below us. The silence was a little eerie, especially after the rowdy shouting we'd heard just a few moments before.

We reached the bottom of the steps. The men sat in their chairs around the tables. There was plenty of liquor in the glasses on every table, but they were ignoring it for now. Right now, all eyes in the place were on us. We had clearly just interrupted something.

I wished I hadn't brought Gertrude down here now. I glanced around, taking them all in. I didn't recognize anyone, of course. I was extremely hot suddenly. I didn't know if it was the musty air in here or the tie around my neck. My collar itched, though, and I could feel my face flushing.

"Who the hell're you?" a slurred voice came at me from somewhere.

"Hey, Cobb," Willie's voice came from the other side of the room. I was relieved to hear it, but I couldn't tell exactly where he was. Then he stood up at a table in the corner. I recognized a few other guys from the train yard now.

Willie had a drink in his hand, and he was smiling strangely. I watched his eyes come to rest on Gertrude, and his expression slowly changed. It was still a smile, but it was a very confused one. His tone of voice changed as well.

"What do you need, friend?" he asked. I looked at him, trying to ignore the eyes of the entire room on me. "We served together," he said to the room. "This guy served with me."

"Why don't you take a seat," said another voice. "Take a seat there in the back…we were just talking." This man was standing near the bar. "Lou, get a couple chairs," he said.

The man who was speaking looked familiar to me. He was dressed in a full three-piece suit, and the chain of his pocket watch dangled from the front of his vest. He looked like a young kid all dressed up, pretending to be an old man. He was smiling, and his eyes were locked on us as Gertrude and I sat down. I was sure that she was just as confused as I was.

"I want to apologize now for some of what you may hear, Ma'am," the kid said, eyes now focused tightly on Gertrude. "We're just working class gentlemen here, discussing some of our own problems. But you're welcome as a guest. Both of you are welcome as customers of mine." I saw that he was holding a thick cigar between two of his fingers, waving it toward us now. I could feel Willie's eyes on us, but I didn't dare look toward him. I was sure everyone else was looking at us, too.

"But where was I?" he asked now, and most of the eyes returned to him. I recognized him then as the kid who had sold Gertrude her fabric at the textile factory.

"For anything you do, there's a standard wage," he said to the group. "But your employer…if he can get the job done by somebody who'll do it for less than the standard wage…well, then, you know he's gonna do it." He spoke matter of factly, as if he was addressing one or two friends. But all eyes in the room were on him.

"And if one man will do two men's work for the wages of one man, well, then…he'll do that, too. If your employer has a good year, guess who sees the profits. It's never you. You probably don't know when there is a good year. I don't know too much about the railroad business, I'll tell you. But I'll bet you boys haven't seen the results of a good year in a long while. Except for overtime, you're not going to see any of the profits. But you know what? You'll be the first to know if there's a lean year, because you'll be let go just like that," he snapped his fingers. "And somebody else'll replace you…somebody who'll do it for less than the standard wage."

The room was silent, except for the occasional clinking of a glass on a table. Out of the corner of my eye I could see Gertrude sitting beside me, very still. The doorman lit a cigarette and leaned on the bar.

"It doesn't matter how long you've been loyal, see, because that's not important to him. There'll always be niggers and bums and 'unskilled workers' to take your job for less money. And that means more money for the boss. But think about what's going to happen then, to America. You want those kind of men doing your jobs? In the long run, that factory's going to close, or that train's going to wreck. And men like my boss and yours call themselves industrialists and say that they have the best interests of America in mind. They put a man like Eugene Debs in prison…a man nominated for president…just because they don't agree with his views. They say America shouldn't interfere with the rest of the world. Well I don't know about that. I think it's easy for those old men to sit around and say that because they didn't just fight for this country."

A few men made grunting noises.

"As I say, though, I'm not really into politics." He shifted his weight against the bar, smiling broadly. "This isn't an organized meeting of any kind…I'm just talking, and whoever wants to can listen. But the truth is, it's not only better for you to organize, but it's really better for America, too. And there may be some people who don't see that, but that's just because they're not living in the modern world…they're living in the past." He paused for a while, taking a drink from a glass on the bar. His expression became solemn after he put it down.

"Now I don't know too many of you boys," he started again. "I know a lotta you work at the train yard. That's about all I know. The railroad is organized everywhere right now…but the local chapter is what's important for you. The Esch-Cummins Act was passed just this February. And that means the railroads are privately owned now, and you've got a Labor Board. But you got to use it. Now I work in textiles myself. And I have for a few years. But I'm nobody, really…I'm nobody official, I'm just talking about my experience in textiles. A lotta you've probably heard about the things going on in our industry lately."

He moved his eyes over the crowd as he spoke, so it seemed as if he was addressing each and every person in the room. He puffed on the cigar between sentences.

"The American Textile Workers was started by the AFL about ten years ago," he said, taking another drink. He set the glass down slowly and quietly, and looked around. "But this is no history lesson. The important thing is that that organization was the first time we divided the skilled workers from the unskilled workers. And that's the first step…that's an important step, 'cause like I said, the world will always be full of unskilled men ready to take your job away from you for almost nothing. Well, I don't know about you but I'm not out to give any bums or foreigners any free gifts."

A few grunts came from around the room. My eyes strayed to Willie. He was drinking from a flask and looking around at the guys at his table.

"There've been a lotta strikes in my industry around here in the last few years. A whole lot. The economy isn't what it used to be. Our local chapter has been busy. But a lotta people still don't get it…they still don't get what we've been trying to do.

"Before the war President Wilson came out in support of labor. But then he changed his mind…because the workers don't run this country, gentlemen. The employers run this country and they've got the ear of the mayor and the president. I'm not trying to teach you history…I'm just telling a story. Whoever wants to listen, can. It's a story about what happened when my friends in textiles got organized and started our own local chapter.

"The boss didn't like it. It's bad news to him and the owner and all those men who don't do the real work. That's probably no surprise to you. But you have to be ready for what they do...to fight back. The textile companies in Greenwood and all over the state, they started their own unions...not in the name of labor but fake unions, pretend ones. So they could say they had a union and they didn't have to recognize anything else.

"What could we do? We went on strike a few times, just like a lotta our boys have been doing lately. We went on a strike, and the company hired strikebreakers. They had some of the big detective agencies down here. Agencies you've probably heard of. And these detectives didn't have anything better to do besides breaking our strike. And the county sheriffs? You think you can count on them to stand up for your right to stage a peaceful strike? This is a right granted by the Anti-Trust laws passed by the president himself. It's been law for six years now. But the county sheriff doesn't care about that. He's out there deputizing the workers that are loyal to the company. So now these strikebreakers have the law on their side, and they can do whatever they want, because they stayed loyal to the boss. They didn't care about their fellow worker trying to bring home enough wages for his wife and baby, and breaking his back in the factory all day long.

"The whole town was against us. This very town, your town. The place you and your father worked to build. The place you call home...if you say the wrong words, they won't even let you rent a meeting hall. They wouldn't let us. Because the people running this country are afraid of treating their fellow man with respect. They're afraid that if they pay us what we're worth, we'll be able to compete with them and someday have a factory of our own and maybe take some of their precious profit away."

The men were getting more and more agitated now. I thought of Gertrude sitting next to me and started fearing for her safety. The mood of the room was shifting quickly.

“Who works at the train yard here?” he asked. “I know some of you boys do.” A few tables let out shouts. One overzealous young kid raised up out of his chair, only to stumble onto the ground. His drink spilled under the table, and coarse laughter erupted all around him.

Willie’s table had all raised their arms. I only recognized a few of them. Had it been that long since I’d worked at the yard? Willie kept looking around, smiling, his eyes glassy and rimmed in red.

“The railroad’s the backbone of this country,” Jack continued, sitting on a barstool now. “I don’t know much about it, but I do know that. And you boys are at a perfect time to organize. A lotta you do repairs on cars, and that’s a skilled worker if I ever heard’a one. I couldn’t do that. But the truth is, everybody here is skilled, so everybody here is entitled to organize. I know a lotta you heard about the railroad strikes back in July. That happened ’cause they tried to cut the wages down a whole lot. You’re in an industry that’s just aching to pull a fast one on you.

“I don’t know how many hours you work in a day, but you should know that there’re laws that say you get to stop after a certain amount of time. They can’t make you work any more. Just like the laws that say you have to make certain wages, no matter what the boss says. And you know what? They don’t want you to know that. Your boss doesn’t, and the railroad doesn’t, and the county sheriff and the detective agencies don’t. But you’ve got to be smarter than them. There’s no pride in getting cheated for the rest of your life. At the end of the day, the boss goes to his nice house, and gets his wife something new to wear and his kids get new toys, and you’re slaving away still. There’s no pride in that. You got to be smart and stand up for your rights. These are rights that this country already gave to you.

“You know all about rights, don’t you?” Was he looking at me? Slowly, impaired by their growing drunkenness, the men began to turn toward the back of the room.

"The Nineteenth Amendment…just this August," he said. I could see now that he was actually addressing Gertrude. I'll admit I was relieved that it was her instead of me.

"That amendment says you can vote, young lady…just like a man. You can vote for the president this November. Just like a man."

Most of the room groaned audibly, and several shouts and complaints were heard. He smiled and nodded, and I thought I even saw him give a little wink to some of the guys that were close to him.

"But I wouldn't take that to mean that you should start frequenting establishments like this one." Most of the men laughed. I didn't dare turn to see her reaction.

"But my point, gentlemen," he said, raising his glass and using it to point toward Gertrude, "is that this young lady has been given the right to vote by her country. But that doesn't mean the president's going to come out here and hold her hand and take her down to vote."

"He wants to hold more than her hand!" a shout came from somewhere, and the room erupted into laughter. I thought about getting up and taking her out of there. For all I knew that would be more embarrassing to her than staying, though.

"No, no…what I'm saying is it's up to her to use that right. It's up to her to educate herself about what's really going on, and use that right. And that's just like the right to organize. I can get you started if you'd like, but I can't hold your hand. And I know a few of you boys would really like to hold my hand." More laughter, and a bunch of drunken movement around the room.

"Thanks for listening," he said then, and stepped over to a table. He started talking with some guys there, and the rest of the room got louder and louder.

I turned to Gertrude at last. Her ears were flushed a bright red.

"You all right?" I asked quietly. I don't think she heard me. I cleared my voice and asked again. She smiled bravely and nodded. We sat there for a few moments, surrounded by the loud voices.

She was looking around at the drunken men, who were very boisterous now. They spilled things, bumped into each other, and accidentally tipped chairs. It wasn't a mob scene or anything, but I'm sure it was a new environment for her. She was definitely the only woman present.

I turned and looked for Willie, but he wasn't where he used to be. Everyone had moved. A lot of them had approached Jack when he was done talking. They wanted to continue the conversation, I guess.

"I don't see him," I said after a while.

"Hmm?"

"I said I don't see him. I don't see Willie, do you?"

"No," she said, looking around as if none of this bothered her.

"Do you want to go?" I asked finally.

She looked at me strangely, but then she nodded slowly. We stood and made our way through the hanging cloud of smoke and up the stairs. No one noticed our exit.

Outside, the night was cold and clear. We walked toward the Delgrew house.

"Well," I ventured after a long silence, "I hope that's the last time I have to go there." She smiled weakly. "You know, I thought they treated me pretty well down at the yard when I was there."

"That's easy for you to say now because you have a better job than any of those men," she said, the steam of her breath pushing forward in front of her.

"You think so?"

"Of course. You have a good job because you're willing to work and you're smart enough to do it. That's not very common in men."

"Well," I said, "just as long as you promise me you won't keep hanging around places like that."

She smiled a little. She had wanted to go to get money from Willie, I remembered. I pulled out my own wallet and removed a few bills.

"I know you don't want this," I said. "But you should take it."

"No," she said. "It's not that bad."

"It's just a loan," I said. "I bet I'll see Willie again before you do, so I'll get it back from him. It'll be the same as you getting it from him tonight."

She wouldn't take the money, though, no matter what I said.

CHAPTER 13

❀

I stopped at the drug store late one Saturday afternoon to pick up a few things for Mrs. Delgrew. She didn't leave the house very often. Except for church on Sunday, she didn't have a reason to go anywhere.

I was in no big hurry, so I got an ice cream soda for myself and sat down at the little counter. The place always smelled as if Mr. Barnes had just scoured it. The phonograph was sitting in the corner, and a disembodied orchestra played through the shining metal horn.

The advertisements hanging behind the counter were painted in bright colors, meant to attract the eye. *Where was Moses when the lights went out?* asked one. It had a picture of a pack of Mecca cigarettes. —*Groping for a pack of Meccas.*

The one beside it displayed the name of *Dr. Jeanne A. Walter. Reduce your flesh exactly where desired by wearing Famous Medicated Reducing Rubber Garments*, it said. *Brassiere—$6, Chin Reducer—$2, Bust Reducer—$5.50.*

"You like the Opus 96?" Mr. Barnes asked. He had noticed me listening. He approached slowly, a stout man with wisps of white hair on each side of his head. He wore a heavy white apron, and a shirt with a bow tie. His large ears and his nose had always seemed impossibly thick and round to me.

"It's…it's great," I said, waving toward the phonograph.

"You're right," he said, walking away from me now and toward the machine. "You're right. Beethoven is great. But this, this is fantastic." He took another black wax record from below the counter, and replaced the one that had been playing. "*The Crazy Blues*" he said with a broad smile as the music started.

I smiled and nodded to the music, as Mamie Smith crackled toward me from the horn. I read another smaller sign behind the counter, warning customers to buy medication against things like *cigarette throat, acid teeth, B.O., and wallflowerism.*

"I should have known you'd know good music when you heard it," he was saying now. "You got yourself a good job, too…working for Durham. Making yourself a good life."

I just nodded and smiling and kept sipping my soda.

"And that's tough to do," he said. "That's tough for a young man to do in this day and age…with inflation and the cost of living up so high and all. There's a lot of kids in this town running around who don't care if they disgrace their own mothers. You know that?" He wiped the counter top with a greasy rag.

"Well, the U.S. Army teaches you a few things," I said. It sounded like the sort of thing he'd want to hear.

"That's right," he said. "That's absolutely right. They need to ship all these kids overseas for a while…like you, then they'd shape up."

Someone placed a pack of Mecca cigarettes on the counter beside me.

"I'll have what Moses is having," a voice said.

Mr. Barnes appeared startled, as if he'd forgotten he was running a store. He rang the cigarettes up. I took the opportunity to pull Mrs. Delgrew's list from my pocket and check it again. *Cheese, Underwood sardines, Kellogg's All-Bran…*

"I'll have one of those ice cream sodas, too," said the man who bought the cigarettes. He sat beside me, and Mr. Barnes moved away.

"Cobb Whittier," the man said. I looked up. "How ya' doin?"

It was Jack.

"I'm good," I nodded, surprised that he remembered my name. "How are you?"

"Swell, just swell," he leaned back and dropped the cigarettes into his jacket pocket. He was wearing a wool overcoat with a white shirt underneath it. "Have a good time out on the town the other night?"

"I was just out looking for my friend," I answered, smiling.

"Who's the gal?"

"That's his sister. I just...I told her I'd take her to him. She wanted to go in."

"Aww, that's okay," he responded, sipping his drink. "It was good for her. She looked like she could handle herself."

"I'm sure she could," I said.

"Well, listen, Cobb," he said, placing a hand on my shoulder, "you probably came in in the middle of things and everything, and I know you used to be at the yard yourself, so I just want you to know that that was nothing but some boys talking. Talking about work...you know. I'm nobody official, I mean. Just spreading my opinions to a room of guys who are probably too drunk to recognize their own mothers." He laughed loudly.

"Sure," I said. The record ended. He turned his glass upward, gulping down hunks of ice cream and swallows of soda. Mr. Barnes put on *I'll See You in C-U-B-A* by the Ted Lewis Orchestra.

"So you go down there often?" He stared at me. It took me a few moments to realize that he was talking about the speakeasy and not Cuba.

"No," I said. "No."

"Me neither. That was my first time. You gotta gather where you can, though, nowadays. Nothing wrong with some boys having fun."

"I understand," I said, smiling.

"You look like a guy who's had some fun in his time."

"Sure, sure," I sat back on the stool a little. "But I'm getting old now."

He laughed as if he thought this was hilarious.

"You know," he said, "a lotta times I wish I'd made it over there with you boys. Second registration...June of nineteen eighteen," he said, pointing a thumb at his own chest. "I just wasn't quite enough of an old timer like you," he chuckled.

"Well, I'm sure you had a gal or two that would've missed you back here," I said, draining the last of my drink.

"Oh, no, not me," he said with a wink. He put his hand on my shoulder once again. "You take care, Cobb," he said as he got up. "And let me know when you're going to stop by and surprise me at a talk next time." He left the store, smiling at a young girl as he passed her in the entrance.

I got up and gathered the items from Mrs. Delgrew's list. Mr. Barnes was waiting for me at the counter again when I stopped to pay. A jar of assorted Charms candy and a box of Baby Ruth bars sat near the register. I picked up one of the candy bars but then thought better of it.

"You know those are named after Grover Cleveland's daughter?" Mr. Barnes asked.

"Really?" I said. I had never heard of them.

Mr. Barnes looked around and lowered his voice as if he was about to tell me a secret.

"You a friend of Jack Wolfe's?" he asked, placing the items in a sack.

"No...not really," I answered, surprised by the question.

"Good," he said. "Good for you. Because he's no friend of yours, believe me."

"Why?"

"Did he talk to you about the war?"

"No," I said. "Not much." I took the sack from him.

"He was a draft dodger," Mr. Barnes said, his pudgy nose bobbing toward me. "Or he encouraged it. Draft dodging. Called the war a capitalist plot. I know it...I have it from good sources. You know the

Myrtle boys? They told me all about it. Did you go to school with them? No, you were probably older."

"He said he went through registration," I said.

A young woman stepped forward and placed a bag of Campfire Marshmallows on the counter, along with a can of soup and a few other things. Mr. Barnes turned his attention to her, and I started to go.

"Wait there, young man," Mr. Barnes said without looking up from the woman's money. I stood there until they finished the transaction. He watched her leave the store, then turned back to me. There was no one else in the place now.

"I've always said that boy is no better than a Russian revolutionary. That's what he is…he isn't American, I know that. I mean, he isn't a foreigner or anything, but he might as well be."

"I'm sure he's harmless," I said. I was remembering his speech about the industrialist employers, actually. Maybe Barnes was the type he was talking about.

"Oh no," Barnes said. "He's far from harmless. You remember the Espionage Act in nineteen seventeen?"

"No," I had to admit I'd never heard of it.

"Look," he said. "They used to say that kid was some sort of genius. That's what his teachers would say about him. But they wouldn't say it now, because he wasted it all. He had to be a smart kid though…a real dynamo. Head of the local chapter of the textile workers when he was nineteen years old. Can you believe that?"

"Really?" I wasn't really paying too much attention to what he was saying. In those days there was a lot of talk from people who thought of themselves as "traditionalists." They were all big on small town Protestant values, and scared of anything else. Barnes was probably like that. Like my Aunt, I thought, just a little over the top.

"I remember it," he was saying. "People tell me a lotta things in here. I can remember the cops talking about it, and you better believe I got to know a few of the detectives they brought down to deal with him and his boys. But he lost it all...President Wilson saw to that."

"What do you mean?" I set the bag back on the counter now. The Ted Lewis Orchestra played on.

"The Espionage Act...the judges could order raids on homes and businesses and any places where these labor people organized. Just like they did to the radicals the beginning of this year, don't you remember? Well he got burned the last time...Jack Wolfe got burned by the Espionage Act. I don't know what happened, but they supposedly got some papers...now don't tell anyone this, okay? You're not going to tell anyone this, are you?"

"No," I said.

"Well, see that you don't. They say they found some papers tying him to the Wobblies. Somebody turned them in...turned these papers in to his boss while the judges had men out looking for just that sort of thing. Somebody must have turned on him. And then the superintendent down there, well, he didn't even blacklist him, because a lotta those boys who are outta control scared him. I would've done it just like that," he snapped his fingers. "He would've lost his job with me. Somebody like that's dangerous to have around. But they were scared down there...they thought those boys would come after their families. So he lost his place in the union...he stepped down as head, but he got to keep his job at the factory. Only in America," he shook his head slowly, as if he still couldn't believe the turn of events.

I was finding a lot of it hard to believe myself.

"So who'd you hear all this from?" I asked, picking up the sack again.

"People who know, that's who I heard it from," he answered, trying to look severe. He rubbed the surface of his ear with a large index finger. "A good kid like you shouldn't have anything to do with Jack Wolfe, and that's the truth." He wiped the finger on a corner of his apron.

"All right," I said. "Thanks." I turned to go.

"You say hello to your family for me," he said. "And you can come listen to Beethoven anytime. Next time I might have a record of Enrico Caruso…that's what I want to get. My brother saw him in *I pagliacci*, you know."

I thanked him and made my way out, in a hurry to deliver the goods to the Delgrews. I was sure they were waiting for me by now.

CHAPTER 14

My Mother gave them permission to bury Henry over there. I guess his squad got blown up pretty bad in the skirmish. When something like that happened the army asked the next of kin if it would be all right to bury them there rather than bringing them home, since it was difficult to separate them or to tell who was who. Sometimes the place where a battle occurred would get bombed afterwards, and it was hard to put the bodies back together.

I decided to visit the graveyard on my way out of the country that spring. I went alone, while everyone else was having their last hurrah before leaving France. They had given me permission to jump a small French supply train that was headed in that direction, since they knew it might be my only chance to see my brother's grave. The train would be unloading there for an hour and then returning. It would only be a day's detour in my trip to the coast.

I sat outside smoking and watching the French soldiers loading the train. Most of them would be going home for good on this trip, and they looked happy.

They folded up the tents that displayed the tricolor, and pitched them on a nearby truck. This was a French artillery unit, with a lot of weapons. I had seen French soldiers before, of course, but never this close.

I watched one cavalry officer who wore a blue coat braided with gold lace on the collar and cuffs. It was definitely fancier than anything our officers wore. The rest of the soldiers looked pretty much like any doughboys, except for their baggy, bright red pants. That was how you could tell French boys from a mile away. The coats had long skirts to them, too, but nothing could hide those red pants.

Most of them carried the flimsy French knapsacks. I saw one fellow near me pack his with a few flannel shirts, a deck of playing cards, two fagots of firewood, and a canteen. Their canteens looked really strange to me. They were covered in a grayish blue cloth, and they had a little horn on top. You could never have mistaken them for ours.

"You all right?" Sergeant Clark was standing beside me now.

"Sure," I said. "Thanks for getting me on this train."

"It wasn't too tough," he replied, spitting tobacco on the ground. "They owe us. We moved so many guns around for 'em they'll never be able to pay us back."

"Really?"

"Their horses were always tired out after all the moving this summer," he said. "At least that was the story they gave us. But I'll bet the real story is there were no horses. Enemy shell fire kills so many they don't have enough left to move around," he gave me a wink. "These boys weren't as good as hiding as we are." He seemed proud. "If you ask me, some of 'em would never've even found the front if we hadn't pointed to it."

"Hmm."

"See ya later."

I jumped onto a car toward the back of the train that was filled with packs and supplies. The Frenchmen were in other cars, and I steered clear of them. I wouldn't be able to understand what they were saying anyway. I slept for a while, and ate some of my rations. I watched the country go by.

When we pulled into the little town I found the graveyard without help from anyone. A few thin trees and a little stone wall surrounded the tiny plot of ground. The markers were simple, and the American names were easy to see. It was one of the sunniest days I'd experienced over there, without a cloud in the sky. But it still felt like winter, and the air was freezing. I pulled my hands from the pockets of my wool overcoat and breathed steam on them, trying to keep them warm. The tips of my fingers felt cold and dead, as if death itself was trying to bring me down with the rest of the soldiers in the yard.

I found Henry's marker and stood over it for a while. It was difficult to think that he was physically there, underneath it. This was just his name, carved in dead stone, to remind the world that he had existed. I stared at it, tracing the name with my eyes until my vision blurred. I swear I could feel him then, just for an instant. I could sense that he was somewhere, right now, watching me. I was going home, and he wasn't. He was staying here.

I felt no anger at his death as I stood there. I didn't think about the war or blame the archduke or the president or anyone. I guess I just accepted that this was how it was meant to be.

I tried to memorize the whole setting, knowing that my Mother and my Aunt would have a barrage of questions for me about his final resting place. I also knew that I would probably never come back here again, and I wanted to be able to remember it for a long time. I studied the other markers, and the position of the trees, and all the details of the crumbling stone wall. I took a final look at his name, and then made my way back to the train, ready to go home.

CHAPTER 15

I stood inside the train station, watching the huge clock on the wall. The train was due in at three o'clock, and it was already five minutes past.

I kept my eye on the windows and the platform outside. I'd thought about waiting outside, but it was just too cold, even with the midday sun bathing the splintered wood of the platform.

The man sitting on one of the shiny benches directly in front of me was reading a newspaper. The headline was something about the New York school commissioner dismissing public school teachers for membership in the Communist Party. The man with the paper was dressed sharply, in a black suit and tie, and I began to wonder what kind of person dressed like that to catch a train at this time in the afternoon on a Wednesday. Mr. Durham had been nice enough to give me the day off, but I wondered why these other people weren't at work somewhere.

I thought about getting a paper from the rack, since they were only two cents each. But I was sure the train would be here any minute now.

Standing there made me think about the bandaged man waiting for the train at the hospital. I wondered if he was living somewhere in England now. I thought about him coming home to his parents and his girlfriend. I'm sure they were all very nice, but things would be different. I pictured his girl trying to think of an easy way to leave him.

I thought about whether I would rather be killed or lose my face. I wondered if the man in front of me with the newspaper would pretend not to notice if I was standing here with no face right now.

I was still thinking about it at eight minutes past when the hulking locomotive finally arrived, chugging in slowly, vibrating the entire station. As soon as it pulled to a stop, people began to climb off and enter the building from the platform. It was a pretty sparse crowd, since most people came to Greenwood during the summer rather than the winter. I watched a small family with two children dragging their suitcases. The father looked like he was about my age. There were a few other men who had the sooty look of migrant workers, and then a few businessmen back from the cities.

He was one of the last people off the train. As soon as he stepped inside, something told me that this was him.

He was about my height, with a rather unremarkable face. He didn't resemble anyone in the family I'd ever met. Brown eyes, brown hair, and eyebrows that were straight as a level across each eye. His hair was parted on top of his head, and two long strands had already fallen in front of his face as he struggled with his two small cases. He brushed the hairs aside and looked around. He wore a chesterfield coat with a muffler tied in a round knot around his neck, and a gray sweater underneath. A well-starched white collar peeked out above the sweater.

He pulled the cases toward me, smiling and looking around. I stepped forward, taking a gamble that this was my cousin.

"Hello," I said. He didn't seem to hear, so I cleared my throat and repeated it.

"Hello there," he responded, moving toward me now.

"Ambrose Bentham?"

"The same," he said. "Cousin Colbert?"

"Yes," he dropped the cases and pumped my hand cordially. He had a narrow nose, I saw now, and the slightest impression of a dimple in the middle of his chin.

"Is this all you have?"

"Yes, this is it. Is it not enough?"

"No, no," I said. "It's fine." I picked up one of the cases. "I guess we didn't really know how long you'd be staying." We began to walk toward the exit.

"I'm not sure myself, Colbert. I'm not sure. My mother insisted that I spend some time out in the country with the family. Not that you are thought of as country people." He brushed back another strand of hair.

"Well, Greenwood may be pretty different from what you're used to."

"I'm counting on it," he said. He followed me through the front entrance. Outside on the street, the cold wind swirled around us. He held his coat closed with his free hand. "That sounds like just what I need." He looked around, taking things in. It was the middle of a sunny but cold afternoon, and horses clomped in both directions, pulling carts and passengers. He seemed to suddenly realize that I was walking away, and fell in step beside me.

"You can call me Cobb," I said. "That's what people have always called me."

"Why do they call you that?"

"I don't know, really. I think they started it when I was little, in school, and just kept it up."

"All right."

"So how was the trip?" I asked.

"Oh, I'm not much for traveling by train. It was all right, though, I suppose."

"Have you traveled a lot?"

"Mostly between New York and home…well, Boston…that's home. Just for business, I used to go back and forth a bit."

We walked on for a while. I didn't want to do all the talking, since I had never liked people who talked too much. I didn't want him to think that I was trying too hard to be his friend, either.

"It's very generous of you and your family to take me in for a while," he said. He was breathing hard, straining to keep up, even though I wasn't moving that fast. Probably out of shape, I thought.

"Well, it's the least we could do…we don't have much family."

"No, that's true…I always said we have so few relatives on my father's side. My mother…well, she has the whole city it seems. But I never met many of my father's side."

"I think my Mother saw you once."

"Yes…she came up for the funeral."

I didn't know him well enough to say anything about his father's death. My father had died also, of course, so we had that in common. I'm sure he knew that without my saying so.

"So what do you do around here for fun?" he asked suddenly.

"Oh, I don't know," I said. "Not too much, really. My Aunt and my Mother…they want us to go to a church social tonight. I think they want me to introduce you to some people."

"That sounds fine," he said.

"They think I still know a lot of people around here, I guess." He was a few years older than I was, so I figured him to be about twenty-eight or so. I didn't know enough about him to tell if he would consider a church social a fun activity. I don't think I would have. "But I told them you might be tired, and all…from the trip. You did just get here."

"Oh, I don't need much rest," he said. "My friends used to say I was the only person they knew who could go a week without sleeping."

"Really?"

"Hmm. That sounds good, though…tonight."

"All right," I said.

My Aunt and my Mother greeted him warmly when we got home. He was extremely polite to them, and I could tell that my Aunt was impressed, despite her misgivings. They had been preparing a large dinner all day, so as soon as his things were put away in Henry's old room we sat down to eat. He removed his jacket and sweater and wore just the starched shirt to dinner.

He talked mostly about the shape of things in the city of Boston. He seemed to be very well versed in the politics of the city, and who was building what. My Aunt asked him if he had been to New York recently, and he talked for a long time about that city, too. Both my Aunt and my Mother asked him about places they remembered from New York. I didn't remember a lot of the city, since I had been so young when we lived there.

He kept thanking them for having him and for preparing the wonderful dinner and for just about everything else he could think of. They waved off the compliments, but I could tell they were both happy that their hard work was being recognized. I had heard all day about how the store had the gall to charge my Aunt thirty-eight cents a pound for the leg of lamb.

It was a long, drawn out meal, and the sky outside the windows grew dark. It would be one of those cold winter nights, I knew.

"Well I suppose you boys will be going to the social down at the church," my Aunt said at last.

"That sounds just fine to me," said Ambrose. "I assumed you lovely ladies would be joining us, though."

"Oh, we have plenty to do here," said my Aunt, giggling like a young girl.

"Are you sure you're not too tired to go?" asked my Mother.

"No, no, as I was telling Cobb…Colbert here, I can usually get by without a whole lot of rest. That's what a few years in the banking business will do for you."

"My husband was a bank accountant when he was living," offered my Aunt. "So I know all about it."

"I'm sure you do," he said. "Hard work pays off in the business, though. I'll bet your husband knew that much."

"He did, he did," she said.

"It's an interesting business," Ambrose said. That seemed to be all he had to say. My Mother interrupted the silence.

"Well, it's cold out there, so make sure you dress warm."

"Oh yes, yes, don't let us old ladies keep you here if you're finished. You run along and meet all of Colbert's friends." My Aunt thought I was close friends with anyone who attended my church and was within ten years of my age. She also thought that any friend I had played with when I was little was still someone I had a close relationship with. She would drop me bits of gossip about kids I had gone to school with all the time. It didn't matter that I no longer knew them at all.

As we got up, Ambrose suddenly bucked to the side and grabbed the table for balance.

"You all right?" I asked. My Mother and my Aunt looked at him in horror.

"Sure, sure," he said, smiling at all of us. He winced a bit and limped away from the table. "It's just an old injury from my days as a runner. I won several championships. But the knee's just never been the same."

"Is there anything we can get you?" asked my Mother.

"No, no, Ma'am. Thank you though. Sometimes it just acts up…must be the weather here."

"The weather has been dreadful lately," my Aunt nodded.

He put his sweater and coat back on, and I got out a jacket and tie myself. When he came from the bedroom he was walking with a straight malacca cane. It was a fancy cane, with an ivory dog's head on the top, and a point at the bottom. We all saw it, but none of us said anything about it. He had slicked his hair back, and looked ready for a night on the town.

"Be careful," they called after us.

I pulled my overcoat tighter when the night air hit me. I was walking slowly at first, so he could keep up. After we'd gone only a few yards, though, I noticed that he was walking along just fine. He was still letting the cane hit the ground with each step, but he certainly didn't look like he was using it for much support.

"They're a couple of very nice ladies," he said.

"Yeah," I answered. "I hope they didn't bother you too much."

"Not at all. So you have many friends from church?"

"Not really. I probably won't know too many people there very well."

"Well, neither will I, so we'll do splendidly." A few moments of silence. "So tell me about the war. You don't mind talking about it, do you?"

"No," I said. "I don't mind. There's not a whole lot to tell, though…I don't really have any good stories."

"My injury prevented me from going," he said. "So any story will sound grand to me. I had to sit around back at the homefront while you boys had the time of your lives."

"It was fun, sometimes," I smiled. In those days the war no longer stood out to me as a trip across Europe with a group of guys. I saw it only in the context of Henry now, like the rest of my family did. In fact, the war didn't seem like anything that had happened to me at all. It was just something that had happened to him.

"So," he was saying. "Did you ever see anyone…you know, get killed over there?"

"I didn't see much real action at all, no," I smiled. "It was just a lot of training. Just training in different places."

"I'm sure you saw some bodies, though," he said.

I thought about the soldier hanging in the barn, and I wondered if anyone ever cut him down. Was he still there now, across the world, on this very night? For some reason that struck me as a terrible fate. To just hang there, in the sky. I wondered where Willie was, too, since I hadn't laid eyes on him in a while, either.

"I didn't see much of anything," I said.

It was a cloudy night, but a few stars were faintly visible in the cold blackness. Looking up at night always reminded me of being over there. I wondered if any of the other guys were looking up and seeing these same stars right now.

The church wasn't too crowded. It was probably too cold for many people to be out. The gathering was in a small atrium off of the entryway, and a fire roared quietly behind the black metal grating of the fireplace. The room itself was very warm, and as soon as we arrived we gave our coats to Mrs. Arthur, the minister's wife. I introduced her to Ambrose, and she brought us over to a long table with crackers, cheeses and fruits spread out, along with some bottles of soda. She seemed to think that this was just what we'd been looking for. We promised her that we would help ourselves later on. We had just eaten an enormous meal, after all.

Besides the fireplace and the table, there were three stuffed chairs in the room, and that was about it. A picture of the church itself hung above the mantle. Three girls stood in one corner talking to each other, and there was another, larger group of about six or seven girls and as many young men gathered near the table. They looked familiar to me, but I didn't really know any of them well enough to start a conversation. They were all a few years younger, I think.

We stood there for a little while, and I asked Ambrose if he wanted to sit. I asked because of his knee, but he said he was just fine. He started to tell me a story about a fellow he met on the train who owned a munitions plant during the war. Then Mrs. Arthur got everyone's attention and thanked everyone for coming. A few families had arrived now, and two little boys were running in circles around and under the table. The little girls were dressed like tiny versions of their mothers, in church dresses and matching hats. Mrs. Arthur smiled at all of them and made a few general announcements about the church calendar as another large group of people came huffing out of the cold and toward the fire.

Ambrose began to talk to me some more about the exorbitant amount of money this man on the train had made from munitions. This guy had been praying that the war would go on forever, and was now hoping that the United States would get involved in another war.

Two married couples arrived and greeted Mrs. Arthur as if she was their long lost mother. They looked about my age. Most people my age in town were married, and a lot of them even had kids already.

I looked around, desperate for someone I knew well enough to introduce to Ambrose. I didn't want to stand there the whole night without introducing him to anyone. He didn't seem to mind, though.

He talked to me about a friend of his who was thinking about investing in air travel companies now that the war was over. This guy thought there was a real fortune to be made in manufacturing and parts for planes now. Ambrose was thinking about going in on it with him.

Then he was telling me about an airplane race that had been held on Long Island a few months before, but he wasn't looking at me anymore. He seemed distracted by a girl who was at the table picking through some grapes. Her hair was short and waved, and she wore what looked like a man's overcoat. I had seen her come in earlier with a group of men and women. Ambrose kept talking loudly. She looked up and noticed us standing there.

"Hello," she said.

"Hello," said Ambrose.

"You boys've been over here for a little while. Are you talking business?" She asked this question suspiciously, as if a lot depended upon the answer. Her lips were wide, and her nose was long and sharp. Her eyes were small, but they were a nice blue color. She was wearing makeup. Below the coat she wore a pair of low black pumps.

"Just talking," I answered. Her hands looked lost in the coat sleeves as she popped a grape into her mouth.

"What do you do for a living?" she asked, moving toward us.

"My cousin is in the insurance business," said Ambrose, waving toward me. "You know about insurance, right?"

"Of course," she giggled.

"And I'm here on vacation myself, but I'm in banking. I'm an investor, really. We were just discussing a potential investment in airplanes. Do you think I should get in on this investment?"

"Sure," she said, rolling her eyes. "I think you should invest in everything. I can show you a diamond I'd like you to invest in, too."

"Really?"

"It's down at Kline's Jewelry, just down the street."

"Well, I'll think about that."

"If you get into the airplane business, I could go to work for you."

"You look a bit young," he said.

"How old are you?" she asked, popping another grape.

"Guess," he returned.

"I'm not good at guessing," she said.

"You have to guess. Part of being a good investor is good guesswork."

"Do you go to church here?" She was looking at me now.

"Yes, I do," I said.

"Sure. I think I've seen you before."

I happened to look up, and I saw Gertrude enter. She was wearing a thick brown coat and a matching hat. A gray scarf was twisted around her neck. I had told Gertrude about the social, and that I might be bringing my cousin. She hadn't really sounded interested, though, and I was surprised to see her. Mrs. Arthur approached her and looked confused. She looked around, as if she couldn't believe that a young girl would come across town after dark by herself.

"You have a car?" the girl was asking Ambrose.

"Back home," said Ambrose. "I have one of my own. A Packard. I don't have it here, though."

"I'd like to ride in it."

"Why don't you wait until I get my new one. I'm going to get a Lincoln. A Model L. It's a permanent car…I'll never have to replace it."

"Excuse me," I said, and left without seeing their reaction. I'm sure Ambrose was fine with the idea of me leaving, anyway.

There were probably twenty or thirty people here now. I passed one fellow who was talking with his friends, but I noticed that he kept turning to glance at Ambrose and the girl in the corner. He didn't look happy.

Mrs. Arthur was still fluttering around Gertrude when I approached.

"Hello," I said.

"Hello," answered Gertrude.

"Well," said Mrs. Arthur to me, "let's make sure Miss Delgrew gets a proper escort home, or I'll have to do it myself. I know she thinks she can do anything, but a night like this simply isn't the place for a young woman to come walking."

"It isn't far," Gertrude said.

"Well, let's just hope you don't ever get lost," said Mrs. Arthur. "Then who would help me with my sewing?" She laughed as if she'd just made the funniest joke in the world. Finally, she left.

"I didn't think you'd come," I said.

"I wasn't going to, but then I thought…I deserve it, right?"

"Sure."

"I never go anywhere…I just take care of Mama. So I decided to come," she looked around. "I don't think I'll stay too long, though."

"Why not?" I asked.

"Oh, I don't know. I probably won't have fun at something like this," she kept looking around. She wouldn't look at me.

"You should've told me you were coming before," I said. "We could've picked you up on the way over."

"Is your cousin here?"

"Yes," I said. "Do you want to meet him?"

"Is he interesting?"

"He seems to be."

"Good. A lot of these people don't look very interesting. See that group? I know them from school. They won't have a word to say to me, though."

"Why not?"

"I don't know. It's all right, though…I don't have a word to say to them, either," she looked at me finally when she said this. "So what is he like?"

"Who?"

"Your cousin."

"Oh…he seems nice. I don't really know a lot about him yet."

"Where is he? I'd like to meet him, and then I may just go home."

"He's right…" but Ambrose was no longer where I'd left him. I looked around, but I didn't see him anywhere. "I don't know where he went."

"Maybe he went out the back door," she said. "Are you sure you don't see him?"

"Where?"

"Through the door there." I saw the door in the back of the room now. I looked around some more, and then headed toward it, confused. She followed.

I turned to see if Mrs. Arthur was watching, but she was busy talking to a group of women. I opened the door and quickly slipped through it, with Gertrude behind me. The hallway beyond was completely dark. I couldn't see a thing. Gertrude was still in the doorway.

I heard an explosion of laughter from somewhere in the darkness. It was definitely a girl.

"Come on," I said to Gertrude, turning back toward the party. I wanted to get away from the dark hall now. I didn't know much about my cousin, but I know that I wanted to protect her from whatever he was doing.

"Hey Cobb," A whisper came from the darkness "Hey. Come here." It was Ambrose, all right. Gertrude stepped in the rest of the way, closing the door behind her.

"Where are you?" I whispered. Another giggling sound, louder now. I heard the pull of a chain, and a light bulb came on to my right and a little down the hall. They were standing outside of a small storage closet, and the door was ajar. I could see a long broom handle leaning against the wall in the closet. "What are you doing?" I asked.

"Just come here," he said again. The girl had a broad smile on her face. She tried to look past me at Gertrude.

"Ambrose, this is Gertrude," I said. I'm sure this wasn't the way she had planned on being introduced. "I served in the war with her brother." I felt strange saying it, since she and I hadn't mentioned Willie for a long time.

"Hello there," he came forward and leaned down dramatically, kissing her extended hand.

"Hey, come see what we've got," the girl said, giggling again. Gertrude was wide-eyed, probably as confused as I was.

"We'll certainly share with friends," Ambrose said. He raised his cane toward us. "I'm always prepared for a night on the town." The ivory dog's head floated between us in the dim light of the bulb, and its open mouth and bared teeth cast strange shadows on the wall.

Ambrose grabbed the head of the dog and twisted it around. I thought he might break it, but then I realized that it was coming free easily. He pulled a thin, rounded flask from beneath the head.

"The perfect place to store the hooch," he said proudly. The girl laughed some more. She reached out for the metal flask and he gave it to her. She tipped it up and drank.

"Save some for the guests," he said. "You like it?" he asked me, waving the cane. "I picked it up in New York, actually." He turned to the girls. "Cobb here thought I was a real cripple," he laughed loudly. "Here." He took the flask from the girl and thrust it toward me. "It'll make this party a little jazzier."

I took it reluctantly, and held it under my nose. One sniff was all I needed. I'm sure I was wincing visibly as I returned it.

"No thanks," I said.

"Are you kidding? This is great stuff…my bathtub gin is famous in Boston. Don't you drink?"

"Well," I said, "I do sometimes…" This was an uncomfortable subject to be discussing in front of Gertrude. "No thanks," I said again.

"Here, darling," he placed the flask under Gertrude's nose. She took it. She looked at it for a while, and then sniffed it like I did. Her nose wrinkled.

"Go ahead, honey…it's really good stuff," the girl was saying. I didn't like her talking to Gertrude.

"Nobody's gonna know…I'll bet you never see a cop around in this town, huh?" Ambrose said with a laugh.

Gertrude looked at both of them and then sniffed it again. She smiled, and started to bring it to her mouth.

"No," I said, and took it from her. She looked at me strangely.

"Ambrose…no."

"Aw, come on," he said. He turned toward Gertrude. "The American Medical Association prescribes this stuff for certain ailments. Really."

"Look," I said. "We're gonna be back in there, so come get me when you're ready to leave. Be careful. There are policemen in this town, whether you think so or not." I felt silly after I said it. I didn't want them to think I was against having a good time. I thought Gertrude might be mad at the way I'd grabbed it from her, but she looked fairly indifferent, as usual. I held the flask up toward Ambrose, and he took it.

"Okay," he said. "You're not going to tell anyone, right?"

"No," I said. "I think I'm gonna walk Gertrude home. Then I'll come get you here on my way back. Is that all right?"

"Fine," he said.

"So you'll be here?"

"Where else would I go?" He turned to Gertrude. "It was a pleasure meeting you, my dear," he bowed and kissed her hand once again.

"Nice to meet you," she said quietly.

"I certainly hope to see more of you at a later time," he was saying.

"How long will you be in Greenwood?" she asked politely.

"Only until you break my heart," he said. The other girl didn't laugh.

"See you later," I said, and we moved away from the dim circle of light and back toward the door. The girl was already giggling again by the time we got to the door and slipped back through it.

No one paid any attention to us on the other side, and I was convinced that we had left and returned without being noticed. Gertrude looked around and then grabbed a cracker from the table as if nothing at all had happened.

"Sorry about that," I finally said.

"Are you ready to go?" she asked.

"Yes…I thought I would walk you home. But you don't have to go if you…"

"No, that's fine. I did a lot of work today and I'm tired. Just let me say goodbye to Misses Arthur."

"Sure." While she talked to Mrs. Arthur I kept one eye on the door, but they never came out.

When Gertrude came back we got our coats from the closet and went out into the cold night.

"Well, he seemed like an interesting man," she said right away.

"Yes...you're right," I laughed a little. "Sorry you came all the way out just to meet him." Her boots made clicking sounds on the walk. I think they were the same boots she wore the night we went into the speakeasy.

"Oh, I didn't, really. Like I said, I deserved to go out."

"This probably wasn't very much fun, though."

"Is going out in Greenwood at night usually fun?"

"I guess not."

"Did you read the book?" she asked. She had given me a book to read called *Martin Eden*. It was about a guy who was trying to become a big writer, like her Mr. Fitzgerald. I had liked it.

"Oh...I was gonna give it back to you, but I forgot."

"That's all right. You can just bring it back to Mister Marshall's when you're done."

Mr. Marshall's store had a little lending library in it, where you could check books out for a nickel a day. Gertrude owned more books than anyone I knew, but she also borrowed a lot from Mr. Marshall. This was because hardbound reprints of books cost fifty cents each, and a book in cloth binding was around two dollars. I never would have known this, of course, before I met Gertrude.

"I read it already," I said. It had only taken me about a week and a half to read.

"What did you think?" she asked.

"It was pretty good." I tried to sound nonchalant, as if I read books that were almost five hundred pages long all the time. The truth was, I don't think I'd read a book since I was in school. I had liked it though. It was sort of fun sometimes. I had read from it in bed almost every night, often staying up later than I should have when I had work the next morning. My Mother had been worried that I was sick, because I would go to bed early to read it. I don't know why I wouldn't tell her that I was reading a book. I guess it was because I knew my Aunt would ask about the book and find something wrong with it. The guy in it was a sailor, after all, and he got in fights and drank sometimes.

"Did you know that it was autobiographical?" she said. I didn't know what that meant, but I didn't say anything. "Jack London was writing about being a writer."

"Hmmm," I said. "Well, I didn't really understand why he wanted to write so much. I wouldn't starve, no matter what." For most of the book, everyone was poor and starving. It had been kind of depressing.

"But that was him putting his need to create above everything else. Haven't you ever had something you wanted to achieve and put it above everything else, no matter what?" I wasn't thinking about myself, now, though. I was thinking about the book.

"He would have been much happier if he'd just gone with that girl," I said.

"Which girl, Ruth?"

"No, no," I said. "Not her…I couldn't stand her. The other girl. I don't know why he didn't end up with her." I felt kind of silly, talking about them as if they were real people.

"Why do you think he didn't?"

"I don't know…he got kind of strange when he started being a writer…he and that other guy. Something was wrong with that guy."

"Well, it doesn't sound like you really enjoyed the book at all," she sounded a bit offended.

"No, I liked it…I did." We walked a little more in silence. Then I spoke up again. "When he was working in that laundry place…boy, I can understand why you'd get drunk at night after working there."

"But Martin got past all that."

"I know, I know he did. But my favorite parts were the parts with Cheese-Face. That was my favorite." Cheese-Face was a guy who thought he was tough, and tried to beat up Martin a few times. The parts of the book with Cheese-Face were the best.

"And what did the ending say to you?" She sounded frustrated now, like an old teacher or something.

"I hated the ending," I said. "It was a terrible ending. I don't know why that would've happened...I don't know why Martin would've done that. That was the worst part of it all."

"I'll bet you don't even know why he did it. Because you didn't feel anything you were supposed to feel with the book," she said. I had never heard her this agitated before.

"I felt what I felt. I read it," I said.

"Do you know anything about Jack London?"

"No," I said. "Why do I have to know about him?"

"Because it's autobiographical. Did you know his mother was a spiritualist and his father was an astrologer? And he grew up to be an intellectual anyway?"

"No." A spiritualist. I thought about the Pilford sisters then. I had thought about them a lot since they had been in my house. I couldn't help wondering where they were. Did they live in Greenwood? I never saw them. And then I felt kind of sorry for Gertrude. She was a smart girl, and nice, but men would always be looking at women who were pretty like the Pilfords before they ever looked at her.

I wasn't a really handsome man, after all, but I was a nice guy, so people liked me. I tried to be nice to people, for the most part. Gertrude's problem was that she wasn't nice enough. A girl who isn't really that pretty should try harder to be nice.

"Well," she said, as if proving my point, "I don't think you're the type of person that Jack London is writing for." The Delgrew house was in sight now.

"I don't think he should be so particular about it," I said. "I read his book, didn't I? I mean, all he's doing is writing books. Did you know that Roger Hornsby hit three-seventy last year, and that George Sisler, in the American League, hit four-oh-seven? No matter how hard Jack London tried, he couldn't hit like that. Maybe Martin Eden could have, before he started becoming a writer and starving to death." I realized how dumb I sounded now. I wanted to rectify it, so I just kept on talking. "But I guess Martin just wanted to do one great thing in his life. Like Bill Wambsganss. You know who that is?"

"No," she said, of course.

"He plays second base for Cleveland. He made an unassisted triple play in the World Series last year. Nobody's ever done that. He's not Babe Ruth or anything, but I'd be happy being him. And that may be the best thing he ever does. So he could just go ahead and retire now…kind of like Martin."

To my surprise, she was smiling. She looked ready to laugh. The tip of her round nose had turned red in the cold air. I was glad I had stopped her from drinking Ambrose's stuff earlier. I told myself that I would have a word with him later about that. We reached the fence.

"Well," she said. "We'll have to pick out another book for you."

"Sure," I said. "Thanks for letting me read that one…I'll take it back tomorrow. And tell your mother hello for me."

"All right," she said, and went inside.

I turned and retraced my steps. She hadn't said thank you or good night or anything. She was a strange girl.

When I got back to the church, a lot of people had gone home. Mrs. Arthur moved toward me when I entered, ready to greet me all over again. But then she realized that I had been there already, so she moved off with only a smile and a wave.

Ambrose wasn't there. Neither was the girl, of course. I was frustrated, because now I'd have to sneak into the back hallway again and get them.

When Mrs. Arthur started cleaning up some of the remaining food from the table, I took my chance and went through the door again. The hall was totally dark. I was angry at him for making me sneak around the church.

"Ambrose," I whispered. I said it again, louder. And then again. There was no answer. I listened closely for giggling, but heard nothing. I reached out and felt my way along the wall in the direction of the closet, trying to remember if there was anything on the floor. I didn't want to bang my shin against something and curse or anything. I was in the church, after all.

Eventually I felt the closet door, and opened it. It took me a little while of flailing my arms about to find the thin hanging chain. I pulled it, and the dim bulb came on.

The closet and the entire hall were empty. My anger flared up. He was completely gone, and here I was sneaking around in the back hall of the church looking for him. What could I possibly say if Mrs. Arthur came through the door right now?

Maybe he went back home without me. I couldn't think of any reason why he would do that, though. Then I thought of his hidden vial of whiskey. Maybe he was drunk and lost, wandering around somewhere.

I pulled the chain again, and the darkness returned. My eyes didn't have a chance to adjust, and strange reddish shapes squirmed in front of me, floating back and forth, moving with me. I closed the door and began to feel my way back along the wall. I made the decision that I was going straight home now. Ambrose knew where we lived. He could come back home whenever he wanted.

But what if he didn't remember the way? I had led him here, after all. He'd never been to Greenwood before in his life. It was quite possible that he wouldn't be able to find his way home, especially if he'd been drinking.

I got to the door, and stood there with my hand on the knob. If anyone saw me come out, they'd probably think I'd been robbing the church or something. I imagined trying to explain that to my Aunt. My anger collected itself and swelled up again, like one of the reddish, purplish shapes floating there in the darkness in front of me. I didn't care if Ambrose was drunk and lost. It was his own fault. He should've waited for me.

I don't think anyone saw me come out of the door. I wouldn't know if they did, though, since I didn't look at anyone. I just went straight out through the atrium and left. I stepped back into the cold darkness, took one last glance around outside of the church, and then strode home quickly.

The house was dark when I got there. Thankfully, my Mother and my Aunt were both asleep. I crawled out of my clothes and into bed. I felt as if I'd gone straight from the dark closet to my dark bedroom, from one to the other without stopping.

I had trouble falling asleep. I started to think that maybe I should have searched for him.

The house was completely silent. It was chilly in my room. I had several layers of blankets over me, and their collective warmth was only now starting to seep into my body. What would I say in the morning if he never came home? I imagined his wealthy Boston family descending on us in a search for their lost son. They would ask me all sorts of questions. I couldn't blame them, though. I would have to explain how I had just met my cousin, proceeded to take him out on his very first night in a strange town, and lost him completely.

The thing I feared more than any wealthy citizens of Boston was my own Mother. Had I lost her only blood relative in America? I imagined how disappointed she would be. I was thankful all over again that I had managed to get in the house and into bed without awakening her or my Aunt.

I would probably be in trouble either way, but at least I knew that this wasn't entirely my fault. All he had to do was stay where I told him to stay. I had to take Gertrude home, because it was the noble thing to do. I'm sure she would have walked home without me, but that was beside the point. I imagined myself calling Mrs. Arthur as a witness before my Mother and my Aunt, asking her to confirm that the girl had come out all alone and was in need of an escort.

I thought about Martin Eden some more. I imagined myself as Martin, telling the other girl, Lizzie, that I would marry her. I was finally warm all over now under the covers, and my thoughts came heavier and more slowly, dragging themselves across my mind in a downward spiral, making less and less sense. I saw Lizzie there in my mind, and she looked a lot like a girl named Susan that I'd known before I left for the war. The reddish shapes had returned, but this time they were on the inside of my eyelids. Was one of the Pilford sisters named Ruth? No, neither of them was. Why had I thought of that?

Lizzie was gone, but now I could see Beth Pilford before me. She was making strange moaning noises and breathing heavily. My own breaths came quicker, and soon they overlapped with hers. Her body was thrashing around, but her eyes were staring right at me the whole time. She was rocking back and forth, and her hair was long and flowing now, and all over the place. She was lit only by a candle. There was a picture in front of her, but it was a picture of me. And then it was me. She was telling me that she wanted to be with me, just like Lizzie in the book. I could pick her to devote myself to, or I could refuse her completely. She waited there for my answer. I could fight my arousal or give in to it. The open question sat there, stretching out into forever.

It felt good, being halfway asleep with my mind freely floating, thinking about what it would be like to be close to a girl like Beth. To be able to say yes or no like Martin. I thought of Sue again, and tried to remember what her perfume smelled like. I saw her face just as I did when we had been together. Somewhere deep down inside I was warm and comfortable. I had a rigid, unbending core of absolute comfort inside of me. I pictured Beth again, and Eleanor. I thought about the girl with the wide mouth who had talked to us at the church just that night. I rolled over in bed, and then over again. I was pressed against the warmth of the bed beneath me. I pressed harder, my lower body tingling, and pictured them all again. My hands were both under the covers.

The thoughts grew into each other and became more and more blurred as I drifted. And then, a noise came at me from somewhere. I snapped back into reality. I realized how warm I had become under the mountain of covers.

It was a rapping sound. I was frightened then, thinking about the rapping on the table when the Pilfords were here. I heard it again. It was definitely coming from somewhere nearby. I felt a presence again. The sound was directed at me, and it wasn't going to go away until it was acknowledged.

But this tapping was quieter than what I'd heard that day in the dining room. This sounded like glass being tapped.

My eyes shot open. There it was again, more insistent this time. Taptaptaptaptap. I saw movement out of the corner of my eye. Was it the tree outside my window? Sometimes its branches moved back and forth in the wind.

I turned my head toward the window. I could see a silhouette through the white curtains, and it wasn't that of a tree. I traced the lines and saw a raised arm, and the curve of a torso, and finally a head that was turning slowly. It was a person, about the size of my missing cousin.

I crawled out from under the blankets and all the warmth I had collected dissipated into the air of the room. I moved to the window and pulled the curtains open. He was looking inside, trying to see into the dark room. When he saw me he waved and smiled.

I undid the latch slowly, my mind still foggy from my flirtation with sleep. I saw his steaming breath escape as he looked around. I opened the window slowly.

"Hey there," he whispered. The cold night air invaded the room. I'm sure I made my best attempt to smile back weakly. "Look out," he said, and handed me the cane. I noticed that the dog's head was screwed on tightly again. I threw it on the bed. He pulled himself over the sill and inside, brushing a loose hair from his face. I closed the window quietly.

"Thanks, friend," he whispered, beaming. He rubbed his hands together and breathed on them. He didn't look like someone who had disappeared and ruined my night at all. He smiled as if there had been a conspiracy between us, a joke we were both in on. "Are the ladies asleep?" he asked. I could smell the strong liquor on his breath.

"Yes," I said. "They were sleeping when I got home."

"Good," he whispered. "Good. Hey listen," he put his hand on my shoulder. "I had a good time tonight. Thanks for letting me come along. Greenwood's not so bad, you know?"

"Sure," I said. It wasn't what I wanted to say, but it's all I said.

"Is it all right if I have a cigarette?" he asked, reaching into his jacket.

"You'll have to go outside," I whispered. "You can't do it in here…they'll smell it."

"Okay, okay, I'll wait until tomorrow. It's too damn cold out there…I'm not going back out. It's funny, really."

"What?"

"Well here we are, sneaking out of our own houses for a cigarette. You're just like me…living with the old lady. We're gonna have a good time, cousin."

I forced another smile. I wanted to ask where he'd been, but he might actually enjoy recounting the tale, so I decided not to give him the satisfaction.

"You know I knew a gal who was expelled from college for smoking? She went to school in one of those states where it's illegal. Did you even know it's illegal some places?"

"Yes," I said.

"Not here, though?"

"No."

"Hmm. Well, I'll see you in the morning," he gave me a wink, and picked up the cane. "It's that way, right?" he pointed toward the hall.

"Yes, to the right."

He pushed back another strand of hair. Then he turned and put his hand on my shoulder again.

"It was nice to finally meet you," he said. I gave a tired smile. "I wish I could've met your brother," he said. He nodded seriously and looked right into my eyes, suddenly very sincere. Then he loosened his grip, turned, and slipped into the darkness of the hall without a sound. From what I could see, he was smiling happily the whole time.

CHAPTER 16

I was eating my lunch at Myrtle's one day when Jim Garrison stopped by my table again. It had been a couple of months since the last time I'd seen him. Once again, I was alone with my paper, watching the clock and savoring each minute of freedom before I had to return to work. I had just finished a piece of lemon chicken.

Jim approached with a smile and a clap on the back, but he didn't sit this time. He was dressed smartly in a belted Norfolk jacket, linen knickers, and oxfords. I had looked at oxfords just like that in the store by my office and I knew that they cost at least six dollars. I wondered why he was dressed so nicely. He must have had a big meeting that day, I thought.

"How've you been?" I asked. He stuck by his decision not to sit.

"Fine, fine," he said. "Things are picking up down at the mill."

"Really?"

"I never thought things could get so busy. There's just so much to do." He tried to smile, but something about his face seemed tense.

He talked a little about things down at the mill. I noticed that there was a scowl that would work its way onto his face every few seconds, no matter how much he tried to erase it. It kept creeping back, commandeering his features. Things must not have been going as well as he was letting on.

I let him do most of the talking and didn't question him. To my surprise, he invited me to continue the talk over lunch Saturday at his home. He stood there, awaiting my response. I agreed to the invitation, just so the awkward conversation would end and he would leave me to reading my paper and counting my minutes.

He gave me the address and then left, chewing on a cigar aggressively. I wondered what the two of us could really have to talk about over an entire Saturday afternoon. As my coffee and orange arrived I sat there, puzzled.

CHAPTER 17

After I'd been working there for a while Mr. Durham hired another helper. James Cordell was about sixteen years old, and he'd just left high school. He wasn't from Greenwood, but his father was a friend of Mr. Durham's family. He was a good enough worker, and always had a pleasant demeanor. He was a heavy guy already, even at that age. His face was usually flushed a bright, dewy pink, and yet he always claimed to be cold. There were certain days when we had the fire going when it wasn't even cold, just to put an end to his complaining. When I returned from lunch on one spring day, I wasn't very surprised to find him wearing a heavy coat inside.

"How was your lunch?" he asked happily, sitting at his desk by the window.

"It was good, actually. Did Mister Durham come back?" I sat down.

"No, he hasn't come back. Out in the field. You think that's what you'll end up doing?"

James had developed his own theory about Durham's future plans for us. He thought that he had been hired to replace me in my clerical duties so that Mr. Durham could ask me to join him in the field, selling policies. It was an interesting idea, but Mr. Durham had certainly never expressed anything like that to me. It was true that I had been training James in my work ever since he'd been brought on, but neither of us really knew what the long-term plan was.

"I'm not sure I'd want to," I answered. This was always my response to the question.

"Oh, sure you would. You wouldn't have to sit here all day...you could go visit the girls in their homes instead of having them come here."

I smiled and laughed a little, looking over the mail on my desk. But the more I thought about what he said the less sense it made to me. I looked up again.

"What do you mean?"

"Hmm?" His pudgy finger scratched at the end of his nose. I noticed a string of tiny sweat beads on his upper lip. He was still wearing his coat.

"What do you mean, girls coming here?"

"Oh...there was a girl here for you while you were at lunch. You didn't see her outside?"

I thought of Gertrude, but I didn't know why she would come here. She did know where I worked, though. I was hoping there hadn't been an emergency.

"Who was it?"

"She didn't give me a name."

Gertrude wouldn't have come by without letting me know. Who could it have been?

"What did she say?"

He put his paperwork down now.

"She said she was picking something up from you."

"Picking what up?"

"I don't know...I thought you'd know."

"How long was she here?"

"Not long. She wanted to look around, at your desk and everything. Tried to charm me. She was a real looker."

"What did she look like?"

"I don't know. Brownish hair, nice figure. A girl, you know. You weren't expecting her?"

"I don't even know who you're talking about." My mind raced. Did it have something to do with Ambrose? Maybe this was some girl he was running around with. But what would he have sent her to get from me?

"She really wanted to look around...said there was some paperwork she needed to see here at the office. I almost let her, but then I thought I probably shouldn't with Durham gone. I told her to come back when you were here. She'll probably be back."

"She didn't give you a name at all?"

"Now that I think of it, I guess she didn't. I'm sorry, I thought you'd know exactly who it was. Maybe you have a secret admirer."

I tried to get more out of him, but it was clear that he wasn't able to help any more than he already had. He seemed disappointed now that I didn't know who it was. He couldn't even give me an estimate of her age. When I asked, he just said that she was about "our age," even though he was a good six or seven years younger than I was.

Whoever she was, she didn't come back that day. Maybe the whole thing was a trick and it was someone I didn't know at all. Were there any important documents in this office that someone would want to get their hands on? I shuddered to think about having to tell Mr. Durham that something had been stolen.

"James," I said.

"Yes?"

"If that girl or anyone ever comes back, don't ever let them in."

"You still thinkin' about that?"

"Seriously...if you don't know the person, don't let them in."

"I didn't let her look through anything."

"I know, I'm just thinking...we should both remember that our files are no one's business."

"OK," he laughed.

CHAPTER 18

Saturday was gray, with the sort of gently oppressive humidity that can only be found in the spring. It had been raining lightly since the night before. I set out across town to meet Jim Garrison for lunch at his home. His flat was on the north side of town, in a newer district, and it was a longer walk than I'd anticipated. I brought an umbrella and wore a rain jacket, wondering all the way there how I was going to fill an entire afternoon conversing with Jim. I was hoping he wouldn't want to talk about the war the whole time.

Garrison's flat was made of a brownish brick, and the name on the mailbox indicated that he lived in the first story rather than the second. I could see the stairs to the upper flat around the side of the building, concealed by well-manicured bushes. I wondered if Jim took care of the grass and bushes himself, but then I decided that a place like this probably had people who did that for you.

I stepped up onto the porch and closed my umbrella. I shook it and set it in the corner so it leaned against the house. I knocked on the door. It opened, and Jim's wife Kate stood before me.

"Hello Cobb," she said. She had blonde hair and a nice tan. Her white skirt was shaped like a barrel and ended a good four or five inches above her flat shoes. Her sweater was white as well, and there was another white shirt underneath it. She looked like a real athlete.

"Hello," I answered, "Jim asked me to stop by today."

"Oh," she said with a broad smile. "Come in, come in." She held the door open.

"It's been a while since I've seen you," I said with a smile.

"It has," she said.

"You were still Kate Sherwood back then."

"Yes," she smiled warmly in response.

She looked exactly the same as I'd remembered her. The skin of her face was a little shiny, and a group of freckles were collected on the tip of her nose. Her eyebrows were so thin that they almost weren't there, and her lips were covered with red lipstick. The corners of her mouth curved downward even when she was smiling.

"Let me take your coat," she said. Her perfume was strong and flowery as she moved toward me and then away again with my jacket. "Isn't this weather dreadful?" she called as she opened a closet door in the hallway.

"It sure is." I was in a sitting room that was quite spacious. The flat turned out to be much bigger than it appeared from the outside. A long couch of gold fabric and dark, almost black wood dominated one wall, and a few lighter chairs surrounded it.

"I was supposed to play tennis today," she said, coming back in the room. "That's why I'm wearing this," she looked down at herself. "Do you play tennis?"

"No, actually…I don't."

"Neither does Jim. He's not much of an athlete at all."

I smiled in response.

"I'm afraid he's not home just now," she said. "He did say you'd be coming by, though. I'm afraid I just forgot…I was just getting ready to take this off when you knocked…I'm sorry it took so long," she waved toward the door. "You must've thought we forgot all about you."

"No," I said. "It wasn't long."

"Well, he should be home any time," she said. "Please, sit down." I sat in one of the chairs. She leaned on a chair. "Things have been tough down at the mill lately. Has he told you all about it?"

"No, I don't think so," I said.

"Jim's going to take over from his father," she said. Her eyes were large and round, and she had a habit of really staring with them, so they seemed to grow even bigger as she told you something. I remembered that she'd always had this way of looking at you. "He's been working very hard," she said.

"I see."

"Let me make some sandwiches," she said, turning the eyes down a notch. "I've got some tea and I'll make some ham sandwiches. Is that all right?"

"Well, if this isn't a good time…if Jim's busy I could come back," I said, getting up.

"No, no," she said. "No, sit down. I'll run off and make some sandwiches so quick you won't even know I'm gone." She smiled and breezed out, skirt shuffling.

I thought of her playing croquet on the lawn with all of the other blonde girls back in school. Back then, of course, she never would have revealed so much of her legs. But women were changing now. I tried to imagine what my Aunt would say about having a guest in your home and serving tea and ham sandwiches. She would probably make a connection between the way girls dressed today and their lack of homemaking skills.

I felt a wave of exhilaration at being here, in her house. I was too young when I was in school to really have much courage with girls, so I had been shy around her for the most part. It was strange to be alone with her now.

There was a window directly in front of me that faced the street, and I watched the rain fall through the sheer white curtain. Why had Jim invited me over and then not even bothered to be here? Maybe he had just forgotten. If that was the case, it would be silly to stay.

I looked around the room. There was a gold and green clock sitting on the mantle, with an oval shaped mirror trimmed in matching gold above it. It all looked very expensive. Here I was, sitting in a house made and maintained by two people who were my age. It was a real home. I tried to imagine marrying a girl and having a place like this.

I could hear Kate humming faintly down the hall, in the kitchen. The rain pattered lightly on the roof. I felt like an intruder. This wasn't my world. And yet, why couldn't it be? These two people were both my own age, but they seemed so far ahead of me. Maybe it was easier when you came from money like both of them did. Maybe it was easier to put together a place like this and sit in here and talk about having kids and taking over your father's business. Maybe you weren't embarrassed to throw together some ham sandwiches for a guest when you knew you would always have money. You'd know that the guest who hadn't done anything with his life since school would consider himself lucky to be eating your sandwiches.

I opened a magazine that was sitting on the coffee table, and turned right to an advertisement for Jantzen's one-piece bathing suit. *The suit that changed bathing to swimming.* The girl wearing it in the picture was beautiful, of course, with impossibly large blue eyes and hair so blonde that I wondered how they made ink that color. Still, the suit looked kind of silly, decorated with broad stripes. *Men's and Women's Styles Available.* She was looking at me, begging me to gawk at her in her one-piece bathing suit and to buy a hundred of them when summer came. I wondered if this was the sort of thing Kate would wear when she was swimming instead of playing tennis.

I reached over and flipped the page. Another ad had a picture of a huge refrigerator. *Yes, Frigidaire, the electrical home refrigerator, actually freezes your own favorite drinking water into cubes for table use.* A woman stood by the refrigerator. It looked like the same woman from the other ad. It wasn't a real woman, of course. It was just a drawing. I wondered if Kate had looked through the magazine and pictured herself standing by the refrigerator in the bathing suit. I was sure she had decided that she and Jim could buy all of these things someday, after he took over the mill.

"I'm afraid I'm not much of a cook," she said, entering with a tray, "but ham sandwiches are a specialty of mine."

"They look delicious," I said as she put the tray down on the coffee table. There were four sandwiches cut into triangular shapes. She handed me a glass of iced tea and sat on the couch.

I watched her sit and stretch her legs, and wished I'd been figuring out something to talk about instead of looking at a magazine. I took a drink of the tea so I wouldn't have to say anything. She reached over and delicately picked up a sandwich. Her fingernails were painted a dark red, like her lipstick. Should I talk about myself? I couldn't even pretend that she cared. About Jim? I didn't really even have that much to say about him. All I could come up with was the house and the food.

"This is very good," I said, after swallowing a bite of the sandwich. It tasted like every other ham sandwich I'd ever had. "And the house...sure is beautiful."

"Thank you," she said. As she put her glass down I noticed a ring of lipstick on the rim. She looked around the room absently. "We weren't sure about the area at first. They were saying that it was going to be quite nice, but you never know." She was staring at me in that intense way again, eyes rounded to full capacity.

"Yes," I said. "Well I'd heard great things about these new buildings. They really are very nice. How long have you lived here?" It didn't even sound like my voice.

"We got married right before the war," she said. "We moved in right away. Jim's father wanted him to be closer to home, I think. But my parents thought this would be a nice place for a new couple starting out."

"Yes, it is," I smiled, taking another bite. She turned toward the window.

"What is it you do for a living?" she asked, suddenly turning back to me. "I know Jim told me, but now I can't remember." She was rubbing her hands, one over the other, very slowly in her lap.

"I work in insurance here in town," I said.

"Oh that's right," she said. "Jim said you were working with Mister Durham."

I couldn't imagine them having any reason whatsoever to talk about me. Maybe he'd just mentioned it in passing when he told her that I might be by today. But if he'd remembered to tell her that, why wasn't he here?

"Yes," I said after another sip. The tea could have used more sugar. "I've been working with him for almost a year now. It's very rewarding." It sounded silly to me as soon as it left my mouth.

"Hmmm," she said, scratching her leg with the red fingernails. She looked me in the eyes again, putting her unfinished sandwich back on the plate absently. "So you served in the war too?"

Her hand landed softly on my knee, and I felt a shot of something that made my heart pick up its pace. I'm sure it was just a reflex of hers, but it was exciting to me, of course. At that moment, when she placed her hand on my knee and looked at me with such interest, I began to see her differently. She struck me not as the pretty, wealthy girl I remembered from school, but as someone who probably didn't get many chances to talk to people besides her husband. That was the only way her interest in me made sense. I glimpsed a bit of her unhappiness right there in that moment, the weight of Jim and his parents, probably, or maybe just the loss of the freedom she'd enjoyed when she played croquet on the school lawn with the other girls. I couldn't get over the strange surprise of feeling sorry for someone like this.

"Yes," I answered, as her hand floated back over to her own lap. I wondered if she even realized that she'd touched me. "Jim and I talked about it a little. He was in another part of France, but we were both there at the same time."

"And you didn't fight at all?"

"No," I said, "not really."

She took another gulp of her tea, adding to the sticky mass of lipstick on the glass. I finished the last bite of my sandwich. She sat back on the couch, smoothing her skirt and rubbing her hands again. The mass of freckles on her nose danced and wrinkled as she made a pouty face.

"I really do feel silly in these clothes," she said. "I should wear something a bit nicer."

"It's perfectly fine," I said, realizing that I never used the word *perfectly*. "Please don't change on my account." She smiled at me then, her eyes reflecting the rectangles of the windows. She shifted her weight in the chair again, and looked outside. She bit her lower lip in a way that was really quite attractive. Then she looked back at me, and her eyes dropped a bit.

"You know I'm supposed to ask you something now," she said quietly. She was smiling at the floor rather than me.

"I'm sorry?" I asked politely. I put the glass of tea down, thinking that a matter of importance was coming up. She looked up at me again, and let out a great sigh.

"I'm supposed to ask you something," she said. "But I don't know. I don't know if I can do it."

"Well, you can try," I said with a smile, trying to sound encouraging. My heart had sped up again.

She leaned forward then. Her fingers were interlaced, and her body was pointed directly at me.

"Jim couldn't be here," she said. "He couldn't be here for something like this, and I don't blame him. He's been through a lot, Cobb. He went through a lot over there in the war. I don't know if he told you about it?"

"Well," I said. "He did tell me a little."

"Jim was injured in the war," she said quietly. I became aware of the sound of the clock and the perpetual rain. "It was pretty serious," her big eyes were boring into mine again. "He almost lost a leg, you know."

"No, I didn't know that," I said. A few moments of silence passed between us. She was looking at the window again, a wetness welling up in her eyes. I felt like an intruder in their house again. I shouldn't be sitting here, talking about something so personal with her. She rubbed her smooth leg absently. I wondered if she was thinking about the leg that Jim almost lost. I really hadn't known that his injury was that serious. He had told me all about the field hospital, but he'd never really said anything about his injury.

"Would you like to see the house?" she asked suddenly, her voice breaking into my train of thought. She was looking at me again, aiming her eyes like cannons, and they were already completely dry.

"Sure," I said, standing up and trying to hide the confusion on my face.

"I just realized that I didn't show you around. That's so rude of me," she said. "Come on."

I followed her through the hallway and into the kitchen, floating through the trail of her perfume. It was a small kitchen, with a metal table where two people could eat. She showed me how the table could be folded down when not in use. Of course, she couldn't actually fold it, since it was covered in the ingredients of our sandwiches. A clock in the shape of an owl hung above the white porcelain sink, and a pile of dirty dishes sat beside it.

She just sort of waved her hands around at everything. Back in the hallway, she opened a door and pointed out the basement, and I was just able to see the wooden framework of a staircase descending into darkness below.

"You have your own basement?" I asked, the answer being obvious. She seemed flustered or nervous now, so I asked when she thought Jim would be home.

"Yes," she said, without looking at me. "It's nice for storing things." We turned down the hall again. "In there is the bathroom, and this is the bedroom."

She waved toward it and I saw that it was neat and orderly, almost the exact opposite of the kitchen. It was a large room, with the same sort of furnishings as the sitting room. The bed had a canopy over it, and everything was decorated in a faded yellow color. It was very rich looking. A mound of pillows sat atop the tall bed. She ignored the bed completely, and instead concentrated on showing me a picture on the wall. It was a reproduction, she said. Her father had bought it at the New York Armory Show they'd had in 1913.

"What do you think of it?" she asked, smiling.

"It matches the room," I said. "The colors, I mean." I didn't know quite what to say. I could see that it was supposed to be a person of some kind, but the whole thing was just a bunch of connected shapes and rough lines. It didn't look real at all. It was just a series of strokes, each one starting and stopping, interconnected to make an image that was more like something out of a dream than real life.

"Can't you see her?" she asked, giggling a bit.

"I think," I said.

"She's going down the stairs," she said. "But she's not wearing anything. Don't you see?"

"Yeah," I said, smiling a little. Actually, I couldn't see that at all. She just laughed at me.

There was a Beaver teddy bear leaning against the wall on the dresser. Its expressionless black eyes reflected the light from the windows. She laughed some more when she saw me looking at it.

"You like him? Jim gave him to me for my birthday," she said, stroking the bear. She was like a little girl who had grown up, and was now playing house. For some reason, I felt as if the bear was something personal that I shouldn't have seen.

"It's a very nice place," I said when we were back in the hall. "Really."

"Jim wanted to have another room to work out of," she was saying as we returned to the sitting room. "You know, he likes to build things...I'm sure you knew him when he was very good at wood working." I hadn't known that, actually. "Of course, he's still good...he just doesn't get around to it that much any more." We entered the front room again, and we both sat on the couch now. "We thought he would be able to work out of the basement...even though it's moldy down there...you really wouldn't want to go down there...but when he first got home, he wasn't able to go down stairs, you see." I nodded. "His legs are better now but he won't even try anymore, I don't think. He could do it if he wanted to. He spends most time at the mill, though."

"I didn't notice anything," I said. "About the way he walks. He seems fine."

"Would you like some more tea?" she asked, noticing the empty glasses on the coffee table.

"No, I'm fine," I said. One of her half eaten sandwiches still sat on the tray.

"Cobb," she said, serious again, "I have to ask you something. It's a favor...a big favor that you can do for me...for us."

I thought of Gertrude then, asking me to go find Willie for her. Was Kate going to ask me to find Jim? To get him to stop spending so much time at work? Or maybe she wanted me to help out around the house. Maybe I was going to be handyman for the whole town. I thought about how much Gertrude looked like her brother. Some women, when you look at them, you can just see how they'd look as a man. You can just imagine a brother or a father with that same face. Kate didn't have one of those faces, though. She was very feminine.

She was looking at me in a strange way, her pretty eyes desperate and in need of help, her turned down mouth twisting in deep concentration. Her legs were nice and long.

"Whatever you need...I'd love to," I said. Boy, did that sound stupid. The way she was sitting there and looking at me made me want to be very serious, as if we'd been close friends for a long time.

"Listen," she said. "This is going to sound strange...however I say it," she smiled then. She looked down and we both watched her sliding a ring around on her left hand. It had stopped raining outside, or at least I couldn't hear the rain anymore. She started speaking again.

"Jim's injury was very bad. He doesn't tell anyone about it. But there are certain things that Jim can't do anymore. Because of the war. Because of what happened."

I nodded slowly.

"We always talked about having children," she said, looking at the floor and smiling. "It was just something we always said we would do, when Jim took over the mill and things were going smoothly." She looked up at me again, eyes wide. "But we can't now. Jim can never have children...that's what the doctor told him. They told him that over there and they told him that here. And you know, his father was willing to pay any amount to any doctor from New York that could help him. But no one could. No one could help him." She reached down and scratched her leg just above the ankle.

"I can't believe I'm telling you this," she said. "I can't believe I'm asking you this. Jim and I made a decision. We want a child more than anything...we need one to stay happy. When I think about not having one for the rest of our lives...I don't know..." She trailed off and turned toward the back of the couch, the heel of her hand covering her mouth. I wanted to touch her.

She looked at me sideways then, and let out a little peep. I didn't know if she was about to cry, but when she moved her hand, she was laughing. She put her hands between her knees and leaned forward again, all smiles now, but with the corners of her mouth still maintaining their vigil.

"I wanted to adopt a baby," she said. "Go to the city and pick one out and everything. But Jim says no. He doesn't want that. He wants a baby that's really ours. Or really mine...that's related to us by blood. He knows he can't have one...but he won't let me adopt one. He just won't. He wants me to carry one and give birth...really. I do too, I suppose. There's no reason why I shouldn't be able to, just because Jim can't. I want to be a real mother." She was shaking her head now, but still smiling at me. "You're going to think I'm very silly. But this is what Jim and I both want. We talked about it a lot. We don't know a lot of people who stayed around in town...from school. We don't. And a lot of Jim's friends were hurt or killed in the war." She was smiling again. "But you...you came back all right. You're his only friend who came back just like you left. And, you know, it would have to be someone he didn't really see around anyway. It couldn't be someone down at the mill or anything.

"Jim couldn't be here," she was saying. "He won't be here today. It's too difficult for him. You understand. And I don't want you to lose his friendship, but you have to understand...he doesn't want to see you anymore. If you say yes. You can come here once a week...maybe twice depending on how long it takes. It can't be a Saturday after today...he's not normally at the mill today. Just some day during the week...whenever it's easy for you to come during the day, at lunch or something. I'll even make you something to eat...instead of going to Myrtle's."

"I'm sorry," I finally said. I shrugged a little bit, showing that I didn't really understand. She was going to have to say it, to really put it in words. She probably knew that already, though.

"Cobb," she said. "I...Jim and I both, we want you to...we need you to help us. To help me have a baby."

No matter how much I'd suspected it, hearing her say it seemed unreal. Could this be a joke? Why would they do that to me? I barely even knew them.

"Don't worry about Jim," she said. "He knows, of course...it was his idea to talk to you." She laughed a little, her hand on her forehead. She looked up and ran her hand through her sand-colored hair. "If you agree, then he doesn't want to see you ever again. You understand. Just come at the agreed time, and he won't be here. It would be too hard for him to see you. This is all so hard on him."

I started wondering what she thought of me. What if she thought I was ugly? Maybe that's why this was so difficult for her. Had Jim picked me out for her? It was too strange to even think about. She seemed very serious, though. That's how some women are with babies, I knew.

"If you don't want to, that's all right," she said, her fingers brushing my knee again and then swiftly retreating. "Just, please...don't tell anyone about this. It's very embarrassing for us. Please don't tell anyone. No matter if you say yes or no...please keep it between us. And..." she seemed to falter a bit, "and if it...if it does work, then, you can't see us either...you can't see it. The baby. That wouldn't be right...this way would be easier for everyone."

It's hard to recount exactly what was going through my mind. This was so far from what I'd expected to happen that rainy afternoon. She was prettier than anyone I'd ever gone around with. And here she was, asking me to do this thing with her. Asking me to come over and do it to her once a week, and even throwing in a plate of sandwiches each time.

She was watching me, waiting for my reaction. Her smile was just a bit sly, like she was in on a joke. That's what was really throwing me. There was a confidence about her that I wasn't really used to in women. Most women had no confidence and never talked to you, or they flirted with you to hide the fact that they were empty on the inside.

But she was different. I thought about what it would take to put this proposition in front of a strange man alone in your house. She didn't seem nearly as flustered as she should have been. I wanted to fluster her, suddenly. It was exciting to me, to be in this position, with a girl who looked like her waiting for my response. I held the proposition in the air, wanting to stretch the moment out as long as I could. This girl barely spoke to me in high school.

"So what do you think of me?" I tried to say it casually, but I could tell right away that it took her by surprise. Her hand was resting on the back of the couch in an unnatural way. It just lay there, in front of us, like the question.

She started laughing. It was such a little sound. I could tell by her eyes that something had changed. My question had broken into something, and now she looked like the girl in school again.

"I don't know…" she said slowly, drawing out the words and looking at the wall. Then she turned back to me. "You look like you could have a wonderful child." The eyes again. "Like you could really help us."

"Would you rather it be someone else?" I wanted to get to the heart of it, to figure out if Jim had really picked me on his own or what. It was so strange, I still didn't really believe it.

"You seem very nice to me," she said then. "And no, I'm not disappointed at all. We both want you to help us. But I…I really want you to. I'm here asking you to please do this. I don't know if you really care about my husband or my marriage or anything…but I want you to do this for me. And I know we haven't really known each other for a long time…I know that. I'm just asking you."

I wanted to say no, right then and there, and end it all. I wanted to end the tingle of flattery, and my feelings of infatuation, and all of the confusion. I very much wanted things to return to how they had been this morning when I'd gotten out of bed, before this bizarre joke was placed in front of me.

But I couldn't look away from her. She was asking so sincerely, and I couldn't help but imagine what she was asking. To know her so intimately, with her complete permission, on a regular basis. I wondered how long it would take to get someone pregnant. How many times? I found myself hoping that it was a lot. I was more excited about the level of intimacy that there would be between us, not physically, but just the regularity of it, and the secret and everything. There would be something real between us. A real bond no one else would know about and that neither of us would ever lose.

The pregnancy part was a bit more frightening. The idea of my child running around here in this house in a few years, another intruder like me, but never knowing it, was too strange to even contemplate.

I knew that there was no way I could give her an answer today. There was too much to think about. And if I ended up saying no, I still wanted to enjoy my imagination for as long as I could. I wanted to savor the imagined, possible intimacy that was being dangled in front of me.

I saw the tight ring on her little hand, and the tiny bumps on the surface of her arm, and a small smudge in her lipstick. She reached up and smoothed a strand of hair behind her ear. This was another man's wife I was looking at, contemplating. I wanted to be nice to her, then, and to let her know that I was thinking about it seriously.

"You're a very beautiful woman," I said, placing my hand on top of hers. Would she pull her hand back? She was married, after all. But she didn't move at all. Her hand was warm. Mine was too, and I hoped it wasn't sweaty or anything. "Any man would love the opportunity to help you in any way possible," I realized that I was sounding a lot like Ambrose now. She was looking into my eyes. I wondered if she really found me attractive. She would have to, wouldn't she? "I want to think about it," I said. I didn't know if I was making sense. She was certainly listening though. "I really respect what you're asking...I really do. I need to think about it and see." She was nodding slowly. "And I want you to know that this is a real secret...no matter what, no one will know about this."

"Thank you," she said quietly. I took my hand away and we sat there in silence. I started to feel hot under the collar, really embarrassed by it all. I was worried that my face might start to flush. She looked like she didn't know what to say, either.

"Well," I said finally, "I guess I'll be going." I wanted to get out of that room more than anything then. A rainy and dreary day outside had never looked so inviting. I just wanted to be in a bigger space, with plenty of time to relive everything she'd said over and over.

"All right," she said. She went and got my coat and then walked me to the door. She was so small.

"It's a nice place," I said stupidly. "Thank you for lunch."

"You're welcome, Cobb," she smiled. And then, as I was stepping out the door and back into the humid spring air, she started talking again. "It probably wasn't quite what you expected."

"The sandwiches were good, though."

She laughed again, nodding. I liked to make her laugh.

"Thank you," I tried to get serious all of a sudden. "For everything." I looked into her big eyes as I pulled on my jacket.

She stood there as I put it on, looking at me but not saying anything.

"How about Thursday?" she said then. "There's no way for me to know what you decide, so we'll just say Thursday at noon. I'll be here. If you don't come, then I'll know you've decided against it."

"Right," I said. Thursday suddenly loomed close, as if it was only minutes away. Somehow I'd thought I was going to get more time to decide. I agreed, though, since any longer than that might be too long. I really didn't want her extending the offer to anyone else before I could decide.

I walked home, deep in thought the whole way. When I got there I realized that I'd left my umbrella on the porch. I found myself hoping that Jim wouldn't notice it there for some reason.

CHAPTER 19

In June of 1918, we boarded an enormous boat in New York City, and we stepped off the same boat in Brest. I don't remember seeing too much of Brest, but there wasn't much to see. We spent most of our time in the railroad station, which was a mass of smells and flies. We boarded a train there and were shipped off across the countryside. All the railway stations looked exactly like that first one to me, and they all had the same smells and flies. We commanded a lot of attention, and the people would look at us and chatter in their language. There were always a few people who spoke English, and every one of them, it seemed, had a brother or a sister or some relative living in America. They really thought that we'd be able to tell them how their family member was doing over there.

The train ride was dark, and we spent a lot of time stumbling into each other. When my eyes had adjusted, I cleaned and prepared my weapons, still under the impression that I would be firing them at someone soon. The best thing about being a member of the American Expeditionary Force was definitely the weapons.

We each had a British 1917 Enfield rifle, which had been chambered to use the same type of ammunition as its American equivalent, the old Springfield 1903. The guns, like the sides in the war, were hybrids of different countries. I hadn't known much about weapons before training camp, but I learned the names quickly, along with what I could expect from them when I pulled the trigger. I had been worried about loading and cleaning before I knew what I was doing, but in reality it was pretty easy. I was proud that I'd picked it up a little quicker than some guys.

Each one of us also carried a revolver that had been designed to use the same ammunition as a Browning-Colt. I liked the feel of the pistol, but I had been embarrassed by how difficult it was for me to aim accurately. The first time I fired it, I kept thinking that something was wrong. No holes were appearing in the target. Was anything coming out of the gun? I got better with time, of course, and soon I could make the holes appear closer to where I wanted them. But I always liked the rifle more than the pistol.

One of the strangest things I had to carry was the ugly mask, with its stretched animal snout and insect eyes. It was surprisingly heavy. Back at Devens they told us it could save our lives. They told us this thing was the only chance we had to breathe once the gas was dropped. They told us horror stories about how breathing the gas might not kill you right away, but it could catch up and get you years later.

I never really understood how the mask worked. It was our most interesting weapon, though. Strapping it on completely was eerie, like going inside myself. All I could hear was my own breathing. The smell of rubber and sweat was overpowering. The bumpy panes in front of my eyes let through a greenish, twisted image of the world.

After a stop in a grime-covered station, we moved to another train. This was, without a doubt, the slowest train ride I'd ever been on. We never picked up any speed, and the engineer seemed to stop in every little town on the way. At least our new car had spaces between the wooden slats where we could watch the country go by, even if it was flat and boring.

At each town we passed, a gang of small children would come running out and follow alongside our car. No matter what the town, they all looked the same. They had dirt on their faces, their clothes were falling apart, and they would call out to us for "beeskits" and "seegarets." We had picked up a few of both things in Brest, and one time I did finally hand a cookie out through the slats and into one of the little hands. It hadn't tasted very good anyway, and I wouldn't have felt right about giving them cigarettes. Bridges didn't mind, though. He tossed a bunch out over their heads. As soon as the children stopped to pick them up, they shot away into the background, and I was reminded that we were in motion.

CHAPTER 20

As my Aunt and my Mother cleared lunch from the dining room table, they began to methodically transform the room without saying anything. It was as if one thing just flowed into another. Clearing the plates became smothering the table in the heavy quilt, and from straightening the kitchen they moved right into drawing all of the curtains.

"What are you doing?" I asked my Mother.

"Just getting ready for the Pilford girls," she said. It had been a long time since I'd met them on that first strange Sunday afternoon. I watched my Aunt get out the candles, wondering how many times they'd done this in the meantime. It was a Sunday again, but maybe they normally came over while I was at work.

"You're still seeing them?" I asked. Neither of them answered. We hadn't ever really talked about what happened the last time I'd seen them in this room. Time had passed, and so much else was happening, with Ambrose being there and everything. But I guess not that much had changed for them. They were still trying to wake the dead. Thinking of Ambrose, I suddenly wished he were here. I wondered what he'd think of the Pilfords and the whole thing.

After a few weeks of doing nothing, Ambrose had taken a job at a local bank. I suspected it was just because he must have been bored during the weekdays while I was at work. Even though it was a Sunday and the banks were closed, he had taken off after church, insisting that he had a few things to do. My Aunt had no problem telling us that she didn't like it one bit. Working on a Sunday wasn't the worst sin you could commit in her mind, but it was a sin nonetheless. Ambrose wasn't her child, though, so she couldn't really reprimand him. Instead, she lectured us about his shortcomings when he wasn't around.

"How often have they been coming?" I asked again.

"We see them from time to time," said my Aunt. "Things have been going well, actually. Last time they used special cards to tell me my future. Can you imagine? Maybe they could tell yours, Colbert."

"Colbert, you can stay," said my Mother. "But please don't disrupt anything. We've really been making progress."

"How much do you pay them for this?" I asked. My Aunt smiled and told me not to concern myself with that. We heard a knock on the door.

Beth's hair was cut short like Eleanor's now. Otherwise, they looked the same. Eleanor smiled politely as my Aunt removed her jacket. She talked to my Mother and my Aunt about how wonderful they both were looking.

"Mister Whittier, what a surprise," she said. I smiled and nodded. She smiled in return and all of my recent concerns over their fees faded away.

"It's nice to see you again," I said to both of them, stepping forward. Beth looked around. She seemed to be in a trance of some kind already.

"We've missed your presence in our sessions," Eleanor was saying. "Have you decided to join us today?"

"Would that be all right?" I asked. She and Beth looked at each other. Beth had a scowl on her face, her eyebrows tilting severely downward. I was struck by how young she appeared. She looked like a spoilt child.

"You'll have to do as we say," Eleanor said to me, a taller and darker version of her sister. "We don't want to undo any of the progress we've made lately."

"Colbert will cooperate," my Aunt said. "And I think it would be a good thing to have him…it would help the positive energy. He's very positive, really," she was speaking to them as if I wasn't there.

"Are you sure?" Beth was asking in her breathy whisper, looking at Eleanor. "We've come so far."

Eleanor looked at her crossly and then smiled and nodded at the rest of us.

"Well," my Aunt was saying. "Would you like something to eat, or drink perhaps?"

"Thank you," said Eleanor. "We're just fine. Shall we begin?"

I followed them into the dining room. The picture of Henry was sitting on the china cabinet in the corner this time. I hadn't seen the picture since the last time they were here. We had no images of Henry anywhere in the house, and it was startling to see him again after such a long while. Here he was, sitting in that same chair, staring across time at me with that somber expression.

Beth arranged four candles around the table, and my Mother lit each one as she set it down. They did this silently, as if it was a very familiar routine. My Mother placed a bowl in the center of the table now, and I saw that it was one of her white china bowls with little yellow roses on it. I had just eaten soup out of one of these bowls a few days before. Beth produced a small cloth bag from somewhere on her person and dropped what looked like several dark pellets into the bowl.

"I'm sorry, Mister Whittier," Eleanor was saying as they took their places in the candle lit room, "but you cannot join the circle. We have had success lately by remaining in fixed places, you see. You are welcome to sit outside, as before."

I nodded quietly. Sitting in the chair by the doorway, I was able to fade into the rim of darkness that surrounded the flickering light. I felt comfortable there. It was as if I was watching a scene unfold far away.

Everyone grew quiet, and a few moments passed. They were all seated at the table now. Beth seemed agitated. She was shifting around in her chair with quick movements, looking back and forth around the room. I half expected her to start waving away the imaginary bugs that seemed to be buzzing about her head.

There was a candle in front of each of them, and wisps of smoke were now emerging from the bowl in the center. The smell wafted toward me, assaulting my nostrils. It was a strong incense of some kind. The room quickly became enveloped in the scent. It reminded me of church.

"Henry has grown more comfortable with our contact," Eleanor said, breaking the silence with a strong voice. "We have not been successful often. And yet his last message was clear…we will no longer need a separate spirit guide to reach him. He awaits our contact. This does not mean that he will always be ready to speak. He may not be in the mood to interact with us at all. But he has grown trusting…Beth is now his chosen medium, and he has learned to occupy and manipulate her."

Beth's lips were open slightly, and I watched her breathe. I thought I'd liked her hair better the other way, but it didn't really matter. She was beautiful. I had some trouble with the idea of her being connected to Henry, though. This girl seemed so far from my memory of him. I glanced at his picture.

Why would he communicate with her and not me or my Mother directly? I reminded myself that these were professionals, though. They took their spiritualism very seriously, and they were devoted to it completely. I wasn't devoted to anything like that. Perhaps that was why he chose them.

I thought about the knocks on the table and the presence that I had felt in the room the last time the sisters were there. I hadn't really talked about it since then. There were a couple of times when I almost told Gertrude, but I couldn't bring myself to say anything. I guess I was afraid that she would react with scorn or disbelief.

"He has also grown impatient with us before," Eleanor continued. "He does not like our questioning his identity. He is not comfortable with our attempts to get him to answer specific questions to prove who he is. He has instead expressed an interest…a near obsession…with the circumstances of his own death. This is normal, of course, and should not be taken as a lack of love or respect for those in this room. When he chooses to communicate, we must consider ourselves honored, and allow him to discuss whatever it is he wants to."

I watched her mouth intently. The shadows around her lips jumped as she spoke, like liquid being stirred.

"Henry is still a lower level spirit, so his interest in the world of the living is understandable. But he is showing signs of wanting to move into the middle level, and we can help him to do this. He has chosen a few spirit guides who are attempting to show him the way. It is crucial for us to help him at this time to aid him in his quest for the next level of existence, even if it means that he will be further from us. Ultimately, the decision is always his, and even as a middle level spirit, he will be reachable by my sister and myself…but at greater cost to our own abilities and our own minds…"

Beth drew in air sharply, interrupting her sister.

"Something is happening," Eleanor said. "We need concentration from all members of the circle. Everyone in the room must close their eyes and help us."

I didn't really want to close my eyes. Still, the last thing I wanted was for my Aunt or my Mother to blame me for something if it didn't come out the way they wanted. I closed them tightly, and the streaks of light left by the candle flames remained on the insides of my eyelids. I pictured Henry again, as he appeared in the portrait, in the dark suit, turned toward the camera with a serious expression. I wondered if he was looking at me now, sitting in my chair, head bowed and eyes closed. I tried to imagine him looking down from his spirit level. How would we look from there?

Part of me didn't want to feel the presence again. I breathed in the heavy incense. Minutes passed in silence. I opened my eyes and peeked around.

Beth spasmed and squirmed in her chair, her forehead slowly contacting the table and then quickly lifting again. It reminded me of one kid who used to fall asleep in class all the time when I was in school. His head would slowly approach the desk just like that, and then suddenly snap back up.

"Has the spirit of Henry Whittier been contacted?" asked Eleanor. There was no response. Beth was sitting there, rigid, eyes pinched shut like two clenched fists in her face. "Those who love Henry Whittier are in this room, gathered again, at the same places in the circle. We await your contact. Is Henry Whittier present?"

"Yes," Beth finally spoke. Her voice was low, and she exhaled strongly as she said it.

"Do you speak through my sister?" asked Eleanor.

"Yes," came the response again. My Mother and my Aunt reached out, grasping hands across the tabletop. Was that voice hers or his? I hadn't felt anything yet, but I was beginning to experience the creeping sensation along my spine again. I watched Beth sitting there, calm now, her face totally relaxed. It was as if she had given in completely to something.

"Is there anything you wish to speak about today?" asked Eleanor to the room. "Will you allow us to maintain contact with you?"

"Yes," moaned Beth in the strange voice again. Her lips were no longer tightly drawn. They looked completely relaxed now, and when she wasn't speaking her mouth fell open. She looked hollow, somehow. She was sitting back in the chair, her body slumped to one side just a little.

"Is there any message that you have today for Jean or Edna?" Beth's lower lip quivered, but no sound came out. I had forgotten that I was supposed to have my eyes closed now.

"There is a new presence here, as you will detect," said Eleanor calmly. "Your brother during life is with us, although he is not in the circle. We can bring messages to him as well."

More silence. The incense had reached every corner of the room and the scent sat in the heavy air, draped over all of us.

"Please tell us if you do not want to communicate at this time."

Beth shrieked and leapt in the chair as if she'd been pinched.

"What is it?" whispered Eleanor. My Aunt's knuckles tightened around my Mother's hand.

"No, no…" Beth was whispering quietly.

"Please," said Eleanor, "do not torment our medium. Show us what you show her."

"I…I'm sorry," Beth was saying now, shaking her head and using her own voice.

"Is contact broken?"

"No…no, he's not speaking through me right now but he's showing me things. He's still here. He doesn't want to go. He wants to show you, through me."

"Tell us what you see."

I closed my eyes again, breathing the incense in and out of my nostrils, feeling it fill my lungs.

"I see…I see a land of green trees and blue waters, blackened with blood and death. The countryside was once beautiful, but now it is filled with noise. Shouts and screams, and the growls of the earth itself. It is as if the gods are calling their children back with these explosions…oh! I can't describe it!"

I opened my eyes and saw that she was slumped over, head and shoulders on the table. Eleanor's eyes were open too now, and her hand was on Beth's shoulder.

"Are you all right?" she was whispering. Beth looked up suddenly. Wet streaks glistened on her face in the candlelight. My Mother and my Aunt were looking at her too, now. "Please...please Beth, Henry wants to show us this. You must help him to show this to us. It is important to him that his Mother and his Aunt see this."

"All right, all right," whispered Beth.

"Now let's all close our eyes again...he is still with us...he is showing us this patiently, like a teacher. This is difficult for Beth. We can both feel how important this is for him...this is so central to his being right now. You may feel this also." My Aunt's head was nodding silently. Beth resumed, and my eyes closed again somewhere during her speech.

"They are like children shouting and running. Just as they used to play in the schoolyards. But they hold weapons now. Things that make them men."

She sniffed a bit, and the room was shrouded in silence. A few moments passed.

"There is a town nearby. A small town where I can sense the throbbing power of life going on. And here...only a short distance from it, is so much death."

I pictured the small town in the French countryside where Henry was buried. Was this the town she was referring to? I had seen it with my own eyes. My heart pounded.

"There is a silence, where we are. We are waiting in our long hole dug in the ground. Man after man. Each of them young and full of life. The unseen enemy is over the hill in front of us.

"The bombs drop. Both sides drop them, and we can't even tell who is dropping them. They go on, unstoppable. Night and day. And then one day, the bombs stop. And we're ordered forward. We're pushed from behind, like animals led to slaughter. They don't want us to have time to think. But I did think then. Of all of you. Somehow, I knew already that it was coming. That death was rising to meet me over that ridge."

I peeked again. Tears had now appeared on my Mother's face.

"I know so much more now. Different things, in the place I am. So everything seems different now. But I have to tell so you'll understand. I have to take out the spirits that floated there. And the angels overhead that waited patiently as the sky opened up. I see them all now as I remember. They were always there. They are always with you, waiting for that moment when you can finally see them. And then, when that moment comes, you know it's time to go with them. And it all seems so simple, then." Her voice had picked up in speed, and was less clouded. She was moving more smoothly, barely faltering, as if she had truly lived all of this herself. I couldn't even think. I knew there would be time for that later. I just listened.

"We advanced, and they were waiting for us. The angels and the enemy. Death waited for us. They launched their bombs from their holes in the ground. And the world started to explode around us as we moved forward. Their cannon on wheels lurched and spewed death before us. I can see some of the others burning and withering, their beautiful spirits leaping from their bodies and into the arms of the angels waiting above them. The angels cannot be described before you are ready to see them. But they are beautiful, and natural. And those men that died, I knew all of them. All of them were my kindred spirits. And each one that left me weakened me as I ran forward.

"And then, somehow, those of us that remained reached the enemy. We got to them, to their hole and their cannon. They looked as surprised as we were that we had reached them. And I felt dead already. And we struggled with them, fighting to rid the earth of spirits we both believed were evil.

"I remember the eyes, mostly. Their eyes as they died in front of us. Surprised in their hole, running away from us and toward us. And we fought them right there, up close, our flesh against theirs. The white of their eyes is all I can see of them now. And we all killed each other. Right there. One of them stood across from me and unloaded the death from his weapon into me.

"I crawled in the dust, a fitting place. And looked up at the sky as the animal life flowed from me and back into the dirt where it had begun. I was aware of that sky as being absolutely full of all manner of things. Things I had never seen before. And my sight grew sharper and sharper as the life left me. Some of the things were airplanes soaring way above the earth. They were the enemy's planes. And they were dropping their bombs on everything. The field was littered with the dead men I had known, and now new men fell on top of them. Everything spun around and around. The field and the dirt and the bodies spinning and mixing together. Over and over as they exploded and exploded in the frenzy of death dropped from the skies.

"And then I saw that some of the shapes weren't planes. They were spirits rising, and angels descending. The clouds opened slowly, and a brightness shone down. It was a brightness that destroyed all shadows. Everything was bleached the color of the clouds. The spirits of the others rose all around me. And then I felt that mine was rising too. And the beauty of the angels was almost too much. It was too much to bear. But they never left my side. I remember no pain, only their beauty as they guided me upward. Surrounded by the spirits of those I'd known on Earth in that field. And the spirits of our enemies were there, too, but we were not enemies anymore. And we all rose together."

She was silent now. My Mother was crying quite steadily, and I heard her muffled sniffling. I opened my eyes and saw tears on my Aunt's cheeks as well. And then I saw that Beth and Eleanor both had shining streaks on their own faces. I tried to stop the wetness pooled in my eyelids from overflowing down my face. I sat there, completely still, but a drop ran down the left side of my face.

"And so we know he thought of his loved ones," Eleanor was speaking now. "On that day. During that very battle, only moments before his passing. That love feels strong to me know. Those who are at this table and in this room can feel it, too."

"There is more," Beth said in a choked whisper.

"We know he has a lot to tell us," Eleanor answered, "and we are grateful. Some must be saved for another day…it is too difficult."

"Something happy, I think," Beth was then saying. "There is more to say at another time to those at this table, but there is something else that I am feeling. He wishes to communicate an idea to one who is with us here. One who is not in the circle."

"I see," Eleanor said. "Henry is now at a point in his spiritual journey where the faces and lives of his loved ones are in focus. He may have special messages to those who are present. He may have something to say from the other side to his living brother."

"Yes," said Beth. "Yes."

There was another silence, and she began again.

"He is sending me another vision. I can see a day in winter, not far from the place of Henry's death. It is the same place but a different time. He sees you at the site of his grave. He sees his brother there, before him, at his grave marker in that countryside, the air cold but the sun shining overhead." I could feel my Aunt and my Mother looking at me. I didn't dare look at them now, not wanting to betray to them just how emotional I was. Beth's words were causing me to shiver, and I felt more tears coming.

"He watched you there, that day. From where he was. And that was the moment at which he truly knew that life went on back on this side, and he was no longer here. And he saw you as you stood there as one man sees the other in the mirror before him. As a counterpart on the other side of the mirror. I'm seeing…I'm seeing something else now. An image that he is sending me…something that he is using to help describe it…or maybe something he thought of on that day. It isn't clear."

I waited, not daring to breathe.

"I see…" she sounded truly frustrated. "I don't know…it may not make sense to me…it may be meant only to you. I don't understand. But I see a horse…I see two horses. Two that are the same. They are toy horses…carved of wood, for children. But they are not really toys, somehow, that is what he is saying. They are meant for something else. For holding books. But they are a set."

I could hear my own breathing now. The hair on my neck stood at attention, and I truly felt the presence. This was a message intended specifically for me. I was no longer embarrassed to cry in front of the sisters. It was simply too much.

"It is gone," Beth said then. "The images have faded. I've lost him, too." A few moments passed in silence, and I tried to regain my composure.

"It's all right," Eleanor's hand was on Beth's again. I wiped the salty tears from my face and glanced down at my Waltham wristwatch to see how much time had passed. The presence of that watch made me comfortable, somehow. The fact that it had moved forward regularly during this strange experience reminded me that there was a world outside of this room.

"You have served us well as our medium," Eleanor was telling Beth. "There is more…clearly Henry will have more to say later. But he understands now. He knows that he cannot exhaust you entirely. This is enough for now."

Everyone exhaled deeply. All four of them looked at me from behind their candles. I wiped my tear-stained face again and sniffed. I returned their looks, not knowing what to say.

"We're glad you could join us today, Mister Whittier," Eleanor was saying now. Beth sat back in her chair and closed her eyes, relaxing completely as if she'd just done a day's work. "I believe it was good for Henry and for all of us to have you here."

I nodded silently, feeling as tired as Beth looked. Slowly, as if time had ended altogether, we stood and blew out the candles and straightened the room, letting the light of day stream back in and reawaken our senses. I refused to look at the picture on the china cabinet. I just couldn't bring myself to do it. I was afraid that I would start crying again.

The Pilford sisters put on their jackets quietly.

"We'll leave you to interpret the messages of today," Eleanor said in the entryway. "These are personal, after all, and are meant for you."

"Thank you so much, dear," said my Aunt, clasping her hand tightly. Eleanor smiled and nodded back.

"I am glad for you that we were able to reach him today. I'm very proud of how far we've come," she said. Beth still looked exhausted.

My Mother came from the back of the house and pressed some money into Eleanor's hands. She looked down at it, still smiling in the same way. She and Beth exchanged a quick look.

"I'm sorry, Jean," she said. "You remember...we discussed an increase after five sessions. I'm so sorry, but with the progress we've made..."

"Of course, of course," my Mother said, moving back down the hallway. Eleanor looked at my Aunt now.

"I'm truly sorry...this is our only income, though...you understand."

"Yes, yes I do," said my Aunt, smiling as well. "It's perfectly all right. What you are doing for Jean...for all of us, for our whole family is worth more than you know. It's perfectly all right."

My Mother returned with the rest of the money and gave it to Eleanor. It looked like a lot of money to me, but I had other things on my mind at the time. Eleanor smiled politely at me and nodded as they left, thanking me once again for attending. I mumbled my thanks in return. Beth said nothing.

I sat in the house for the rest of the afternoon in a strange, disjointed state. Nothing felt quite real. I held the newspaper in front of me, staring at words over and over again. Each time I reached the end of a line, I realized that I couldn't remember what I had just read. I concentrated on a quote in front of me on the page. The prime minister of Belgium was saying "*Since the Crusades I do not know of any enterprise which has done more honor to men than the intervention of America in the War.*" I couldn't feel anything about this at all. I felt numb, and no matter how hard I tried to concentrate on anything, I couldn't bring the world back into focus.

My Mother put the picture of Henry away again, and she and my Aunt went about cleaning the house vigorously. None of us said anything to each other about what had happened.

I thought about the presence in the room again, wondering if it could really be Henry. The voice hadn't really sounded like him. I wanted to discuss everything with my Mother and my Aunt. I wanted to know what they thought about what he said to me. I wondered how they felt about him telling us about the battle and him bringing up the horse bookends like that. But Ambrose came home right as my Mother was preparing dinner, so we didn't say anything. I knew instinctively that they would be uneasy discussing such things in front of him, and I was right. They were silent, and so was I.

Ambrose was a whirlwind of activity and discussion, as always, so our dinner certainly didn't lack conversation. I couldn't help searching my Mother's face throughout the meal for any sign that she was thinking about Henry, though. She looked tired, and the few times that I caught her eye she just smiled her sad smile, the corners of her mouth drawn tightly.

CHAPTER 21

❀

I was invited that week to have dinner at the Delgrew house. I ate there every once in a while. Gertrude would usually catch up with me when I was leaving work, sewing cases in hand, and let me know that her mother would like me to come again.

The three of us sat in the little kitchen eating butterfish and conversing politely. The green paint on the walls was no longer peeling, since I had covered it with a new coat. The crucifix remained on the wall, but now there was a clock as well. It was a round clock with two robins painted on its surface, their wings spread as if in mid-flight. Mrs. Delgrew had chosen it from the clocks at Mr. Marshall's store and had me pick it up a few months before.

Mrs. Delgrew smiled when I commented on how delicious the meal was.

"Do you like your job?" asked Gertrude. "It seems to me that it would really be boring." By now I was used to the things she said. That was just how she was.

"Gertrude," said Mrs. Delgrew. "Colbert has a good job."

"No," I said. "It is pretty boring sometimes." Mrs. Delgrew looked at me. I swallowed another forkful. "But any job is, I think. My old job was boring sometimes too."

"If you were an artist you wouldn't be bored," said Gertrude.

"Maybe not, but you wouldn't get as much work done," I secretly enjoyed sparring with her. It was always funny to watch Mrs. Delgrew look back and forth between us.

"What do you mean by that?"

"I don't think being an artist counts as having a job. I don't think an artist is contributing anything to his country."

"Well, that's interesting," she said, sitting back a little and taking a drink. "I don't think you even know any artists. I would really like to psychoanalyze the mind that would say something like that."

"Oh, Gertrude," said Mrs. Delgrew. Then she looked at me. "She's always on about this now. Psychoanalyzing everything. I've told her it's just a fad."

I didn't know what she was talking about.

"He hasn't read Freud," said Gertrude. "He doesn't like to read about anyone who doesn't hit balls with wooden sticks."

Mrs. Delgrew looked confused.

"Who is Freud?" I asked with a smile.

"He's a man who might say that you have a repressed artist inside," Gertrude said, as if teaching a class. "This artist is a more expressive and interesting person, but you keep him in your unconscious."

"So do you have an artist in your unconscious?"

"It's different for women."

"Why?" I asked, glancing at Mrs. Delgrew. She was eating quietly now.

"It just is. We don't have as much freedom to repress our natures."

"Really?"

"Colbert," Mrs. Delgrew interrupted, reaching across and touching my wrist. "Tell me about your cousin. He's staying with you now?"

"Yes…Ambrose. He's gonna be with us for a little while. He's started working at the National Bank now. He was a banker when he lived in Boston."

"So what else is he doing while he's in Greenwood?" she asked.

"Gertrude got to meet him," I said, glancing at her. "He's very social, really…more than I am."

"Is he a Catholic?" Gertrude asked me.

"Who? Ambrose? No. Why do you ask?"

"A lot of city people who are against the Volstead Act are Catholic."

"He's not Catholic, is he?" asked Mrs. Delgrew, quite seriously.

"No," I replied, taking another bite of fish.

"Good," Mrs. Delgrew continued. "I don't know why those people just can't leave the country if they want to drink so much. The trouble is, they all come from countries where it's perfectly fine to drink all day long. Imagine saying that you can't worship the Lord without the use of alcoholic drinks."

"But can you imagine how confused they are?" Gertrude was saying. "Foreigners, I mean?" she turned to me. "You know what William was saying last time…last time he was here?" I shook my head, not daring to look at Mrs. Delgrew at the mention of his name. "He was saying that this nation has allowed a religious majority to make the laws."

"You mean against drinking?" I asked.

"Yes…it's just Protestants. People like us…small town people. Think about it. This Amendment's not about the evils of alcohol…it's about one religion trying to discourage the practice of another one by immigrants. That's the truth. That's what William was saying, and he's right, if you think about it. Why else did they do it?"

"I don't know."

"If wine wasn't a part of what Catholic people do, there would be no Eighteenth Amendment. That's that."

"What's wrong with that?" I asked. "We've been nothing but immigrants ever since the country was started. Now we're finally becoming one and the same, right? We're finally putting down rules to bring everyone together. So we're not just a jumble of different people and religions and things."

"Really?" she continued. "What if they started passing laws against going to your church on Sunday?"

"They won't do that here," said Mrs. Delgrew. "Because we're not foreigners." She gave me a little smile as if we'd triumphed together, and then stood up to clear the dishes. She usually ate little, and ate it very quickly.

Gertrude was shaking her head slowly. I just smiled.

"In college, you're allowed to talk about things like this," she said loudly. Mrs. Delgrew's back remained unexpressive over by the sink. Gertrude looked back at me then. "Do you think we should interfere in the affairs of Europe?"

"I think we just did."

"I mean now…from now on. Do you think we should let them fight their own wars next time?"

"I don't think they'll have any more."

She looked annoyed. I wondered if she thought about these things all the time, and just waited to bring them all out when she had someone to discuss them with.

"You know what I mean," she said. "Well, do you think we should set a certain number of immigrants who are allowed in our country every year? And then tell the rest they can't come in?"

"I'm not sure. Are they thinking about that?"

"You probably do," she said. "You probably think that this country is just for you, just because you fought in a war."

Mrs. Delgrew turned toward her daughter slowly then. There was a moment of silent communication between them. Gertrude turned back to the table, expressionless. She took her plate and my own and rose.

"Well," I said, "thank you so much for the wonderful meal."

"You're quite welcome," said Mrs. Delgrew.

"Excuse me," said Gertrude.

"Where are you going?" asked her mother sharply.

"I'll be right back," she said, disappearing into the hallway.

"So how is your Mother, Colbert?" Mrs. Delgrew asked. She always asked me how my Mother was, even though I don't think she knew my Mother at all.

"She's doing well, actually," I said. "It's nice to have Ambrose in the house…it makes it a bit busier…" I trailed off, realizing that a missing presence in the house might not be a good topic to bring up here.

"Well, we could say the same thing about you in our house," she said, and then turned back. It shocked me a little, since it seemed so unlike her.

I stood up and Gertrude returned.

"Here," she said. She placed a worn hardbound book down on the table. I could tell that this was a book she actually owned, so it must have been a favorite. I picked it up. The front said *O Pioneers!*. I looked at her, waiting for an explanation.

"You'll like it," she said. "It's a good book. About Americans. It's by Willa Cather." I knew that the book was a peace offering.

"Thank you," I said.

I had enjoyed the last book she'd given me to read, but I found myself unable to choose things to read on my own. I'd looked at all the books at the lending library in Marshall's store, but there were so many, I had no idea which were good. They always had a bunch of books by Zane Grey, and some others I knew nothing about. I remember one that I almost borrowed called *The Sheik*. I didn't know anything about it, but Ambrose and I had seen a movie called *The Sheik* with Rudolph Valentino, and we loved it. The young girls in the theatre had gone crazy for Valentino, and Ambrose even went to the bathroom and slicked back his hair afterwards, just like the Sheik himself. It was quite a little craze. They even came out with a brand of birth control device named after that Sheik. But I wasn't sure if the book was about the same Sheik. So I never really borrowed anything from Mr. Marshall's library.

When I got home that night I started reading Gertrude's book right away. It was a lot shorter than the last book, but it was good. It was about Swedish people living in Nebraska. It was about a girl, though, instead of a man, and I thought that this was probably why Gertrude liked it so much. In fact I pictured Gertrude as Alexandra in the book while I read it.

It got to be a love story between a kid named Emil and a girl named Marie, who I pictured as looking a lot like Lizzie from the other book, for some reason. I liked the parts with Frank Shabata though. They were all foreigners, mostly Catholic, but Frank I could understand. He had a really bad temper, but he had a good reason to.

Only a short while after I finished that book and gave it back to Gertrude, President Harding passed the Emergency Immigration Act. Apparently, the things she was talking about that night at dinner were real issues. This law restricted the number of immigrants from each country in Europe. They were limited to a certain percent of the number that had been here in 1910, or something like that. My Aunt was in favor of it, of course. I couldn't believe Harding had just become president only a few months before, and he had already signed something like that. I'd even heard that he had ridden to the ceremony in a Packard. He obviously had no problem showing off a little.

After I finished the book I used to picture myself as a pioneer, with a wife in a tiny home somewhere on a huge farm. I thought about how I would treat her, and what things would be like, night and day. I imagined coming in after a hard day's work and her having dinner ready and everything. It made me think of a song I'd heard, sung by Englishmen in a war hospital. And then I remembered that the song I was thinking of was Jim Garrison's song about having a little wife.

CHAPTER 22

Thursday morning I sat at my desk and watched the sluggish movement of the clock.

I took off before noon, heading north as fast as I could. I should've left earlier. As I approached the front porch of the flat, I realized that I was sweating from walking so quickly. I hoped it wouldn't show.

She didn't really look happy or sad to see me. I don't even remember what she was wearing. We didn't say too much. She had made something for lunch but I said that I wasn't hungry yet. So she led me down the hall by the hand, and I swam through the lingering, twisting trail of her perfume. We walked slowly.

I kissed her a little bit on the bed, and she put her hand under my shirt. Her hand was cold. I wondered if she was as nervous as I was. I tried to imagine that she was Marie, from the book.

I remember her small body under me, and the mass of freckles on her shoulders. Her breasts weren't much more than curves in her skin as she lay back. In those days, large breasts weren't fashionable on women, and they didn't want them. They even used to tape them down. She was very skinny and little, almost like a boy, which was a good shape for the time.

I thought it might feel different to be with a married woman, but it didn't, really. Of course, it had been a long while, so maybe it did and I just couldn't remember how it had felt before. It was pretty enjoyable with her, though. She was silent the whole time.

She put on her clothes afterward, facing away from me. Her back looked so small and white, with its sprinkling of freckles around the shoulders and neck just under her blond hair. Her arms and legs looked so thin as she dressed. I looked at her body and wondered if she could be pregnant already, at that very moment, while she put her clothes back on. Could it happen that fast?

I started to feel a little guilty then. This was another man's wife, after all. For some reason, the picture on the wall made up of all the shapes and lines made me feel terrible. I thought about her father buying the picture for her in New York. He was probably even bragging about his little girl to the man who was selling it, and the man was listening and nodding because it was a customer. But really the salesman knew that she was just another girl somebody would sleep with. Then I imagined Jim and his wife sitting in their bedroom and looking at the picture, thinking about how cultured they were for having it. I left the room, averting my eyes from the teddy bear.

Neither of us said much of anything afterwards. I grabbed something to eat on my way out. She handed me my umbrella at the door, and reached up to wipe some lipstick from the corner of my mouth. There was something nice about the way she touched me to do that. It was strange, but that contact seemed more intimate than anything we'd just done.

As I walked back to the office different people climbed through my head, their images lit up like in a movie. My Aunt and my Mother and the Delgrews and Mr. Durham and Ambrose. Just about everyone appeared. I was thinking about how they'd all feel about me, if they knew what I just did. I imagined what my Aunt and her friends from church would say.

I tried to remember how Kate's perfume smelled. I pictured her back in school with all the other girls. I reached up and touched my mouth where she'd wiped the lipstick off.

CHAPTER 23

We unloaded our packs from the train and met the captain near another small town. A lot of our boys must've already passed through this town, since there were several YMCA tents set up.

The only memorable thing about the town itself was the church that stood at its center. An enormous tower rose from its top and pointed to the sky, and on the very tip of it was a statue of Mary with Christ in her arms. I had always associated that sort of thing with America. Before I saw that church I never thought about these people having a religion at all. I wanted to go have a look, and Willie followed me, like he did a lot.

In the window of a little cottage nearby was an etching of the church, with the name printed in English underneath. I thought it would make a good gift for my Aunt. We went into the shop, and I picked it up. The place was full of little pictures and post cards. There were even some larger drawings of the countryside. I wondered if the little woman behind the counter had drawn them.

When I brought the etching to her to pay for it, she began pointing and gesturing at the tower in the picture. She kept looking me up and down and gesturing, saying something in French.

"That's a very famous statue," a voice said in English. It was one of the YMCA workers. He was a middle-aged man, with a large, curling mustache.

"I don't know what she's saying," I said.

"It's a well known statue in France. Have you been inside the church?"

"No," I said. "It looks very nice." It had been a long time since I'd spoken to a civilian.

"She's telling you that the French have a saying about the church," he said, taking the etching from me and looking at it intently. "As long as the Virgin and the Christ don't fall, things will go well with the allies," he looked at me now, handing it back to me. "That's why she's telling you…because you're a soldier."

Willie seemed very impressed with this new knowledge, and he mumbled his thanks to the man. We smiled at the woman and left. Willie was in awe of the church, and he couldn't resist another glance at the statue in the sky as we passed it. I knew he was a religious guy, and I didn't bug him about it.

Willie and Henry and I had all trained at Camp Devens in Massachusetts. We'd been paid twenty-one dollars a month for living expenses. That was where they put everyone from the selective service of the National Army from our part of New England. Each division there had a thousand officers and almost thirty thousand men. People at camp hadn't paid much attention to Willie because he was quieter than most of the guys who came through the first registration. He got done what he needed to get done without complaining about it. He was a good guy to have around.

I had heard about his father dying by then, of course. I think my Aunt had probably told me about it. She knew that I had known Willie in school, and therefore she felt that it was her duty to tell me anything she heard about his family. Maybe she thought I would get along better with another guy whose father had died.

Willie and Henry never really became friends, though, even at camp. I was the only one Willie really wanted to talk to and be around. I have no idea why. Henry was a fast moving guy sometimes, though, and we weren't always together.

As far as I know, the top of that church stayed intact throughout the entire war. I don't know if it's still there, but I like to imagine that it is.

CHAPTER 24

We were wilting in the little office. It was warm everywhere, but at least outside there was a nice breeze. Inside, even James was wearing only one layer. His blue shirt was decorated with a dampness under each of his arms.

Beads of sweat formed on my forehead and slid downward toward my eyes. I dragged my hand across my brow and then watched the dampness bleed from my fingertips onto the papers in front of me, smudging the ink. The windows were open, and the faint sounds of the street below had come floating up, reminding us of the world outside and adding to our desire to end the workday.

Mr. Durham had told us he was taking the second half of the day off, since it was his birthday. We could go home too, of course. Now he was taking care of paperwork, moving things around, and watching the clock to see when the halfway point of the day would come. We had to stay there until noon to be able to count it as a day of work for the main office.

My Aunt had baked some spiced cookies for Mr. Durham's birthday, and she insisted that I bring them in. He had been crunching on them all morning. He had a strange, sideways way of chewing, as if his jaw was made of two separate pieces, each one sliding past the other and then back again.

While he was waiting for the morning to end Mr. Durham sent me out to get supplies. I cut through the park, taking my time and enjoying the scenery. A group of children ran around in circles, teasing a horse that was tied to a post. Nearby, an old man was selling fresh buns and apples from a cart. I bought one of each. His toothless mouth sucked at an imaginary object while he put my coins in a small pocket in his jacket. I wondered if he had ever had a job indoors and wished he could be outside on a day like this one.

When I got back to the office James was still at his desk. Aside from the fact that the wet spots under his arms were slightly bigger, I wouldn't have known that any time had passed at all. Mr. Durham was still floating around the files, putting things in order, and trying to steal his glances at the clock quickly so we wouldn't catch him looking.

"Plans for the afternoon, Colbert?" Mr. Durham asked as I came in. He smiled at James. It had been a long time since I'd seen the old man so happy. He ran his thick, brownish hand over his white hair absently, waiting for my answer. The skin on his hand looked just like the wrinkled brown paper bag they had put the supplies in at the store.

"Oh, I think I'll just get some relaxing done," I answered as I pulled the items out of the bag and lined them up on my desk. I shuffled the new packages of paper and carefully unloaded the bottles of ink.

"Really?" he asked, still smiling.

"I wish I had some a' that relaxing planned," James said from his corner. There seemed to be a joke going on between them.

"What?" I asked, smiling faintly.

"I think she came by a bit early," Mr. Durham said, slowly lowering his frame into his own chair now. I was confused.

"Who?" I asked him, sitting down in my own chair. He pulled his pocket watch out and adjusted it, studying the clock over the little fireplace. He shook his head.

"I'm sorry. It's not our business, of course. She was lovely. It was her story that gave it away, I think."

I just looked at James, waiting for an explanation. I noticed that he had a small pile of the cookies on the corner of his desk now.

"A girl came by for you while you were out," he said with a smile. He wiped sweat from his forehead with the back of his pudgy hand, showing me the extent of the armpit stain. He had succeeded in plastering some damp hair down above his eyes.

"Who was it?"

"Come on…you don't know who it was?" James asked. Mr. Durham had gone back to the papers on his desk. He probably felt as uncomfortable discussing girls with me as I did with him.

"No," I answered again. "What did she say?"

"Well…she acted like she wasn't waiting for you, but we thought she probably was. We thought she was just a gal waiting for you to get off today. You sure you weren't expecting her?"

"No," I answered. "I'm not expecting anyone. How could anyone know I'm leaving work early today?"

He shrugged.

"What did she say?"

"I didn't really talk to her," he said, looking past me at Mr. Durham.

"Mister Durham, did she say something to you?" I asked. He looked up.

"I thought she might have a message for you, but she didn't," he said, his bony shoulders rising and falling again in a shrug. "She didn't even knock on the door…I opened it to get some air and she was standing there, at the top of the stairs. I think I probably frightened the poor thing as much as she scared me."

"She was waiting for me?"

"Well, she said she was a friend of yours. And then she sort of told a little story. But I'm sure it was a lie, because she had to think of some reason to be standing out there. You boys would never believe it, but wasn't that long ago when a young girl like that would be waiting for me to get done with my work here at this very office. I know, you don't believe it." He had a smile now and a far off look. "She was very lovely." Now I wasn't sure if he was talking about the girl he saw today or one from a long time ago.

I looked back at James, who shrugged as well.

"What did she look like?" I asked.

"She was tall, I suppose," Mr. Durham answered. "And pretty. She wore a hat though, so I couldn't see her hair, although I think it was dark."

"We just thought it was some gal meeting you, Cobb," James said.

"What was the story?" I asked both of them. "You said she told you a story about what she was doing?"

"She said," Mr. Durham started with a slight smile, "that you had asked her to get something for you at the office. I'm sure it was just the first thing that came into her mind to say."

"What did she say I'd sent her to get?"

"You didn't send her, right?" asked James.

"No. I don't even know who it was."

"Well," Mr. Durham began, his arms folded across his chest, "I believe she said you told her to come here and get copies of the life insurance policies for your family members," he was still smiling.

"Poor kid," James said. "I'll bet it really sounded like a good excuse to her. What do you think she would'a done if we'd said 'all right, we'll just get them for you,'" he laughed.

"Why would I send someone to do that?"

"Well that's what I thought," said James.

"I told her you would be back soon," Durham said.

"We thought she'd stick around outside and wait for you," said James. "She didn't wait for you out there?"

"No," I said.

"I told her you would be getting done with work early today and it wouldn't be long," said Mr. Durham, leaning back in his chair and studying his pocket watch. "I hope that's all right."

"Sure," I said absently.

"A boy your age ought to start looking toward settling down," Mr. Durham was saying, rising from his chair and wiping cookie crumbs from his lap. He must have been in a good mood because of his birthday, because he had never talked to me about anything personal before. "That way they don't have to chase you at work."

I smiled a little, but I didn't respond.

"Well, boys," he said then, pulling on his jacket, one thin, wiry arm and then the other. "I believe I will be going. You can go whenever you'd like...please lock up, if you're last to go."

"Sure," said James. "Happy birthday, sir."

"Happy birthday," I said as well.

"Thank you, and I'll see you tomorrow," he said, making his way out the door. I wondered briefly what he would do for the rest of the day. Neither of us had even asked him.

I sat there at my desk, deep in thought, trying to replay the scene they had described. Then I had an idea. I got up and went to the policy files.

"You gonna stick around?" asked James. He was still at his desk, watching me carry a stack of files over to mine.

"Just for a little," I said. "Why don't you go?"

"I'm on my way in just a second here," he said, turning back to his desk. "It's either get it done now or have it tomorrow morning. I'm gonna do some fishing this afternoon, myself, and I need to be totally relaxed to be at my best. No thoughts at all about this place, right?"

But I wasn't really listening anymore. There was something tugging at the back of my mind. It was something Mr. Durham had told me a long time ago.

There were insurance documents for my own family here, of course. Just about the whole town had files, since there weren't many companies with field offices in Greenwood. I had never really looked over our own policies, though, as I couldn't imagine there would be anything of interest there.

I found the home insurance policy that my Aunt's late husband had taken out on the home I was now living in, as well as a few other papers of my Aunt's describing pieces of jewelry and items that he had given her. I was sure I had seen the flashy jewelry on her all my life, and yet the descriptions brought no images to mind. It just wasn't the sort of thing I would have paid attention to. Some of it was certainly expensive, though.

I came upon the life policy that I was looking for. It was in the name of Henry John Whittier, and it bore the stamp of the Indian Creek Textiles Company. It was a certificate of life insurance. In the event of Henry's death, it was payable to Mrs. Jean Whittier. The company had offered these policies on all the workers years ago, when Henry had just started, because of the hazardous working conditions in the factory. My Mother had never said anything about it, but as far as I could tell the policy had been kept active. It was a basic accidental death policy, and it had no exclusion for war. I looked at the amount of money again.

The claim form was behind the certificate. I had seen countless forms like this one since I started to work for Mr. Durham. And yet, I couldn't help being affected by it. There was his name, home address, and date of birth. The claim was filed by Mrs. Jean Whittier. The information on the bottom half of the page had been filled in by Mr. Durham. I knew his tight, orderly handwriting anywhere. He had written in the cause of death as *casualty of war*. The date of death was listed only as *October, 1918*. In the section for notes, he had written *Mr. Whittier perished on a battlefield in France. Official notice reached his next of kin on November 15, 1918. See attached.*

Attached was a telegram from the United States Army. *We regret to inform you...*I put it away. It was just like my Mother not to want the official notice in the house. She had turned it in to Mr. Durham for his file. Here was an amount of money with the value of Henry's life attached to it.

"So what do you think?" James was saying.

He was looking at me expectantly, munching on a cookie.

"What?" I asked, putting the forms back in the file slowly.

"You think Landis should have banned 'em all? The White Sox boys?" He held up the front of a newspaper.

"I don't know," I said, still distracted.

"The judge said they weren't guilty, though, right?" He took a bite.

"Yes," I said. I could talk about baseball in my sleep, no matter how distracted I was.

"Then I don't get it," he said.

"Some of the testimony just disappeared," I said. "Grand jury stuff. Remember that. Landis is new...he's still new to being commissioner. You would've made the same decision...you have to, for the game."

"I don't know," he said, shaking his head. "I thought he was supposed to let the judge decide. And the judge ruled, but now Landis says they can never play ball again. I don't know."

"Well it's a good thing you're not commissioner," I said.

He laughed and folded the paper. He stood up then, walking around his desk.

"So tell me something else," he was smiling broadly now, as if in on a secret with me. "Who was the dame? Really. You can tell me."

"I really don't know," I stood and walked away from the files, not wanting him to see what I had been looking at.

"Too bad," he said, smiling broadly and wiping his forehead again. He headed toward the door. "I just thought if you really were meeting up with her that you might need someone for her friend." He laughed a little, and shrugged. "Remember to lock up, okay?"

"What friend?"

"Well, Durham couldn't see, but I saw the other girl from the window," he motioned with his head toward his desk, which sat below the window that looked out onto the street.

"There was another girl?"

He nodded.

"I couldn't see her that well from up here, but she looked like a gal I'd like to get to know. Had blonde hair, I think. Lighter than the other one, anyway. Hey," he said, his eyes lighting up in the middle of his pudgy face, "maybe they're sisters. Wouldn't that be something for you and me?"

James left, excited about his day of fishing, and I paced around the office a little. I pulled out Henry's life insurance policy again and looked at it. I held it in my hands, wondering why they would want it. I would have a talk with my Aunt and my Mother, of course. But aside from that I didn't know what I could do just then.

And it was a nice afternoon, anyway. I wanted to take advantage of my half day of freedom. My Mother and my Aunt had no idea that I was being dismissed from work early today, so I was in no real hurry to get home. I made sure to lock the door securely behind me.

As I left the office I couldn't help thinking about the life policies issued by the textile factory. Mr. Durham had mentioned them before, but who besides himself and the policyholders would know about them? I knew that some factories encouraged them and some didn't, depending on the unions. Outside my own family, though, the only people who would know about Henry's policy would be the other guys who had worked at his factory. Unless, or course, my Mother or my Aunt had talked to someone about it. But I couldn't really imagine them doing that, since they hadn't even said anything to me about it.

I knew just the thing to get my mind off of all this. It being a Thursday afternoon, I went straight to the Garrison's flat, as was my routine that summer. Kate seemed as distracted as I was that day, though. She hadn't even been bothering to put together lunch lately. But today I had eaten cookies all morning and then the bun and the apple I bought when I was out getting supplies, so I wasn't hungry anyway.

We exchanged our normal greetings, and performed our normal tasks. I saw her so often now that there wasn't much to say. I was still enjoying it quite a bit, though, and I found that it really helped to relax me toward the end of the week.

Having finished in the bedroom, we walked toward the front door, and I told her about how I didn't have to go back to work that afternoon. She had a glass of lemonade in her hand, and she was wearing a nice summer dress that she had put on afterwards. She told me about how she had to go over and visit her sister and her family, and she wasn't looking forward to it because she didn't get along with them very well.

As we said goodbye by the door, I thought about the time she had reached up and wiped the lipstick from my face. Right then, something made me bend down and kiss her lips softly. It wasn't a good idea, of course. I could tell it had taken her by surprise, but she didn't do anything. She didn't really kiss me back, but she didn't pull away, either. As I pulled my face away from hers, she just smiled a little bit, as if I was a small child and she was tolerating my misbehavior.

As I walked home under the flat summer sky, the events of the day swirled around inside my head. I thought about the invasion of my office and the life insurance policy and the kiss and it all stirred together and baked under the hot sun.

The Pilford sisters were coming out of the front door of my house just as I was making my way across the grass, deep in thought. I wondered if there had been another attempt to contact Henry in the dining room or if they had just come by to ask for more money.

They hadn't seen me yet, so I quickly moved around to the side of the house and hid behind the bushes. I stood there, waiting, listening to my own breathing.

I brushed against the bushes. I had just cut them with the oversized shears a few evenings ago. I noticed an uneven spot, a branch of green longer than the rest. I had missed it the other night.

The sisters were moving across the lawn and into the street now, and I decided to follow them. No one would miss me at home, since they thought I was still at work.

They walked up the street, sharing the same erect posture and brisk pace. I crept along, staying back a little bit and keeping to the trees beside the road.

I watched the backs of their heads, one slightly taller than the other, noting how similar they were. The hair on both was in the same short, bobbed style, but the color of one was a true brown, while the other was a little lighter than sand. From the confident way they walked, one might think they were on their way home from visiting some poor charity case rather than stealing money from old women. I was flushed, but I couldn't tell how much of it was anger and how much was the heat.

I couldn't tell if they were talking quietly or just walking side by side in silence. Their heads never turned toward each other. Eleanor produced a dainty umbrella, trimmed with lace of some kind. She held it above them, shading them both from the sun.

I moved slowly through the wooded area, never more than a few yards back from the road. They never turned around though. As long as I was quiet, I told myself, they would have no reason to turn around.

I had fantasized about both of them, as any man probably would have. They were around my age, after all, and were more attractive than most women I saw. For some reason, this fact made me like them even less now. I blamed them not only for coming into my home and my work, but into my dreams as well. They knew me personally, and they knew my family. I had even cried in front of them. And even though they weren't from around here they had found out where I worked and come there. What had they been looking for? It must have been Henry's policy. But why? There wasn't a whole lot of information there.

The woods were beginning to give way to the buildings on the outskirts of Greenwood. We were approaching my old school, which was across the street now. The low, squat building of dark brick was very old, and I remember my Aunt telling me that it had been here when she first came to Greenwood. Her first visit here was for a summer at her husband's vacation home, the house we now lived in. I wondered what she must have been like then.

I watched the Pilfords walk around to the back of the building. I saw a few people walking down at the end of the street, but otherwise all was quiet. The town was suspended under the blanket of heat and sun, stirred only by the occasional breeze.

What could they possibly be doing behind the school building? There was nowhere to go back there, unless they were going to cross the back yard and creep through town in the grassy spaces between the buildings. I thought about what Mr. Durham and James were each doing right now, with their afternoon off. Neither of them would believe that I was following two girls around town.

I moved slowly along the side of the school, feeling the rough brick with my fingers as I went. It reminded me of the times I'd played cowboys and Indians in this very spot when I'd been here as a kid. As soon as the teacher let us go outside to play, I would creep around the building just like this, an Indian assassin, hoping to surprise my friends in their cowboy camp.

We used to have to finish our afternoon prayers before we went out to play. I can remember days when I wanted to get outside so badly that I told them I was done praying even when I wasn't. I always felt guilty about that, and I wondered if I was short-changing anyone that I should be praying for.

I rounded the corner and the first thing that caught my eye was the automobile. It was a black Columbia Six sports car with white wall tires, staring at me with two large, round headlights. The engine was running, the top of the car was down, and a man was inside. He saw me first. Beth was facing away from me, and was already up on the running board. Eleanor was behind her.

He had very light yellow hair that was almost white, and I saw that a few strands had blown down in front of his eyes. He pushed them back and looked at me from his driver's seat, squinting in the sun. His skin was tanned, and he wore a white shirt. A lit cigarette was in his hand, hanging over the side of the car. He took a puff. I thought about jumping back behind the corner before the Pilfords turned around, but it was too late now. He had definitely seen me and was trying to figure out who I was. He probably wasn't much older than I was. I wondered, for a fleeting second, how he could afford such a nice car.

I don't think he said anything to them, but Beth and Eleanor saw him staring and turned, following his gaze. Beth stepped down from the running board and onto the ground and they both turned toward me. Eleanor leaned over and whispered something to them.

I stepped forward now. Something about the way the man was looking at me made me feel embarrassed for having followed them at all.

"Mister Whittier? Is that you?" Eleanor sounded as if she was the hostess of a party and a surprise guest had arrived. I smiled and nodded, but then I thought better of it and quickly banished the smile from my face. Beth just stood there looking, as if she really wasn't all that interested in what was going on. I turned toward the man in the car, and gave him a little nod of my head. He didn't move at all, though. He was just watching, like Beth.

"I followed you," I said, speaking up over the growl of the car. It wasn't what I had wanted to say at all.

"I see," Eleanor said. I was only standing a few yards in front of them in the shadow of the school. The car was parked on a little dirt drive that cut through the grass behind the building.

"Is there something we can do for you?" she asked. I just stood there. "We'll be back at your house next week, Cobb," she continued without waiting for my response. "I know it's difficult sometimes...but you should really talk to your Aunt and your Mother rather than us. Normally we don't like to see family members outside of..."

"Okay, just...just stop," I said. Her eyes widened a little. She was surprised at how strong my voice had come out. I was, too. I stepped toward her, leaving the shadow of the building completely. The man in the car flicked some ashes from his cigarette onto the ground.

"You're not...you're not helping my family," I said, almost shouting now. "That's not what you're doing. You're just taking money from people. They don't want to see you anymore."

She wore an expression of patient disappointment. It reminded me of the way my teacher had looked at me at this very school only a few years ago.

"Now, I don't think your Aunt or your Mother told you that," she scolded. "We'll keep helping them as long as they want to be helped."

"No."

"Listen," she said, a new sharpness in her voice now. "People react differently to our work. If anger is something you feel, then that's fine. But blaming us won't..."

"You know about the life insurance policy, don't you?"

Her mouth closed slowly, but her eyes betrayed her. Before her reaction, I hadn't been absolutely sure that it had been them at the office. But now I knew.

"That's the money you want...that's the money you're cheating out of my family. The money from that policy." It didn't even sound like my voice. "Have you been coming to my work?" I asked, squinting in the sun. I stood there in the unkempt, brownish grass. No one took care of it this time of year.

"Your work?"

"Yes, you've been coming to my job…where I work, trying to get that policy…I don't know, trying to see how much it's for maybe, so you can keep raising your price or something. You've both been seen there…they identified you." It wasn't entirely true. But they didn't need to know that.

Beth turned and climbed into the car as if I wasn't there. I felt the sudden urge to strangle her, or throw something at her, just to get her to react to me.

"What we do," Eleanor was saying, "is something that you don't fully understand. We have a power that you do not. So we help people."

"Who told you about that policy? How did you know…those things about my brother?" I was letting my anger show now. The way that Beth had turned away infuriated me.

Now Eleanor turned and stepped up onto the running board of the car as well.

"Hey…I'm not finished…"

"I think you are," the man said, taking a drag on his cigarette. He had a strong accent. It was English or French maybe.

Eleanor was in the car now. My heart was pounding. I don't know what I even wanted from them, really.

"You poor thing," Eleanor said. "You know you felt things in that room, Cobb. You did. Don't deny those things. Don't turn your back on Henry when he's trying to get through to you."

"He wouldn't choose you," I said. "I don't believe it. He wouldn't choose someone who's just in it for the money."

Eleanor sighed and shook her head. She looked at the man beside her.

"Let's go," she mouthed quietly. And then back to me, "We'll see you next time." Beth smiled at me then. It was a little, unnatural smile. The car lurched past.

I wanted to shout something at them as they pulled away. I wanted to say something like "if you ever come to my home again…"

but I didn't know how to end the sentence. I wasn't sure how to threaten them, because I'd never met anyone like them. Who was the man? Their brother? Husband? I had no idea.

So they drove away on the dirt road, back around the building and onto the street. I was left standing there in a cloud of dust.

I walked back home. At least I'd let them know that I was onto them, and that I knew they'd been coming to my office. The things they'd talked about in our dining room both times were things no one could possibly know. Maybe they'd gotten the information out of my Aunt somehow by getting her drunk or using hypnosis or something. She wouldn't be that gullible, though.

I *had* felt things when they were in our dining room, just as Eleanor said. I decided that it didn't matter, though. It had to have been them at the office, and that gave it away. No matter what they were doing, their motives weren't pure.

I thought about the man in the car and the way Beth smiled. The only thing I knew for sure was that I didn't want them around my family any more. But how could I tell my Aunt and my Mother about this? Would they even believe me? As far as I could tell, they thought that the Pilfords could do no wrong.

CHAPTER 25

Ambrose was thinking about buying a car, so we went to see Mr. Womack one Saturday when we heard that he was selling one. Mr. Womack wanted to sell his car to someone besides his son. He explained to us that his son didn't deserve to ever inherit the car because of the rotten way he treated his family. Ambrose had been enthusiastic all morning, but once we got there and started talking to Mr. Womack it became clear that he hadn't really intended to buy anything today.

In fact, as we left the old man behind Ambrose told me that now he had decided to get a new car back home. He wanted a Model A Duesenberg, which was a new American car with all sorts of things that sounded good, like an overhead camshaft and hydraulic brakes, and a straight-eight engine. They were new this year.

Looking at the car hadn't taken as long as I thought, so Ambrose and I went and saw a movie called *The Three Musketeers*. I walked out wishing that our country could have a war with swords rather than guns. It would be much better to watch. Even Ambrose agreed.

When I finally arrived at her house, Mrs. Delgrew had acted disappointed that I hadn't been able to come earlier. But she soon got over it when I started working. Now she was in the little yard with me, silent as usual. We took comfort in each other's presence, I think.

The Delgrews had a yard that seemed to sprout new weeds as soon as I tore the old ones out of the ground. I pulled and pulled, wiping my brow in the evening heat, placing the weeds in a pile on the ground beside me. Locusts were making the buzzing sound that I always associated with summer. The sun was almost below the horizon, and a slanted evening light came through the fence, casting long shadows across everything.

The weeds held on, grabbing handfuls of dirt with their twisted tendrils. I imagined them slowly balling their roots into little fists, fixed and ready to resist my pulling. I wondered what it would be like to be a plant. I remember how shocked and amazed I was the first time I learned that plants were alive, just like us. They moved and worked, just as we did, but they did it all so slowly. And now here I was, pulling and tugging at them, trying to loosen them from the positions they had worked themselves into.

Mrs. Delgrew moved to the other side of the yard silently. She was in the process of displacing some flowers from the front of the house to the back, and she had carried a number of bulbs and clippings in a fold in her apron. She wore gloves and the same cream-colored apron she wore when she cooked. It had small brown flowers stitched in the corners.

She knelt down with her digging tool. In the fading light of the day, it looked as if she was digging a series of small graves, one for each flower. I realized that I'd seen her planting flowers in this same spot many times before, but I had never seen any of them come to fruition. Her yard just wouldn't support them, somehow. I admired the patient way that she went back to that same place and tried once again to make life grow and thrive. But it never did. Could a plot of earth be completely dead?

The shadows stretched into each other and formed a web of darkness, and the sun disappeared from sight completely. I finished up the weeding and threw the casualties away.

"Thank you, Colbert," Mrs. Delgrew said, passing me on her way inside. She pulled her gloves off and smiled at me, rubbing her back. I couldn't imagine my own Mother doing as much physical work as Mrs. Delgrew did.

"You're welcome, Ma'am," I returned.

"I believe Gertrude wants to see you before you leave," she said then. "I'll tell her you'll be out front."

I walked around the house and sat on the steps in front of the little porch. I looked around the street. People who had been outside on their lawns and porches were starting to go in now, as the sky grew darker.

The front door squeaked open, and I heard the sound of Gertrude's footsteps behind me.

"Mama wished you could have come earlier."

"So do I," I said. "I was looking at a car with my cousin. I think I got everything done that she wanted, though." I was still looking out into the street. She was standing behind me.

"You're going to buy a car?"

"No…he was thinking about getting one here. He has one back home."

"He's rich, isn't he?"

"I guess so. He has a telephone in his house in Boston, too." Not many people had phones in their houses.

"They say they're going to have telephone service from coast to coast before the end of this year," she said.

"There won't be that many people who have them anyway," I said. "I can see having one at work or in an office or something. But what do people have to talk about at home in such a hurry? They could just send a telegram."

"Do you think you'll ever be rich?" she asked then.

"Probably not."

We were both quiet for a while then, listening to the insect buzzing swell as if it was inside my ears.

"There's a little rally going on Friday night," she said. "You should take him there, if you want to show him something interesting." I knew that she wanted me to ask her about this, so I didn't. I was growing tired of her company by then. Nothing ever seemed to change between us. It was as if every time we talked, we had to start over. "It's something going on right under everyone's noses here in this little town," she kept talking when she realized that I wasn't going to ask. "But I'll bet no one knows about it. It's not the sort of thing that small town Americans pay attention to."

I stood up then, with a bit of a sigh, and turned toward her. My leg muscles ached from squatting in the yard for so long.

"You don't like this town?" I asked.

"I don't know."

"You want to go off to college somewhere, right?" I said.

"Do you think I'm smart enough?"

"I think you're probably smarter than most of the kids in college now," I answered.

"Well," she said, stepping forward then, "I just wanted to lend you a book...if you want it." She came toward me, Willie's face on a girl's body. Her hair was still curled tightly, and her mouth was closed beneath her small, rounded nose. I thought about her mother's large nose, and how different they were. And yet, in some ways, I could imagine her growing up to be a lot like her mother.

"Sure," I said, "what is it?" I was always flattered when she gave me a book.

"I don't know if you'll like it," she said. "It's not really a novel. But it's very interesting."

She handed it to me and I saw that it was a slim green volume. *From Ritual to Romance*, it said in gold, important-looking letters. *Jessie Weston*. Another woman.

"It will really make you think...about a lot of cultures and stories," she was saying. "I don't know if you'll like it, though. I don't really know anyone else who's read it."

"Thanks," I said, turning it over in my hands. A dog barked in the distance. "I'll read it," I said.

She nodded.

"Well, I guess I'll see you later," I said.

She turned and headed inside.

"And thank you for the book."

She closed the door.

CHAPTER 26

❀

Early Sunday morning the sun began its climb across the sky overhead, and our family prepared for church.

I wasn't sure if Ambrose was going to make it. He'd been out late the night before with some friends from the bank. I watched him sway back and forth as he tried to straighten the medium-wing collar on his shirt. The skin around his eyes looked slack and yellow. His face was sweaty and clammy, and as I helped him with his shirt I noticed that the smell of liquor lingered in his sweat.

"Have a good time last night?" I asked him.

"A little too good," he replied. I finished with the collar. "Thanks." He moved to the mirror, pulling on a double-breasted jacket that went well with his striped trousers. "Oh boy," he said, looking at himself. He began to slick down his hair, sighing heavily. "That's the last time I bring a hip flask to one of Mr. Drake's parties." He was smiling though. His regret wasn't so great that he wouldn't do the same thing next weekend, I knew. Mr. Drake was the owner of the bank, and he had a home a few miles up the river. His parties were legendary, but I had never had any reason to be invited to any of them.

"You haven't been sick or anything yet this morning, have you?" I asked as I straightened my own tie.

"I never get sick," he replied, sitting on the bed and pulling on his spats. "That's one thing I'll guarantee you...Ambrose Bentham never gets sick."

"Really?"

"I guarantee it. Not from drinking. I'll even bet you. If you want to, I'll bet you money I won't be sick today even once. Come on."

"I'll take your word for it."

"You don't want to bet? You sure?"

"I'm sure."

"Suit yourself. I feel just fine."

But he sure didn't look fine as we entered the church. I could swear he looked even worse than he had when we left the house.

My Aunt was beaming, as she did every Sunday. Attending the service was the highlight of her week. She turned this way and that, greeting everyone as they filed into the building around us. My Mother smiled and said her hellos as well.

Mr. and Mrs. Arthur stood in the doorway, and I watched them grow very animated as they greeted my Aunt. She, in turn, seemed to get even more excited herself. It was an ever-escalating contest to see who could be happiest.

"Edna, Edna," Mrs. Arthur cooed. "How are you? And how about this weather?"

"Delightful," my Aunt returned. "The heat doesn't bother me a bit as long as the air is dry, and it has been dry, hasn't it? Of course, with these two men around the house, there's not much for Jean and I to do outdoors," she winked at Mrs. Arthur. I winced inwardly at the reference to us, because it led to more attention from Mrs. Arthur.

"Boys, it is so nice to see you as always. I have no doubt that you have the house running in ship shape."

We nodded and smiled.

"And Jean," she continued, "you look more and more lovely, it seems, no matter what kind of weather. I was just telling someone the other day about how good you've been looking lately...making the rest of us look bad. The heat doesn't bother you a bit, does it?"

We were holding up a line of people that were trying to enter, and the line was moving impatiently now, like a snake twisting in the sun. I wondered if everyone there came to church because someone else made them. I suppose I came because I knew that it made my Mother happy, and she needed that.

Mr. Arthur was a tall, thin man with two or three wads of dark hair remaining on his scalp, spread out in different areas. The sweat on his head had caused these strands to lie in a strange formation, each one somehow perpendicular to the other. I had always thought that his eyes were too close together, too. He smiled and nodded, pressing each of our hands as we got past his wife. As anyone might expect, he was a quiet man. He would have to be to live with Mrs. Arthur. I could remember when the long flowing white robes he wore seemed gigantic to me. Every Sunday for almost as long as I could remember he would shake hands with me right here, and yet the two of us had barely ever exchanged a word.

As a young child, I had spent most of my time in church listening to his voice and waiting patiently for the service to come to an end so that I could go outside. There had been summer days like this one when Henry and I had been almost unable to control ourselves. I can remember Henry seated in the pew with his legs swinging above the ground. Both of us would stare longingly out the little stained glass window on the opposite wall at the summer day that awaited us.

Today my Aunt led us right toward the third pew from the end on the right hand side, as always. One time Mr. Arthur told my Aunt that he could always tell where a new family in church was going to sit based on what they looked like. The most sheepish always sat in the back, he said, along with those who knew that their commitment to the church activities left something to be desired. They would sit in the back so that they could be the last ones in and the first ones out. After that, my Aunt had tried to make us sit closer to the front.

She was convinced that Mr. Arthur had been trying to bring into question our own family's commitment by telling her this.

I turned to Ambrose. He seemed to be in motion even as he sat, his head swimming in whatever it was he'd downed the night before. He shot me a glance and wiped the sweat from his brow. I wondered if my Aunt or my Mother would notice his condition. His wild Saturday night of drinking was overflowing into their carefully planned, well-dressed Sunday morning. The two worlds were mingling for him now. I felt sorry for him, and also glad that I hadn't done any drinking last night.

"Our nation is still waking up from the Great War," Mr. Arthur was saying. His voice was low and strong, but it had a nasal quality that I had always found distracting. He rubbed his palm across his forehead and continued. "And the fate of our nation has been decided by God. We have triumphed, but it has changed us forever. And that is God's doing and God's will. So all of us, here in Greenwood and all over our nation must now decide what it is we will take with us, from this war. Now that we have the hindsight of a few years. What has Jesus Christ told us through the war? What was his message for us?

"There was much talk during the war about the opportunity of the Church. Some of you may have heard this phrase…the 'Church's opportunity.' The role of the Christian Church during war is a difficult one. It is to bring peace to those who are engaged in fighting. To those who have loved ones that are sacrificing themselves for a cause. To bring peace and the teachings of Jesus Christ into the battlefields and all of the miserable places that people go during war.

"We live in an age where the Church has much difficulty. There are large numbers of our flock who are in error, and who are wandering far from the safety of the fold. The war was an opportunity, then, for the Christian Church to bring those back into the fold. So now we stand here and ask the question: did we take advantage of our opportunity? Did we do all in our power, to turn a time of war into a time of triumph for Christ and his followers?"

He stopped, looking around at all of us. My Aunt and my Mother sat at attention, fanning themselves with the folding flowered fans that they pulled from their purses each Sunday. Poor Ambrose was starting to fidget. He gulped and looked around.

"Many fighting men have told me they felt that Christ was 'on their side' during the war," he continued. "Some of them may not have even been baptized in the Church. And yet, with death all around them, they knew…they felt, the presence of Christ walking beside them. He was, indeed, on their side. And he carried them through it. He carried us. Some of us lost our loved ones, and that was the will of God. But Jesus Christ never left our side…whether in the war or here, at home.

"In a few weeks, the United States and Germany will sign a peace treaty…the first treaty officially recognizing the end of the war." I knew that this was true, but it seemed so strange to me. The war itself was something that happened a lifetime ago. But the U.S. had never agreed to the Versailles treaty, so there had never been a piece of paper that said it was over. I wondered if having one would make any real difference.

I turned and caught Ambrose's eye. He was starting to look desperate.

"So now that our nation has triumphed, what can we bring back to our own lives from what our brave young men have done? I believe the true opportunity for the Church is now. We are living in an age of amazing feats. The 'Noble Experiment' that is the Eighteenth Amendment to our Constitution is a cause that must be upheld by the Church. Some members of our Church are even trying to push for federal laws on the subject of marriage and divorce. Our country is deciding where it stands on these issues of morality. The youth of our nation do not know how lucky they are to be growing up in this wonderful time. It is up to us to bring more young people back into the fold, though. They felt and experienced the marvels of Jesus Christ Almighty all around them during the dark hours of war. And now they are ready…ready to learn and be taught by their parents about how to live a good Christian life."

I was thinking about the battlefield where Henry was killed now. I wondered if he saw the Angel of Mons. I imagined it as Beth Pilford had described it, the air full of angels and spirits. I wondered what Mr. Arthur would think about that.

"If you will be so kind as to bear with me, I have a quote," he said, looking down at a paper in front of him. "This comes all the way back from the year eighteen-thirty, and it was coined by a man named Alexis de Tocqueville…I probably didn't pronounce that correctly, but he was a Frenchman. So, I'll put it in my own words. But Mister Tocqueville said this about our nation of America…he said that American life is characterized by three things: continual movement, lack of tradition, and rootlessness. Now these may be harsh words spoken by a European, but let's think about them. Perhaps he's right. I see a lot of this nowadays, in America. My own parents were born, lived and died right here in Greenwood. The same town, for all of their lives. They never even thought about leaving. But children today are different. They have trains, and automobiles, and even airplanes to take them across the world. And many say that they are, indeed, lacking in tradition. Young men and women are wearing things and behaving in ways that defy the imaginations of many present in this room."

I could hear the silent agreement of the congregation. I turned and saw that the color had left Ambrose's face. His lips were almost the same color as his skin. He looked over at me, his eyes wide.

"So now is the time for us to bring these people back to our own flock. Movement, lack of tradition, rootlessness," Mr. Arthur raised a long finger for each of these items as he counted them off. "Sounds like life during the war. And life in America? Perhaps. But Jesus Christ created a religion that works…that flourishes, in fact, in just these times. And he has left his charge to you and me, to show this religion to those who need it. To those who have only a dim recollection of our traditions and roots. Tradition, it seems, is just what these young people are calling out for. They need it…they require it to save their lives and their souls. And they are ready for it, because they understand that Jesus Christ will always be on their side. In war and in peace. Amen."

Ambrose stood and ran for the back door. He shut it quietly behind him, but the rows around us couldn't help but notice. My Mother and my Aunt looked at me for an explanation. I just shrugged, and wished that I had taken him up on his bet.

CHAPTER 27

When we got home, I decided that it was as good a time as any to discuss the Pilford sisters. My Aunt and my Mother were in the kitchen, wondering aloud about what was the matter with Ambrose, and why he was back in his bed, asleep.

They stopped talking and looked at me as I entered the room.

"Is he all right?" asked my Mother, nodding toward the back of the house.

"Sure," I said, trying to be nonchalant, still standing in the doorway. "He just wasn't feeling well. I think it was just something he ate that didn't agree with him. He needs to sleep a little."

They looked at me suspiciously.

"I saw the Pilford sisters on Thursday," I said, changing the subject. "Were they here?"

"Yes," said my Mother, nodding.

"I think maybe it would be better if you didn't see them for a while," I said. They looked at each other. "I think it may be better for us...for our family."

"Why would you say that, Colbert?" asked my Aunt.

"Just...just trust me," I said. "I was able to speak to them outside of here...away from here."

"About what?" asked my Mother.

"A lot of things, I just…I think that they've done all they can for us, don't you?"

"Well," said my Aunt, "they seem to think we have more to accomplish with the next spirit level. At least that's what they told us on Thursday. What did they tell you?"

"I don't really want to go into it," I said. "They'll want to keep coming over…I'm sure they'll ask you if they can keep coming. I'm just saying…I want you to say no."

My Mother sat down at the table in the corner. She was looking at me, but I could tell she was deep in thought. My Aunt remained standing.

"Well," said my Aunt. "It's always up to you if you want to be here for their sessions, dear. But I don't see why your Mother and I can't continue to see them…"

"I just think that we're doing fine without them," I looked at my Mother as I spoke, but I could read nothing on her face. "I think we're fine now…with Henry. I think they just make things worse a lot…stir things up, when they're fine."

"Don't be selfish," said my Aunt. "What if we're fine but Henry isn't? How can we stop communicating with him now?"

"Maybe Henry's fine too."

"You don't know that."

"Edna," my Mother said. She looked tired. "Maybe he's right," she shook her head slowly, rubbing her temples with her other hand. She wasn't looking at either of us. My Aunt turned to her now, her mouth open in astonishment.

"Just trust me," I said. "There's something going on. I can't really explain it. I'm trying to figure it out. But I don't trust them. I have reason not to trust them right now, and I think you should tell them you don't want to see them for a while. Tell them you're busy…I don't know. If everything's fine, then I'll let you know and you can do whatever you want."

"You know," said my Aunt, "I think this is just what Mister Arthur was talking about today...no sense of tradition. Here you are, telling your own Mother what to do as if you're in charge of her."

"What would my father think?" I asked, looking at my Mother now. I knew that this was dangerous territory as soon as I said it. "What would he think about the Pilfords and what you're doing and all the money..."

"Don't you talk about that," my Aunt said, throwing her hands up and turning to the sink, facing away from me now. "You can't really talk about that. I know my brother and what he would think," she said over her shoulder.

"What if I know *my* brother?" I asked. "What if I know him well enough to say let it go. Let him go. These women have nothing to do with our family. They have nothing to say." I could see that I wasn't getting anywhere with her. I had no choice left.

"I know I'm the man of the house, and I know I'm not bringing in all the income," I said. "I know about the insurance policy. And they do, too. When they raise their prices and tell you they have to come back again and again, that's what they're thinking about." My Mother was looking up at me now, her mouth slightly open. "I know that's what they're thinking because they've come around Mister Durham's office, trying to get a look at the policy. Trying to find out just how much they can take from you."

My Aunt's back was still to me. She struck me suddenly as a frail woman. I normally didn't think of her that way, but she was, really.

"And that's the truth," I said. "I wanted to save you from it, but I had to tell you. That's the truth. And I don't care if we ever talk about them again. But they have no place in our house, and they shouldn't be allowed to come back."

I looked at them both again. They didn't deserve this. It was the loudest I'd raised my voice to them in all my life. All they wanted to do was say goodbye to Henry.

"I'm not telling you, I'm asking you," I said. "Because I love you both, very much." I swallowed, and tears welled in my eyes. "I'm not saying they haven't helped us at all. They've told us a lot of good things. And they told us a lot of things that had to come from Henry...that only Henry knows. It may not have been about the money at first...but they know about it now, and that's what they're after...I know it. And if that's the way they want to be, then we don't need them. I think Henry understands that." I wiped a tear from my face.

"All right," my Mother said quietly. My Aunt reached out to her and placed a hand on her shoulder. "I think they've done enough," she continued. "I was just thinking that there might not be that much more to do." She reached out to me, and I stepped forward and held her hand for a few seconds.

Then I nodded and left quietly. I wished that I hadn't had to speak to them that way. More tears came in the hallway, and my anger at the sisters grew.

CHAPTER 28

During the middle of the week I stopped at the post office to get Mr. Durham's mail and to send off a few forms to the main office in New York. The incoming mail was made up of the usual letters from policyholders and paperwork from New York.

I shuffled through the envelopes quickly, trying to get a grasp on just how much work I would have this afternoon. Then I came across one that was addressed to me. My name was handwritten on the front, and the words *c/o M. Durham* were underneath it. There was no postmark or stamp. Someone had dropped this note directly into our box at the post office. I had never gotten a personal letter of any kind at work.

I stepped into the shade of a large tree just outside the post office, and slid the other pieces of mail under my arm.

Who would address a note to me at work? The sender obviously didn't want to risk having it arrive at my house and be opened by my Aunt. Which meant it was possible that the sender knew my Aunt. Could it be from the Pilfords? Why would they write me a letter? As I ripped the envelope away and pulled the single sheet of paper free, I couldn't have been more surprised by what I read. The handwriting was firm and neat.

~

Mr. Whittier,

Please allow me to buy your lunch for you tomorrow, as I must discuss an urgent topic with you that is of a personal nature. Please meet me at The Brown Cafe on Main at twelve-o-clock sharp. I will be seated outdoors, waiting for your arrival. I trust that this is not too mysterious for you, as I assure you that this manner of invitation is necessary only to protect us both from embarrassment regarding this personal matter.

Yours,

Jonathan Crowe, M.D., Retired

I had absolutely no idea what Dr. Crowe could want to discuss with me. My best guess was that it had something to do with the Delgrews, since their household was really the only thing that we had in common. He hadn't really allowed any way for me to return a response to him, so he must have just assumed that I would be there.

CHAPTER 29

Our squad headed toward training camp, passing a six-armed French signboard that pointed the way to six towns I'd never heard of. It was flat, boring country, with an occasional farm or orchard. We passed a group of tethered observational balloons, hanging overhead like giant bloated sausages in the sky. It was easy to gauge how far we'd walked by keeping them in sight. Miles and miles of telegraph poles stood along the roads, as well. They were our constant companions whenever we stuck to roadways. I imagined the orders coming from General Headquarters to all of the camps along those hanging lines. It was difficult to grasp how it worked.

We did a lot of hiking across the countryside, and a lot of camping outside under the stars at night. I can remember one evening as we lay awake in a barn loft, smoking cigarettes quietly, listening to the silence. The dry, sweet smell of hay was all around us. There was hay in my hair, my clothes, even my boots. Every once in a while, I'd raise my head and look around, and see bright orange pinpricks all around me, waving about as the guys talked, and then dancing to the floor with the flick of a butt.

Each of us carried a rope of dried onions, a can of alphabet noodles with a few stale and broken macaroons, string beans, and sometimes a little pot of strained honey. We were just finishing up a typical dinner. We discussed weapons as the inky blackness of night grew darker and darker around us.

"What do ya think it'd be like, to get hit by the gas?" Lovejoy's voice asked the darkness. We carried the fear of the gas with us always, represented by the bulky masks that we couldn't leave behind.

"It's just like you're chokin'…that's what they say," O'Malley answered. "And gettin' tired at the same time."

"I think you'd rather get shot. I know I would," Bridges said.

"You know what I think'd be worse than gettin' gassed?" asked Jarret. Everyone smoked silently. "There's this bomb that the French have that'd be even worse," he said. I watched his orange point of light jumping up and down as he spoke. I had to go to the bathroom. "It's a bomb filled with these darts…metal darts. They were telling me about 'em back in town. They're about the size of a pen. That length and that thick. So the bomb explodes at about a thousand feet. And these darts are scattered all over the place, and then they come down."

"Ouch," said Lovejoy's voice quietly.

"A couple guys were telling me they saw a squad get hit by one a' these," Jarret continued, "and these darts went all the way through a couple guys and into the ground."

"What do you mean, all the way through?" Lovejoy asked. I got up and moved toward the ladder to go relieve myself.

"I mean through 'em…from the top of their head down into the ground." Jarret answered. "I def'nitely think that'd be worse than any gas."

"So what would be the best way to go?" asked Bridges. They all began arguing about whether they'd want to be shot or blown up or gassed. I missed the consensus, since I was outside by that time.

The smell of the cold air was alive all around me, forcing its way up my nostrils and separating the little hairs inside. We were in a foreign land, and I had grown used to the smells there, including the different way that the air smelled in winter.

The stars seemed clearer than usual, through the dome of cold that was above and around us. The sky was full of them, sprinkled like salt across the blackness. My life seemed so tiny and far away that it was no more significant than one of those stars.

I thought about the points of orange light in the barn and the way that each one of them represented a guy I knew. I looked up at the stars and wondered if every one of them could represent a kid who was over here fighting.

CHAPTER 30

The Brown Cafe was a restaurant on Main Street in an area of Greenwood that normally catered to the wealthier citizens. I had eaten there once before, actually. It was shortly after the war, when my Aunt decided that we should have a nice evening out to celebrate my safe return. We had enjoyed the food, all the while pretending that we felt truly fortunate to have one of the two family members that went to war come home.

During most of the year, The Brown Cafe had seven or eight tables outside, under a large green awning in front of the restaurant. As I approached it, I noticed that Dr. Crowe was seated at one of these tables, as he promised. There was a large Durant parked on the street nearby, and I imagined its owner was spending a great deal of money in the stores that surrounded the restaurant. These included Klein's Jewelry, Main Street Furs, and a bunch of other places I'd never set foot in.

Dr. Crowe didn't see me at first. He was perusing the menu through a pair of small glasses that sat on the end of his nose. His thin hair was so white it almost looked incandescent. He wore a dark brown three-piece suit with a black bow tie. I wondered how he could stand it in the heat. I approached slowly, moving into his line of vision above the menu.

His eyebrows raised a bit, and he cocked his head back to look at me through the glasses.

"Mister Whittier," he said. I had forgotten how loud his voice was. I was sure that the rest of the lunchtime crowd on the terrace had all turned to look at me now.

"Hello," I said.

"Please," he stood slowly, shaking my hand. His grip was tight, and I felt the dry, creased skin of his palm. I smiled and nodded. "Sit," he said, and I did. A single pink flower drooped in a glass vase in the center of the table.

"How is the insurance business?" he asked.

"It's fine," I said. I picked up the folded cloth napkin that sat on the table before me. It was a dark green color, the same shade as the awning.

"Durham doing all right?" he asked, with a slight cough.

"Yes," I said, "yes, he's doing well. In fact, he took on another young man a short while ago."

"Really?"

"Yes."

He put the menu down, and nodded toward mine. I picked it up and looked through it.

"Well," I said, "thank you for the invitation to lunch. I don't get to eat here often."

"Yes," he said, reseating his glasses on his nose. "I used to eat my lunch here everyday, did you know that? My practice was very near here."

I studied his face, trying to determine what he may have looked like as a young man. The eyebrows would have been strong and dark rather than unruly and white. And he would have had more hair, of course. He just seemed like the sort of man who had always been old, though. I couldn't help but think about what my Aunt had said about him. I wondered what he would say if I asked him about my Aunt.

He began to talk a little about the days when he had first come to Greenwood from Chicago, where he had gotten his degree in medicine. We ordered our food. He talked about the Greenwood fire of years ago, and the growth of the town, and when each church was built, and what this very area where we were sitting used to look like when it was the Baker farm. Our food arrived. He talked about the little known fact that Dr. Morris had been strictly an animal doctor before he came to Greenwood. He talked about the changes in medicine, and the doctors who were practicing now and how they were letting them out of school much too soon, and how they didn't really know how to care for families any more. They may know how to cure diseases, he said, but they're not being taught how to care for people.

"I'm sure you know that I am currently retired," he said. I nodded, working on my small piece of steak. I moved the sprig of parsley to the corner of the plate. "But you may not know, Colbert, that I do still see a few families in town. Just a few of the old families. It's difficult to let go, really. When you've really cared for these people for years…when you've seen the babies that you cared for grow up and have babies of their own. You feel as if you have a real investment in the well being of these families. I don't know if people your age understand that."

I nodded, to show that I did indeed understand, but I don't think he was paying any attention to me now. He took each small bite gingerly, as if he was worried about upsetting the delicate balance of his insides with food. I thought about what it would be like to be retired. What would you do all day? I suppose you'd have time to eat as slowly as you wanted to. His watch chain hung from his vest pocket, swinging back and forth as he spoke. I hoped he realized that I didn't have as much time for lunch as he did.

"When I first retired," he continued after a sip of tea, "I thought I could walk away from the old families. But I couldn't. I thought about them too much. The Garrisons and the Sherwoods…those are two of the old families." I realized then that when he said "old families" he meant rich families. "Now that was a nice match…a good marriage between two good families. Good Christians. I cared for both of those children from birth, did you know that? James and Katharine."

"No, I didn't," I said. I felt a low, dull sort of panic begin to take shape in the back of my mind. His voice was stern, but it always sounded stern to me. He sat there in silence now, fixing me in his gaze and breathing steadily. The nasal whistling sound of his breathing seemed to me to be the loudest sound on the entire street. He removed his glasses and laid them on the table. He rubbed the bridge of his nose in a circular motion, and then looked downward, deep in thought. I looked at his wide hand, fingers spread across his forehead, and I noticed the two large rings he wore. They were both the same dull gold color, but one had a green gem in it. The surface of the other one was silvery, and I thought I saw lettering of some kind, maybe his initials.

He raised his head then, looking at me expectantly now. One heavy eyebrow was raised, and in a way I felt that this was the first time that he was truly acknowledging my presence. Was he waiting for me to say something?

"You know James and Katharine?" he asked at last.

"Yes," I said, smiling a little.

"Mmm," he nodded slowly, and looked around at the people seated at the other tables. "Well." He said it dismissively, as if it were the end of a sentence. But then he continued. "Even though I am retired, I do still see both of them. I take care of young Katharine as if she were my own daughter…I always have." I nodded. "And James as well. I saw him several times when he returned from the war. I even recommended a few colleagues in New York…I thought they may be able to help him. They could not, of course. I knew even then that there wasn't much chance. It's a shame to see a promising young man limited by his injuries. I believe you may know what I'm talking about."

"I think so," I said quietly. Why was he talking to me about this?

"It's families like theirs that made this town. The mill's been under the Garrison name for many years. It's a shame when an atrocity puts an end to a young couple's prospects for bearing children and continuing their own good family name."

I knew where this was going. But I couldn't figure out his involvement. How did he know? What did it have to do with him, anyway? Had Kate discussed our arrangement with her doctor? I had been convinced that as long as I kept quiet, no one would ever find out about it. But this was a danger I had never imagined. Would she talk to someone? The thought had never even entered my mind.

"I think you may know already what I'm getting at, Mister Whittier," he said, clearing his throat dramatically. I couldn't help but hear the contemptuous way he pronounced my name.

And then his voice dropped to a normal volume. It was the softest I'd ever heard him speak. He leaned in a little.

"I know Katharine well. I am her doctor, after all. And I know about...well, things that are going on. Things that gentlemen do not discuss over lunch. As her doctor, it doesn't feel entirely right for me to bring these things up at all. But sometimes, when one examines a patient, one finds things that the patient and others do not want to hear. And yet, when these things are for your own good...for the good of the patient...well. I know that, unfortunately, young Garrison's injuries have left him unable to perform certain duties of a husband...things between husband and wife. And I believe I know from examining Katharine, that she has nevertheless been acting the role of wife with someone else."

He was looking around at the food on the table now. His face was flushed slightly, and the pink skin shone beneath the white of the eyebrows and the scalp. He rubbed the bridge of his nose again. A few moments passed and I began to think that he had forgotten I was there. He was staring at the remains of my steak now.

I felt a lot like the time I'd been caught as a child swinging from the curtain in our old apartment. My Mother had warned me several times not to do it, and I'd promised that I wouldn't. But I did it one more time, with Henry there watching and laughing. And then I noticed that my father was standing in the doorway and he'd seen the whole thing. I had the same feeling now. It was that instant when I knew I had been caught, and there was no way to deny anything. I felt like a child again sitting across from the loud old doctor. And what I'd done with Kate seemed like a foolish, childish idea.

"I know what's going on," he was saying, his gaze lowered directly at me now. My eyes dropped to the tabletop. "But I see a lot around this town that people don't know about." I nodded slowly, unable to look up at him. I felt my own ears flushing red now.

"I just wanted to talk to you here today about it," he went on. "I don't know if any of your generation listens to your elders anymore or realizes the importance of the integrity of things like family and marriage," he was motioning toward me with his hand now, rings gleaming. "God knows young Katharine must be having problems with that. She's a nice Christian girl, too. The Lord has tested that family…He's tested her. And right now, she's weak. We can't blame a woman for being weak. Maybe she feels as if she's missing out on a part of…being in a marriage. I'm not sure. And I don't know which of you started this whole mess, or how long it's been going on. I really don't. But what I'm giving you today is a warning," his finger was extended now. "You won't be able to fool James Garrison for long, you know. A man cannot be cuckolded in his own house without finding out about it eventually."

Something lifted. He didn't really know what was going on. No one had talked to him at all. Maybe he'd seen me go over there a few times, but that was all he knew.

I felt sorry for him in a way. Here he was, lecturing me so earnestly, thinking all this time that I was engaged in an illicit affair. The truth would probably shock him beyond comprehension. He seemed to have aged a great deal to me in that instant. I looked up and into his eyes. He was past the age of an authority figure, despite his voice. I saw this now. People probably never realize when they pass that point, I thought.

"The Garrisons are a good family," he went on, "and they have power in this town...power over employment, say. They have a good deal of influence. Not to mention the Sherwoods. I shudder to think about Misses Sherwood. Nothing is worth breaking up a good Christian family for, Colbert. Nothing. I don't know what feelings you may have for Katharine and she for you, but they must be put aside, at once. I'm sure such things are taken lightly by children of your age, but I assure you, they are grave things indeed."

His large, wrinkled hands unfolded on the tabletop, and his palms shrugged up toward the sky. He was waiting for my response. What could I say to him? I think he took my momentary lack of a response as insolence, because his face grew redder again, and the fingers of his hands interlaced tightly once more, rings glinting.

"I believe you did good things in that war...you children. And son, I believe you've been doing good at the Delgrew house. Lord knows you've helped that woman. But I hate to think about the young girl that lives there as well...and I just hope your motives are pure. I hate to think that you may see fit to break up another household. I just hope your motives are pure. Pure..." I watched him mouthing the word a few more times without sound, shaking his noble head and looking down at his hands.

And suddenly, I realized that I owed him no explanation for anything. His speculations about the Garrisons seemed merely silly, but once he brought up the Delgrews he began to strike me as pathetic. I got my courage up. He was still sitting there in silence.

"Well," I said. "I don't know what to say, Doctor Crowe. You said earlier that this is none of your business, and I agree with you. I appreciate your advice, and thank you for the lunch. But I don't feel any…any responsibility to explain myself to you." I stood up then, and he looked at me, utterly shocked.

"I'm glad to see that you're concerned about your patients," I said then. He looked very old. "And I'll give some thought to what you've said," I continued. "You…you may not know all that's going on with the Garrisons, and things may not be as you think they are. Unless one of your patients talks to you about something, or asks you something, I don't think it's your job to…to decide whether or not they're living their life correctly." His expression was frozen, mouth slightly ajar.

"But as for the Delgrews, I take offense at what you've said, to be honest. I don't feel that I owe you the slightest explanation."

And I walked away. I didn't look back until I was up the street and almost around the corner. When I did I saw that he was still sitting there. And I could also see, even at that distance, the pinkish bald spot on the back of his head.

I worried a little that he might talk to Mrs. Delgrew about me. They were neighbors, after all. What if he told Mrs. Delgrew and Gertrude that I was having an affair with a married woman? What would they think of me then? I couldn't imagine the disappointment. Now that I thought about it, I was glad that he and my Aunt hadn't spoken in so many years. Otherwise I might have been scared that he would say something to her.

Kate and Jim had every right to do whatever they wanted. All three of us were adults, and our agreement was no one's business. I decided that if Dr. Crowe told anyone that I was having an affair, I would just deny it. It wasn't strictly true, anyway.

When I went by Kate's that week I was especially observant. I was trying to see if there was any sign that she knew about my meeting with Dr. Crowe. She seemed normal, though, so I didn't say anything about it. I was afraid that it might upset her and make her decide to put an end to my visits.

CHAPTER 31

It was a Friday evening, and Ambrose had asked me to meet him after work at one of the drug stores in town that sold illegal pints right at the counter. Mr. Barnes wouldn't allow this at his store, of course. But the younger clerks at the newer store would sell it to you as long as they knew who you were. They all knew Ambrose, of course.

As soon as I saw him I knew it would be quite an evening on the town. His jacket had padded shoulders and narrow lapels, and was tight around his waist. He wore a long black tie in a sailor knot. No one would have mistaken him for someone from Greenwood.

His skin was tan, now that summer was here. I looked pale by comparison. I wondered when he was getting all this sun.

"Things sure have picked up at the bank," he said.

"Really?" I asked, taking a sip of my pint of beer. We sat at a tiny counter in the store.

"It's amazing how careful a few years of poverty makes these farmers. Some of these fellas want to see every dime they have in the bank right then and there. Just to check on it. This guy asked me if I could show it to him. All his money, in cash. He didn't want to take any of it out, he just wanted to make sure it was there. Can you believe it? People have no idea how banks work."

I laughed along with him, taking another drink. I didn't really know what was so outlandish about the request that the farmer made. I suppose I was one of those people who didn't really know how banks worked.

I thought back on how strange the last few weeks had been, while the beer swirled around in my head. I had raised my voice to the Pilfords, my Aunt, and Dr. Crowe. The more I thought about it the more I felt as if I had been watching someone else's life unfold.

Ambrose knew nothing of the Pilfords or their visits to our house, since none of us had ever raised the topic around him. We drank more and more, and I told him all about them.

Ambrose was a better listener than I would've predicted. Part of the reason for his rapt attention was probably the way I described how attractive the girls were. But when I talked about the sessions and Henry, he was respectfully serious and quiet, just nodding, his forehead furrowed.

A few people shuffled in and out of the store, some of them drinking beer out of soda cups like we were. The kid behind the counter kept his distance from us, sensing a serious conversation.

I described the two seances I'd seen and what I knew of the sisters' visit to my work. I ended the story with the man in the car behind the school. That had been the last time I'd seen the Pilfords.

"Hmm," he said, nodding slowly. He took a large swig of his beer.

"Who do you think the guy was?" he asked. "Their brother?"

"I don't know. He didn't look like it."

"You don't think he's…you know, in with both of 'em, do you?"

"I don't think so."

"So I'd have a chance then," he said.

"I suppose so."

"I'm just kiddin' around," he laughed. "I didn't know you had people like that here. I used to know some fortune tellers up in Boston, and in New York there's a whole city of them."

"They're not really fortune tellers, though."

"No, I guess not," he said, a far off look in his eyes. "Fortune tellers are old hags. But these don't sound like hags. Maybe if you see them again, you can let me know, and I'll be sure to question each one thoroughly. Or, both at once, right?"

"I'm glad you think it's funny," I said. I was smiling, though. The more I drank, actually, the funnier it did all seem. It was a relief not to take it so seriously.

"No," he said, the serious bank teller face returning. "No, I know it isn't funny. Those crooks were taking advantage of your Mother and your Aunt, and you and I won't stand for that. We're the men, right?" He smiled broadly then. He looked a little drunk. Then I realized that I probably was, too.

"So you want to take me up on that bet now," I asked, "about you getting sick? What're tomorrow's odds?"

"I couldn't tell if it was the liquor from the night before or that sermon that did it," he said with a chuckle.

I turned around on the little stool and looked around the store. A large picture of a bowl of oatmeal hung on the end of an aisle. *FOOD UP 85%*, it said. And then, *One cent buys not much more than a bite of meat or a bit of fish; 1/5 of an egg, or a small potato; a slice of bacon or a single muffin.* And then, below the bowl, *One cent buys a big dish of Quaker Oats.* I wondered if the farmers Ambrose was talking about knew how much Quaker Oats they could get for their money.

I turned toward the large front window of the store now. I watched the twilight of evening rising on the street outside. I was happy sitting there, my head buzzing quietly like a motor. The sky had an orange pallor, and life seemed good. I thought about Eleanor and Beth and Kate. A few people walked by.

Ambrose was talking to me again, but I was distracted. A man had walked in the store, and I was busy watching him. He bought some cigarettes at the counter. I was having trouble concentrating. Something screamed from my insides, but I couldn't react. And then he was gone.

"Hey," I said then. There was silence. Ambrose had been saying something, and I had interrupted him. I turned toward him.

"What?" he said. "You sweet on that guy?"

"No," I answered, ignoring the jibe. "No, I…that…that was him."

"Who?"

"That was the guy." I saw now in my memory what I had failed to recognize when he was in the store. The bright, almost white hair, the way he lit the cigarette as he left. "That was the guy from the car. I'm telling you, that was him."

"That guy you were just looking at?"

"Yes. That was the guy with the car who picked them up."

"The sisters?"

"Yeah. He just left," I pointed toward the door, raising myself up just a bit. Ambrose gulped the last of his beer and stood, steadying himself on the counter.

"Let's go," he said.

"Where?"

"Let's get him. That guy. Come on, we're gonna lose him."

I stood too quickly. I was dizzy, and I felt for the stool. It wasn't where I thought it would be, but then the heel of my hand jammed against it. I straightened up.

"Let's get him," Ambrose said, pushing a strand of hair back. "He's got some explaining to do." Soon, we were out in the summer night, on the street, walking quickly in the direction we thought he had gone. We were moving smoothly, unimpeded, in the direction of the kill. He was no match for us in my mind. In reality, we probably looked like two men who had obviously been drinking.

I did feel strong with Ambrose beside me, though. And as I thought back to the last time I'd seen this guy, I got angrier and angrier. Right in front of the sisters, he had acted as if I was of no importance. He hadn't even known that I had a legitimate complaint against them. He had brushed me aside. Now he was going to be sorry that he had stopped in that store for cigarettes.

I wasn't sure what Ambrose would be like in a fight. I figured him for tough because he was from a big city. I didn't know what I would be like though, since I hadn't really been in a fight since I was thirteen and one of the Myrtle boys knocked my hat off. It was a hat that used to be my father's. That must have been why I launched into him with my fists going. One of the teachers had put an end to that one, but not before I drew blood from one of the Myrtle noses. That was the only fight I could remember being in.

There were a few people out walking through the dusk. We passed the post office and the hardware store on Rose Street. I was already getting winded, although I never would've admitted it to Ambrose.

"There," I said, pointing. I had seen the light head of hair disappear around a corner ahead. We turned the corner.

He was already quite a distance away. He had crossed through the alleyway behind Marshall's store and was now on the dirt road that led west away from the center of town. There wasn't much in that direction. He was moving into the wooded area, toward farmland. We were out of sight of the main streets now, and it was almost completely dark. This would be a good spot to jump him, I thought. But he was so far away, and I was tired.

"I wonder where he's going in such a hurry," I thought aloud.

"You think he saw us?" Ambrose asked.

"No," I said. "He hasn't turned around. What if he leads us to them?"

"Who?"

"The sisters. Maybe he'll lead us to them."

He shrugged in agreement. We kept our current pace up, just to keep him in sight, but we didn't try to gain on him now.

The dirt road twisted into the sparse woods, and after a short time we could see his destination right in front of him. A section of the woods was glowing, as if it were on fire. He stepped off the road and into the woods, walking toward the light. It was a clearing that I knew. I had been there before, myself. It was owned by a bootlegging farmer who was known for managing a few whiskey stills on his land. If I had my bearings right, his barn wasn't too far away beyond the trees.

There was a fire going in the clearing. Maybe a few, by the look of the glow. Large sparks rose slowly and became one with the stars that were now twinkling in the low sky.

The man we followed had already disappeared into the clearing itself, and we approached through the trees cautiously. My hand brushed against the rough bark of a tree.

Strange shadows were cast among the branches of the trees that surrounded the clearing, and we heard voices shouting and talking. Ambrose and I glanced at each other. Maybe the Pilfords were here, I thought. Maybe we were being led into some sort of spiritualist camp. Would they be performing sacrifices? Did they do that? I listened some more. It didn't sound like any kind of organized ritualistic event, though. It sounded more like a large party.

As we moved closer we saw that the field was full of people. Most of them were a bit younger than us, and they were all men. The smell of burning wood assaulted us in the summer air. The wind brought a wave of heat in our direction. A film of sweat was forming on my forehead. It was a hot night already, and the bonfire only added to it.

Ambrose stepped into the clearing, exhibiting no fear at all. I followed him. By the look of things I was beginning to think it was just a party anyway. We stood near each other, looking around, but the guy we'd followed had disappeared into the crowd.

Men laughed loudly and pushed each other near the two large bonfires in the center of the field. Ambrose had a smile on his face.

"Looks like we found the big event," he said loudly over the voices.

I smiled back, nodding.

"You know whose land this is?" he asked. I nodded again.

"I can't remember his name now," I said. "A farmer. I think I've actually been around here before with some boys from the train yard...he makes some strong whiskey."

"Sounds like my type a' guy."

"I'm sure."

I watched the sparks cascading from the fires in a frenzy of motion up toward the sky. I could actually see a line of bluish light between the treetops and the black of the night sky above. It was a nice night.

When I looked back down, Ambrose wasn't next to me anymore. It would be just my luck if the guy came over to me now and started a fight, while Ambrose was off wandering around looking for a drink or a woman or both.

I saw a few men who looked to be in their thirties, and then another three kids talking together who must have been about seventeen. They were dressed in workman's clothes, as if they had just come from jobs. A dark, low shape moved through their legs and trotted toward me.

Green eyes stared up at me like a couple of full moons glowing in the darkness. They flashed with light, and then turned downward. It was a large dog. He walked circles around everyone, tongue hanging out and bouncing with each step. He moved toward me, and I saw that his fur was a dark brown color, and his ears were pricked up as if on alert.

I remembered my Mother always warning us about dogs when we were little. If we ever ran into any farm dogs along the road we were to walk away slowly, because if we ran then they would chase us. I got along well with dogs, generally, though. I remember Henry had been bitten by one on the way to school once. But that had never happened to me.

This dog rubbed its snout against my leg, sniffing curiously. I leaned down and stroked his short fur. He kept sliding his head against my hand and leg, and I felt the long whiskers of his muzzle and the cold wetness of his nose. His tail waved back and forth slowly, like a fan.

Then, suddenly, he decided he had somewhere else to go. His ears pricked up and his head snapped to attention, and he moved away quickly, solid torso floating above four scrambling legs.

I stood back up, my hand still tingling slightly from the feel of his fur. A large insect of some kind buzzed around my head, and I waved my arm at it. I had been prone to being eaten by mosquitoes ever since I'd lived in Greenwood, and I knew that this was just the sort of night that they would be out in numbers. I thought about moving toward the fire to avoid them. I turned to look that way, and then I noticed Ambrose talking to someone nearby. He threw his head back and took a drink out of a large flask. I moved toward him. He had removed his jacket and loosened his tie now, and he held the jacket over one shoulder with a crooked finger.

"Hey, pal, have a drink," he said happily, clapping me on the back. "Is it all right?" he asked the other guy, having already handed me the flask.

"Sure."

I took a little nip. It was a homemade mixture that tasted just as I imagined poison might. Rather than kill me, though, it just filled my head and body with a light, airy feeling.

"This is my cousin Cobb," Ambrose said, leaning toward the other man. "This is...what was your name?"

"Ralph Lockehart," he said with a deep voice, leaning toward me. I handed him the flask and we shook hands.

He was at least a head taller than I was. His nostrils were round, gaping caverns in his face, and the rest of his large nose looked like it had been shaped around them. His eyebrows were dark and thick, and his lower lip and jaw looked as if they were a little too big for the top half of his face.

He shook my hand with a terrible grip, and I found myself thankful that Ambrose had made a friend out of this guy and not an enemy. His shirt was unbuttoned, and his sleeves were rolled up to his elbows. He looked ready for manual labor at a moment's notice.

"You boys local?" he asked loudly.

We both looked at each other and nodded slowly.

"What's your chapter?" he asked.

My mouth opened, but then I realized that I had no answer. Had we stumbled upon a secret society or something? Ambrose looked at me, his eyebrows raised.

"Or are you just here for the hooch?" Ralph asked with a laugh, holding up his flask.

We both smiled and nodded.

"Really? You dunno what this is about?" Ralph asked.

"We just heard about a little shindig, that's all," said Ambrose.

"Whudda you boys do for a living?"

We told him, and he still looked confused.

"You're not lookin' to organize? No chapter affiliations?"

"No, no…we're looking to defy the Eighteenth Amendment, and that's it," said Ambrose.

"What do you do?" I asked Ralph.

"I work with Jack," he said, pointing a thick thumb behind his head and in the direction of the bonfires.

"Who…" I started to ask, when a loud chorus of shouts interrupted me.

"Attention! Attention!"

The shouting carried over the heads of everyone, and the crowd of unruly men slowly began to hear it. They stopped laughing and patting each other's backs with drunken abandon and turned, one by one, toward the center of the event.

"Let's get started!" came another voice, hoarse with overexertion.

A man stood above everyone else then. I moved from side to side, and my vision cut a momentary swath through the bodies. I saw that he was standing on a little wooden stairway that had been pulled up next to one of the fires. It put his own face a good four feet above most of the heads.

His face was lit from underneath by the fire, and his nose cast a shadow upward, distorting his features. Still, he looked familiar to me already.

He raised his arms and then pushed them downward, as if fanning the flames. He was calling for quiet, trying to control the crowd. Most of them were cheering and shouting.

"All right, all right," he started with a smile. Some of the shouts continued, though. A disembodied hand lifted from the group of men nearby and offered him a flask. Everyone thought this was the funniest thing in the world. Whoops went up on the wind as he grabbed it and took a swig. He wiped his mouth with the entire length of the back of his arm in an exaggerated gesture, and returned the flask to the sea of hands.

This made them shout even more, and he smiled, positively beaming out across them. He was dressed in a dark jacket. His butterfly bow tie had been untied, and hung around his neck.

"All right," they were quieting down now, at last. "I think most of you know me," he rubbed his eyes, obviously irritated by the smoke. "But for those of you who may not, my name is Jack Wolfe, and I'm just going to talk to you a little bit tonight…just one man to a bunch of other lazy, shiftless men." They shouted and laughed some more.

"We're here…" he started, and the voices quieted somewhat, "we're here 'cause we have the right to a gathering place." The crowd swelled again, and he raised his arms to quiet them. "And they can tell us that we can't gather in the town hall or in the middle of town, but we'll find a place. Because there will always be American citizens who own their own land who know that our cause is just. We're here for all the boys who can't be here right now, because the government of the good old U.S. of A. has put them where they can't cause any more trouble. Men like Sacco, and Vanzetti." Shouts and arms were raised. "Oh yes…two boys with foreign names. They sound foreign to me. But what they've proven is that the American government are the real petty criminals. Those men are gonna be condemned now.

They have no chance. But not because of the murder of some bank guard. Because of who they are, and because the government can put a label right there on them…'red anarchists,' and make it stick, because they can't defend themselves against a nation that's drunk on its own fear of the world. Those men have no hope of a fair trial. There's enough proof that they did it. And you know what, maybe they did do it. Maybe they did." When he paused, we heard only the sound of the fires crackling and popping as they consumed the piles of wood.

"Maybe they did do it," he repeated. "I don't know. But the thing is, they won't get a fair trial. And that's what America seems to be about these days. Nothing here is fair anymore…don't fool yourselves…nothing. My father and yours grew up in a country where he could speak his mind. He could gather with his friends and they could speak their minds. That's what this country was all about. Our founders made that a part of this country…a big part, so the English couldn't come in and stop them from gathering and speaking.

"But not any more. You and I, friends, we live in a time when that freedom is gone. We live in a nation where fear of anything and everything has made our government into a bunch of hired thugs, coming down on anyone who tries to make his own life a little better." He looked over the crowd. There was no doubt in anyone's mind that he truly believed these words that he was saying. He seemed ready to die for his cause, and the crowd was starting to go with him.

For my part, I still wasn't sure what it was all about. I knew about Sacco and Vanzetti, as everyone did. Last year they had been arrested in Boston when some bank workers were killed during a robbery. Ambrose and I had talked about it a few times because he had known a man who worked at that bank. It had been a big controversy. But the newspaper said that they were foreign radicals, and that was all the reason they needed to have done it. I'd never really given it any thought until now. I remembered reading that the two men were going on trial soon. Jack was certainly getting the crowd excited over this, but I wasn't sure what his interest was.

"The American government is going to exterminate those men," he said. "But they won't be removing two men from society...they'll be removing an idea. That's what they do now. They wipe out ideas that scare them. Let me tell you a story about a group of men called the Industrial Workers of the World," a great shout was raised from the crowd in reaction to this. Ralph, still standing beside us, nodded his head slowly along with them. Ambrose took this opportunity to tip the flask back again and take another gulp. He looked at me, smiling, and gave a little shrug as if to say that he had no idea what was going on either. He seemed happy enough to be sharing this man's liquor, though.

"These men had ideas...now I'm not saying I agree with all of them. But they had ideas. And ideas are what move this country forward. And the party of people who call themselves Socialists, well they just weren't committed enough to the cause. But the men of the IWW are pledged to their cause. Because maybe it's time for America to become a place where we can all have what we need. Maybe it is." The crowd listened in utter silence. "Then again, maybe it wouldn't work. I don't know. I'm just one guy. And I'm nobody official. But I will say that these men...these men they called 'Wobblies'...at least they had a cause that they were devoted to. And the outcome of their devotion was strengthening men like us. Giving us the strength and the power to organize, and tell the employers of the industries of this country that they do not hold all the power," the crowd began to make noise again. "That we hold the power, my friends. That it is our cause and our destiny to get what we need, to ask for what we deserve, from those men who employ us...who take the best years of our lives in their factories and mills.

"But the government...once again, the government of this land has decided that the IWW, like Sacco and Vanzetti, are just too different. They're saying things that the government doesn't like, so it's time to exterminate, right? That's right," he was smiling, but anger flared in his eyes. "It turns out that a few of the boys in the IWW in Washington were trying to have a peaceful meeting, just like this one. This was a few years back...you remember. But their hall got attacked. They had to fight, to defend themselves from people who called themselves 'anti-radicals'...people who didn't know or understand what those men were really fighting for." Silence again, except for the popping of the flames.

"Well, those men defended themselves, just like you or I would have to do tonight, if the town came down on us." He paused, letting this sink in. "And some people got shot. And now, because those boys defended themselves against attackers, the IWW is going down. It's being taken down, by a hysterical government. They say out in California they're even hiring fake 'witnesses' to speak against these boys. What kind of a country are we living in? Right now...right now, if the town came crashing down on us...attacked us right here in this peaceful gathering, we couldn't do a thing. What're we supposed to do? Let them beat on us and not retaliate?"

He looked around, slowly. Even Ambrose was listening. I felt very sober now.

"This is a government that won't even allow you to think for yourselves," he started again, quietly, contained. "If you organize, or go on a strike because you're trying to feed your family and your fat, rich boss isn't giving you what you deserve...well, the American government is going to come down on you. Of course, when they need you...when they want you to fight their damn capitalist plot of a war for them, they expect you to line right up, and lay right down and die. And I admire those boys who got outta that draft, and decided that they just didn't want to lay down and die for a government that wouldn't even let them earn what they deserve to earn.

"Now we're not here tonight to change anything," a few groans came from the front. He smiled and continued. "No, no, we're not...I know some of us get agitated and we're ready to go right out there and fight. But we're not doing that, you see. We're in the position that we can't even defend ourselves if they attack, now. But what we have is each other. This is about organizing together, and keeping the power of our labor unions alive in this town." Shouts and cheers went up. "Because that's all we have, friends. Make no mistake…this isn't Russia. There's no revolution that's gonna happen here, no matter how scared they are of the Bolsheviks who tore up the Socialist party. That's not happening here, and maybe it shouldn't. Maybe it shouldn't. What we're getting here tonight is a renewed power…a power that comes from gathering and talking and drinking with men like you who work hard…who have skills to offer, and who have families to feed. And if you feel a power, here tonight, among all of you, then we've succeeded. Because they can't stop us, no matter how much legislation they put through…no matter how many strike breakers they send. Because we have a power that they can't touch…and this revolutionary power is just what started this nation, and made this nation great." The crowd of men were shouting and cheering and patting each other's backs.

"And it's hard," he said, raising his arms again to quiet them down. "It's hard to keep up the fight…but draw strength from each other and don't quit. And some of you men may be blacklisted in the process. That's right. It happened to me." Everyone was silent again, serious. "They tried to tell me that I was blacklisted and I was out of a job. And I lost my place in my own union…lost the position I loved. But they couldn't fire me. You know why? Because there were too many men on my side. It would've been too dangerous for them…they were scared. We had them scared. And that's power. That's controlling our own destiny and our own lives. That's what this is about tonight. Because I'd be out of a job…a job I've worked hard at for years…if not for the support of all you boys. But they can't stop me from speaking to you. I'm not official at all…but I can always speak to you.

"We've got to be loyal to each other. We've got to be loyal. You can't support the cause of labor halfway. It's all or nothing, just like war, or else you weaken us when the time comes and we need you. Right here, tonight, in fact," any trace of a smile left his face and he stared the crowd down slowly, his eyebrows severe, "there are men who'll betray us. Oh yes, there are. You may know who you are, or maybe you don't know yet. There'll always be cowardly types in every crowd. The men who'll break at a critical moment during a strike, or be afraid to go all the way for their cause. And there are even men who'll smile to your face and call you friend, and then turn you in to your employer as soon as you turn your back." He nodded slowly, everyone at attention. "It happened to me. It could happen to any of you. So those boys you know down at the factory that aren't here tonight...you better watch them. You better get them involved in the cause as soon as you get to work on Monday, because if they're not with us, they're against us. They're either on our side, and ready to stand with us, or they're the enemy...just as bad as the boss."

I turned toward Ralph. I wasn't sure what he was thinking about the speech, but he certainly seemed serious about it. Ambrose was looking around behind us, distracted. As for me, I must admit that Jack had captured my attention completely. I felt a sort of power emanating from him, along with a palpable response from the crowd. I knew that he could call them to battle right now and they would follow. He had them completely under his control. There was something dangerous about this.

"So take that away with you, tonight," Jack was saying now. He wiped his forehead, and I could see, even from where I was standing, that the smoke from the fire had mingled with his sweat and created a dark shadow above his eyes. "We have the strength, in the name of the laboring men of this country, to get whatever we want. Now, speaking like this gets me all riled up, and I'm sure it does you, too. But we don't need to walk away from here and take that anger out on our own town and our own loved ones. That would be a mistake. I don't want to hear about any destruction tonight, or any family quarrels. We're welcome to stay on this land as long as we like...drinking and talking and strengthening our brotherhood. But when we leave here, let's conserve our energy for the cause. Gentlemen, I appreciate your attention, and your devotion to the cause. Take that devotion, and offer it to your labor leader...to the leader of each of your chapters. Together, we can make this nation great again...we can make it the same place our fathers grew up and loved...and we can make them proud of us and all we do."

The roar seemed to go up to the heavens, and he was mobbed by the flowing crowd as he stepped off the platform.

"Whudda you boys think about that, now?" Ralph was asking, his large face turned to us, smiling.

"Sounds good to me," Ambrose said, laughing a little.

"Yeah, he sure riles 'em up," Ralph said. "Need some more?" he motioned toward the flask.

"I never turn that kind of offer down," Ambrose said. "You can pledge me to any cause, as long as I don't go dry."

Ralph chuckled and disappeared into the crowd. I turned to Ambrose.

"What do you think?" I asked.

"About what?"

"I don't know...this, all of this."

"I don't know," he said. "I guess what he says makes sense. I don't really care, though, if you wanna know the truth." He lowered his voice and moved closer to me. "But I sure wouldn't want to make enemies out of these guys." He smiled.

I nodded, still shocked that something like this was going on right here in town. It wasn't anything terrible, it was just the fact that these people were so devoted to a cause, and so ready to fight. I didn't associate this sort of thing with Greenwood, and I never had.

I caught sight of Ralph making his way back toward us with his flask in hand. He was speaking in a very animated way to two other men, both of them older.

"How long do you wanna stay?" I asked Ambrose.

"It's up to you," he said. "In case you haven't noticed, there aren't any women here."

"I noticed."

"You sure?"

"Yes."

"Because you looked pretty interested in what that kid had to say. Like you're ready to sign up. Maybe you just thought he was pretty."

"Shut up. Here comes your new friend with some more for you."

"Just what I need."

Ralph handed him the flask.

"So whudid you say you did for a living?" he asked me.

"I work in insurance."

"Oh. Not much need for organization there, huh?" he said with a smile.

"No. But it was very interesting," I said, waving toward the place where Jack had been. Unlike Ambrose, I still felt as if I needed to apologize for my presence here.

Ralph smiled back.

"Jack's a smart guy," he said. "Probably the smartest guy I ever met. You should'a seen him last year...Amalgamated Clothing Workers went on a strike against sweatshops. Lasted about six months. I never seen anybody work a group a' guys like he did. I'll tell you somethin', though." He looked around to make sure no one was listening. The nostrils were like two holes that could swallow me up. "I work right next to 'im every day, and I don't listen to a lotta what he says. Don't get me wrong, I understand the cause and everything, but sometimes he's...well, he goes pretty far, sometimes. That's why he's been in trouble before."

"These guys really believe him," I said.

"I know. It's a little scary what some of 'em would do for him. I really can't talk about it though. Don't get me wrong…I'm on his side." He seemed worried that he had said too much to us. "So what are your names again, fellas?" he asked now, looking back and forth at us. He still seemed concerned, and kept looking over his shoulder.

"Cobb Whittier," I said. Ambrose was busy drinking and looking around absently. "This is my cousin Ambrose Bentham."

"What was your last name?"

"Whittier."

His eyes went wide, but just for a moment. He looked around, then focused back on me.

"Why'd you come here again?"

I had almost forgotten about the guy we'd followed.

"Actually, we got here sort of by accident. We were following a guy…" I thought better of telling him the whole story. There probably wasn't any connection between the Pilfords and these people, and it would just seem like a long and crazy story. "It was just a guy I was after. We'd had a little scuffle before. So Ambrose and I went after the guy. He led us here."

"Is he here?"

"Probably," I said, looking around. "I haven't seen him though. It's nothing, though, really. Nothing big."

"I've actually met Jack a few times," I said. "You work with him at the textile factory?"

"Yeah, I've…I've been out there for a while," he said, his eyes dropping a bit.

A short, stocky man approached Ralph. He wore a tight cap that looked too small for his head. They talked for a while about where everyone was headed now. Ambrose and I just looked around.

"What are you guys up to now?" Ralph asked, turning back toward us.

We both shrugged.

"Mister Drake's throwing a party up at his place...that's what summa these guys said."

Ambrose's eyes lit up.

"I'm a friend of Drake's," he said. "You boys want to head up there?"

"Really?" asked Ralph. He looked like he didn't believe him.

"Sure. Stick with me, boys. Drake and I are gonna show you the time of your lives."

"Let's go," I said. I had never seen one of Drake's legendary parties, and I was excited at the prospect.

"All right," said Ralph. "Why not?" He said something else to the short guy, and then came back.

"I sure appreciate the hospitality, Ralph," said Ambrose, handing him the empty flask. Ralph took it and returned it to his hip pocket. The three of us stepped back out between the trees and over their roots. The fires still burned behind us, and most of the men were still there, buzzing loudly.

We walked back toward town, and the noises of the gathering grew gradually softer behind us. It was late, and there weren't many people out on the dirt road. The few men we saw were all coming from the gathering, as well.

"You said you met Jack before?" Ralph asked me as we walked.

"Yeah," I said. "I don't know him well or anything...but we've met a few times."

He was silent again for a while, thoughtful. A group of men laughed loudly behind us.

"Where do you live, Ralph?" asked Ambrose.

"Over toward the factory," he said.

"Any girls out there?"

"Not really," he answered, smiling.

"You're not married, are you?" Ambrose said it as if he was asking if he'd been convicted of a crime.

"No," he said, still smiling. "I got a gal who has her eye on me, though."

"Get out of it as fast as you can, pal," answered Ambrose. Ralph laughed a little. Just before we got back to town, we crossed over onto the little road that led upriver.

"Just a second...wait," said Ambrose, who had been leading the way. We stopped, and he left the road and walked to the line of trees to relieve himself.

We stood there, waiting.

"Gotta make room for the next party," Ambrose shouted up to us from the trees.

I smiled, but Ralph seemed preoccupied.

"Did Jack ever say anything to you about your brother?" he asked me suddenly. I felt my smile fade slowly.

"No," I said. "I think he told me he knew him. Did you know him?" I studied the shadows on his face. The left half of it was in darkness, and the other half was illuminated dimly by the moonlight. The only sounds were the summer insects of the woods and Ambrose shuffling around below.

"Yeah," he said. "Did he ever talk to you about things at the factory?"

Ambrose came back up.

"That's better," Ambrose said, exhaling loudly with a smile. He looked between us then, realizing that something serious was being discussed. We stood there, in the darkness between the dirt road and the trees, not moving. Half of the moon floated overhead. My eyes had adjusted fully to the darkness now, and I could make out their faces clearly.

"No...not really. He didn't say much about it," I answered.

"Hmmm," said Ralph. He nodded silently, as if something was on his mind.

"What are we waiting for?" asked Ambrose. We started walking again.

"Now you boys've probably never seen anything quite like Drake's place. Just stick with me, though, and I'll get you as much wine and women as you can stand for one night."

"Yeah, toss us a few of your leftovers, please," I said sarcastically.

Mr. Drake's house was huge, and it was covered with lit windows. I had seen this place before, when I used to explore the woods and the nearby river as a kid. But that was always during the day, and it had looked deserted. I'd never seen it lit up and full of life like this.

We approached from the road and made our way across the driveway. A shiny new car was parked in the front, and it had to be the most beautiful automobile I'd ever seen. It looked like a silver beast, crouched and ready to pounce, smooth and rounded all over. It had definitely been placed there to be admired by the guests.

We could hear voices and music flowing out over the front lawn from the house. As we stepped onto the porch, Ralph and I looked at each other, unable to control our smiles. Ambrose led us, still playing the professional.

I had always wondered who got invited to these parties. Now I realized that the front door was literally open. Maybe Drake had never really been concerned with invitations. That was odd, since Ambrose always went out of his way to tell me he'd been personally invited to the parties here.

The entryway was small, but there were a lot of people crammed in it. Most of the men wore shirts with ties and flannel slacks. Some of those with jackets had colorful handkerchiefs in their breast pockets that matched their ties. Two men in the corner wore the type of large knickers I saw in pictures from the city. These pants were so wide around the legs that I imagined they must have made it difficult to walk.

I was still a little anxious over the fact that we hadn't really been asked to come in. I was ready for someone to come up and tell us to leave at any moment. That would be embarrassing, especially in front of all of the women, who stood around in the entryway wearing shiny dresses that squeezed their shapes as flat as they would go. Ambrose looked around at everyone, nodding and smiling. Others nodded back, but I couldn't tell if they really recognized him or if they were in the mood to nod at anyone.

We moved through the crowd, jostled softly on all sides by shoulders and elbows. The entryway opened out into a great room with a very high ceiling. A large, expensive-looking Arabian rug dominated the center of the room. Several couches and chairs were arranged on top of it, and they were all full of people. I caught sight of a large decorative fireplace where several guests stood and talked. The walls were lined with books. I never would have pictured the Drake I'd heard of as an avid reader. I decided I'd have to get a look at his books later. I'd be ashamed to admit it to that crowd of revelers, but I was actually interested in books now. I blamed Gertrude.

The source of the music was a grand player piano in one corner of the room. People surrounded it, talking and laughing, setting their drinks on its shining black surface. One man with large glasses sat at the bench and waved his hands over the keyboard as if he were playing it. He clearly found this hilarious, and he kept tugging at the sleeves of the men standing nearby to get their attention and show them what he was doing. I watched a few young girls dancing together to the music. I think it was playing *Kitten on the Keys.* I had never seen a player piano in someone's home before.

"What do you think?" Ambrose asked. He had to raise his voice quite a bit to be heard.

We just smiled and nodded. I didn't know anyone here. Most of the men were older than I was, although a lot of the girls looked like they were about my age. This had to be the summer vacation crowd, I thought. Drake himself supposedly split his time between this home and a penthouse in New York.

"You know anyone here?" I asked Ralph.

"No," he said. "Summa the boys said they might stop by…maybe they're not here yet. You ever been here?"

"No," I said. "Always wanted to, though."

Ambrose had already gotten the attention of one of the young-looking dancing girls. Now he brought her over near us.

"This is my cousin, Cobb," he was saying loudly into her ear. I could hardly hear him from where I was standing. "And this is our friend Ralph." She smiled at both of us and took a drag on her cigarette. Did Ambrose know her, or had he just grabbed her?

Her hair was short, and so was her dress. It may have been the shortest dress I'd ever seen on a girl. None of these women could walk down the street in town dressed like this without being arrested, I thought. I remember there was one state that was trying to pass a law about skirt lengths.

The girl's body was still dancing, but her head was still, smiling at us. Her tiny round teeth sat close together on a large surface of gums. They looked just like the string of pearls around her neck, in fact. She shouted something at us, but I couldn't hear. Ralph and I both leaned in.

"You boys know how to dance?" she was asking.

I looked at Ralph, to see how he would answer. He seemed to be looking at me for the same reason. Then he nodded a little.

"My friends and I are looking for some men who dance," she said, shouting at us from a few inches away. Her smile looked vacant, somehow, and her eyes had the look of someone who was well into a night of heavy drinking. "Not these old men," she said. "Old men can't dance," she broke into hysterical laughter, then, doubling over, unable to stop. We just kept smiling.

"Sure these boys dance," Ambrose said into her ear, leaning over. His hand was resting on the lower part of her back. "But let us get ourselves something to drink first...we'll be back, don't worry."

She didn't seem worried, though. She went back over to the other girls, still laughing. The piano played *Ain't We Got Fun?* and the girls danced with themselves. Ambrose was smiling broadly, celebrating an accomplishment of some kind.

"I'm gonna go find Drake and say hello," he said to us, and moved away through the crowd.

We looked around for somewhere to sit or someone to talk to. I wondered how Ambrose did it. I wished I could be like him, just walking right up to them and starting the talk. But it all sounded so fake to me, somehow. I had never been able to do that.

"How long have you lived in Greenwood?" I asked Ralph.

"Since I was about sixteen," he answered. "I grew up near Pittsburgh…my father was in steel up there."

"You like it here?"

"Sure, it's all right."

Someone bumped into me from behind. I turned around.

"You should salute when an officer's present, soldier," said a slurred voice. Willie was holding something large. He stumbled into Ralph now by accident.

"Willie," I said with a smile. It had been a while since I'd seen him, and he was the last person I had expected to see. He was wearing a shirt with no tie, and it wasn't buttoned all the way up. It didn't look very clean, either. His face was greasy with sweat, and it looked as if he hadn't shaved for a few days. He wasn't wearing his glasses, I noticed.

"You know Drake?" he asked, his breath heavy with liquor.

"No," I said. "My cousin does…we're here with him." I asked. I don't think he heard me, though.

He just looked at me with a goofy expression on his face.

"Look at this," he said, holding up what was in his hand. It was a hot water bottle, just like the one my Mother used to lay across my chest when I was sick as a kid. He was grinning from ear to ear, showing it to both of us. "This is where I keep the good stuff," he said, tipping it back and drinking from it. "I'm telling you," he wiped his mouth on his sleeve, "you can take these things anywhere and nobody asks you a thing."

I wanted to ask if he had spoken to his mother lately. I had no idea what he was doing these days. I doubted he was holding down a job, so I couldn't imagine where he could be living. Was he sleeping outside? Did people do that in this town? I had seen a few hoboes around the tracks when I worked at the train yard, but I couldn't imagine someone I knew living like that. They did always seem to be drunk, though.

Maybe he was living here, I thought. A reveler in Drake's house who always managed to stay the night or two until the next party. It was possible. Maybe he could even hide in the house without being found, and come out for the parties. The place was big enough.

Ambrose returned, still smiling. He handed me a glass of something. It was a nice glass, with an inlaid pattern of wheat around the base. I took a drink. It was a mixed drink of some kind, and was actually quite good.

"Ambrose, this is Willie Delgrew." I started to tell him that this was Gertrude's brother, but I stopped. I didn't want Willie to think I'd been running around with her or anything. They shook hands.

"Cobb and I were in the war together," he said loudly toward Ambrose. "Did you know that?"

Ambrose shook his head.

"No," he said. "I don't think so."

"You and I should'a been draft dodgers," Willie said, his eyes slipping to the sides, focusing on everything but me. "Just like old Jack," he guffawed, as if this was the funniest thing he'd ever heard.

I took another drink rather than saying anything. Ambrose had brought a drink for Ralph, too, who was downing it quickly. Willie stood there, shifting his balance, and his eyes settled on Ambrose.

"You from around here?" he asked.

"No, I'm from Boston originally," Ambrose responded.

"Really...I'll bet they've got some strong home brews up there."

"I used to make few nice varieties myself," Ambrose said with a smile. Willie clapped him on the back as if they'd been friends forever.

"Hey Cobb," he shouted. "Where're you working now?"

I started to answer him, but Ralph grabbed my elbow. He was looking around again, anxious. The piano played *I'm Just Wild About Harry.*

"We need to talk," he said. "Maybe in the kitchen…over there," he nodded toward another room.

"All right," I said. "Hey, Willie," I got his attention again. I knew that it was going to sound silly, but I had to try. "Why don't you go see your mom tonight or something? We could walk you there."

His reaction was slow. At first I wasn't sure if he'd heard me. Then he broke into a broad smile, and put his arm around Ambrose's shoulders.

"This guy…" he said to Ambrose slowly, "this friend of mine is always trying to get me to stop having fun…he's worse than my mother. Worse than my father. Can you believe it?" he asked Ambrose, laughing a little forced laugh. Ambrose was busy looking around for women, though, so I don't think he really heard him.

"Leave me alone," Willie said then, moving away from Ambrose. "If you're my friend, come out with me and we'll have a good time…don't tell me to go home. Don't tell me where to go. You can't tell me…" he stumbled a little. His voice was growing louder. "I'll see ya," he said to Ambrose now. "My night's just beginning. You boys go home to mommy. I'll see ya." And he was gone, back into the crowd.

"You ready?" Ralph asked me. I thought about going after Willie, but it wasn't my job to chase him down.

"Hey," I told Ambrose, "we'll be right in there, all right?"

"What're you talking about?" he asked. "Look at all these women. Look at those gams over there." He nodded toward a girl who was leaning against one of the bookcases with her long legs crossed. She was drinking from a tall cocktail glass and talking to a man whose back was to us.

"That's probably her husband," I replied.

"He can have her for life," he answered. "I just want one night. There's plenty here for you boys, too."

"Well, get a few warmed up for us...we'll be back," I said.

"All right," he said with a shrug, moving off toward the woman by the bookcase.

The kitchen was large, and everything in it was a bright white. A collection of half-emptied glasses was scattered across the large table. People milled in and out, trying to get some air or just taking a break from the main room. I saw more people through a window near the table. They were outside on a deck of some kind, where a few white electric lights had been strung. I guessed that the river was probably below.

A man and a woman were whispering in one corner of the kitchen. It looked as if they were in a fight of some kind. The man raised his hands animatedly, but the woman matched him gesture for gesture. Another man was slumped on the ground in the corner near the cabinets. A line of drool went from his open mouth, below a large mustache, down to his starched collar. He was out cold, and everyone was stepping around him.

Ralph seemed distracted. He was looking the place over as if someone might try to listen in on our conversation.

He pulled a chair out from the table and sat down, and I did the same. He looked around some more. The woman in the corner shouted loudly and stormed out, and the man followed. For this brief moment, it was just us and the unconscious man in the corner.

"Listen, Cobb," Ralph started after a long drink. "This probably isn't the best place, but...I gotta talk to you about something."

"Sure," I said.

"You saw how those guys were tonight...with Jack," he said. "So I gotta be careful."

I wasn't accustomed to hearing a large man like Ralph declare himself afraid. I nodded.

"I've been tryin' to get away from it…from that part of it, for a while now. Jack just has too much power, I think." He stopped then. A man had stuck his head in, and looked around the room.

"You fellas see a girl come through here?" the man asked.

"No," I said. He looked at me suspiciously, as if I was hiding her. Then he turned and left. Ralph made sure he was gone before he continued.

"You seem like a good guy," he said. "You shouldn'a come there tonight. You didn't belong there."

"I know…"

"No, you don't," he said. "You don't. I wish I hadn't found out you're a decent hardworking guy. 'Cause I wouldn't have to…to give you the whole truth."

There was a loud bang then, and Ralph jumped in his seat and turned around. It was just some drunk outside who had fallen against the window, though. Ralph turned back, looked around some more, and then went on.

"I got a brother," he said. "That's why. You deserve the truth. I got a brother and I'd wanna know the truth.

"I guess Henry didn't talk about things that much at home…but there's some things you don't know. You should probably know. We all get along fine at work. And Henry and Jack got along just fine for a while."

He slid his glass back and forth on the table, and I took another large gulp of my drink. It was sweeter toward the bottom. A song I didn't know floated in from the main room.

"There was one strike a few years back…it was in 'seventeen I think. Jack was head of our chapter. Things got rough. The sheriff was against us, they had detectives breakin' the strike. The factory had their own fake union, so they wouldn't hafta recognize us. This was back when I was just startin', so I didn't know a whole lot. It was my job, and I just walked into it, and Jack was in charge. Nobody did a thing unless he told 'em to. He's a good guy, but things went too far. The town wouldn't give us a meeting hall. But you could tell Jack was just lovin' it. He was havin' the time of his life. And the worse things got, the more he fought. That's how he is. And he could talk so everyone would be with him...you heard him tonight."

I nodded slowly, taking another drink. The piano played some song. *Second Hand Rose,* maybe? I heard a woman giggle hysterically in the main room.

"Things got bad," he went on. "This was when the gover'ment started taking support away. We had less and less guys on our side. But Jack wanted us ta fight the police and everybody else and maybe get shot. A lotta the guys had families they were supportin', though. So it was tough. But...but Henry, he got a few a' the guys...the guys who'd been around for a while, to step down. I mean, he wasn't crossin' the line or nothin', he just said he wasn't gettin' shot over this, and he said he'd just wait and see what happened. I don't think he was tryin' to take guys away from Jack, but a bunch of them went with him. They just did. I think they'd just been waitin' for someone to stand up to Jack and say it, and it was just him that did it."

The liquor had settled in pools in my brain, slowing things down, calming me. Right now I was just listening.

A few men came into the kitchen loudly, and Ralph stopped again. They went through the cabinets, stepping on the man who was passed out. Then they knocked on the window, shouting at the people outside. They stumbled around the table, looked at us, and smiled. We watched them, waiting until they left. I wondered what Ambrose was doing right now.

"Anyways, after the strike, things got rough for Jack," he went on. "I dunno what was really goin' on, but a lotta guys were sayin' Jack and Henry really had it in for each other after that. I dunno if it was true or not. Henry probably didn't care. He did his work, and that was it. I never saw 'em together, but I don't know what was really going on. But it was right after that…right during summer, I think, when the judges started lookin' into the unions all over. The Espionage Act. And Jack was under some real heat then…real trouble. They raided places we'd met, and somebody told me they raided Jack's place and everything. That's what I heard.

"There were some…things that tied Jack to the Wobblies. The IWW. And these got turned in to the cops. These documents. That's why Jack had to step down…that's when the boss almost fired 'im. But he couldn't fire 'im 'cause all the guys were still followin' 'im. So he hadda quit being head of the chapter, but he was still the same, because everyone was afraid a' all those guys…you saw tonight."

He was quiet now. He took a drink, and looked at me. Was he waiting for me to say something? I didn't know what to say. I just kept nodding.

"I didn't know," I said finally. "I didn't know about any of that at all."

"I know," he said. "I could tell that you didn't know nothin'…you wouldn'a been there tonight if you did. But then I wasn't sure. I wasn't sure if you were there to start trouble over what happened."

I shook my head.

"Well," he said, sliding the glass back and forth slowly again. His drink was almost gone. "I don't know what really happened…but a lotta the guys said that…that it was Henry who turned those documents in. To the investigators. I dunno, but that's what the guys said. And Jack…you could tell that's what he thought. I could just tell."

He leaned in closer, putting his glass aside now.

"Do you wanna know about all this?" he asked.

"Sure," I said quickly. I looked up at him. "Sure. Did you know Henry?"

"Yeah. Not that well, though. But I knew 'im. I dunno if its true. I dunno if he had anything to do with it…with the papers."

I nodded.

"Listen," he said, looking around suspiciously. "You seem like a good guy. Like I said, I got a brother myself. But you let me know if you don't want to hear any more."

"I'm fine," I said.

"No, listen," he said, his voice dropping almost to a whisper. "Really." He looked down, shaking his head. He breathed heavily, and his brow was furrowed.

"Listen," he said again. "I'm gonna tell you this…I'm gonna tell you the truth. But you gotta wanna hear it. If you're happy…right now. If your family's fine, you may not want…there might be things you don't need to know. It's not my business to tell you things you don't need to know."

"Here you are," Ambrose shouted dramatically, entering the room. "I've got several ladies out here wanting to meet you guys, and you're sitting in here…" he stopped, sensing that the tone in the room was serious. "What's goin' on, boys?" he asked.

Ralph looked at me. I guessed that he didn't know if I was comfortable with this being discussed in front of Ambrose.

"We're just talking," I said. "About important things. Sit down, if you want." Ambrose sat, and I nodded at Ralph. "This is our family," I said. "We want to know everything you know." I'm sure Ambrose was thoroughly confused, but, to his credit, he knew when to keep quiet. He just sat there, looking back and forth between us.

Ralph leaned in again, voice dropping.

"I can get in real trouble for tellin' you this," he said. "Real trouble…dangerous stuff. I just want you to know that. But you deserve to know. You should know. God, I dunno what I'm doin'." With a movement so quick it made me jump, he threw back his glass and emptied the remains entirely into his mouth. He gulped loudly and slammed the glass back onto the table, his eyes brimming with red.

"I can't answer no questions," he said. "I'll tell you all the stuff I heard, but that's all I know."

I nodded. A few seconds passed. His hands were folded in his lap now. The tinkling sound of the piano came from the main room.

"You dunno what those boys'll do for Jack," he said, shaking his head. "He was real connected, too…to other chapters." He stopped, unable to continue. He looked at both of us. Ambrose looked very confused.

"There was a contract," he said. "That's what I know. There was a contract, after…after what happened with the documents. A contract out on Henry. And they got 'im. He was killed in the war, but he wasn't killed by no German. It was a guy from our goddamn union, collecting the contract. That's it, guys. That's all I know. They got 'im." He stood up and walked to the window. "A guy named Murdoch. Tommy Murdoch. I don't even know the guy. I never seen him. But that's who Jack got to do it. Some guy from another chapter…not far from here…the type a' guy who could do somethin' like that."

He shoved his chair across the room in anger. He wouldn't look at us. I could feel Ambrose looking at me, now, but I didn't look back.

"What the hell…" came a slurred voice from the corner. The chair had slammed into the man who was passed out on the floor. He'd been roused now, and was looking around, red-faced and confused. He wiped the drool from his mouth and stood slowly, taking his time. Collecting himself, he swayed as if he had never walked before. He slouched by us, asking all the while if we knew where some girl named Jane was. We ignored him and he lurched out the door.

I felt like that man must have felt, as if I'd been awakened from a dream, and I wasn't sure what was real yet. All I remember is a slowly building anger. I was angry at everyone and everything. I was angry at the world and the country and all of it. I was angry that I had stumbled into the meeting that night, and that these people existed here in Greenwood. The next thing I know Ralph was speaking, trying to calm me down.

"Listen," he was saying. I heard the sound of people talking and music and laughter in the background again. "I told you this 'cause you need to know. But there's nothin' you can do, all right? Don't think there's anythin' you can do. That's what I was scared of when you came to the meetin' tonight. Don't get in that kind a' trouble...there's nothin' you can do." He turned to Ambrose now, hoping to get through to him. "Really. Don't get nobody else killed. I just thought you should know, that's all."

"What was the guy's name again...who did it?" It was Ambrose. He sounded composed to me, more serious than I'd ever heard him before.

Ralph shook his head.

"Murdoch...Tommy Murdoch, I think. I don't even know 'im. I don't even know who he is. And ya know what? Maybe he was there tonight. But don't...just stay away from it, guys. Really. I shouldn't even tell ya the name. Just stay away from it. That's what I'm tryin' to do. That's what I'm gonna do, from now on. I've been trying to put some distance between me and Jack ever since it happened. Ever since I heard about it. A lotta the guys who know just keep their mouths shut and act like it's nothin'. I can't do that. But right now, I gotta keep the job. I'm lookin' for somethin' else, but I gotta keep it 'til I find somethin'. I need the money. But there's nothin' you can do. Listen...there's nothin'."

His face was right near mine now. I looked at his large nose and I wanted to break it. I stood up, my own chair tipping back and landing on the floor behind me. I was right up next to him, and I didn't care how big he was.

"Get outta my sight," I said. "Get the hell outta my sight," I was shouting now, my voice like a low, growling animal. I blinked at him through tears, my throat filling with a lump of pain. "Just shut up..." I said. "Telling me nothing...don't tell me about nothing. You're telling me that because that's what you did...nothing, when you knew all about it."

Ambrose was beside me now. I was in a rage. The alcohol and the anger were working together, and I felt like a stranger behind my own eyes. But I didn't care about anything now. Why would I?

I exploded, violently attacking him, throwing my fists with as much strength as I could. I don't really remember much after that. I remember some broken glass in the kitchen, and a pain in my back. I remember people coming in and looking at me as if I were crazy. I remember little things, like the way one ugly girl looked at me and said "Who is that?" with a stupid expression on her face. And the next thing I remember is several arms pulling and dragging me outside.

I was sitting on the side of the road, the buzzing of the insects in the night woods around me, the sound of the party in the distance. Ambrose stood over me.

I crawled over toward the trees and felt a burning in my stomach shoot upwards into my throat. I choked and heaved and vomited into the woods, tasting the bile in my mouth. I coughed and sputtered and wished I had some water. I heaved again and again. Nothing came up now. I was doubled over, and I could feel Ambrose's hand on my back. There was a sharp pain in my elbow, and I saw that it was bleeding. I had no memory of when or how it was cut.

I stayed down there, in a crouch. In front of me was a small collection of branches and leaves. I studied the way that the leaves were attached to the branch with little bulbs of green that held them there. I could've grabbed them and ripped them away so easily, but I didn't. That was the size I wanted my world to be. Just those leaves on that one branch. But I knew even then, in the back of my mind, that I had to retreat from this little place eventually. I had to come back to the world.

Ambrose pulled me back, and we walked along in silence, toward home. The taste remained in the back of my throat. I had no water, and no way to wash it away. It burned back there, no matter how many times I swallowed or spit. It felt as if it would go on burning there forever.

I was in my bed then, staring up at the darkness, feeling a great emptiness inside. Ambrose had gotten me home without waking anyone. I knew that I had washed my mouth out, but I barely remembered doing it. I remember now that it took me a long time to fall asleep. And yet, I have no memory of what I thought about as I waited for oblivion to take me.

CHAPTER 32

I never saw anyone get killed in the war. Lovejoy saw a man die through a telescope, though. We were in a support trench, during the big battle. The closest thing to us on the map was Verdun. The real fighting was in the distance, but when we first arrived there was some activity less than a mile to our east. We were on high ground, with the Argonne Forest behind us, so we could see pretty far with the telescope.

The captain talked to HQ through the thick rubber disk on the big hand telephone. Then he took a few guys and went to meet up with someone else, and left Sergeant Clark with us. We sat there and listened to the distant roaring of guns and the whining sound of a monoplane, trying to judge how far away we were.

"Hey Sarge," said Jarret. "If the Fritzies get back here to us, we might as well learn to speak German, right? I mean, if we're all that's left…"

"You haven't learned it yet?" Clark asked, smiling at us. He was a short, stocky guy with slick dark hair and mustache. He always claimed to be part Italian, but no one believed him, with a name like Clark. The strange thing about him was that he never wore his helmet. He used to tell us that if a bomb dropped on him or a bullet had his name on it, a helmet wouldn't do him any good. I often wondered how the captain felt about Clark not wearing his helmet while he was making sure all of us did. He never said anything about it, though. Clark knew he would survive, he said, because he was going to go to the Virginia Military Institute after the war. This had been his goal all his life.

"General Pershing and the boys have been pushin' out there since late September," he said, looking around at all of us. I think he got a kick out of lecturing us. He was probably just repeating the things that the captain told him. "Over forty days. GHQ's throwin' every American division out here at 'em. We're in the last stage. We're not gonna see anything ourselves today." I think he was as disappointed as the rest of us. We were one of the support trenches, and we were only there in case the enemy somehow came through the rest of the Americans and undid the last few days of eastward movement. We were backup troops, brought in after the last stage of the offensive had already begun.

Our dug-out was our home for many days, and the days were usually short and rainy that time of year. Our drinking water was brought to us in cans strapped to big packhorses, who would slosh through the mud toward us, usually at night. Sometimes the Services Of Supply men who led the horses could give us small tidbits of information about the surrounding country and what was happening. It was one of these SOS guys who told us that the real fighting was going on about five miles east of us, and that our boys had already reached the far bank of the Meuse.

It was twilight when Ted was squinting through the telescope. A lot of rainwater had gathered at the bottom of the trench. The rain had stopped that afternoon, but the air still felt damp all around us. The sun was slowly descending beyond the trees of the Argonne.

"Those guys just got hit," he said suddenly.

"Get down!" Sergeant Clark was yelling.

Something happened to the end of the dug-out far behind the sergeant. The ground and walls twisted and jumped on their own. An enormous boom materialized out of the air around us, and dirt and rock were thrown everywhere. We all got down.

Another shell hit at the same end of the dug-out, and the ground itself appeared to jump toward the sky again. Dirt rained down on us from all around. I think most of the guys just stared, dumbfounded, like me. The end of the dug-out was torn to bits now. There was just a hole in the middle of a big pile of ground. Then more shells struck the same place, over and over, upending the ground again and again.

And then, there was silence. Our eyes were on the gaping hole in the ground, and then the sky around us. No one said anything. Our weapons and masks lay strewn about. We all knew that there was nothing we could do with them now.

Then an area of the dug-out that was much closer to us belched into the air with a deafening explosion. Some of the guys were closer to it than I was, but luckily it was still a few yards away from us. Then there was another strike in the same place. The explosions were certainly loud, and I started hearing a high pitched ringing in my ears after each one.

Another area of the trench was gone, and now, the silence came again. I knew now, as we all did, that the next set of explosions would probably be even closer to us, or on top of us.

I realized that the next wave could be in my lap, and my first instinct was to flee. Everyone looked around in alarm.

This was the one scenario we never could have dreamt up when imagining the war. It was a situation in which we had absolutely no course of action. To run down the dug-out in the opposite direction of the hits could put us right in the middle of the next set just as easily as sitting where we were. Leaving the dug-out, of course, would present us as easy visual targets.

They had to be hitting us from a distance with their big, long-range guns. It looked as if each set of five or so shells was dropped another twenty yards down. They had measured their distance and direction, and they were firing methodically, trying to put an end to any life that may have been in our dug-out.

We could've easily been in the middle of a twenty-yard interval. Or they could've hit us ten yards long or short. There was nothing we could do but wait to see if we would be lucky or not that day. Time stood completely still, and everything was wrapped in a thick silence.

The wait seemed so long that I started to think they had given up. Then another explosion occurred around us, too deafening to even describe. After the noise I was able to open my eyes and unclench my teeth, so I knew that I wasn't dead. The newest area of ground to be turned inside out was actually a few yards past us. I slowly moved down the trench toward the already destroyed sections, along with everyone else. I knew then that we were okay.

The hits kept coming, then moved down another twenty yards and started again. They'd missed us. We all sat there, staring at the other end of the trench and watching it explode over and over again. Every time the dirt and debris settled, it would jump again.

And then, finally, it was over. I don't know if they moved on to another dug-out or ran out of shells. That was the closest I ever came to dying, though. I heard later that two out of three American soldiers saw battle. I don't know if my experience counted or not.

This was a new kind of war, though. It was thoroughly modern, and the enemy could get you without you even seeing him. There had been a lot of talk about that kind of thing, but now I believed it. This was a whole new way of fighting.

We stood up and wiped the mud off our trousers. We were silent for a while, and then someone let out a snicker. I don't know if it was a sound of disbelief, or true laughter. I think maybe someone just needed to make a noise, to be sure we were alive.

"Everybody okay?" asked Clark. There were a few nods, but no one really answered. There was a hollow ringing sound in my ears. For the next few nights I would lie awake listening to it. It took a few days for my hearing to return to normal.

The sergeant looked through the telescope cautiously now.

"I saw the boys over on the south end of the field there get hit before us," Lovejoy was saying. I moved closer to them. Sergeant Clark swung the little telescope around.

"That's too far," he said.

"I'm tellin' ya…I saw it," said Ted. "A couple of 'em were clownin' around on top of the dug-out." He turned toward me. "I saw one of 'em get hit," he said.

"Where the hell are they?" the sergeant asked no one in particular.

"I think they had to be east of that other trench, maybe in those trees on the high ground," said Ted.

"What high ground?" I asked.

"That ain't high ground," answered Clark at the same time.

"It was one a' those big guns," Jarret said. We hadn't heard him approach. I don't think any of us could hear much.

"What?" asked Ted, leaning toward him.

"I told you," said Jarret. "They've got these forty-two centimeter boys. Huge. Takes a team of thirty horses to haul 'em. And it takes a whole mess of mechanics and engineers to fire it."

"Bill…" Willie Delgrew had been standing there listening as well.

"What?"

"Where do you get your yarns?" Willie asked, shaking his head. I laughed.

"How else could they've hit us from that far?"

"We don't know how far they are," Sarge said loudly. "So just be quiet for a minute and I'll try to find out." He handed the telescope to me and leaned over the field telephone again.

"Jarret, you capture yourself one of your famous forty-two centimeter guns," said Lovejoy, "and I'll personally pin on your Distinguished Service Cross. Better yet, I'll give you a night with my girl back home." Jarret was always talking about these mythical guns. I'm not sure where he got the idea. The truth is, I'd heard of them from a few other sources, but I didn't want to ruin anyone's fun, so I joined in the ribbing.

CHAPTER 33

❁

There was truth in Lockehart's story. I knew that, somehow. Not that I wanted it to be true. I wracked my brain for memories of Henry right before we left for the war. I thought back to the times when we were in training. But he'd never said a word about Jack or any of it. Maybe he had no idea of the trouble he was in. Maybe, when the bullet hit him that day, he died truly believing that it had come from a German gun.

I had never tried to imagine Henry's killer before. I hadn't thought about putting a face behind the gun that shot him. Maybe it was because I hadn't really seen the enemy when I was over there. My family had always just known that he was killed in the war, killed *by* the war.

What Ralph told me changed everything, of course. Not even the Pilford's communication with him from beyond the grave had revealed this. But this should have been the first thing Henry told me. There was no way he would have wasted our time with our dead brother or the bookends.

Would Henry hide this knowledge from us during the seances? He had been hiding quite a bit from us before he left from the war, if what Ralph said was true. The Pilfords had said that his personality would remain the same. Perhaps he wanted to protect my Mother and my Aunt from the knowledge of what had happened.

I could understand this. So many people they loved had lived and died. The world they'd known was changing so quickly now. Nothing would be gained by telling them the truth. The war killed Henry. Anything else was just a gruesome detail.

But I couldn't hide my own selfish disappointment and anger. I could understand my Mother and my Aunt, but why had he hidden this from me? We hadn't talked very much about his job, but I always thought that was because nothing new really ever went on. That's how my job was, anyway, and I'd just assumed the same was true for him.

Maybe he was scared, I thought. Ralph certainly had been afraid of Jack's followers. If Henry was really in that much trouble with Jack, he had probably been scared as well. He'd never acted afraid, but perhaps he hid it from me before we went to the war because he didn't want to get me involved.

It felt as if a great, empty hole had opened up in the pit of my stomach. I was underneath something that was holding me down. And I was rolling over and over, trying to get out.

My dreams were like that all weekend. I can't remember anything specific that happened in them, but I was left with a feeling of darkness and helplessness each morning.

Without the presence of Ambrose, without the simple knowledge that he knew what I knew, I might have been swallowed whole by the despair. The knowledge that he was in on this too was like a lifesaver thrown into the void for me. It was something to hold on to, at least.

On Sunday afternoon, we sat in the little rowboat on the lake, our fishing poles loosely seated in our hands. We had rowed out to the center to cast our lines at the deepest point. It was one of the few places where the bottom wasn't visible, and all we could see was the greenness of the lake water.

The lake glistened with sunlight, but I spent most of my time staring at the bottom of the boat. I watched two little pools of water flow and change shape, sliding around my shoes. My own legs and feet looked dead to me. They were so still that I began to think that I couldn't even move them if I wanted to. I studied the splintering paint on the little seat in the center of the boat. The oars were crossed on the bottom, one over the other. The wood on one was slightly warped, giving the oar a strange curve. It had been like that for as long as I could remember.

We hadn't said much to each other the day before. I'd spent part of it recovering physically from the night of drinking. I assume that he had covered for me with my Mother and my Aunt, as I had done for him before. Dinner was quiet. We exchanged looks every once in a while, but I don't think either of us could assemble our thoughts in a way that would mean anything.

Birds chirped in the distance.

"You been thinking about the other night?" he asked. I could feel him looking at me, but I didn't return the look. The sun was behind him in the sky, and it was just too bright.

"Sure," was all I could say.

He turned back to his pole.

"Well what do you think?" he asked.

I just sat there.

"You're not going to tell anyone, are you?" he asked.

"I don't think so," I said, shaking my head slowly.

"This…this is strange," he said now, still looking out over the lake. "But, I…I know this is going to sound crazy, but I think I may know something."

I waited for him to go on, but he didn't.

"What do you mean?" I asked finally.

"I mean…about this guy Ralph was talking about," he said. "I'm gonna find out more. I don't know if you want to, or not, but I do. I'm gonna talk to Ralph again."

"Why?" I asked. But I did want to know more.

"Because...I don't care what he thinks. There may be something we can do. You know...maybe we can find this guy. What do you think?"

Revenge had passed through my mind, of course. But something about it seemed so pointless now. I had imagined confronting Jack, but that was where my imagination stopped. I'm sure he'd just talk his way out of it.

"There's no proof," I said.

"Well...right. There's no proof tying it to that kid who gave the speech the other night. That's how they would've done it. But I mean...what if we could find this guy, Murdoch?"

I didn't answer. I hadn't been sure if I'd remembered the name correctly. That was it, though.

"Because," he went on, "that's what I wanted to tell you about. You're not gonna believe this...I know it seems impossible, but I think I may know this guy."

I looked up then. We were both squinting at each other. The sunlight was reflected upward from the sparkling surface of the water.

"What?" I just shook my head.

"Really...well, I don't know him, but I think I may've met him. I'm not sure. I'm gonna check on it this week...I'm gonna send a wire back home to the bank. It may just be a guy with the same name. But I think it was Tommy Murdoch. And that would make sense...it would make sense. He was one of the last customers I saw at the bank up there. In Boston."

"Are you sure?"

This was the most serious I'd ever seen him.

"I'm gonna have them check this week...to look up the file. I remember, though...I remember because I had to refuse him a loan. I mean, I did that all the time, but for some reason I think I remember this guy. I've been thinking about it for the last few days."

"Maybe someone had the same name."

"Maybe," he nodded. "That could be. But the more I think about it, the more I remember what he was talking about. He was a young guy, and he'd just come back from the war. He was coming through Boston on his way home. I remember that, though…this wasn't long after the war. That's probably why I remember him, because we talked about the war a little bit. He seemed close to my age…maybe that's why he came to me when he got in the bank. A lotta the other guys are older."

I slid my shoe through one of the little pools of water, leaving a dark smear behind on the wood. I listened without feeling. Very little would surprise me right now. Still, the odds that Ambrose had somehow run into this same person were pretty slim.

"The strange thing is," he started again. "Well, the thing that's unbelievable is I think it must've been him. It must've been this guy. It all makes sense to me now…with what you were saying about the sisters and all."

"What?"

"I've been thinking about it a lot," he continued. "I don't know what made me think of it yesterday…but the name just came back to me. It must just be because I talked to him about the war…that was the first person I met who'd been over there…just come back…and he was telling me about it. That must be why he stuck with me, somehow. That, and because he was one of the last customers I saw about a loan there."

Four birds floated across the sky, black shapes against the sun.

"He was asking questions about life insurance," he went on. "That's why I think it must be him. He was asking me about how it could be collected…I can't remember exactly. He told me he wanted to know for the mother of a friend who'd been killed over there or something. I don't remember his story. But he was asking about how an insurance policy could be collected for someone who'd died in the war. It had to do with that, because I remember asking a guy I worked with to come over and help me out, because I wasn't sure."

"In Boston?"

"Yes."

I couldn't believe what I was hearing. Was this even possible? The man who killed Henry was asking about how to get the money from his life insurance policy?

"My God," I heard myself saying softly.

"I know, I know," Ambrose said. "It had to be the guy. It would be a big coincidence if it wasn't."

"What do you mean?" I asked, louder now. "It would be a bigger coincidence if the guy happened to go to you, out of everyone at every bank in the world."

"I know that," he said, shrugging a little. "I know. But think about it. That's what he wanted to know about. He would know about the insurance because he knew everyone at the factory…he was working for the guys at the factory. I don't know if it's him or not. But just think if it is. If somehow, that guy came to me. I think he's still around. He's still around somewhere."

I may have been getting carried away, but it started to make sense now.

"Maybe he's got the Pilford girls working for him," he went on. "Maybe he's still around…and he's trying to get some of the money from the policy. He couldn't get it…I couldn't help him, so he's using them to get it from your family."

"But a lot of people would know that my Mother collected money for Henry's death. It could be anyone trying to get it."

"But someone must have told the Pilfords about it…they were looking for the policy at your office."

"I know, but anyone could have told them. It could've been anyone at the factory."

I had pulled my pole in without even realizing it. I wasn't going to catch anything anyway. We sat there in silence for a while, Ambrose still nursing his own pole and staring into the water.

"So you're gonna send a telegram back to the bank?" I asked.

He nodded.

"You know," he said, "I never met your brother. So I don't think I have a whole lot of say…in terms of what we do here. It's up to you. All this is pretty strange if you ask me…not what I expected on my vacation at all. But…I just want you to know…if you need help. If you want to go after this guy and try to find him or something, I'm with you."

I nodded silently.

"Like I said, I can go talk to Ralph…see if I can get anything else out of him. I'm pretty sure I can find him. Some of Drake's friends were pretty mad at him…I think they escorted him out. They were ready to do the same for you, if I hadn't told 'em I could take care of you. His kitchen was torn up pretty good." He tried to smile. A few moments passed in silence. "But it's really up to you. It was your brother. If you want to leave it alone, I'll respect that. You might not have anything to gain from doing anything. You might be best just forgetting about it. I never had a brother, so I don't know."

He pulled in his pole and sat there, dragging a finger along the skin of the water. I watched him pull it out and flick the water droplets from it. Then he plunged it in again.

I picked up one of the oars. He picked up the other, and we rowed back toward the house.

"I'll think about it," I said quietly as we pulled the boat onto the embankment. "Just find out what you can."

CHAPTER 34

We were ordered to move back toward the forest after nightfall. I think they just wanted us out of the way when the FA boys came through with their Browning machine guns. They brought in a lot of Field Artillery at night in those days, trying to wear out the enemy and make sure they couldn't sleep. When the darkness was complete, we sat there and watched the flares go up, lighting the sky red every few seconds.

The next day we heard that there were a few small pockets of German soldiers that had hidden during the American advance. They were camped much further west than anyone thought. They must have been aiming at our dug-out, desperately trying to blow their way out the back end of the American troops. During the early hours of the morning, before dawn, our boys flushed them out and took care of them, though.

Late that morning the captain came back and told us we were pushing east across no-man's land toward everyone else. We were supposed to pick up any other groups that were left behind the offensive line. Apparently this had been decided the night before, but news didn't always get around quickly out there. We marched out that day, moving toward the battle, knowing that it would probably be over by the time we got there. Our troops must have already been able to see the outskirts of the Sedan while we were being shot at the night before.

"Once they cut the Sedan-Mezieres, we're goin' home, boys," the captain had said that afternoon. He seemed happier than usual. The Sedan-Mezieres railroad was the main German supply line to the Western front. Our goal was to cut it so they couldn't maintain troops there any more.

We met up that day with another unit that was heading in the same direction we were, and they brought the first rumors that the railroad had already been taken. A short while later the orders came through for us to stop heading east, so we camped for the night, along with two other squads. Morale was pretty high as we traded stories back and forth. Discipline was still maintained, of course. Even well after it was all over, we would be kept on strict, separate training regimens through the year's end.

By the time we awakened the next day and started moving, I swear I could almost sense a new feeling in the air. At last, word reached the captain that the armistice had been signed just before dawn that morning. That was the twelfth of November, and all fighting was to stop by eleven o'clock that day. The terms were that our troops would start advancing toward the Rhine on the morning of the seventeenth.

This was no surprise to us, of course. We all knew that President Wilson had been exchanging messages with the German government for some time. There were other divisions that didn't get the word until well after we did. And, in fact, some German prisoners were actually taken after eleven, and had to be returned. It was like a game, that way. Our boys returned them, playing by the rules. It was a lot like the cowboy and Indian games I used to play in the schoolyard.

CHAPTER 35

I had been seeing Kate every Thursday for four months now. I used to dream about her being my girlfriend. When I was with her I would imagine that we had met in school, and had been dating ever since. In my mind she had waited for me patiently during the war. I thought about what it would be like to ask her to marry me. I won't say I fell in love with her or anything. I was just using my imagination to escape the other things that were going on in my life.

During my happy imaginings, though, it was only a matter of time before I would think of Jim and remember that I was in another man's house. Sometimes I was actually angry that I knew Jim. I wished I'd never met him, so his face wouldn't keep popping up in my mind.

I wondered if they talked about me, or if I was a subject that they avoided. I imagined her bringing me up somehow at the dinner table, even if it made Jim angry. I hoped that it made him angry, for some reason.

I had never mentioned my lunch with Dr. Crowe to her. Right after it happened I'd planned on saying something about it, but I just couldn't. Truthfully, I was worried that it might cause her to end our arrangement, and that was the last thing I wanted to happen. I kept an eye out as I walked to her flat each week, trying to get a glimpse of anyone who might be watching me. I never saw anyone, but I'm sure that Dr. Crowe got his information through the grapevine of wealthy gossips in town. Any of her neighbors could have been looking out their windows at me as I came or went.

I remember one day at the end of summer very vividly. It was still warm, but there was a strong, blustery wind in town that would come up suddenly and remove men's hats, carrying them away in swirling circles on the street. As I walked I felt the bulk of an object in the inner pocket, against my ribs. I reached in and drew out the book that Gertrude had given me. I'd been reading it the day before during my lunch break. Today I'd meant to leave it back at the office.

I hurried over to Kate's during my lunch. Her street seemed silent and empty. The whole town sometimes felt deserted this time of year, when the summer vacationers headed back home.

I was ready for her as soon as I hit the porch and knocked on the door, as usual.

She opened the door with her little smile. But the corners of her mouth were turned down a bit more than usual, and her perfect eyes held another secret as they engaged my own. I studied the faint freckles on her neck and imagined where the trail continued down below her pale yellow dress.

"Hello there," I said.

"Hello," she said. But she didn't let me in. She just stood there in the doorway for a few seconds. I'm sure I looked foolish, eyes raised expectantly, like a dog waiting for its supper.

"Listen, Cobb," she said, eyes cast downward. Was it that certain week of the month? I could never keep track. But no, this was different. Somehow I knew that already.

As I waited for her to go on, I heard a dragging sound behind me. I turned and watched a trash can lid being blown up the street, dancing drunkenly in the wind, scraping against the hard ground. She was watching it too. Her eyes followed it as it blew up the street on its frenzied course. Then the eyes came back to me. I waited patiently for her to speak.

"You…you don't have to come anymore." That's how she chose to say it. As if it was something I was being forced to do. She couldn't have really thought that, could she?

I just nodded slowly. Inside, my stomach felt as if it had dropped toward the ground. I think I had seen the blow coming but didn't want to admit it to myself.

"All right?" she was asking, looking at me now. She tried to smile and look happy.

I just kept nodding like an idiot.

"Thank you, though," she said. "Thank you."

"You're welcome," I said.

"Well," she said, "good luck."

"Thanks," I replied. "I'm sure I'll see you sometime, right?"

She just nodded and closed the door. I turned and stepped off the little porch and walked back down the street for the last time. I was angry that it was over, but also because I had to go back to work unsatisfied now.

I wished I'd said something else to her. It had been so unexpected, though, that I hadn't been able to think of anything to say, really. I should've asked why. But that was the one thing I couldn't ask. I didn't have the right to, somehow. She had started it all, and I always knew, deep down, that she would make the decision to end it.

Had Dr. Crowe said something to her? Maybe he'd let her know that he knew about me. That would be too much for her to take, probably. He knew her parents and her husband's family as well. Maybe he'd made her promise him that she would put an end to it. Even though he didn't really understand what was going on, I was sure his interference would be enough to scare her into stopping.

Or maybe it was Jim. Maybe he just couldn't take the thought of it anymore. For all I knew, he could have been hating me all summer long. Even though it had been his plan, maybe the thought of his wife and me together had just been too much. But if that was the case, I would've expected him to put a stop to it much sooner.

Perhaps Kate just couldn't take it anymore. Women in general were still a mystery to me, and I suppose they always will be. She had always seemed content to me, and every Thursday was like the first. We got to be a little more comfortable with each other as time went on, but her attitude was basically unchanged. She was fulfilling a contract. We would talk a little when I first came in, and maybe eat something quickly, and then go to the bedroom. It was always the same.

And then there was the chance that it was over now because we had succeeded. How did a woman know if she was pregnant? I had no idea. She hadn't looked any different to me as she stood in the doorway. I should have looked at her stomach more closely, I thought. Would she have told me if she was pregnant, though? Would she have said anything?

And then I had another thought. What if it was Dr. Crowe who had to tell her that she was pregnant? I felt sorry for her suddenly. I could almost feel the guilt she would have experienced with the loud old man. He knew about Jim's condition, and he knew, whether he told her or not, about me. And then, if he was the one to tell her that she was pregnant…what could she say? I wished desperately that he had never found out about me. He could make a really big spectacle out of this in town. Everyone might know soon, including my Mother, my Aunt, even Mr. Durham. He wouldn't do that to Jim, though, no matter what he thought of Kate and me. He wouldn't upset his "old families," would he?

Did Kate and Jim's parents know the extent of Jim's injuries? I had never thought about this before. Was her sudden pregnancy going to astound the rest of her family? I hoped that she and Jim had been smarter than that. Even if their parents knew how injured he was, though, I suppose they would just think that a miracle had happened. If people want to believe something like that enough, they'll choose to ignore the truth no matter how clear it is.

I saw pictures in my mind of the Garrison family gatherings of the future, everyone thinking that my child was Jim's. A strong feeling of jealousy crept over me. This child was my intimate connection to Kate, and no one would ever know about it. They would all just think it was Jim's.

I forced these thoughts out of my mind, because even then I knew that they were dangerous. This was the deal I had agreed to. She was Jim's wife, and now I might never see her again. Neither of them ever wanted to see me again. Even though it had come suddenly and I'd had no time to prepare for it, I had to accept the fact that it was over. All I had now was the memory of the things I'd done with her. I desperately tried to recall each and every time then. I wished I'd written things down somewhere. I wished I'd somehow recorded each and every moment, so that I could play them back, slowed down and stretched out, like one of the old, scratchy recordings that Mr. Barnes played at his store.

I dreaded lying awake at night and thinking about her. I knew how easily that could happen, starting tonight. I was the only one to blame, too. I had entered into an agreement, and now I had to be man enough to realize that it was over.

I came upon the trash can lid, which had now settled down in the middle of the road. It was just waiting for the wind to pick up again and carry it. I kicked it, and it slid a few feet in front of me. And suddenly I thought about how I was like that, too. I was just sitting in the same place, waiting patiently for the wind or whatever to push me around.

Kate closing that door made me realize that there was nothing keeping me there anymore. That was when I made the decision, at last. I had been weighing it for weeks before then, but at that moment I knew. I was ready to leave all this behind, if not for good, then for a while.

Ambrose had found Ralph Lockehart again and questioned him. Apparently, he hadn't been very happy to talk about it, but eventually Ambrose had convinced him to say more. I don't know how he did it, but I'm sure alcohol was involved. Ralph told him everything he knew about this Tommy Murdoch, but it wasn't much. Ambrose tried to get Ralph to describe Murdoch, since he was still wondering if it could be the same man he'd met in Boston. But Ralph said that Murdoch had never come to Greenwood after the war. That would have made his connection with Jack too obvious. So Ralph had never seen him and couldn't describe him.

He was, however, able to give the name of the town where Murdoch was now supposedly hiding out. Apparently Jack had mentioned to him that Murdoch was in a town called Dunville, just beyond the state border. Dunville was south of Greenwood, about a day and a half by train. I'm not sure what Murdoch would be hiding from, since it sounded as if his plan had gone off without a hitch.

Ambrose told me all this without offering any advice whatsoever. He stated the facts and left it at that. Between the two of us, we knew that there was a decision left in the air, and that it had been left to me. We had the name of a town now. Perhaps I could find the truth about in this town that I'd never even heard of. I'd thought long and hard about it in the days and weeks since our first meeting with Ralph, and Ambrose had waited patiently for my answer. In fact, by now he probably thought I was going to let it rest.

For a while I thought that I might let it rest, too. It was all still very difficult to believe. I reflected back on the last few years, and everything that had happened. I thought a lot about my first few meetings with Jack, and the way he'd behaved. Had he said anything about Henry? I couldn't really think of anything.

Overall, I knew that no matter what decision I made, Henry was gone and I couldn't bring him back. If I got involved in all of this I would be in trouble myself, and maybe they would even try to kill me or something. I had survived the war, and I'd never thought that my life would really be in danger again. I just didn't seem the type to get killed, somehow. Henry was the type who could get killed, I thought, and Jack, and maybe even Ambrose. I could imagine that. Their deaths would make their lives meaningful, somehow. I couldn't imagine that with me, though. If I died people probably wouldn't really know what to say about me.

I was going after Tommy Murdoch. Nothing was keeping me in Greenwood anymore, and I had to find out what had really happened. I had to confront this guy. It was my turn to have revenge now. For the first time, I had room for a thing like that in my life. It gave me a new sense of purpose, something I hadn't really felt since the war. I was on a team again. I had my place in another fight.

When I got back to the office James was sitting on the steps outside, next to the clothing store. His thick hands were wrapped around an enormous sandwich of some kind. This was perfect, I thought. I had planned to throw some gravel at the window and get his attention so that he would come down. But he was here already.

"Hey there," he said.

"Is Durham here?" I asked, pointing up the stairs.

"Yeah."

"Listen, James…I need a big favor."

"Oh really?"

"Yes. Tell him I got sick."

He looked at me strangely.

"Tell him I got sick and had to go home. Just say you saw me out here getting really sick. Tell him you wouldn't be surprised if I didn't make it to work tomorrow. All right?"

He just looked at me, a blank expression on his face, the half-eaten sandwich trapped in his chubby fingers.

"What've you got going on?" he asked, his face spreading into a slow smile. I knew he'd lie for me already, but his price would be the details.

"Nothing," I said. "Will you tell him?" I was whispering, looking up at the window. Any minute now, I thought, Durham would look out the window and spot me, or else start down the stairs.

"You going on a trip with someone?"

"Yes," I said. "A little weekend getaway. You know how it is...living with your mother. A man needs some private time."

"Who is she?" He thought everyone was hiding a woman or two. In this case, though, it was to my advantage.

"You don't know her," I smiled. "Look, I'll owe you for this, all right?"

"That's right," he said, pointing toward me with the sandwich. "You will. And that means when you get back you introduce me to one of her friends. And not an ugly one. Deal?"

"Sure," I said. "All right. So you'll tell him?"

"All right."

"See you later." I took off toward the bank. I knew that Ambrose would be surprised to see me since I had never visited him there.

When I got there he was out front, talking to a tall man in a three-piece suit and bow tie. They were laughing together in the shade beside the square building. They puffed on their cigarettes and leaned against the dark, grimy brick as if they were in no hurry to get back to work.

He turned toward me as I approached, and I saw his smile diminish a little. The other man looked at me then, and murmured something to Ambrose as he watched me approach.

"Hello," I said when I got there.

Ambrose introduced me to the man, who shook my hand limply. I don't even remember his name. I wasn't really listening. He said something else to Ambrose and then went back into the bank.

"Cigarette?" he asked me after the man had left.

"Don't you want to know what I'm doing here?" I asked.

"I want to know if you want a cigarette," he said. "Then I'm sure you'll tell me." Ambrose was in a good mood. I'm sure he'd been entertaining his fellow worker with amazing stories of wine and women before I'd arrived.

"What did Ralph tell you?" I asked. "About Murdoch."

"He knew the name of the town. That was about it," he said. I'm sure he could tell that I was agitated. I had walked quickly, and I was still breathing hard. I was probably flushed, and I could feel a little sweat on my forehead. I wiped it away.

Ambrose didn't look warm at all, of course, despite his jacket and tie. He blew smoke into the heat, and watched it curl and fade into the sky.

"But, you know," he said, "I'll bet we could find this guy if we wanted to. If we went there."

"Do you remember what he looked like?" I asked. "If it's the same guy that came to you at the bank."

"Not really," he returned.

"He didn't have light hair and an accent, did he?"

"No. He had darker hair, I think. Like yours. I'm not sure, though. I think if I saw him I'd probably remember him. Have you ever been to Dunville?" He spat out the name of the generic small town like any true city boy would.

"No," I said. "But I'm ready to go."

"Are you really?

"Yes. What do you think?"

"I'm coming."

"That's what I was asking...what do you think about going?" I needed him, of course. I couldn't say that, though. Besides, I knew he'd be ready to go as soon as I was. I'm sure he'd found his trip to Greenwood boring so far, and here was a chance to make something happen.

"When do you want to go?" he asked.

"I'm ready now," I said. I waited for him to call me crazy. And yet, as soon as I said it, I could tell that he liked the idea.

We were all set to have an effect of some kind on the world, at last. I had no idea what we would find, but we were looking for revenge. We deserved revenge. It was like a movie.

He nodded slowly, and broke into a smile.

"How are you gonna get away from work?" he asked.

"I already told them I'm sick."

He kept nodding, unable to find anything wrong with the plan.

"We'll stop right now," I went on. "On our way to the station, and send my Mother and my Aunt a telegram. I'll tell them I had to go in the field with Mr. Durham...for work." Even as I said it, though, I knew that the idea wouldn't work. Why would Ambrose be going with me? Why would I be traveling with Durham over the weekend?

Ambrose was still nodding quietly. He crushed the end of his cigarette against the brick wall of the building, driving it in, ripping the paper and spreading the ash. It left a black mark on the wall.

"No," he said. "We'll tell them we went somewhere together...on a trip with...someone from the bank. Tell 'em a friend of mine has a cabin somewhere and he was going right now and we had to decide. We'll probably be back in a few days anyway."

"All right," I said. "How are you gonna get away from the bank?"

He looked at me for a second as if he hadn't thought of that at all.

"Well...how long will we be there?" he asked, even though he had already given me his estimate.

"I don't know."

"It shouldn't take more than a few days," he repeated. I wondered what he was envisioning when he said *it*. "I'll tell them I'm sick or something."

It sounded good to me. There were details we were neglecting, of course. There were the questions of where we were going to stay when we got there, and what exactly would happen once we arrived. But those things could be worked out later.

Ambrose said he'd tell them he was sick and had to leave for the day, and then he'd meet me at the station. My heart pounded as I walked to the post office, and it was all I could do to stop myself from running. I wondered when the next train came through that could take us south. We would have nothing but the clothes on our backs and the money in our pockets. It was perfect.

I hastily composed the note to my Mother and my Aunt. It was a little silly to pay for a telegram from such a short distance, but it was the only way I could be sure that the note would be delivered to them right around the time that I would normally be getting home from work.

Mother and Aunt Edna,

Ambrose and I had to go away for the weekend. I apologize for not being able to tell you in person. Ambrose's boss invited us to his cabin to go fishing. He was leaving right away. We will be back before Monday. Sorry.

Colbert

Ambrose arrived at the train station shortly after I did. It reminded me of the very first afternoon I'd come there and met him months ago. Nothing had changed. In fact, the train station in Greenwood never changed. It had been exactly the same since I had arrived there on my first trip from New York as a young child. It was like the whole town in that way, I thought. A few of the magazines on the rack even looked the same.

A train was coming through in a little over an hour. We were lucky, as it turned out, because there wouldn't be another one until late that night. We bought the tickets and the man asked if we wanted a sleeping car. We said no since it would have cost a lot more money, and I couldn't imagine sleeping anyway.

Ambrose told me the story he'd given them at the bank. He'd said he must've eaten something bad at lunch and was going to see a doctor. He also showed me a small hip flask he had hidden in his pocket for the trip. He seemed to have an unending supply.

I paced around the station while Ambrose sat on a bench and attempted to start a conversation with a woman seated across from him. She was clearly waiting for someone, probably her husband.

But Ambrose didn't seem to care. She looked familiar to me somehow. She was probably someone who had been a few years ahead of me in school or something. Everyone around here looked vaguely familiar. They were the same people I'd seen all my life, with the same little kid faces pulled tighter and leaner into adult faces now. She didn't seem interested in talking to him.

At last the train pulled in, and we crossed the wooden platform outside. The air was filled with a powerful, metallic smell. Steam poured from the huge cup on top of the locomotive, and the sunlight shimmered on its sides.

It wasn't a very popular travel time, so there were only about six or seven people that boarded with us. I felt strange boarding with no luggage at all. We climbed on the nearest car and sat down on a padded bench. There were a lot of empty seats on this car, and most of the men were stretched out across the benches.

It seemed as if we sat there forever. One of the men in our car said something about them loading freight. That must be what was taking so long.

Finally the station lurched and slowly began to slide across the window. The train chugged to life, and I watched as the trees outside picked up speed and moved off.

There was no turning back now, I realized. The station itself was almost out of sight already. I knew we would be heading south out of town, but nothing outside looked familiar to me, even though we had just started moving. The man came into our car with his blue velvet jacket and matching cap, and we surrendered our little pieces of paper.

Nothing but flat, grassy land stretched outside the window now. The grass was more yellow than green, and it was long enough to wave in the wind. We were moving, and everything felt different now.

This part of the state certainly wasn't much to look at. I thought about the train I'd been on in Europe, and even the trains I'd cleaned back home. None of those were anything like this one. This was the sort of train my Aunt and her husband used to take from New York to their summer home, which was now the home we lived in. I imagined that Ambrose rode in these trains all the time. He was reading a newspaper to my left, uninterested in the world that flew by outside the window.

A page of his newspaper sat on the bench beside him, and I picked it up. There was a story about a new holiday called *Armistice Day*. If congress passed it, President Harding was planning to make a speech about it from the Tomb of the Unknown Soldier. The tomb said *Here rests in honored glory an American soldier, known but to God.* I wondered how many unknown soldiers there were. I pictured them all buried together, the arms and legs of their skeletons twisted and mismatched. I suppose it didn't matter who they were. The country was in love with peace now. They were even putting the word *Peace* on the quarters.

There was something about Sacco and Vanzetti in the paper, too. They had been convicted of murder and sentenced to die, of course. Hadn't Jack predicted that? I wished that they would die, now, just because it would make him angry.

"Have you talked to Drake since the party?" I asked Ambrose.

He lowered the paper. He actually looked relieved to put it down. I don't think he'd really been interested in it.

"No," he said. "No…I haven't." He looked at me for a while. I just nodded. He smiled a little then, and his eyes dropped. He raised them slowly and looked around the car.

"I was just wondering if he ever said anything about me," I said. "And what happened that night."

He sighed and looked out the window. I watched the tiny daylit squares of window glass reflected in his eyes. I could almost see the blurs of discolored grass flying by, framed beyond each of them. All of this detail was on the surface of his eyes. He had a strange look on his face.

"You know," he said quietly. "I don't really know him."

"Who?" I was confused. I hadn't even remembered what I'd asked.

"Drake," he answered. He turned to me now. He was looking at me with a wily grin suddenly, as if he was letting me in on a plan of some kind. He brushed a strand of hair back.

"What do you mean?" I asked.

"I…" he was still smiling, but he was looking around at everything except me. "I never really knew him."

"Oh," I said.

"I never really worked at the bank."

"What?"

"I never really got a job…at the bank."

"Never? All summer?"

"Nope." He smiled broadly now, as if he was about to break into laughter. But his eyes weren't smiling. I couldn't believe what I was hearing.

"But I just saw you there today."

"I was just talking to Jerry," he said with a sigh, sitting back. "I know a lot of the boys there. Some of them get me samples of Drake's brew." He lifted his shirt a bit, showing me the silver top of the flask protruding from his hip pocket, and then dropped it again. "But I don't work there."

"Where have you been going every day?" I asked.

"Just out and around," he said with a little shrug. "Having a little fun. I'm on vacation, right?"

"But why'd you tell us you were working there?"

"I could tell your Aunt wanted me to get a job. Everyone did. And you were busy. I thought I'd spend some time and get to know the town."

I couldn't believe it. He had kept up this charade all summer long. He'd come home at the same time every day, and talked to us about the bank every night at dinner. I began to realize that my cousin was a truly talented liar.

"So what were you doing?" I asked. "You had to be doing something."

"I did a lot of drinking...let's put it that way," he chuckled. "And, I must admit, I've made a few lady friends since I've come to town. No one you know."

"I don't think it sounds like anyone I'd want to know."

He laughed again. Like any small town, Greenwood had its share of loose women. I imagined Ambrose with one of them and almost shuddered. His standards had to be higher than that, though. Maybe he was spending time around the schools and meeting younger girls. I had heard a few interesting rumors about the girls at the new high school. I felt a pang of jealousy then. His smug smile didn't help.

"I'm on vacation," he said.

"You could've told me," I said.

"I just did. I didn't know you that well for a while, though. But now, we're in this together. I found something to do, finally."

He just hadn't wanted to work, that was all. I could understand that. I was surprised by the lengths he had gone to maintain the lie, though. I admired that in a way, because I knew I could never do that. I just didn't have it in me. Henry had been a little like that, I remembered. It had always been easier for him to tell lies when we were kids.

I thought of one day when we'd skipped school to go collect frogs down by the river. During a certain time of the year the place was overrun with little brown spotted frogs. When we got home, all it took was my Mother asking what we'd done in school, and I was ready to confess. But Henry stepped right in and made something up about him losing one of his books and us having to explore the riverbed to find it.

Ambrose had to be the champion, though. I leaned forward toward him, my elbows resting on my knees.

"So what other lies have you told me?" I asked. I imagined Ambrose making up stories everyday about work. He would have gotten a peculiar sort of fun out of that, I knew. He must have been really bored with us.

He laughed a little. Then he sat back, sighed, and stared out the window for a little while.

"Well," he said at last. "I know I told you that my mother wanted me to take a summer off and go to Greenwood to give me a change of scenery…to get me away from the bank."

I just nodded. The train rocked back and forth a little.

"Well," he continued, still smiling. "That wasn't entirely true. It was really my idea…to come."

"Really?"

"I've…been having some problems with my family. For a while now, I guess."

I nodded again. He touched the newspaper, which was folded next to him on the bench. There was a little twitch in the corner of his mouth. Then he leaned back toward me and continued.

"I didn't do too well at the bank after my father died," he said. "And my mother and I haven't been getting along that well. I don't know if you know, but my mother…her family is one of these old, rich Boston families. Supposedly they go all the way back to the Boston Tea Party, and one of my ancestors was one of the Sons of Liberty or something. You know who they were?" I shook my head. Maybe that was the day I'd skipped school to collect the frogs.

"It doesn't matter…it's just one of those families everyone knows," he went on. "After my father died and I had some trouble working at the bank, I tried a few other things, but then I registered. I wanted to go to the war. This was in…well, it would be…" he thought for a second, "…'seventeen, whenever everyone was registering. I really wanted to fight," he shook his head. "I just wanted to see Europe. See where my father came from. I was tired of my mother's family history.

"But I didn't get to go. So I decided to come visit my father's sister down here…as the next best thing. To learn about him a little, since I couldn't see where he came from."

I hadn't heard Ambrose ask my Mother anything about her brother, though. Maybe they talked when I wasn't around.

"So they didn't call you…to camp, even? When you registered?" I was confused. Ambrose would've been about twenty-five then, I figured.

"No," he said, looking back at me now. "When you come from an old Boston family and your grandfather knows the mayor, things happen…that prevent you from being called. Even if you want to go. If your mother and your grandfather don't want you to go, they're not gonna call you."

"Really? Is that what happened?"

"I never found out for sure," he said. I could see that he was still angry about it. "But I think so."

"Did you get along with your mother?" I asked.

"I don't know. Sometimes. I wasn't raised by her. I was raised by a nanny." He exhaled sharply, and I thought he was going to laugh. But he didn't.

"What about your father? When he was alive?" I asked.

"We got along all right," he said. "I don't know. He gave me a job at the bank when I decided to quit going to college after less than a year. People used to say we were alike." He had a far off look in his eyes now.

"How old were you?" he asked me. "When your father died?"

"About nine or ten, I think."

"Mmm," he nodded. "You know," he said. "I never told anybody this, but…well, I'll say this first…they didn't get along very well the times I saw them together. My father and my mother. I don't think things were going that well for the last few years he was alive." He paused for a second, and snickered. "There was one day, I followed him to his nurse's flat. He'd been sick for a little while, but he wasn't that bad. So I followed him from work one day at lunch. I was just a kid, really…just quit college. And I caught him…he was at his nurse's building."

He smiled broadly. He was looking past me, out the window.

"And I just stood there, outside, waiting for him. I knew he'd come out any minute and I had no idea what I'd say. I wanted to leave, but something held me there. And he did. There he was, coming out of her building, pulling his jacket back on to go back to work and pretend he'd been off at a lunch meeting. And I was just standing there, on the street."

"What happened?" I asked. He glanced my way and continued.

"Nothing, really," he said. "He didn't really say anything. I could tell he was surprised. Then we just walked back to work. He didn't say anything to me."

He pulled the thin flask from his hip pocket, twisted the cap off, and threw his head back, taking a swallow. He grimaced and held it toward me, but I gave a quick shook of the head, and he returned it to his pocket.

"I wasn't very good at banking," he said. "I know that now. But he gave me a chance. I inherited a lot when he died. But I'm sure they were only tolerating me at the bank because of him. So they let me go right after the war ended. Really, I was done for a while before then. I took time off, and then came back for a few months after the war, but everyone knew I wasn't going to make it as a banker. Even me. I told 'em I was taking a leave during the war…it was easier for all of us that way. I just traveled around and got into trouble. I didn't want to be here. I wanted to be over there fighting."

I wanted to tell him that he hadn't really missed much. But I couldn't think of anything to say that would sound good.

"I think he was like me," he was talking about his father again. "Or I'm a lot like him. He liked to drink and he liked women, I'm pretty sure."

"That doesn't sound like you at all," I said with a smile.

He let out a small chuckle. Then his serious expression returned.

"I'll bet you and your brother were good kids," he said. "You know, I think it's better not to be raised around too much money. Then it has some meaning for you, when you get it. I went to the best private school in Boston...did you know that? But I wasn't interested. I've been interested in the same two things for as long as I can remember. Women and liquor.

"Seriously," he said. "That's my trouble. I know that." He started smiling now. "You know, my first experience with the opposite sex was when I was eleven years old. My nanny had a daughter, and she would come over sometimes after her school. We played doctor one time...can you believe it? Eleven years old. And I was interested in that stuff...I can remember it. That's all I thought about in school all day for the next few weeks, was when I was going to get a chance to play doctor with her again. I could never keep my mind on studying, in high school either. How'd you do it?"

"I wasn't in high school for all that long," I said quietly. "I had to quit to go to work." I could tell that this took him by surprise.

"I'll bet you did better than I did," was all he said. "I'll bet you would've jumped at a chance to go to college."

I didn't answer. I'd never really thought about it, actually. Something told me it would have been a waste of time. Colleges should save room for people like Gertrude, who really wanted to go and could do well.

"The first time I raided my old man's liquor cabinet..." he started, studying the ceiling of the car in thought. "I was about thirteen or so. I never did stop, after that. I couldn't believe it when they outlawed the stuff. What were you thinking when you heard that?"

"I guess I really couldn't believe it either," I said.

"It didn't seem fair to me, somehow," he said.

I nodded. I suddenly felt close to him. We were allies against the rest of the world, and we could depend on each other. It was a silly thought, I know, but it just came upon me as we sat there in silence. I looked toward the window. The afternoon sun was beginning to dip toward the ground, out across the trees. Sunlight was streaming into the car from the side, resting on the faces and raised newspapers. Tiny dust particles swam around in the rays of light. The bottom half of Ambrose's face was touched by the sunlight now, and I could see a few hairs on his chin that had escaped his razor.

"Well," I said. "I hope this vacation has been…has been all right, for you. I know Greenwood isn't the most fun place."

"My whole life's been a vacation for a while," he said with a little laugh. "I've been a mess for a little while," he said.

I kept nodding.

"Really…you wouldn't believe it. I know every damn speakeasy in every city in New England. I've been in trouble since the war. I have. I've been with a bad crowd…I know that. And I've been pretty much drunk the whole time…just gambling and getting in trouble, all up and down the coast."

"Sounds like Greenwood is just what you needed," I said. I don't think he was listening, though.

"I inherited a lot," he said then. "From him. And it's all gone. I'll bet you didn't know that. I don't have anything left. I threw it away. That's why I'm here. I've got nothing…just the clothes I brought. I even sold my car back home."

I wondered what my Mother and my Aunt would say if they knew.

"What about your mother?" I asked.

"She doesn't know how bad it is," he said. "A lot of it was just bad investments…when everyone was doing bad, after the war. And I don't want her help. I'm too old for that."

He sat there, slumped over in the unforgiving light of the sun. That kind of money was something I didn't understand. Maybe he was right about being better off not growing up with it.

I realized that almost everything I'd thought about him had been a lie. I thought about the day we'd looked at the car that was for sale. He had truly acted the part. And now that I thought about it, I realized that I had never really seen him buy anything while he was here, except for liquor. His clothes were very nice, but he had brought them all from home.

"You'll get it straightened out," I said.

"Sure," he said. He gave me a smirk then. It was the same crooked, confident smile he had shown me so many times. I remembered it from the time he brought out his cane at the church social, the time at Drake's house, and even that first night when he'd come in through my window. He turned away then, looking out the window on the other side of the car. His head tipped back and rested on the bench. He was done talking.

That was the first time he really talked to me. I hadn't even missed it before, because he'd seemed just like a rowdy friend come to visit. But now I wished that I had known more of my family growing up.

I turned and looked out the window now. The sky was a mixture of orange and bright pink. I couldn't believe how flat everything was here. There was nothing but an occasional squared off field of corn or wheat or something. Every once in a while I caught sight of a barn, and wondered what it would be like to live out here. I imagined a pretty girl, living on one of these farms, hidden away from everyone else. I could come and take her away, and show her the places she'd never seen. But I knew she'd probably choose to be with some guy over on the next farm, so she'd never have to go anywhere. People were like that. Maybe that's why I liked Ambrose so much. When I had come up with the crazy idea of jumping on this train, he was right there with me.

Now all the questions rose up again. What would we find there? What would we do? If we even found this Murdoch, what would we say to him? I had no idea. I tried to force it from my mind again. I concentrated on the window. I slid closer to it, trying to fill my entire field of vision with the swiftly moving scenery. But each time I got close enough, my breath formed a circle of white steam on the window, and I couldn't see.

I turned back toward Ambrose, but he was still staring out the other side. I thought about asking him for his newspaper, but I didn't want to disturb him. Then I remembered that I had Gertrude's book in my pocket. I decided to read it now, while I still had some sunlight. I knew that we would have to eat down in the dining car before we went to sleep in our seats tonight. I should've been hungry by now. I wondered how far we had traveled already.

It was a fairly new book, I could tell, and it wasn't really that long. I was expecting one like the others I'd read, but it wasn't like them at all. It wasn't even a story. Instead, the author was talking about a lot of other stories that I'd never heard of. These stories were full of people with very strange names. Even the author wasn't sure how to spell these names, and she kept giving different ways to spell them. Maybe Gertrude had read the stories themselves that were being discussed. I certainly hadn't. And yet, I liked it, but I'm not sure why.

There was one part that was all about cards, all of a sudden, in the middle of the book. At first it was about a strange set of cards with seventy or so different faces. Then she was talking about real playing cards, and how hearts represented a cup or chalice, and diamonds a lance or wand, and spades a sword, and clubs meant dishes or pentangles. I didn't know what a pentangle was, but it was amazing to me. I had never thought about the four suits in a deck of cards and where they came from. I thought back to all the times I'd played cards, including the times we played over in France.

I got Ambrose's attention and told him about what the four suits represented. He didn't seem as enthusiastic about it as I was, though, so I went back to reading. There was an element of the book that was frightening, somehow. It's difficult to describe. The things that were being discussed didn't quite seem real, but they didn't seem like fiction either.

I liked reading about one hero, named either Gawain or Bleheris, who had undertaken a journey without really knowing what his task was or where he was going. He was taking the place of another knight who was killed or something. He wasn't really successful, though. There was a question he was supposed to ask, but he didn't. If he would have known the question, he could have restored the land, which was ruined. The land was dead, and nothing would grow in it. Everything had died because of the death of the knight, but they didn't know the real identity of the dead knight.

But then in another version of the story they did know who the dead knight was, and his name was Goondesert, or Gondefer, and he was the brother of the king. There were all sorts of different versions of this same story. People back then must have told it to each other in different ways. They could have changed it around every time if they wanted to. And now, in the modern age, this author was trying to piece it together, trying to make sense of it and see what the real message was. And she said that the only thing she knew for sure was that in the original story, one figure was dead, and the task that they undertook was to bring him back to life.

There were religious parts in it, too. She talked about Jesus and someone called The Fisher King. It was strange, but she talked about these things as if Jesus was just a story, like all of these other stories. She felt that some things may be more true than others, but what really counts is the story. She talked about fertility gods, and ancient rituals. At certain parts she seemed to be saying that these old stories were a lot like the stories about Jesus. She was even saying that a lot of stories aren't new at all, and they just come from older ones.

There was a lot of talk about quests, and a great place called the "Chapel Perilous." I wondered why people didn't write stories like this anymore. I wanted to read this story itself, instead of just reading about it. But that wouldn't have captured it, somehow. Part of what was so neat about it was all of the different versions. I couldn't tell which one was right and which one was wrong, because no one knew, so they could all be right. It made me feel good to read, because I thought of myself as on a quest now. Sitting there on that train didn't seem quite so silly while I was reading. Men had gone on quests for a long time. The quests were what was important. A lot of people didn't ever go on one. And here I was, taking one of my own.

Ambrose tapped me after a while and asked if I wanted to get something to eat. I was suddenly aware of a gnawing hunger in my stomach. The sun was much nearer the horizon, and the light had been fading, even though I hadn't noticed that either. I tried to talk to him some more about the book as we went into the dining car.

There were a few tables available now, so we sat down at a little one, complete with miniature white tablecloth. He was listening to me, but I could tell that he wasn't really that interested. When I'd first pulled out the book he looked at me as if I was crazy. I asked him if this was the sort of thing they read about in college, but he said no, the things they read were much more boring, as far as he could remember.

He started talking to me about Fatty Arbuckle and the girl he had supposedly murdered. He must've just read something about it in the paper. I wasn't really listening very closely, though. Then he started telling me about something that had been invented by two cops in California. He even showed me the quote about it in the paper. It was a machine that measured pulse rate, sweating, and breathing to tell if someone was lying or not. I didn't fully believe it, though, and I told him so.

I ordered a salmon steak. I turned the little fillet over with my fork, studying the silvery scales underneath the pink meat. I imagined this fish swimming only a short while ago, somewhere on the Earth.

After the meal I sat back in my chair, feeling very content. Ambrose was talking to me about the World Series now. Both New York teams were in it that year. I was listening, but I was also wrapped up in thoughts of my own. I thought about all the things from the book. I felt like a wise man who had seen a lot of life. What I was undergoing here wasn't a silly chase after revenge, it was a quest for the truth.

"What exactly are we gonna do when we get there?" Ambrose asked now, looking at me over his glass. He looked around and then poured some of the liquid from his flask into the glass when no one was looking.

"Well," I said. "Dunville can't be a very large place. We'll just start asking people if they've ever heard of him."

"What if it's bigger than you think?" he asked. "What if they haven't heard of him? He's hiding, right?"

"I'm not sure," I said. "Maybe he's not really hiding. What would he be hiding from down here? No one's going to come looking for him. He must think he's in the clear by now."

"But he's not," Ambrose said, eyebrows arched.

Back in our seats, I took the book up again. I quickly became engrossed in the author's account of a certain tribe in Africa. It caught my attention right away because the king of the tribe had a lot of wives. I'd heard of that type of thing before, with sultans and kings far away, but I never really knew if it was true or just stories. But now here it was in a book, so I knew it must be true. I thought about what it would be like to be married to a bunch of different women, and to be able to go to whichever one you wanted on any particular night. The other ones wouldn't even really care because it was all legal. To those people it was normal, and having only one wife might seem strange to them. I thought about who I would pick to be my wives. As king, of course, they would have to say yes. It would be an honor.

I was looking out the window at the darkness of night now, making up a list of my wives in my head. Ambrose was further down in the car, talking with a few businessmen. They were playing cards now, I could see. I'm sure Ambrose had offered them a nip from his flask and they'd dealt him into the game immediately. They didn't know they were playing with lances and cups and pentangles.

When I returned to the book, I found that things were more complicated with the king than I first thought. He was a lot older than most of his wives, but when the time came that he could no longer satisfy them, they would actually report to the chiefs of the tribe and let them know about it. Then, one day while the king was taking a nap in the middle of the day, these chiefs would go and spread a white cloth over his face and one over his knees. And once he was marked like this, they'd come along and take him into a special hut, and kill him. And the author of the book didn't even know how they did it. She thought maybe they strangled him, but no one really knew.

So the king got to have a lot of wives, but this was the price he paid. This was their way of knowing when he was too old and it was time for a new king. So the wives had some power anyway. I imagined the pressure he must have had each time he went to see a wife as he got older. He probably went less and less, but he couldn't hide it forever. Maybe if he was really nice he could get his wives to keep it a secret for a while.

I wondered how it must have felt for him to wake up in a world of close whiteness, knowing that the cloth was draped over his face. What would it feel like in that one instant when he recognized what it was that they had put over his face? How would it feel to be picked like that? To wake up and know that was your day?

I wanted to talk to Ambrose about it. His back was to me, though, and he was involved in the card game. I hoped he wasn't betting money he didn't have. We had brought some with us, but not enough for him to gamble any away. I watched the men in the game for a little while. They were quiet and serious, and then whenever a hand was played they would grow louder with laughter or anger. Somehow, I knew that they wouldn't understand if I tried to tell them about the king. They wouldn't appreciate it.

My eyes were growing tired now, and I put the book away. It was almost pitch black outside now. Every once in a while the twisted shapes of trees would jump into being out of the darkness and then fade again. My eyelids grew heavier and heavier. I tried to keep them open. I thought about my Mother again, and Ambrose and his family, and Henry and Murdoch, and the king with his white cloth.

I nodded off sometime after that, and almost immediately I found myself in the midst of a bizarre dream.

The first part of it centered around Dr. Crowe. He was laid out somewhere. He was dead, I knew. His eyes were closed, and his hands were folded peacefully over his chest. I don't remember him wearing anything in particular, but his pocket watch chain was there, and it was very large. It was a huge, thick chain made of golden links, a sparkling version of the rusted old chains that I used to drag across the train yard. The other end of the chain was attached to some sort of shining, golden object. It glowed brightly, but I can't remember what it was exactly, or if it was anything in particular at all. His face looked sunken and strange, and his features appeared to sink in even more each time I looked at him, so I tried not to look, but I had to.

Kate was there, too. She was talking to me, maybe about Dr. Crowe. But I couldn't hear her. Her lips were moving, but I couldn't hear anything. I just acted like I could understand her. And I knew somehow that she was his wife. They had been married.

I tried to touch her but she crumbled in front of me. She was made out of dirt, I saw, and she became mixed in with the ground, so I couldn't find her anymore. I was running across the dirt then. It was a field of some kind. I looked down and saw that I had my rifle. People were shooting at me. And I tried to move out of the way, but I moved too slowly. There was a ton of bricks in each of my boots, and I could barely lift my legs to move them. I couldn't see who was shooting at me.

The whole field was dirt. I fell down, and the dirt was in my eyes and my mouth. I looked around, and saw that there were no trees or grass anywhere. Everything was dead, and covered with this thin, powdery dirt. It was like sand now, filling my mouth. I kept trying to spit it out.

And then I was back where I'd been at the beginning, I think, although I don't really know where that was. And I knew that it was the old people's fault. I blamed Dr. Crowe and all of them, because I knew the whole thing had been a plot. The old men had invented a war, and sent all of the young men to go fight in it and kill each other, so they could take all the young women while we were gone. I would realize that it didn't make sense when I woke up, but during the dream, it all seemed perfectly clear.

I wished I had my rifle but I didn't have it anymore. I couldn't find it anywhere. I went over to look at Dr. Crowe lying there, but it wasn't him anymore. Now it was my father.

When I was young, and they told me that my father had died down at the docks, I imagined what he would look like dead. And that was exactly what I saw before me now. His beard was there, and his huge chest, but he had no eyes. They were missing. If your eyes were open you were alive, and if they were closed you were asleep, but when I was young I hadn't known what they were when you were dead. So he didn't even have them anymore. They were gone. There were just two empty eyeholes. From the side, it reminded me of the two of spades.

I suddenly noticed that I was awake now, and I was staring into the darkness of the window next to me. The lights in the car were off, Ambrose was across from me, his eyes closed, his mouth open wide and his arm flung out to one side across the bench. The flask was in his hand, and he was breathing peacefully. I turned back to the window, but the only thing I could see in the glass was the glimmering reflection of my own eye. I blinked it a few times, studying it. I promised myself that I would remember my dream and write it down somewhere when I got back.

The train made a few stops the next morning at small towns, and I knew we were getting closer to our destination. A few families got on. It was Friday now and people were going places for the weekend.

It was still morning when we pulled into Dunville, and Ambrose and I got off, squinting in the direct sunlight. We hadn't eaten anything, so we walked into the first restaurant we saw, which was a little wood building next to the train station. I was tired and hungry from the ride. I had slept fitfully all night, tossing and turning myself against the hard wooden bench.

The restaurant looked ancient. The flowered wallpaper was yellowed, and the whole place was no bigger than a small living room. In fact, there were stairs leading up on one side of the room, and I guessed that the family that owned the place probably lived up there.

A young woman brought us glasses of dirty water. She had bright blue eyes and crooked teeth. She told us what was available today.

Ambrose seemed to have slept just fine, and was apparently in the mood for a feast. But even he, who never passed up the opportunity to speak to a girl, didn't have much to say to this one. He ordered a bowl of buttered rolls and a leg of lamb. I ate some of the bread, but I didn't really feel like anything else. He convinced me that I should be well fed though, for whatever was in store for us that day. So I ordered some chicken, too.

The food was good, and I began to feel better as I ate. Ambrose seemed cheerful and completely at ease. He traveled a lot, I remembered. I started to tell him about my dream, but I could tell that he wasn't really finding it very interesting.

"So should I ask this gal?" he asked me, a forkful of dark lamb meat in his hand.

"What?" I said. "Ask her what?"

"About Murdoch," he said. "Should I ask if she knows him?"

Somehow I hadn't thought that we would be starting in on it this soon.

"Sure," I said.

But she just looked confused when Ambrose asked her. She pulled her upper lip shut over the teeth, thinking. Then she decided that she didn't know who that was.

We left the little house and walked out into the street. The whole town was nothing but old wooden houses, with their first floors converted into stores. It was a much smaller town than Greenwood. There was an elevated walk made of wooden planks that led between a lot of the little buildings, and I could see that the street was mostly mud. There were two rather thin horses tied to a post across the street. The outline of their ribs shone through the shiny skin of their gaunt bellies. I could see flies buzzing around them even from here.

A very old man sat outside of another of the stores, his chair tipped back. He looked as if he hadn't shaved in years. He watched us carefully. I heard heavy footsteps on the planks, and turned to see another man carrying a large box of something from one storefront to another. Aside from that, there was no one around. It was as if the town was deserted. I wondered what Ambrose thought of the place. We didn't say much, but I'm sure he was thinking the same things I was.

Why would Murdoch want to live in a place like this? I saw a few buildings that looked like old saloons and taverns, though, and I started to realize that this might be the sort of place that came alive at night. I saw a man wiping tables in one of these buildings as we passed. Maybe being in the middle of nowhere had its advantages.

"What do you think?" I asked Ambrose, who noticed the tavern as well.

"Looks like it's open," he said.

"Could they get away with that?" I asked.

"I guess so," was his answer. "Probably aren't a lot of state authorities coming down here."

"Maybe we should ask that guy," I said, nodding toward the man I'd seen through the open door.

He nodded in agreement, and we crossed the street.

It was a tavern, all right. The interior was dark, but the bar and tables were arranged neatly and there was no booze in sight. I'm sure it was hidden during the day. I wondered if they just paid off the county sheriff, or if they had to keep the door closed at night, like a speakeasy. The man we'd seen was nowhere in sight now, but I could see the clean surface of the dark wood table where he'd just rubbed it.

"Hello?" asked Ambrose into the room as he leaned on the bar. He looked ready to order a drink.

The man came around the corner. He still held the greasy rag, but he was using it to clean a glass now. He had a very thin mustache, and was small and wiry all around. His black hair was oiled back tightly against his skull and his thin arms were lost in the sleeves of his white shirt.

"Yes?" he asked with a deeper voice than I'd expected. He kept looking back and forth between the two of us. One of his eyes looked in a slightly different direction than the other.

"Actually," Ambrose began. "I'm wondering if I can get something to drink."

The man looked at him now, his other eye pointing somewhere on the far wall. His forehead furrowed, and then he smiled thinly, and shook his head back and forth in a slow, pronounced way.

We waited for him to say something, and then realized that he wasn't going to. That was his answer.

"Well then," Ambrose said, smiling now. "We're new in town and we're looking for a friend. We served with a fella in the war who's from around here, and I'm just wondering if you can help us out…just let us know where he lives."

The man kept looking at him in silence. Then he raised his eyebrows and shrugged a little, as if waiting to hear the name.

"His name is Tommy Murdoch," he said.

The good eye focused on me now. He looked deep in thought, but then started to shake his head slowly.

"Nope," he said.

"You don't know him?" asked Ambrose.

"I don't know everybody's name," the man said. "But I never heard of 'im." He shrugged a little again, and then started to move toward the back.

Ambrose walked away from the bar and back toward me, as if ready to go.

"Wait," I said. He stopped, and so did the man. "Have you ever heard of the Pilford sisters?"

Ambrose turned back toward him now, and we both watched his eyes scan the room in thought, each one looking somewhere else. Then he started shaking his head slowly again.

"Two sisters," I said. "They're young and very pretty." Ambrose was looking at me now as if it was time to give up. "One has darker hair and is a little taller than the other. The other one has lighter hair…short hair. But they look pretty similar…they're sisters."

I could tell immediately that he knew them. He still looked confused, but something had lit up. The slow shaking of his head stopped.

"I seen 'em," he said. "I think so. I seen 'em around town," he continued.

"Do they live here?" I asked.

"Not all the time. They come and go."

"Where do they come and go?"

He opened his mouth, as if about to tell us, but then it shut slowly and he looked us up and down suspiciously.

"This friend we're looking for is their brother," I said. "I just thought you'd have remembered seeing them if you haven't seen him."

"Didn't know they had a brother," he said quietly. I shot a glance at Ambrose, but his eyes were on the man.

"Their brother lives here," I said. "Maybe they've come and gone to his house."

"Yeah," he nodded again, wiping the glass in his hand absently. "There's a place a little bit east, down the road. Take a right when you see the fence at Foster's land. It's down next to the river. On the river."

"Thanks," I said. When we got back across the street, I could still see him through the doorway, standing there and staring at us with his mismatched eyes.

"You think the girls are here?" Ambrose asked.

"Maybe," I said. "It was just something I thought of…they had to be connected to him."

"Well, they'd have no other reason to come here. If he's seen them here, that's where Murdoch is."

We followed the man's directions down the road and past the rest of the makeshift town. It wasn't long before we came to a little turn-off in the road, near a corner of land that was fenced in with wires. There were no markings, but it must have been the farm he'd mentioned.

We could hear the river before we actually saw it. As soon as we rounded the corner and it came into sight, we saw the house as well. The river flowed through the trees beyond it. There must have been some rocks or an outcropping, because we could hear the water splashing behind the house.

The house itself sat right up against the water, just as the man had told us. It was made of large stone bricks that rose up out of the dirt, which made it difficult to tell where the ground ended and the old house began. There was something European about it. I wondered how long this little structure had been here.

There were a few windows, but as we approached we could see that they were all heavily curtained, and the shades were drawn. Perhaps the Pilfords lived here and the place had nothing to do with Murdoch, I thought. That would be an awful coincidence, though. We had come pretty far, and I knew that we'd probably find what we were looking for in here.

We reached the front door and looked at each other, and I realized how ill prepared we were for this. What if Murdoch answered the door? What were we going to say? What if he wasn't here and the Pilfords were?

I imagined myself stepping up to Murdoch, and telling him that I knew everything, and that it was my brother that he had killed over there. But I had a hard time picturing myself doing that. What would his reaction be? What would I do if he admitted it? Part of me hoped that ten of Jack's friends were inside to beat us up and throw us on a train back home. That would have ended it, at least. Looking back in retrospect, I can only wish that it had been that simple.

Ambrose was obviously waiting for me to knock. I reached up and pounded on the door.

We stood there, listening to the water cutting its way through the woods behind the house. I turned to Ambrose, who was still eyeing the door. What if we had come all this way and there was no one here?

"Did you see that?" Ambrose asked, his voice startling me.

"What?"

"That window right there. The curtains moved…I think someone was looking out."

I looked past him at the window. The curtains were dead still, and there was no sign of movement.

"Are you sure?" I asked.

"I saw them move," he said. "Like someone was looking. I'm telling you, they moved."

I knocked again, but still there was no answer. It seemed as if ten minutes passed. My mind was a blank.

I jumped, hearing a sound from behind the door. Then there was another muffled sound. Someone was inside. Were they scrambling around? Preparing for something? Ambrose reached up and knocked loudly, making three quick raps with the meat of his fist.

And the door opened.

I saw a row of beaming, yellowish teeth smiling out at us, and two eyeballs of the same yellowish white. The shape of a person formed itself in front of me, behind the teeth and eyes. It was a Negress, and the room behind her was shrouded in darkness. Her clothes were dark as well, but she wore a red cloth wrapped around the top of her head, and this one spot of color floated above her in the blackness.

"Come in," she said. Her voice was soft, and it seemed disembodied. She was still smiling broadly.

I cut a sideways glance at Ambrose, whose brow was furrowed in confusion. He was ready to enter first, but I pushed in front of him a little. By now I was wondering if the man at the tavern had played some sort of trick on us, or if we had taken a wrong turn somewhere.

There was a moldy, cavernous smell inside the house. The curtains had been drawn entirely. I couldn't see anything. I moved down a hallway, the red cloth head bouncing along in front of me, Ambrose behind. I could hear my own heart pounding in my ears. I had my hands at my sides now, ready for anything. Still, I realized, there was no way Murdoch could have known that I was coming, or even who I was.

Ahead, at the end of the short hall, I could see a room. The bouncing, flickering light inside had to be coming from candles. The woman led us inside, and then she disappeared into the room somewhere.

I'll attempt to convey the things I took in, in the order that I saw them. It's amazing how much I can remember, to this day.

There were furnishings around the edges of the room, and lit candles sat on many of them. The room itself had no windows, but there was a mirror on the far wall. It hung directly in front of me, and at first, through the shadows, I thought that someone else was standing over there, his face lit by flickering candlelight, looking back at me. It was me, of course, but I barely recognized myself.

Dominating the center of the room was a large round table. A number of golden candelabras sat in the center, all lit and giving the room an eerie glow. Several people were seated at the table. I saw the Pilfords right away, their faces lit by the dancing light just as I'd seen them back in my own house. They both looked serious now, but they were staring at a point somewhere above the center of the table, rather than looking up at us. A shiver of electric coldness danced up my back.

On the other side of the table a man was seated. I didn't recognize him at first, although I should have. This was the guy with the light hair and strange accent who had driven away with the Pilfords. It was the man who had led us to Jack's rally. He, too, was staring at the center of the room, ignoring us completely.

The Negress floated back into my vision briefly now. She was in the corner of the room, and I saw now that the front of her body bulged out at an impossible angle. She was very pregnant. The dark cloths she wore were wrapped tightly around the round package of her stomach, just as the colored cloth was twisted around her head. I watched as she slowly reached out of the shadows and put out one of the candles by pinching the end of the wick. It was as if the shadows themselves came together to form a hand, black as night, that extinguished one of the flames. Then she sat down in an empty chair at the table, as close to it as she could pull herself with her protruding belly. Her skin seemed to shine in the dim light. She didn't act as if she was a servant of any kind.

And then there was the central figure. A man sat there, bathed in candlelight. He alone was staring right at me, a strange, uncontrolled smirk on his face, the architect of it all.

In the days to come Ambrose and I discussed what went through our minds as we entered that room, so much so that I can remember it now as I saw it, and also as he saw it. He looked around a little, frightened as I was, and he saw the two beautiful feminine faces that simply must have been the sisters I'd discussed, as well as the other mysterious woman. The man with light hair he may or may not have realized was the same one we'd followed before. But at the center, seated and looking at both of us, he saw Tommy Murdoch. He saw a young man with dark hair, and almost right away Ambrose remembered him. He remembered the way that he had talked about the war and asked how a life policy would work for a soldier who had been unfortunately killed. He remembered the way that the deep, brown eyes had looked at him unsteadily as he answered. And here was Murdoch now, seated before him at this bizarre table in this inexplicable little house.

Of course, I can never fully convey all of the things that I felt as I stood there and engaged the eyes of the central figure. His features swam in the murky darkness, but the pattern remained in the dim light of the tiny fires around him. This was not Tommy Murdoch. Seated before me, alive and well and returning my gaze, was my brother Henry.

CHAPTER 36

I was paralyzed. After all this time, I thought I'd forgotten the details of his face. But now, here he was, right in front of me. And those details all came rushing back, as if he'd never been gone.

I couldn't look at him. I had to look away, above his head. And I was greeted with the sight of my own face in the mirror. He had never looked that much like me. Now that the two faces floated in the darkness in front of me, one above the other, I was able to see that. The eyes were the same, and so was the hair. But aside from that, his face resembled that of my Mother in certain ways that mine did not. The face that stared back at me from the dim reflective surface of the mirror was shrouded in shadow. It was utterly devoid of expression, as well. The eyelids looked halfway shut, and the lips drooped in defeat. Or was that just a trick of the light? People had told me that I resemble my father, but I had never really known what they were talking about. Now I saw it, though. The face in the mirror looked utterly dead, just like my father's own face in my dream of the night before. I didn't have the beard, of course, but the eyes and the mouth were both just gaping holes of emptiness, filled with nothing but shadows.

I could feel Ambrose's eyes on me now, as well. He had turned toward me, waiting to see what action I would take. He cleared his throat expectantly. I realized that he had no way of knowing who was sitting before us. There hadn't been any pictures of Henry in our house during the time he'd lived with us.

I had to act. The room was waiting to see what I would do. I had to reach down and pull myself out of this paralysis. I felt a strong urge to just fold in on myself, to find the center of my own being there in the warm darkness. Was I about to faint? I don't usually think of myself as being that feminine. I was a bit dizzy, though. They were all waiting for me. I turned back to Henry, and gave a little nod of acknowledgment. This seemed to snap him out of his own spell, as well.

"Please sit down," he said. He was indicating two empty chairs at the round table, directly in front of us. I hadn't heard his voice in years, and yet the memory of it came flowing back as if I'd been speaking with him yesterday.

There was something in the calm way he had said it that made me angry, though. I didn't know what all this showiness was for, the candles and the darkness and these people. My shock slowly subsided into rage, and the anger felt good. It flowed through me, coursing and pumping, looking for a way out. I stepped forward and threw one of the chairs over on its side.

Ambrose stepped forward as well, ready for a fight that he had no way of knowing was now impossible. The act of throwing the chair made everyone in the room look at me now. Perhaps they hadn't been expecting that. Eleanor and Beth were both staring at me blankly now. Their empty eyes only stoked the furnace of my emotion.

"What the hell is this?" I asked, indicating the room and everyone in it. Henry glanced down at the tabletop. He looked embarrassed at my behavior. No one answered. A few moments passed. I hated the silence now. I hated every mysterious moment of silence. "Ambrose," I said loudly, "This is my brother Henry."

I kept my eyes on Henry, but I knew Ambrose was looking between us, back and forth. His confusion was palpable.

"We've met," said Henry then, his own voice still calm. "Sit down and I'll explain it all."

"No," I said again. "We're not gonna do it this way…not this show you've put together. I don't know who all these people are, but tell them to get the hell outta here."

"You can't talk that way to us in our own home," he said quietly.

I lifted the chair I had overturned, and heaved it, over my head, across the room. There was a small table in the corner that was covered with lit candles and what looked like drinking glasses. In an explosion of light and sound, the chair collided with it and the table was smashed in on itself. Everyone stood, their own chairs pushed back. Their faces floated just above the circles of light made by the candles. I hoped that whatever they had planned wasn't working out, and that they were surprised. A glass rolled away from the splintered remains in the corner, slowly making its way across the room.

My heart was pounding violently, and I could feel a film of sweat on my forehead and the palms of my hands. Then the man with the light hair was moving suddenly. He strode around the table toward me, ready for a fight. Ambrose stepped forward swiftly and crushed the man's jaw with his fist. The next thing I knew, the man was on the ground looking up at us, a trickle of blood flowing from his nose and across his lips.

"All right, all right," Henry said loudly. He looked at the corner, where Eleanor and the Negress were picking up shards of glass and overturned candles. They worked quietly and diligently. It reminded me of my own Mother and Aunt, silently cleaning up after us when we had done something wrong as children. Was this some sort of strange family? He had called it "our house," hadn't he?

"Come on," he was saying now, stepping around the table. "We'll go in here." He glanced toward the other man, who was standing again, holding his nose, eyes stabbing into us like daggers.

Henry led us around the table and toward a back door. As I passed, Beth stood there, staring at me with her dumb, lifeless face. I turned and stared back, and her eyes narrowed like those of an animal. I fully expected her to bear fangs of some kind, or let out a hiss. But she also looked like a little girl, with her face screwed up and wrinkled with anger. And I thought of her then, operating her scam in my own living room, with the trust and admiration of my Mother and my Aunt. The whole room became silently poisoned by her presence, then. I couldn't reconcile this foulness with the existence of the two old women who lived with me. Henry's back was turned, and I couldn't help myself as I passed. I reached out with one hand and connected with Beth's breastbone, just below the neck, and I gave her a shove, right back into her chair. She landed in it with a thud, eyes narrowing even more.

My heart was pounding so loudly in my ears that it felt as if my entire being was pulsating, and I was nothing but one large heart. I braced myself, thinking that this shove would make the other man attack again. But he didn't. I just followed Henry the rest of the way out of the room. And when I think back now, I couldn't be happier that I decided to push her like that.

He led us out a door and around a little corner, still in darkness. There was another door ahead, though, and light came from beneath it. We stepped through it and back outside. It was a relief to be out of the stifling atmosphere of the little house. I had been strangled by something in there, and now I felt as if I could think again.

We were standing on a small wooden deck behind the house. The river gurgled below, and the trees of the forest rose all around. The afternoon sun streamed through them, now, and its finger of light almost reached us, but fell short a few feet from the edge of the wooden planks. To our right was a massive water wheel, but it was still and dead. Its wooden surface was crumbling. Rotten pieces of the wood hung there, covered with roots and plants that had broken the wheel apart from the inside.

I examined him in the light of day. He looked a little older, I thought, or maybe it was just that I hadn't seen him in so long. The bottom half of his face was dark, and he obviously hadn't shaved in a few days. His hair was a little longer, maybe. But aside from that, he looked just as I'd remembered him. He wore flannel pants and oxfords and a simple white shirt. The top few buttons were open.

Ambrose stood there too, looking around at the woods and then back at Henry and me.

"You didn't recognize me, cousin?" Henry asked him.

"No," he said, his level eyebrows furrowed in confusion. A strand of hair touched one of his eyelids, but he ignored it, as if he didn't even notice. All three of us had the same sort of thin, brown hair.

"That's because they've got no pictures of me around," Henry said with a little smile, leaning against the splintered wooden railing. Then he turned back to me. "How would you like it…if they hid any pictures of you after you were gone? Some family," he spat. "They don't even talk about me, do they?" His eyes were narrow like Beth's.

"You have no right to say any of these things," I said, thinking of my Mother.

I thought of the Pilfords spying on our own house for him, and telling him that she put the picture away after each seance. I thought about the day I stood at his grave, or the grave that I thought was his. It's a strange experience to stand at someone's grave and then see them alive years later. I can't really describe it, aside from saying that it felt as if the ground had fallen out from beneath me.

"You're not happy I'm alive at all," he said to me. "I didn't think it'd be like this. You think I had a choice?"

"I think you need to explain yourself." I said it loudly and forcefully.

He nodded, smiling a little.

"All right," he said calmly. "All right." He scratched at the stubble on his face. Fingers just like mine. I had forgotten that.

He turned away then, looking down at the stream, deep in thought. The old stone of the house just sat there, still.

"I met Tom Murdoch at the end of training camp," he began, still looking out over the river. "That's who you thought you'd find here, right?

"I had no idea who he was. I'd never seen him before in my life. He was from a little town in Massachusetts. He told me all about it. Said he'd just finished school, he was gonna take over the family business. He told me about an uncle he had…who'd been a professional strikebreaker in the Anthracite strike of ought-two. I don't think that was true, though. I guess maybe that was his way of trying to get me to talk about my own job. I didn't really say too much about it, though. I didn't pay that much attention to what we talked about. I should've. But I didn't know who he was.

"I'd had some trouble in Greenwood. Right before the war. It was about the labor union…down at the factory. There were a lot of, a lot of things going on," he shrugged. "I'd made some enemies there…some things just went wrong. I thought the war was gonna be a break with all that. A way to get away from it for a while. I needed to get away. I was never gonna go back to work there. After the war I was gonna find work somewhere else. Some job with no unions, where I wouldn't have to deal with it. Something quiet. But I didn't know how serious things were already."

He shifted his weight, and turned back toward the house. He must have known how bad everything was before the war. Why hadn't he said anything? He looked small to me, now, somehow. It was as if he had grown larger in my memory since he'd been gone. I had forgotten that he had always been a head shorter than me, and much thinner.

"They put a bounty on me, I guess," he continued. "I'd made enemies with the wrong guys. It's so silly…all of it. There are guys who take it way too seriously. Most of 'em do. Can you imagine killing someone over your job?"

The question hung in the air for a while. Ambrose picked at the splintered wood of the railing, and a bird of some kind squawked in the distance. I saw in Henry's face the young boy I'd spent most of my life with. There was fear in his voice, though. It surprised me. He wasn't in control of everything, and perhaps he never had been.

"Murdoch was the guy who collected it. He set it all up…to get near me and kill me, during the war. That was the only way he could get away with it. We had a lot in common…at least, based on the stuff he told me. He was in my squad, and we got along. I got along with most of the guys. Just about all of 'em are gone now." He coughed a little, and looked at his shoes.

"It happened all of a sudden…there was no way I could've seen it coming. We'd been in a few battles. Just little ones…never anything like the big one that finally did us in. We'd spent the night in a little town somewhere, I don't even know where it was. I haven't looked at a map since I got back. The Kaiser had the area just to the north, and the next day he was supposedly bringing some supplies through. We were gonna stop the supplies from getting down toward the bigger battles. And then, depending on how things were, attack and try to push 'em back…back north, I think.

"I don't know how many battles you saw," he said, looking at me now. He never called me by name. We had rarely ever called each other by name.

"Not many," I said.

"You were lucky. This big one, there was nothing like it. It was contested ground…really both sides just wanted the towns around there. Both sides dropped a lotta bombs. Then ours hit the supply train, and they stopped bombing. We were ordered to charge across this open field to where they were dug in. It was wide open, though…we'd be right there, for everyone to see. None of us wanted to do it. But we had to.

"As soon as we started across, I knew it was a mistake. They started hitting us with everything right away. I didn't think I'd ever make it across." He looked at me now, straight in the eyes, and I fought a shiver. It still felt as if I was talking to a ghost. I thought about everything the sisters had said about the spirit levels and all. It was meaningless, of course, but now, as he stood before me, I realized how much it had sunk in over the past year or so. Part of me had really believed it, I suppose.

"I did make it, though," he went on. "And I slid down toward the trench, too…I think it'd rained the night before. I'd fired some shots while I was running…just shots, out in front of me. So I was out of ammunition by the time I got there. I didn't really fight anyone. Most of 'em ran away. I just looked around for a few seconds, trying to figure out where I needed to go next."

Ambrose lit a cigarette and offered one to Henry. He reached out and took it, and I thought I saw his hand trembling a little. I realized how thin he was now. Everything about him was small and narrow. Ambrose lit it for him, and he continued, blowing the smoke in a cool, straight stream out in front of him. I'd never seen him smoke before. Maybe he always had, though.

"Once we'd cleared across the field, they started bombing it. I think it was our guys…they probably thought it was a minefield. Maybe it was. They started dropping 'em everywhere…pretty close to where we were now. And we couldn't tell who it was that was doing the bombing, but they were doing a pretty messy job," he blew more smoke. "All I remember is looking up, and I saw Murdoch right there, walking toward me," he gestured, the cigarette in his hand. "I couldn't hear anything…my ears were ringing from the bombs. I wanted to yell to him that we needed to find cover…to chase 'em back toward the woods, where our guys'd gone already. He was about as far from me as that tree over there," he indicated a tree not far from the deck.

"Then I saw he was pointing his pistol at me. He was walking toward me, pointing it at me. I thought there was someone behind me or something, so I turned around. But there wasn't. I thought maybe he was just carrying it that way, for some reason. But the thing was, he'd crossed that field with me, and counted my shots, so he knew when I was out. He could've just shot me in the back while we were crossing. But he hadn't. He'd waited 'til he could do it facing me. I think that was part of his deal…to tell me who it was from. I still couldn't hear very well, but he was talking to me…I could see that. And then I swear he said 'Jack Wolfe.' That was the name of a guy back home who was involved in all the stuff, that I'd had trouble with. That's all I could hear, but right away I knew what it was all about. There was nothing else he could've said, no other way he could have known who that was. I knew that he was pointing it at me on purpose, and he was gonna shoot me. I was gonna be killed in the middle of a battle over some silly thing from back home. I'd been out there fighting for my life and my country, and I'd forgotten about all that stuff. But here it was, come back to get me. What made it worse was that this guy had been my friend out there, for a while, just waiting for the right time. It seemed really stupid to me…what they'd done. That's the thing I remember thinking as soon as I figured it out."

He was quiet for a few seconds, looking down at the water again. I heard a noise from inside the house that sounded like a heavy piece of furniture being moved. He flicked the ashes from the end of his cigarette over the railing and down below. Ambrose coughed a little, and I heard more birds.

"I was looking right into the hole of the gun," he said. "And people tell you your life flashes before your eyes, and silly stuff like that. But it doesn't, really. I couldn't think of anything at all. That made me mad, too. All I did was wait, and watch that little hole. I was thinking maybe I'd see the bullet come out and have time to get outta the way.

"I was hit, then…something pushed me back, and I slid into the dug-out behind me." He pushed at the air in front of him with his hands, moving them around wildly. "I checked myself down there in the mud…I thought I could find the place where I got shot. But I hadn't been shot. And then I started hearing explosions…more and more of 'em. They were bombing right around us. I stuck my head up real slowly, and Murdoch was gone. Everyone was gone. As soon as I climbed outta there, everyone disappeared. The only things moving were the planes overhead…it sounded like they were buzzing around right on top of me.

"But then I saw him…he was down, on the ground. Right where he'd been standing. He was on his face now, in the mud. One of his legs was torn up pretty bad. It wasn't really there anymore. I knew a bomb must've hit behind him. That's what had hit us. I checked myself again, but I was fine. If that ditch hadn't been there, I don't know if I would be. But it was a German dug-out, and we were on their side of the field, so that's why they were dropping bombs around us. They thought all our boys had already gone past there. Most of 'em had.

"I saw him moving a little. They were still bombing, though, so I wanted to get outta there. But then I saw the sidearm he'd been carrying. It was on the ground, a few feet in front of him. I went right over and picked it up, and as soon as I did, he lifted his head. And I saw the whites of his eyes, looking at me. I could hear again now, and I heard him cursing me, over and over. I didn't know what I was gonna do…I hadn't planned anything. I could've just left him there. He was dead anyway…they were still dropping 'em everywhere, cleaning up the whole place and leaving nothing. I don't know what happened. But I was just so angry then."

He was looking at Ambrose now, as if he truly needed him to understand. He flicked the cigarette butt away, and put his hands in the pockets of his trousers. Ambrose was listening intently, expressionless. I wondered what he was thinking. I saw an intricate spider web in the corner, between the wood and the stone of the house. There was no sign of the spider.

"When I saw the blood and his leg I thought about how this guy probably had a girl, and a mother and everything. So I just looked at his face…it was covered in mud, but the eyes were so white. If he could've killed me by looking at me, he would've."

He paused for a while, looking between us. He coughed a little.

"So I shot him. I just squeezed the trigger, and felt the gun kick, and I did it a couple times. I don't know how many. I just put a few in his back, right there, 'til his head went back in the mud and he shut up. I thought I deserved to. This guy was gonna kill me over some cheap thing from back home.

"I took off into the woods. I knew I'd be dead too if I stayed there. And I watched 'em turn that field into nothing. They hit it over and over, 'til there was nothing left. I couldn't look away, though. I should've been trying to catch up to the rest of my squad. I should've been scared an enemy patrol would come across me sitting there alone. I'd just sat there and thought about how it had felt to kill him. It didn't feel bad, really. That was the only person I killed over there, as far as I know, anyway. Unless I hit somebody else while I was shooting out in front of me.

"It started to get dark, and the bombs stopped. The planes were gone, and the field was empty. I had no idea how far away my squad was by now. I'm sure they were still being ordered to chase the enemy as far as they could. Then I started to think about Murdoch, and this guy Jack. I was wondering if they had anybody else over there…if any other goons in my squad were out to get me over that stuff. I started thinking maybe Murdoch wasn't really dead. Maybe I just thought he was. I started going a little outta my mind, sitting there, I think. I couldn't remember if I'd really shot him or just imagined it. I wanted to get another look.

"I was scared of my own shadow, then. It got dark quick…real dark. It was totally quiet there…silence, like when you're far from everything. It'd been the loudest day of my life, but now there was nothing. I even said a few words out loud, just to make sure that I hadn't lost my hearing. My voice was so hoarse and quiet that I thought for a second that I had. I had to go look at him, though. So I came out of the woods, real slow. I imagined Jack's friends were behind every tree.

"I knew I was in trouble now. If they could reach me there, they could reach me anywhere. I started to worry about everyone, then, about my whole family. I thought they might even come after you," he said, looking at me.

"Once I got to the field, though, I forgot everything. The sky was cloudy, too…the moonlight was pretty dim, so it took a while for me to make out what I saw all around me. Then I really thought I'd died. I started really thinking that I was dead and in hell or something. I saw bones sticking out of the ground. Really. Most of the bodies I saw were just burned out pieces. I didn't even recognize them…as bodies for a while. A few times I swore I was looking at the charred shape of an animal of some kind. They were all men, though. Dead men who'd been thrown around by the bombs.

"I went to where I thought Murdoch was, and I found him eventually. His whole face was gone. His jaw bone'd come off. His head was totally burned. There was a little skin above one of his eyes, and I could even see the little hairs that had been one of his eyebrows. But that was it. I started to think maybe it wasn't him. So I actually got out his identification…I reached into his pockets and everything. It was him.

"When I looked at what was left of him I knew there was no way anyone else could tell it was him without his ID. Something about that gave me hope right away…I think I was already coming up with the idea. I stood up and walked around a little bit more, thinking about where I was gonna spend the night. But I couldn't concentrate on anything. I was totally alone now…and I liked it. I liked it more and more. I didn't want to find the other guys. As far as they knew, I was dead. By now they were probably far away, and they'd heard on the radio that the whole field had been bombed anyway.

"I knew I could escape from everything then. I could walk into the next town, a dead man, and they would have no idea who I was. I don't know, if you were faced with the same thing, what you'd do. My life wasn't perfect, and I'd made some mistakes. But I knew this was my second chance. I should've been shot right there that day, but I was still alive. And now I could start over. Hell, I had to. It was the only way to make sure nobody would keep coming after me for that stuff. That they'd leave my family alone and consider it over and done. I had to make 'em think Murdoch had succeeded. So I switched with him. I just switched our identification. I switched everything I could. Tags and all. They'd find him there, and as far as they knew, that was me, dead."

He looked back and forth between us.

"Hmmm," said Ambrose.

"There's more," Henry went on. "There're certain people back in Greenwood who could tell you about Jack and his boys."

"We know," I said finally.

"Oh," he said, looking at me. "You know about that?"

"I've met Jack…since the war," I said. "We came down looking for Murdoch because we heard he was here. Ralph Lockehart told us we might find him here. That's what he'd heard."

He nodded quietly, clearing his throat.

"Ralph's a good man," he said. "I knew he'd get fed up with it someday."

"So you started telling people you were Murdoch then?" Ambrose asked.

Henry looked at him as if he'd been thinking about something else entirely. Then he started again.

"Well…what happened right away was I walked back the way we'd come…back toward the town, that night. I can't speak French, but I stayed outside the town just watching and listening. I wanted to go talk to someone…to find out what was going on in the war and where I could go. How to get home, maybe. But I couldn't. Something was stopping me. There was something there, now, between me and everyone else. It wasn't just the language, either.

"I was dead, for a while. I wanted to be dead…it felt nice, really. I wandered around outside the town and slept in barns and under trees. It was a few days, I think. Sometimes I'd cover myself with grass so no one would find me all night. Just like being dead and buried, really. The place was so silent…I didn't hear a sound for days at a time, unless I was listening to the noises of the town.

"One night, I swear I heard an entire German squadron march right by me. I was in the woods, covered with sticks and dirt, and I heard 'em. At first it was just voices, but it was German instead of French. I didn't know if I was awake or dreaming at first. But then it got louder, and I knew I was awake but I was too scared to move. I just hoped I was hidden. They marched right by…they walked right over me. There must've been hundreds of 'em. They were carrying big weapons, too. Heavy things. I started thinking maybe I should warn the town. I wondered if the war was over…if all our boys were dead and they were coming through to claim their new country now."

He looked between us.

"You think I went crazy?" The question hung in the air. Finally Henry reached out toward Ambrose for another cigarette, and he passed one over.

"It was impossible…for Germans to be there. I didn't know that at the time. But I swear to you, I heard 'em. An entire army moving through there. It was on a cold night, I remember. I thought I even saw some signs the next morning…some leaves were moved around on the ground. I'd known just where those leaves were.

"I know, you think I was going out of my mind. Maybe I was. Maybe it was a dream." He shook his head, "It was too real, though, I'm telling you. Maybe it was the ghosts of all the Germans who got killed in the field, though…everyone we'd killed and bombed. Maybe that was all of 'em, passing through on their way to wherever.

"I finally went down to the town the next day, just to see if they were real or not. But there was no sign of any Germans at all. Still, if they hadn't marched through there, I might've never gone into town. I don't know how long I'd been by myself. I had some rations with me, and I'd taken some more food from one of the farms. So it might've been a week or more. I really don't know.

"I went into this taverne and got something to drink and eat. I met a fella there who spoke English. He asked if I was a soldier, and we talked about the battle a little. I asked him if there were any Germans left around here, but he didn't understand what I was talking about. And when he asked me my name, I knew I could tell him anything. I didn't have to be me anymore. I told him my name was Tommy Murdoch. It could be me, I thought. To tell the truth, I was still a little confused, I think. I hadn't been eating enough.

"He told me there were some Americans that had been left there when we'd come through. To watch over the town, I guess. Then I got scared again. I was glad I hadn't told anyone my real name. For all I knew, there were more of Jack's thugs waiting for me right there. I had no idea. Maybe Murdoch was supposed to send him word of some kind when the job was done. Maybe they were onto me already, looking for me.

"So I waited, there in the town. I avoided everyone. The man I met had a friend who let me sleep in his barn if I helped out a little with his farm. He didn't even know any English. I almost froze to death every night in his barn, but he wouldn't let me build a fire. I couldn't blame him…I didn't really do that much work. His wife would put out a little food for me when they ate. I have no idea what they thought of me, or who they thought I was. It wasn't long, anyway. About a month, maybe.

"The war was over now, I'd heard. I was sure everyone thought I was dead. I'd avoided American troops at all costs. They'd come back through there, of course. They'd collected what was left of everyone from the field. The rain had washed a lot of it away, but they took all the piles that had been American boys. I watched them bury most of 'em right there, right nearby.

"No one would've recognized me by now. My beard had grown out, and I could say a few simple French phrases. Even if they would've seen me, they never would've known. They would've thought I was a Frenchman who'd lived there my whole life.

"Some of the soldiers'd already been shipped back, and a lot of 'em were leaving. The place was starting to get quiet again. I still wondered what happened to the rest of my squad…to everyone else I'd known. I'd found some in the field, but a lot of 'em were gone. I wondered if they'd gone home by then. It was strange to think that they would never even know I was alive. They'd always think I'd been blown up there in the field. By then they'd probably told everyone back home I was dead. I didn't know how long that sort of thing took, but I thought by then they probably had. I wondered whether they'd told you yet.

"After that, I wasn't so scared anymore. The Americans were pretty much gone now, and nothing happened to me…no one else had come after me. And then there was the grave. I went at looked at it. My own grave, marked out, right there. When I looked at it, it really felt like that wasn't my name. That name didn't mean anything to me. I recognized some of the other names, though.

"It's tough now, to think about it. I hadn't talked to an American for a long time. I started to think about what it'd be like just to stay there forever. I looked at the grave and thought of everyone back home, thinking I was dead. But then I'd think of Jack, and I was glad that I was dead.

"I don't know how long it was…not more than a couple months. The worst part of the winter, I was there. I did work on the farm there in exchange for food and a little money. I was saving it for when I'd have to get back home.

"I don't know how long I would've been there. I just stayed there. But then I saw someone over by the graves one day. Somebody in town told me there was an American who was looking at the graves. I thought it must've been one of Jack's boys come to get me. So I hid out and watched. I was too far away to see, really. But I could still tell it was you."

He was looking at me now, and I stared back quietly. I saw it through his eyes. I saw myself standing there on that cold, sunlit day, seen from far off. I wondered what I had looked like. Had I made any grand movements? Had I talked out loud to myself? I tried to remember, but I couldn't.

"I wanted to shout out, and run over to you," he said. "I really did. I almost did. But I just wasn't sure. I didn't know if I was just seeing things. I had no idea how you could've been there. I thought you should've been back home by then. I thought it might've been someone come to kill me. I was afraid to get closer. I was afraid we'd both be in danger. I just…" he shook his head, "I just wasn't sure it was you. I wasn't sure if I even remembered what you looked like. I didn't know if I was just looking at some guy and thinking it was you. I don't know." He shook his head some more.

A fly buzzed around my head and I brushed at it with my hand. When I thought about how close he'd been to me that day, I was filled with a heavy, sad feeling. How much of the last few years would have been different if he would have just shouted out as I stood there? I thought about the times my Mother and my Aunt had asked me to describe the grave, the marker, the trees nearby, the town. They had planned to go there someday.

"Then you left," he continued. "And it was too late. I hadn't done anything. But I started thinking about getting back. Just seeing you there made me think. I started thinking that I had to get back somehow. Even if they killed me, I didn't really care. I couldn't just hide there for the rest of my life. I felt powerful now, in a way. I had a secret…I could hide from them. Things were different. So I decided to go, just like that, and I started back. I made my way toward the coast…I jumped a train and went there, back out of the country the same way I'd gone in. I got to the coast, hoping to find a boat that was shipping out to America. There weren't anymore, though…not for a while, from what I could understand. So I got on a boat that was crossing to England. I just climbed on, and no one said a word to me. I just sat there. But I was right there, and they could've said something to me if they wanted. It was a cargo ship, but there were some soldiers on it too. I started thinking all over again that I was a ghost…that they couldn't even see me.

"I got to London. It was quite a place," he smiled now, and looked out over the woods. "The women wear these big, floppy hats, and really long hair. I finally got a shave and a real bath there. What I mostly did there was drink, though. And while we drank and played cards, little girls and old men kept coming up to us, with these tin cans…rattling 'em, asking for money for the families of dead soldiers. For widows and orphans. I gave them some, a few times. The place looked worse than France to me…broken cab windows, poor people always around. And there hadn't even been a war there.

"I couldn't hide my voice though…they all wanted to talk about America. They had all these philosophies about the war, though. One fella used to quote this book that H.G. Wells wrote about the war. He used to always tell me quotes from it. I don't even remember any of 'em now. I was lucky, though…I gambled a little and got more money.

"I met a girl over there, too," he said, looking down a bit and clearing his throat. "One time, when I'd been drinking a little, I went ahead and told her my story. I don't know if she really believed it or not. I just needed to tell it to someone, to see what they'd think. I was worried she'd think I was a coward for deserting my squad. But instead, she told me she was jealous of me. She told me I shouldn't waste this opportunity…that I had a chance to start over. She didn't think I should go home at all. She said if she had the chance to be someone else, she'd never go home again.

"I wasn't sure how to take it at the time. But it worked on me, I think, during the passage over. I paid my way onto a ship that was crossing. I was on there with the poorest people I had ever seen. Most of 'em didn't even speak English, so I couldn't figure out why they were going to America. But it was a long trip. I had lots of time to think. I hardly spoke to anyone, that whole time.

"I'd changed a lot, by then. I was among foreigners, and I felt like a foreigner. I'd spent a while avoiding Americans out of fear, and I'd lived in France and England...I know it was only for a short time, but it didn't seem that way. I looked around at all those people, and I was one of 'em. That was what it must've been for our parents...coming over, to start a new life.

"There was one thing I thought of, though, one night on the deck, smoking and looking at the stars. I remembered my life insurance...the insurance that I had from the factory. I started to think everyone might be better off without me, anyway. They were getting money, now that I was dead. Or at least I thought so. I wasn't sure how it worked. And I think it was right there that I started to really think about starting over, totally new. If there was some way for me to get that money...not all of it, but some of it. It was really mine anyway...money that paid for my life."

He looked at me and knew what I was feeling, somehow.

"Just hear me out," he said, one hand out toward me as if to steady things. "Just listen." He had already gone through the second cigarette and tossed it away by now.

"I didn't know what I'd do. I didn't have a plan. For all I knew, as soon as I saw home, everything would be back to normal. But I wanted to find out about the money first...I wanted to know, just to know, how it worked. So when we landed in Boston," he smiled and looked at Ambrose now, "I remembered hearing about you. I remembered I had a cousin in Boston. I knew my mother's maiden name, of course...Bentham. So I found you real quick...it was easy. I decided I might as well meet you finally. I needed to talk to someone about money anyway. And I knew you were in the banking business.

"When I walked in there, I knew right who you were. I really did. I introduced myself with Murdoch's name and we started talking. It was so easy to be someone else. I didn't wanna tell you the truth, and it didn't really matter. I didn't know what I was gonna do yet. I knew that everyone back home would think I was dead. So I talked to you, and got the information. I didn't think I'd ever see you again, if you want the truth. And to you, I was a stranger…a new face. No matter what my name…all I was to you was a stranger."

"That's true, I guess," said Ambrose quietly.

"But after I talked to you, I knew there was some money down there. So I hadda go back to Greenwood, no matter what. On my way down, I went through New York, though. I went back to where I was born. I listened to the pipers on Fifth Avenue, and watched the people in khaki celebrating…they were so happy about the war. In London, they'd been celebrating in a quiet way, I guess. But there, in New York, it was different. The happier people were, though, the more out of place I felt.

"I started to get worried, too, 'cause I didn't really know where Murdoch was from. I knew what he'd told me, but I didn't believe that, of course. But he was at Devens, so he must've been from around here somewhere. I wondered about his family. But I'm sure they just eventually figured he was dead. There were so many unknown soldiers and unidentified bodies. For a little while I was scared I was gonna introduce myself to someone that knew the real him. I guess that was silly."

He was silent now, a distant look on his face. I tried to imagine him without the stubble. To me, he still had the exact same face he'd had as a little boy.

"I even went down to the docks there," he said, looking at me with a smile. "Back where our father used to work," he told this to Ambrose as an aside. "I looked around all of it. It was old and run down. I saw our old apartment…I think it was the right one. I wasn't sure though. I saw the lot where we used to play all the time," he smiled at me again. "I wasn't sure what I was doing yet, but it felt good. I got somethin' from it. I got stronger from it. I didn't wanna go home."

"Why not?" I asked, tired of listening. "You knew we thought you were dead. You could've made them happy. That's all it would have taken…just to know you were alive." The familiar lump had seated itself in my throat. He had been so nonchalant while telling his story. I wanted to get him excited about something, to prove that he still had emotions. "Instead, you repay them by coming up with a scam to take their money?"

"Listen," he said, louder now but still controlled. "It's more complicated than that. I mean, it is. It really is. Maybe there's no way you can understand, though. I was still hiding. I had to hide. I couldn't set foot in Greenwood, no matter what I wanted. People told me Jack was still around, same as always. So I wrote to him. I thought that was the best thing to do. I sent him a telegram from Murdoch. All I said was that the job was done, and I was gonna stay quiet for a while, so no one could connect us. I worried that the telegram would give it away somehow…that there was a code word between them I hadn't used, or that Murdoch would've talked differently to him. But I had to do it…I had to do something, just to see what would happen.

"I told him he could reply to me down in Dunville. I told him exactly where I was. I had to. I had to get a reply, just to know if I'd fooled him. To know I could go on without being scared everyday. I'm glad I did. Without that reply, I never would've known for sure. When it came back, it felt good. I'd fooled him. That would probably be my only revenge, I knew. That was as much as I was ever gonna get…just knowing that I'd outsmarted him in the end. That I was alive. My name didn't matter."

My emotions were still pitching and rolling. Only now was I beginning to fully accept that he had been living, all this time. I suppose part of me wanted to think that God had returned him to Earth just right now, just as we entered the house. But no, he had been right here, not that far from us. He had watched us all from the outside, and had never returned. He was a part of us, a family member, lost far from the fold. He was a vessel, containing blood that was the same as mine, that belonged with us. But he didn't want to be in the place where he belonged. I didn't understand it at all, and I told him so.

"I can't explain it to you so you'll understand," he said. "Don't you think I thought about coming home all the time? I just didn't think it'd be safe. I needed the money to live, and I knew they'd give it to me if they knew I was alive. So I came up with a better way to get some of it...without putting anyone in danger."

"Lying to us all? That was your better way?" My voice cracked and shook.

"I thought you'd understand," Henry said, staring at me. "Out of everyone. I thought you'd understand."

"Well, I don't."

"Look, the war...it changed you, and it changed me. It probably changed everyone. A lot happened to me over there. The war didn't end for me over there, like it did for you. I couldn't just come home and go back to normal. I still had an enemy, waiting back here."

"That can't be it," I said. I knew him too well. He was trying to justify his actions to himself. "You could've found a way to get in touch with us, without anyone else knowing. It wouldn't be hard at all. You didn't want to come back." I knew it was true, as I said it. I was beginning to grasp how much he had really changed.

"Maybe that's true," he said quietly. "Maybe it was time to grow up...I didn't want to insult you, but maybe living at home with two old women wasn't my idea of adulthood. We had a nice childhood, but it's time to grow up. There wasn't much for me back there...I knew it. I know it...it's true. Maybe if I'd grown up with a father it would be different."

"You did have a father..."

"Not that I can really remember," he said it loudly.

"Who are these people?" I asked, waving toward the door. "What are you doing here, in this house?"

"This is my house. From what I've heard you've been spending some time in other households too. Don't get angry at me if you're still too tied to the apron strings to make a real break. I had a chance to get away from there for good, and I took it. You might've, too."

"Now hold on," Ambrose said, stepping forward toward Henry. "I don't understand everything that's going on here. I don't know much about what things were like before. My dad died too. And I didn't love my home growing up. But you lied to me. You came to my place of business and told me lies, and took advantage of my time and my services." He was calm. Henry looked at him, a bit surprised. "Your brother and I came down here to find the person...we thought had killed you. To get revenge for the family. So this is yet another waste of my time. And now I'm waiting for my apology."

A smile slowly spread across Henry's face. He was truly impressed. He extended his hand.

"Then you have it. I apologize for lying to you." Ambrose shook his hand. "I've told you everything I can. I told you this so you'd understand. You may not agree with the way I did things, but most of it, I had to do."

Then Henry turned toward me, and extended his hand again. The last time I'd shook his hand was when we'd left camp to go our separate ways into the war. I don't think I'd ever shook his hand before then. Here it was, though, offered once again. Ambrose had stepped back now and was leaning on the railing.

"I know this is all hard to hear," Henry said, his eyes on me. "But it's good...to see you again." That was hard for him to say, I knew. But I wasn't ready yet. I just stood there, not knowing if I ever would be. I couldn't help thinking that there had to have been an easier way. He could have let *me* know, somehow. I pictured him feeding information to the Pilfords about our dead baby brother and our childhood and the horse bookends.

He smiled sadly, and his arm fell back by his side.

"I didn't know what to think, when they said it was you at the door just now," he said. "But you know, I've imagined it before. I'd thought about this before. And I hoped you'd understand."

"So what are you going to do now?" I asked. "I'm sure you have it planned out."

"You can come back with us now," Ambrose said. "Now that we know what's going on. We're not afraid of those guys."

"Why?" Henry asked us both loudly. "Why go back? I am afraid, if you want the truth, and I should be. So why risk it? There's nothing for me there but my past. And I left that life behind. I let that life die over there. What's wrong with that? It was my life, I should be able to get rid of it when I say. Most people get killed, and then it's over, and they don't get to plan it. But I got to. I got another chance…that's what they understand," he motioned toward the house. "Why can't you understand it?"

"I'm going to tell them about you," I said. "If you won't come. I have to."

"No," he shook his head. "No, you don't. Why? Why tell them? Just so you'll look good. Just so you can say you found me. That's not the right reason."

"Because they have the right to know. She has the right to know that you're alive, and that everything those…" I pointed toward the house, "everything those girls told them was a lie."

"They're old people," he said. "They need their lies. Don't take them away. It does no good to take them away. Do you know what's happening to the world? I've seen it. Do you know what's going on? Everything's changing. And they still live in the last century…that's where they're comfortable. That's where they wanna be. Hell, most of your town does. I'm just another loss to them. Just let it be that way. Just another loss. That's a small price to pay…to buy me a whole new life. Don't you understand?"

"What life?" I asked. "What are you doing down here? What is this place?" I waved at the house. "Do you sit here and light candles all day?"

He couldn't repress a smile.

"No," he said, his smile fading quickly. "No. That was for show...the candles and everything. They'd told me you'd sat in on a few seances." He looked down for a second, and I wondered if he felt shame. But his tone seemed to only grow sharper. "I have a life down here, whether you like it or not. Don't tell me you think like an old woman just 'cause you're still living there."

"You don't know what you're talking about," I said angrily.

"I'm gonna see the world...I've already seen a lot of it. I'm gonna go back over there, to Europe, I think," he went on. "Just to look at it now. To see the beauty of it now, after everything's over. That was what I liked best over there...the silence, afterward. You didn't get to hear that. You left in a hurry. You know what they say now? What I heard? I heard that the old bombs still go off now, every once in a while. Some farmer'll be plowing his field over there and then...bang!" He clapped his hands, his eyes reflecting the light of the afternoon intensely. "And you know what they say about the fields, like the one where Murdoch died? They say the bombs brought up old flowers and things that were way beneath the soil. Flowers from the time of the knights...really. Blooming there again. They hadn't seen these flowers for a thousand years, and there they are again. That's what's left over there now.

"There's no reason to tell anyone about me," he went on, hitting his stride now. "I needed some money at first, and I'm sorry about what I had to do to them to get it. But from what I heard, it brought them peace. It was a gift, in a way...for them. That money got us started, but we're all right now. I don't need anything else from anyone. All I need is to be forgotten. There's no reason to tell...that does you no good at all. Just leave me alone, here. If you don't understand, then fine. But leave me alone. Let me go the way I want to go. For all you knew before today, I was dead. So just tell yourself that again, if that's what you need to do. You got on with your life. So keep it up. Pretend today never happened, and I'm dead. It's the only way that everyone's gonna be happy."

I looked through the words and saw the little boy I remembered, the person I was closest to in all the world, probably. And I knew there was nothing I could do. He had made up his mind long ago. Our visit had been completely unexpected, and he would have been perfectly happy, going on, without me ever knowing. I could've lived my whole life without knowing the truth, if I hadn't met Ralph Lockehart that night. Or if I'd been afraid of Murdoch, I might never have come. I wondered what other things might be quietly passing us by, so near that we don't even think to look for them.

They were both looking at me now. The week had turned out in a way I couldn't possibly have imagined. And yet, it made some kind of sense. From Kate closing her door on me to the strange woman opening the door of this little house. I had been moving toward this moment.

And with that, I suddenly had the feeling that I was better than him, somehow. I know that doesn't sound good, but it was true. Henry had found peace in the idea that he had bested Jack Wolfe. Now I had a similar feeling. For all of his plans and attempts to hide, I had found him.

I had asked the right questions of the right people along the way. I didn't have to bring him back as proof of my being a good son, or of my being the man of the family. I had proven my own worth to myself, and that was all that mattered. I looked at both of them, and realized that I was at the center of the family now, or what was left of it. It was me that was connecting them all.

I knew things my Aunt and my Mother didn't have to know, things I would save them from knowing. Not because they were so old that they couldn't understand, even though that's what Henry thought. Because they had been through enough already, and they deserved to hold on to their own beliefs about life.

Anyone can run and hide and leave things behind. Maybe I had even done a little of that in my time. But now things were different. Now I had to take care of everyone and hold everything together. Henry could have his fun down here, or wherever he went. Even if he didn't really remember our father, I did. And I knew he would be proud of me.

I reached out my hand then, and he took it. I shook his hand, nodding slightly. He gripped mine tightly in return. His hand was warm. I tried to come up with the right thing to say.

"All right," I said quietly. "If I'm the only person from Greenwood who knows the truth, then fine. If this is how you want it, all right. I don't really understand. I paid my respects at your grave though. That's all the respect I have to give."

Ambrose had moved off, the wood boards beneath him creaking. He was looking out over the little railing.

To my surprise, my brother's eyes were rimmed with wetness. He shook my hand fiercely. His mouth opened, and then closed. He seemed unable to say something.

"I wish it wasn't this way," he finally got out. "But this is how it is." He nodded a few more times.

I'd like to say that there was a real understanding between us then. I don't know if there was, though. All I know is what I was thinking. It was strange, because so much of my life had been shared with this person, in a way that neither of us had ever put into words. When I'd heard that he was dead, and thought that I'd never see him again, I had wished that our last goodbye before the war had been different. I'd wished that it had held more meaning, or been more final, somehow. I'd wished that I could have put into words who he was to me.

And now that I did have a chance to truly say goodbye, it just wasn't like that. We didn't say much at all. The truth was, there was nothing to say. We couldn't put these things into words, and maybe that's what made them meaningful.

Or at least, that's how I hoped it was. That was my optimistic take on things. On the other hand, as I looked at him there, this strange man across from me, I realized that maybe there were no words because we simply didn't have anything to say. Maybe I didn't really know him, and I had never truly known him. I'm sure he had friends at the factory or during the war who knew more about him than I did. Probably the bizarre little group inside the house even knew him better.

I had been so close to him all my life that I hadn't been able to see who he really was. It was like the painting in Kate's room, that way. If you stood too close all you saw were the shapes, but you couldn't make out the picture.

"How is everyone?" he asked then. It seemed like an afterthought.

"Fine, fine," I nodded. "The same, really."

"Good."

"Well...good luck."

Ambrose had floated back over now. His expression was tight, his face giving away nothing. He and Henry shook hands again.

"It was good to meet you," Ambrose said warmly. Henry nodded and smiled.

"Nice to see you again, too. I'm glad I got to meet you."

The three of us stood there for a few moments in silence. I had been dealt quite a blow that day. And yet the birds continued to chirp overhead, and the water still flowed by below. I looked down at the little rocks on the sides of the stream, and watched the water washing over them. They held their ground. I knew from playing in the creek as a young boy that those rocks would come out the smoothest.

I didn't want to go back through the house on my way out. I didn't want to see the Pilfords ever again, or the guy with the light hair, or the obscenely pregnant Negress. They seemed like odds and ends that he had accumulated now.

The ground was higher on one end of the wooden deck, and I noticed that we could easily hop over the railing there and walk back around to the road. Ambrose had been eyeing the door, but as I moved toward the end of the deck he read my mind and turned that way as well. Henry was speaking again.

"Thanks," he said. "Thanks for coming down here…for coming after Murdoch…really." We just smiled and nodded, and climbed over the low railing.

I landed on the soft ground, and Ambrose came over after me. Then I turned and stood there, looking at Henry. We weren't far from each other at all. Only the short railing separated us.

"Take care of yourself," I said. He nodded, and smiled a little.

"You too. Take care of everybody."

I'll always remember him standing there on the deck, giving a little wave and then watching us walk away. The shadowy stubble on his face made it seem longer and darker, somehow. But when I think back the face that I see there is the same one that has always existed in my memory. It's the one from the picture of him seated in the chair, a little rounder and fuller with youth. The boy in the chair always seems to me to have a whole life ahead of him. And every time I look at the picture, he looks happy to me. He is frozen there forever, glad to be alive and a part of the simple world given to him by his Mother.

CHAPTER 37

My Aunt started to feel ill in the spring, and within a few months she was spending her days in bed. I remember it being a beautiful spring, actually. Sometimes I think she simply decided not to participate in yet another rebirth of the seasons. Perhaps she'd had enough of change altogether, and was ready to be cloistered away in an unchanging room. There's a stage that all older people reach, I think, when they make a conscious decision that they've simply had enough, and they give up trying to keep pace with the world.

I can't remember exactly when we realized that she really was sick. I'd always assumed that most of her ailments were imaginary. I'm sure my Mother felt the same way, although the two of us never really talked about it.

As the weather grew warmer, though, Dr. Morris became more and more of a presence in our house. One day, after looking in on my Aunt, he stepped out into the hallway. My Mother and I were both there, and he started to speak to us quietly about her condition. I noticed that he was directing almost everything he said toward me. I had been used to him ignoring me, as he did when I was a child. But starting that day in the hall, he would always talk to me about her. My Mother seemed content with it, and she rarely listened now when he spoke. She just waited for me to tell her about it after he had gone.

Dr. Morris would look at me through his thick glasses, the long hairs of his eyebrows spurting and tangling above the rims of the frames. His thick beard had been peppered gray and black and the lines on his face had been etched deeply ever since I was a child. His lower lip stuck out quite a bit, and it always looked very wet, as if he might start drooling at any minute. I don't really remember most of what he said. In short, her family had a history of bad hearts, and it looked as if she had one as well. She should be avoiding any strenuous movement. But beyond that, there wasn't much he could do.

My Aunt was only too happy to obey. To her, his diagnosis was a confirmation of what she already knew and had accepted. She confined herself to her bed, getting up only to use the bathroom. My Mother doted on her day and night, of course.

She had many visitors. Mr. Barnes came by often, and almost every older woman in town made at least one appearance. Mrs. Arthur came over nearly every week, always bringing vast quantities of food that the three of us couldn't possibly eat. Mr. Arthur came as well, to my Aunt's great joy. My Mother seemed to think it was good to have him there, as well. They would talk and pray together, and I would hear Mr. Arthur's nasal voice lifted throughout the house. I thought back to when I was little and I used to associate his voice with the voice of God. Now, when I overheard him from the bedroom, he just sounded like an aging man, struggling to be heard.

It was good for us all, I think, to have so many visitors in the house, despite my Aunt's condition. Ambrose had left at the end of the year, and we'd missed his presence for a while. He went back to Boston to smooth things over with his mother. His plan, as he told it to me, was to keep an apartment there and return to banking full time. He wanted to get married and have a son of his own. He seemed so set on it that I was sure he would keep his word, and avoid women and wine to the degree that it was possible for him.

He left just before Christmas. I remember it was right before President Harding pardoned Eugene Debs and commuted his prison sentence. Harding pardoned everyone who had been convicted under the Sedition Act of 1918. I thought about that a lot, and wished that Ambrose was around so we could talk about it. Harding forgave them all now. America forgave them. I wondered if Jack felt redeemed.

I began to miss Ambrose as soon as he left, of course. Without him around, my mind was free to roam to places that I wanted to avoid, and there was no one to share these thoughts with. I had gone through a few desperate months following Christmas. These were the early, cold months of the year. I remember they had a conference in Washington on arms reduction and came up with all sorts of treaties. Everyone was forgiving and disarming. But there were some things that I couldn't forget.

Although I never would have wished sickness on my Aunt, the fact was it helped things in our house. My Mother and I had something to concentrate on now, something to face together. By the time summer arrived, my Aunt had stopped coming to the table to eat. Dr. Morris told me that she could certainly make it to dinner, and that a walk around the house each day would even be good for her. But she insisted on being even more vigilant than he suggested, and she made the announcement one day that she would no longer be making the trip down the hall to the dining room. Instead, we moved a small table into her bedroom, which had always been the largest of the house, and we ate in there with her.

My Aunt liked to have the large window across from her bed open as wide as the shutters would allow. It did have a nice view of the lake, and she told us that seeing it made her feel as if she were still out there, in the world, living. At which point my Mother would insist that she was being silly, and that of course she was still living, and had many years to go.

I remember one clear night in early summer when we had eaten dinner in there with her. We had just finished our food and my mother was clearing the dishes. I sat there, staring out the window, along with my Aunt. The sun was only now beginning to approach the horizon, and the view was as relaxing for me as I'm sure it was for her. It seemed as if I worked harder and harder during those days, and I was often faced with fatigue in the evenings. Even on weekends, though, I was beginning to prefer quiet evenings to activity of any kind.

I looked around her room, which had been the same for as long as I could remember. The furniture had sat there, unmoving, for the span of my entire life. That was a strange thing to think about. To me, I had been living forever, through vast changes in the world. But to her, my lifetime had been so short and inconsequential that she hadn't even gotten around to rearranging the room. There were two maroon armchairs, and an old set of dressers of light wood, all of which had been here before I was. I could remember playing around on the large bed as a child when we first moved here. It had seemed enormous to me then, and we couldn't resist exploring it. She hadn't liked that at all.

There had been a small oil portrait of her husband on the wall by the bed then. I barely remember him in real life, but the portrait looms vividly in my mind. His wide, bald skull and tiny eyes stared out at us, pleading with us not to play on his bed. Everything in the house was his. I was familiar with the idea of death by then, of course, because of my father. Still, I didn't like the portrait, and I didn't like to be in the room with it alone, especially after dark. I can't remember when she took it down finally, but I'm sure it was partly as a result of my Mother's influence.

"The days are getting longer," I said aloud, sitting in one of the armchairs in the corner.

"Mmmhmmm," she answered thoughtfully. My Mother carried some plates out of the room. I got up and carried the table away from the bed and over to a corner, and then returned to the chair. She turned from the side of the bed, and slid back into the center.

Even though it was summer and quite warm, she insisted on covering up with the blanket. Her shape under the covers looked smaller than it should have been, as if the bed was slowly swallowing her whole. It was funny how I'd never noticed this before. Her face was the same as it had always been, at least. Perhaps it was a little thinner, but the sharp eyes remained, and her features were completely untouched. Her hair was pulled back and fixed, just as it would have been had she been going out somewhere to dinner. Every morning my Mother fixed her hair just in case she decided to leave the house that day and walk into town. Of course, she never did.

"How is your work, Colbert?" she asked. She took a new interest in my work now. Anything going on outside the house seemed to be of great importance to her.

"It's going well," I answered. "Mister Durham has me in the field with him now every week. I get to go around to all the nearby counties and investigate claims with him." He had given me a substantial raise that spring, as well. I wasn't sure if it was because of my work or because of the condition of my Aunt, though. He asked about her all the time, now, and he had even visited once.

"Good, good," she smiled. "You're doing so well." She looked at the door then, listening for my Mother. When she heard nothing, she turned back and leaned toward me confidentially. "How about a girl? Is there a young lady you're courting?"

I smiled and shook my head a little. I wondered if she realized how often she asked me that.

"You'll be the first to know when there is," I told her.

She was quiet for a while then. Her face always looked so serious now, when she wasn't speaking. There was something about the way that her mouth closed in the light that gave her a somber, almost scowling look.

"You're so good to take care of your Mother," she said then. "But we want you to be happy, too. We want you to start a family of your own. Your Mother may not say that, but we both feel that way. I certainly do. I want the Whittiers to continue in America. I really do," she said quietly.

She saw me as the last hope of her family, of course. I was the only one who could carry on her maiden name.

"Did your brothers in France have children?" I asked. She didn't hear me, though, so I asked again. The air in the room was still.

"Stephen didn't," she said. "His wife couldn't have them, it turned out. She was a shrewish woman." She had a far off look in her eyes, and was quiet for a while. I watched the covers move up and down with her methodical breathing. "You know, she beat me one time."

"When was this?"

"Oh, I must have been about sixteen years old," she smiled a little now, which I thought was strange. "She was a terrible woman. She drove my other two brothers away. We had all been living on the farm together, after my father died. That was when I went to live with my aunt. I ran away, after she beat me."

"How many brothers did you have?" I asked. I felt as if I was doing her a favor of sorts, talking to her like this. My Aunt had always liked to be listened to, and I could tell that lately it was one of the few things that still brought her pleasure.

"I had four brothers," she said with a smile. "Your father was the oldest. Then there was Stephen, and Francois, and Meriwether."

"Were they a lot older than you?" I asked, adjusting my position in the chair.

"Oh, yes. I was the youngest."

"How much older were they?"

"Let me see…" she looked down, as if she was searching for the answer to my question in the folds of the blanket. "Your father was…five years older than me, I believe. And the others were in between. Meriwether was only a year older. People used to think that we were twins. I wish I had a picture of him, to show you."

"Did he have any children?"

"I don't know," she said with her false scowl. "I always thought they would, but I don't know. They had a farm together, the last I knew. Meriwether and Francois. But the things that happened with Stephen and that woman…his wife, that really hurt things between all of us. I don't think they liked me coming over here, following your father, either."

My Mother entered the room quietly now and sat on the edge of the bed.

"He had always doted on me," my Aunt went on. "They all did, of course…I was the only girl and the youngest. I think I was closest to Gerard, though. He always made sure I was taken care of. And my mother, of course. But our parents passed away very close to each other…close in time, you see? And that was hard for us."

"Your father had his accident," said my Mother softly.

"Yes, that was terrible," she said, looking at me. "One of our horses was ill, and he was trying to take care of him. He loved those horses. I always wanted to ride them, when I was big enough. And the horse fell on him somehow, and crushed his leg. Oh, I can still remember it happening so clearly. I wasn't there," she shook her head slowly. "I must have been inside. But he shouted so much and I was so frightened. That leg never healed right. And they could never get me to go near those horses again.

"That's when Gerard started having to do the work, really. He was the oldest, and he had to go and sell the grapes and the vegetables every season. He had to make the trip, it was to Paris, that he'd go. Because that's where the real money came from…selling the things there."

"And that's where I met him," said my Mother.

"That's right, that's right. Of course, he'd been going there for a while. My father didn't like it at all. He didn't like being hurt and depending on Gerard. And he would be so angry. I can remember how angry he always was.

"And then my mother passed away," she said sadly. "And that was so difficult for him. And I know it was hard for Gerard, because our father was never happy after that. He never was. They said she had trouble with her heart," she said, looking at both of us, waiting for a reaction. She wanted us to say something about her own sickness. She seemed almost triumphant, as if she was proud of this connection. My Mother and I just sat in silence, though, waiting for her to go on. We knew her well enough to know that she wouldn't be able to tolerate silence for too long.

"And it was after that that Gerard stayed in Paris, and didn't come back. And I took care of our father…that's all I did. You know, I had never been outside of our town? Just our little farm and a few other farms…that was all I'd ever seen in my life. My father passed when I was only about…oh, I'd say about fourteen years old. And then my other three brothers took over the farm and we all lived there. Gerard had already gone to America by then and he was married to your Mother." She reached out, and my Mother reached her arm across the bed and offered her hand. She took it and held it.

"But Stephen brought that horrible woman back to the farm when he married her. I can't remember where she was from, now. Some other town…I don't know where he found her. But that woman drove off Francois and Meriwether. They went off and became migrant workers for a while…gave up their own father's farm. Can you imagine? Oh, she was terrible. She didn't do anything around the house. She would make me do the cooking and clean everything. And she had the most horrible temper. I never did anything right…she was always yelling and throwing things.

"And Stephen would only defend her. He would never admit that she did anything wrong," she shook her head sadly, still holding my Mother's hand. "There was one time I remember, that she threw one of my mother's dishes and broke it. She didn't drop it by accident, she threw it across the room. I don't remember why. But he kept saying that she had just dropped it. And he would get mad if I tried to tell him that she threw it. But I saw her...she threw that dish. It was terrible. I stayed there for a few years, but then one day...oh, she beat me terribly. And then I left. I didn't even have anything to take with me, can you imagine? I didn't even say goodbye to Stephen. I went to my mother's sister. She lived alone, not too far away. And I never went back to that farm."

"How terrible," said my Mother. "What would your parents have said about their own farm...with that woman taking it over." It was a statement rather than a question. She didn't need to ask, as she knew that it would be greeted with a strong response.

"Oh, my mother wouldn't have liked her at all. I think that's why it turned out that she couldn't have children...just because the Lord knew that she would be mean to them. Things have a way of working out, you know."

"So they stayed there on the farm?" I asked.

She looked up at me suddenly.

"Stephen stayed, yes. I wonder who's there now. I don't really know. He was angry when I left, I'm sure. We wrote back and forth a few times, but you know, as the years go on, that life just seemed so far away. I had new people to love here." She patted my Mother's hand and let it go. She sank back into the pillows.

"When did you come here?" I asked.

"Well, I lived with my aunt for a few years, working in her house, mostly. But I wanted to go to America, even then I did. Gerard had even sent me a book of English, and I was learning it. I really was...I used to read it at night, when no one was around. I would hide it," she laughed for a while at that. "My aunt was a good woman," she said then, unexpectedly.

"She didn't let you out of the house either, though, did she?" asked my Mother, who knew the answers to all of these questions already.

"Well, I was always busy."

"Oh no, she kept you locked up just like Stephen's wife did. It was because you were beautiful. They were jealous of you."

My Aunt smiled. She wasn't about to deny that.

"But you know," she said. "I didn't know the first thing about men. I really didn't. There was a hired hand on our farm when I was little, and I remember him talking to my brothers about me. He must have said something they didn't like, though, because they talked to my father and he was gone the very next day. I was just a girl, though. I didn't know anything."

"How old were you when you were living with your aunt?" I asked.

"Well," she said. "I'm not sure. Let me see. When I finally came over here I was about eighteen. Gerard just sent me the money one day. And I knew I'd never get another chance, and he wanted me to come. So I did."

"It was so important to him," my Mother said. "That money. He wanted his little sister to see America. I was so nervous about meeting you," she smiled.

"I was so embarrassed because I knew that I couldn't speak well," said my Aunt.

"But you learned quickly," said my Mother.

"Yes, yes I did. I don't know how I did it. But I wanted to learn, I think. That's the difference, with children today. They don't want to learn. If you try to, you can learn anything." My Mother nodded silently.

"I hope you always remember your Aunt, Colbert," she was saying now. I smiled a little, ready to protest her talking about herself like that. She wouldn't let me get a word in, though. "No, I mean it. This world's changing quickly. Too quickly. I'm frightened for you young people. Frightened. Have you seen that sermon the Baptist preacher gave in New York last week?"

I shook my head.

"They had it in the paper. You know what it was called? *Shall the Fundamentalists Win?* is what. Something like that. People are afraid of the Fundamental Protestants today, you know that? Those are the people who built this country, and soon they'll have no place. People don't care about the important things anymore. Now the president's got a radio installed in the White House. That's the way things are going."

I thought about the crystal set that they had down at the post office, and how often we all crowded around it after work, listening to the sports and the "Red Menace" news. It was the most wonderful thing I'd ever heard. I thought it best not to say anything about it.

I could hear the growing sound of the insects of summer outside, buzzing as night fell.

"Would you like some water?" my Mother was asking now, standing.

"Thank you, dear."

"What about you, Colbert?"

"No thank you," I said. My Mother walked out. My corner of the room was quickly becoming shrouded in shadow. I sat there, watching her on the bed. She just stared forward, looking at nothing, in silence. I knew that she spoke to my Mother a lot about how she felt. She still saw me as a child, I'm sure, and would never talk about such things with me. She didn't know that Dr. Morris talked to me rather than my Mother about her health now.

"How old were you when you got married, Aunt Edna?" I asked, even though I knew.

She just kept smiling as if she hadn't heard. But then the smile gradually faded into an expression of concentration. She shifted her weight against the pillow and looked at the ceiling.

"Oh, Colbert…" she said. "I was a young woman. So very young. When William and I met, I had been working as a maid."

My Mother came in again and put a glass of water on the bedside table.

"You were working in his office by then," she said, and sat on the bed again.

"That's right," my Aunt responded, looking at her now. "I was a good maid to a man who got me a job cleaning up the accounting office. And he worked there, and that's where we met. He was a widower when I met him."

"Gerard didn't like him," my Mother said to me, shaking her head dramatically.

"No, no he didn't."

"It was because he was so much older. Your father didn't like that."

"Was that it?" my Aunt asked her, as if she had never thought about this before.

"Yes," my Mother said.

"How old was he?" I asked now, genuinely curious.

"He was more than twenty years older, wasn't he?" asked my Mother.

My Aunt took a drink from the glass, and set it down slowly, as if it weighed a hundred pounds. Then she smiled again and stared out the window. A breeze blew the drapes aside and cooled the room.

"He was forty-five or forty-six, I believe," she said at last.

"And how old were you?" I asked.

"I was twenty-two when I got married," she answered, pride in her voice. "We fell in love," she said. "But no, Gerard didn't like that. He said he didn't bring me over here for this to happen."

"Is that what he said?" my Mother asked.

"Oh yes, oh yes. He did. But he was all right, after a while. William was so well-off, compared to us. He had inherited this house."

"They got along, though," said my Mother. My Aunt looked at her strangely. "He and Gerard," she clarified.

"Yes," she said now, "after a while, they sure did. Well, Gerard was already sick when I got married."

"Yes," said my Mother.

"But he never told us that. He didn't say anything until later, but I think he was already sick. And even later, he wouldn't take William's money to see a doctor."

"No," my Mother said, a distant look on her face now.

"He had a lot of money," I said.

"Well, not as much as a lot of people around here think he did," my Aunt answered. I had given her something to gossip about, and she sat up as if she'd totally forgotten about her condition. "We came here in the summers, you know. And the people here in town had known William's first wife, so some of them didn't take to me too well. But I was determined to make friends, and I did. William didn't have good luck in those days, though. His investing didn't go well. I didn't really know about it when he was alive of course. But then, when he passed, they told me about his debt."

"That's when you came here for good," said my Mother.

"That's right. I had to sell the place in New York, and I liked it here better. I had to get rid of one or the other."

"And you took on boarders here for a while, too," said my Mother.

"Really?" I said.

"Yes," my Aunt nodded. "That was the only way to make money then. In the summers. Not many people came during the winters, of course."

I imagined her then, still young, determined to make a life for herself here. She had always been very religious, I knew, and she'd been a member of the sewing circle and several women's groups. By the time we came to live with her here, you would've thought from the way people acted around her that she'd been one of the town's founders.

It was during that time, I knew, right after my father's death, that she and my Mother had become so close. They had brought in money by sewing before Henry and I were old enough to work. My Mother had even sold a few things to the man at the textile factory shop back then. That was how Henry got his job, in fact.

The sun was setting now, and twilight had crept into the room.

"It has been delightful to have my family here with me during these last years," said my Aunt. "This is my real family."

"Now, Edna," said my Mother. "Don't talk like that. You have many years left."

"Not in bed, I don't want to spend them in bed."

"You won't be in bed for long. You're just a little under the weather just now."

My Aunt turned toward me.

"Let me tell you something," she whispered, as if my Mother could no longer hear her. "Those young girls talked to me about my health."

I saw my Mother sigh and shift herself uncomfortably on the bed.

"They did, they did. The sisters. They read all about me in their cards. They told me that I didn't have much time left. That's what they said. And now we see they were right. Now we can see, they were right." Her eyes were wide, as if she had really been granted the vision to see her own future.

"That will only come true if you want it to," said my Mother quietly, looking out the window.

My Aunt shrugged a little and settled back onto the pillows.

"Just lay me to rest next to my brother," she said now. "In the family plot over here, where we'll all go. It sounds so nice to me now…to rest."

She was talking about rest as if she'd been working hard for a long time. I thought she'd mostly been resting for the past few years anyway. I wondered how real death seemed to her now. I wondered if she thought about the different spirit levels and all of that, preparing herself.

I didn't think she was really dying, though. Dr. Morris had said that she probably wouldn't get a whole lot better, but that she wasn't really that bad as long as she didn't strain herself. It was up the air, he had said. She could live for another twenty years. Up in the air, like the world of the spirits, or like a bomb waiting to drop. It was like that for all of us, I suppose.

The discussion of her grave reminded me of Henry. This may sound strange, but their grief over Henry had been completely put to rest by now. It was my Aunt's own health problems that finally allowed the two of them to move on. They had something else to concentrate on now. Ever since she had fallen ill, they had let Henry go at last. It seemed strange now to even think back to a time when they felt a need to contact him on the other side.

Their desire to go see his grave in France had me worried for a while. But now it was clear that my Aunt would never be making a trip like that. And without her forceful energy, I was discovering, my Mother was a lot different. Now that my Mother was a bit freer to live her own life outside of the house, she let go of things much more easily. I think the decision to let them bury Henry over there had come from her, not my Aunt. She had let him lie where he had fallen, because she didn't need the body over here. I understood that more now, and I could also imagine what she went through when making that decision. My Aunt would have been thoroughly against it. My Aunt would have chosen, if she could, to have him buried in the yard so that she live her life weighed down by the grim reminder of death each and every day.

I had spoken to my Mother a few months before about the grave, very briefly. I was only a little surprised when she told me that going to see it had been Edna's dream, not hers. She said that she had the grave of her husband to look at, and it didn't remind her of him when he was alive, or help her to picture his face.

It wasn't as if they had forgotten about Henry completely, but when we talked about him now it was mostly just to remember things he and I had done when we were children. To me he was gone, never to return, just as he was to them. Discussing his life rather than his death just seemed right, and I found that we started to discuss my father more, as well. It took my Aunt's ill health to make our household finally move past the tragedies of death and recognize instead the joy of memory.

CHAPTER 38

That spring the temperature increased dramatically and suddenly. I remember one particular afternoon was so stifling that I simply had to stop in at the drugstore for a soda after work.

"How's your Aunt doing?" Mr. Barnes asked, placing the drink on the counter. He had put a record on. I think it was *Dreamy Melody* by Art Landry. I wore a full suit now on the days when Mr. Durham and I were out in the field, and my jacket was folded on the stool beside me. An advertisement peeked out from behind his head. *Often a bridesmaid but never a bride—For halitosis, Use Listerine.* A woman held a bottle of Listerine as if she were going to marry it.

"She's getting along," I said. "Nothing much changing."

"Well, maybe that's a blessing," he said, shaking his head slightly. "We sure miss her around town."

Aside from church, though, I couldn't really remember my Aunt really ever being around town. I just smiled and nodded. The notes of music floated there in the air of the little store, stirred only by the large fan turning overhead.

I scanned another sign behind the counter. *It is common knowledge today that intestinal putrefaction causes brain fatigue, often reducing efficiency 50 per cent and more. Fight putrefaction with Pillsbury's Health Bran.* A bowl of cereal, not looking very appetizing. Maybe my Aunt had brain fatigue.

Two kids ran in and pointed to some Eskimo Pies, dropping their shining change on the counter. The coins rolled around, spinning faster and faster until they came to rest. I looked over at the boys as they withdrew their grubby hands, and they looked up at me in the same moment.

One had a scrunched up sort of face, and dirt on his elbows. He glanced at me, and then squinted up at Mr. Barnes, waiting patiently.

The other kid was taller, and wore a cap. He had a collection of moles sprinkled across his nose and cheeks. He waited a few steps back from the counter, looking around.

I wondered how I looked to them. Just an old man at the counter, dressed for work, finished forever with the games and rejoicing of summer. I smiled to myself, thinking about what it had been like to be their age.

Mr. Barnes gave them the Eskimo Pies and they left happily.

Ten minutes after using DANDERINE *you will not find a single trace of dandruff or falling hair.* DANDERINE *is to the hair what fresh showers of rain and sunshine are to vegetation.* A picture of a medicinal bottle.

Mr. Barnes was writing something behind the counter now. He raised the pen toward me.

"You seen these?" he asked. "You're a businessman."

I shook my head.

"That's a Lifetime pen from Waterman. Two dollars and fifty cents. It'll last you a lifetime. They charge five dollars for them in New York. What do you think?"

"I'll think about it," I smiled.

"You tell Durham. See if he needs any."

"I will."

"I never would've thought they could invent something like that," he turned it over in his hand. "You know what else they've got now? A self-winding wristwatch. I've seen one with my own eyes. There's going to be nothing left for us to do in a few years. Everything running itself, lasting forever."

I finished my soda and thanked him, then stood and draped my jacket over my arm. As I turned I was surprised to see Mrs. Delgrew in one of the little aisles, looking at something intently.

"Hello, Misses Delgrew," I said, approaching her.

She looked up at me for a few moments, blinking in the sunlight that streamed from the front window. Then she nodded and smiled.

"Hello, Colbert," she said. She had been looking at the fifty-cent Vanity Puffs, I saw. "How is your Aunt?"

"She's doing well, I think," I replied with a smile of my own.

"Well, I'll have to come and see her some time," she said. "I've just had my own hands full lately."

"Of course," I answered. "How is...everything at home?" I had my own reason for guilt now. I hadn't visited the Delgrew house since the summer before.

Early that spring Willie had come home at last. He was home for good this time. He had been working over the winter in the steel mill. One day, as I heard it, he had come to work drunk, which wasn't too unusual. The foreman usually sent him home on those days, but on this particular day, for whatever reason, he didn't. There was an accident with some of the heavy machinery. Willie did something wrong. I wasn't too sure of the details. All I knew is that Willie would never walk again.

I felt terrible when I thought about the fact that I still hadn't visited him at home. But the more time that passed, the more difficult it had become to go.

"Things are fine, thank you," she replied to my question.

"How is Willie?" I asked, more specifically.

"He's all right," she said. "He's been in a better mood, lately. I think we've all been happier."

"Good," I said. "That's good."

"Why don't you stop by sometime?" she asked now. Every single hair on her head was the gray color of steel now.

"I'd like to," I said, holding her gaze.

"Come by on Saturday," she said then. "Gertrude and Willie will both be there. It'll be good for you to see her again, too." Her smile was strange.

I agreed, not sure exactly what she meant. There had been something strange about her that I couldn't really put my finger on. She seemed happier, but in a way that I couldn't quite understand. Perhaps it was just having her son back at home and needing her help more than ever.

CHAPTER 39

Myrtle's had added a few tables in front of the restaurant, in an attempt to compete with some of the more upscale cafes in town. I still preferred my old table inside, though. I didn't have as much time for lunch in those days as I had in days past, now that I worked much more closely with Mr. Durham. Still, it was good to get out and have lunch on my own every once in a while.

I was reading the newspaper one day, finishing up my food. There was a quote about *a change for the worse during the past year in feminine dress, dancing, manners, and general moral standards.* The writer asked everyone to *realize the serious ethical consequences of immodesty in girls' dress.* It was the sort of thing my Aunt would agree with, I thought. I was actually hoping she hadn't read it, because I could just imagine how it might get her juices flowing after dinner. There was something almost funny about it to me, though. I thought about the way girls had dressed when I was younger, and the way they were dressing now. I didn't really think they were behaving any differently than they always had.

Of course, I was older now, and I didn't go to too many parties or meet many young girls anymore. I had more important things on my mind. I wondered if Ambrose was having more fun than I was now. I was pretty sure he was. I hadn't told my Mother yet, but I really wanted to save my money and go visit him sometime in the next few years. I imagined us both meeting all sorts of girls then. Maybe we would even go to New York, and I could see the place where I was born.

In the process of turning a page, I let the paper drop momentarily, and caught the eye of a man who had been looking at me. It was only after I'd reached the next page and resumed my reading that I realized the face had been familiar. I cautiously dropped the paper again, and saw Jim Garrison, sitting alone on the other side of the room. He wore a small pair of glasses and he had a thin mustache now. He was dressed in a smart suit with a vest and fob. I wondered if I looked that old already.

I didn't know what to do. We had both seen each other, and it would be rude to pretend that I hadn't recognized him. I wanted to raise the paper again and hide behind it and wait for him to leave. I had no idea what his reaction would be to seeing me now. I didn't want to know.

I glanced over there again, and he happened to look up as he finished his drink. Now we were looking directly at each other. I gave him a smile and a nod, and looked back down at my paper, which was now resting on the table.

I could still feel him staring at me, though. I felt my ears and neck flush a little. He was still in my peripheral vision, and he hadn't moved. Should I raise up the paper again, as a sort of flimsy wall between us? That might make things more comfortable. As I started to move it, though, I saw him lift himself from his chair.

"Cobb Whittier," he said, standing above me now.

"Hello, Jim," I let the paper drop and stood, shaking his hand.

"I haven't seen you in here for a while," he said. I couldn't tell how he really felt about seeing me.

"No," I said. "I don't make it in that much anymore."

"Me neither," he said.

"Please," I motioned to the other chair. He looked at it, a bit surprised maybe, and then sat down, throwing open his jacket, his brow furrowed. I sat as well, and looked around, hoping that he couldn't tell how nervous I was. I was afraid that he would be able to read my mind somehow. I tried to banish any thoughts of his wife.

A few awkward moments passed, and it became clear that he wasn't going to say anything. His eyes were focused on the newspaper sitting on the table.

"So," I said finally, "how are things at the mill?"

"Oh, the same as always," he said, looking up. "I'm in charge full time now. That's why I don't get over to this part of town that much."

"Hmm."

"How is Durham doing?"

"Oh, he's doing well. I'm doing a lot more fieldwork with him now. It's interesting."

"Good, good. So you'll be replacing him someday?"

That wasn't really something that I had ever thought about. I still didn't know if Mr. Durham liked me that much or not. It was the type of thing Jim would think of first, though.

"I'm not sure about that," I said.

"You wouldn't like to?" he was staring at me directly now. He was one of those men who found real comfort in discussing business.

"Well, I don't know, exactly," I said.

"You never really had a plan for the future, did you?" he asked with a little smile, as if we had been best friends for years. It seemed like a strange thing to say.

"I suppose not," I replied. A few more moments of silence passed. He produced a large white handkerchief from his front pocket, removed his glasses, and began cleaning them.

"Would you like another drink?" I asked, just to say something. He was staring at the tabletop sullenly now, working the cloth around in little circles over each eyepiece, barely aware of what he was doing.

"No, no," he said. I nodded.

"So the mill's keeping you busy?" I asked pointlessly.

"Of course," he said. He held the glasses up toward the window and squinted through them. His eyes looked so small without them, I thought. He returned the glasses to his nose and put the handkerchief away. "Kate and I are doing well, though."

"Good, good," I said, my throat constricting.

"We're thinking about building a home out beyond the mill, maybe."

"That sounds great," I said.

I hadn't seen or heard anything from he or Kate since the day she closed the front door on me at the end of last summer. I hadn't asked anyone about them, either. I didn't really want to know. It was quite a surprise to suddenly be confronted with him now. I wasn't prepared at all.

Still, although I hadn't heard anything definite about them, I knew that she hadn't been pregnant. Or at least that she didn't have a child. The town was just too small. I would have heard something. I still didn't know why they had ended our arrangement, though. I'm surprised that I hadn't been more curious about that. I suppose other things had come up.

"Yes," he said. "It should be good."

"You'll have a lot more room?" I asked. I winced inwardly, hoping that I wasn't reminding him of my familiarity with their current home.

"Sure," he said.

"Well, good."

"Listen, uh, Cobb," he said. "I just…I just want you to know that, that things are all right." His eyes jumped up to mine and then back down a few times. His hands were clasped on the tabletop, and he was slowly rolling his thumbs, one over the other. I just nodded, not sure what he meant.

"Well," I said finally, "I didn't plan on running into you, but that…that's good."

"I hadn't planned on this either," he said quietly, smiling a little. "But I guess I should just at least say thanks, to you, for, well, for keeping things quiet. Kate and I…appreciate that." I nodded.

"Of course," I said. "I don't…I don't want you to worry about that. Don't even think about that."

He smiled in relief and unclasped his hands, placing them flat on the table, palms down. We both sat there in silence. I glanced at my watch.

"Something happened to me over there," he said suddenly, studying the backs of his hands. "Before my injury. It…it might help you understand."

I didn't know if he was waiting for a response.

"Well," I finally said, "you don't owe me any explanations or anything."

"I know, I know," he replied, a few fingers raising a little. "I just…it might help you understand."

I just sat there. His eyes slid back and forth.

"This was…this was before I got injured," he said. "We were making our way in…actually, toward the fight that did me in. There was one fella who I used to pal around with all the time. He and I went into this cottage one day. One of those with a sign hanging over the door that said 'Estaminet.' There were a lot of places like that. I know you saw them. We were tired from carrying equipment, and we went inside and ordered some beer."

He looked at me now, and took his hands off the table.

"We were treated like family there. That's how it always was. It was a French home…a whole family, but without the young men. Monsieur sat there, smoking his pipe by the fire, looking over our uniforms and our gear. Madame would cook for us, while she was watching Bebe playing nearby. The young Mamselle was sewing in the corner, looking us over as well. It was a family, you see?"

I nodded a little. He wanted to convey something, but I wasn't sure what it was. He pronounced the foreign words quickly and fluently.

"It was just like our families over here. They were missing their young men. But they welcomed us instead. The uniforms weren't all that different. We reminded them of their sons. So they welcomed us…trusted us."

He paused for a while, looking toward the far wall. Then he suddenly turned back to me.

"That's what I wanted, I knew. A family, back home. But that's something I'll never have now." He stared at me angrily. I thought he was about to lunge at me.

"And it's my fault," he said then, suddenly calm again. I was confused, to say the least. "You go to church, don't you?" he asked.

"Yes," I said.

"Did you go during the war at all? To see the chaplain or anything?"

"Well…not a whole lot."

"So you just go when your family goes?"

I didn't answer. He smiled a little.

"Don't worry…I was the same way. That's what I found out about myself over there. I was tested, and I failed. I don't know if you believe in all of that stuff…in church and everything…but I do. I definitely do. What happened to me, happened for a reason." He lowered his voice and moved in closer. "My injury I mean. It was my own sin, returned to me."

He sat back now and sighed, quickly at ease.

"I went back to that cottage a few times. I could speak a little French…more than my friend. But language didn't really matter when I looked at Mamselle. I looked at her until she started looking back at me. I didn't think she was going to, really. But she did. And then I knew that things might be bad. I didn't want to go back there. But I couldn't stop. They just made me feel so welcome. Of course, it wasn't that. That wasn't why I was going back…even if I tried to tell myself it was," he shook his head. "It was that girl. She was so pretty. I was still a kid, really…stupid."

I just listened.

"She…she was the school mistress in the town. The school marm. She seemed so young to me. So young to be doing that. But she did. I saw her outside sometimes, and you should've seen how people respected her. There was just something about her. Everything was so different…we were so far away. Another world. Nothing I did there could ever matter back here, in my life or my marriage. That's how I was thinking."

He kept shaking his head as he spoke.

"The school marm was a pretty important person in those towns. I found that out. She explained it all to me as well as she could, in simple French. I didn't understand it all, but I nodded along like I'd been speaking French all my life. And I'd learned a little over there. Whenever the Premier gave a speech, see, there was a Minister of Public Instruction who would send it out across the country to the school marms. Then they would read it to the pupils in school. So she really knew everything that was going on. Sometimes they would even tell us to talk to these women, if we came across them, because they might have news that we didn't even have yet. The three-o-clock telegraph bulletin would come in, and everyone would crowd around the post office for it after lunch everyday. And she could always explain everything to all of them. You should've seen the way they listened to her. Her voice…the way she spoke in French…it just, it did me in."

He was turning angry again now.

"When I think of that wonderful family…I can't even think of that father sitting there, smiling at me happily with his pipe in his hand. We couldn't really say anything to each other, since we didn't speak the same language. But it was just the way he looked at us, in our uniforms. He looked at us as if we were his own sons. And I feel like I really betrayed that trust."

I lifted my cup to my mouth, realizing too late that there was nothing left to drink. My world became the dark inside of the cup, my breath filling it and blowing back out at me. I pretended to drink and then put it back down. I was uncomfortable, to say the least.

"There was this new…this new loan they were trying to sell one day," he said, his eyes sharp with remembrance. "I remember they put up these placards, trying to get everyone to put money in the treasury of the country. She was there, explaining it to everyone. And I kept acting like I didn't understand. I could tell, the way she was looking, that she was interested in me too. I really wish she hadn't been.

"It was hard to tell, though, with the languages. I just wasn't sure, so I…I kept pushing it, just to see. We went back to the schoolhouse, because she had notes there, and she thought she could show it to me on paper. I'm sure she knew that I wasn't really interested in the loan at all. She should've just ignored me. Just another American boy far away from his wife. But she took me back there, and no one was there." He leaned in close, his voice dropping. "And I did what I shouldn't have done there. We both sinned together. We couldn't even really talk to each other, but I knew she enjoyed it, too. And you know, I didn't even feel that bad about it afterwards. That was my real problem…vanity. I still thought it was too far away from here to ever matter. How could my wife ever know? There was no way. There was no way it could come back to get me. I was stupid.

"Our squad moved on, and it was a few days later that I got hit. I knew it right away, too…I knew why it happened. I was being punished by God. You should've seen the way I got hit in the battle. It was so strange, a lot of the boys didn't even believe it until they saw how bad I was hurt. It was meant for me. From God. And I got to lie there in that hospital for the rest of the war and think about it.

"You can't imagine how terrible I felt. And I knew somehow...I knew even before they told me. I could never have a child. I would never have a family. I thought about my parents, then. I thought about what my father would say when they told him that he'd never have a grandson. They said I could never even...I could never even be with my wife again. I knew it before they said it, though. And I...I felt so much for her, out there then. I couldn't believe what I had done. The last time I was ever with a woman in that way...the last time I could ever be. And that girl doesn't even know, either. She doesn't even know that was my last time ever. I wished so badly that I had died out there. But that wasn't punishment enough...God did it perfectly."

He sat back again, his hands clawing at the tabletop, his fists opening and closing. His ears were a bright red, I noticed. He reached up and touched the mustache, as if he had just remembered that it was there.

I just sat there, quietly.

"Maybe you understand more now," he said. "Maybe you can see why, in a way, it was only fair. I wanted to have a child, yes. She wanted it more than I did. But also, also it was only fair for my wife to be...to be with someone else," his eyes dropped. He couldn't look at me now. "I had to punish myself that way. I didn't want to, but I had to. Because I'd never told her. I didn't tell her about it."

So last summer Jim had been trying to right a wrong. I wondered if one day he had simply decided that the debt was paid, and told his wife to turn me away at the door.

Had he ever told Kate his true reasons though? I wondered if I was the first person he was telling. Why would he tell me? Perhaps he simply had to tell someone. Maybe it made him feel better.

"So that's it," he said. "There was more going on than you thought, probably," he tried to laugh a little, but it sounded forced. "But I just thought maybe you'd like to know what was going on."

"Well," I said finally. My mouth was dry, and it came out weak. I cleared my throat and started again. "Well, once again, all of this is…is confidential, with me."

"Thanks," he mustered, nodding. "Listen," he stood suddenly. "I'd better get back. Let me get your lunch," he drew a bill from his pocket and let it fall onto the table.

I tried to protest, but no sound came out of my mouth. I was still thinking about everything else. I wanted to say something, but I didn't know what. So I just stood quickly, before he could leave, and extended my hand. He shook it.

"I…I like the mustache," I said, pointing at it.

"Thanks," he said. He nodded, his lips pressed together tightly. As he turned toward the door his glasses caught the light of the window and flashed, two glinting circles of pure white. And then he walked out.

CHAPTER 40

That Saturday I remembered to get the Jessie Weston book out of my room at last, to return to Gertrude. It had been there for a long while now, and I had found myself turning back to it on numerous occasions. Sometimes at night when I read parts of it, I could remember reading those parts for the very first time. I could almost feel myself sitting on that train with Ambrose, both of us enthusiastic about our silly errand to go find a bully and beat him up.

I felt guilty, of course, that I hadn't given it back to her sooner. My relationship with Gertrude had been strange. The more we saw of each other, the less we had to say, and the less comfortable it was. At least, that's how I would describe it. I wondered if she had that effect on everyone.

Their house was painted a different color. The fence and the porch were exactly the same, though. I found myself sneaking a glance at Dr. Crowe's window, just to see if he was watching me as I walked by. My Mother had told me that his health had deteriorated lately, and that he didn't leave home all that much anymore. He had supposedly put in a telephone, though, although I couldn't imagine who he had to call. Perhaps it was for emergency purposes, because of his condition. Dr. Morris had suggested that we get one this summer for that same reason. But my Aunt, of course, had been against it, claiming that she'd never needed one before.

There was a car in front of the Delgrew house. It was a black Tin Lizzie, sitting there as if it owned the street. I studied the car as I passed it, and my shimmering reflection flashed in its dark surface. The car certainly looked clean. Could it possibly belong to the Delgrews? I couldn't imagine it.

An overturned watering can rested on the grass by the porch, and I reached out with my foot and pushed it upright as I passed. I made my way up the steps, listening for any noise from the house. I heard nothing, though. Mrs. Delgrew hadn't really given me an exact time to come by. Perhaps they were out somewhere. I knocked on the door.

I heard male voices, and then footsteps coming toward the door. I was expecting Mrs. Delgrew or Gertrude. But when the door opened, a man was standing before me. It wasn't Willie, though. He smiled broadly and extended his hand. It was Jack Wolfe.

"Well, hello there," he said. "It's been a little while, Cobb."

"Hello," I mustered. He shook my hand vigorously.

"What do you think?" he asked, looking past me. I turned and saw that he meant the car.

"It's great," I said.

"Sure," he said. "When Durant brought out the Stor, Ford dropped the price to compete. Three hundred and twenty dollars. Can you believe it?"

"No," I said quietly, shaking my head.

"Well, I guess the old boy can afford it. They're calling him a billionaire now, can you believe it? You know how much he makes in one day?"

"Who?"

"Henry Ford. Two hundred thousand dollars. In one day."

"Wow."

"Come in, come in," he said. He was wearing a wool sweater with a colored pattern on it. I stepped inside. His presence confused me. Was this the right house? "We're all in the parlor," he said.

"How've you been?" he asked, leading me through the little room where I'd eaten so many times before. There were a few small differences, I noticed. The wood of the cabinets was darker, maybe. And there were a few flowers on the wall, pressed between glass. I wondered if they had come from the yard.

"Fine," I said. "Fine."

We stepped through the door and into the parlor of the house.

"Look who I brought," said Jack loudly. I just smiled and looked around.

"Colbert," said Mrs. Delgrew with a smile. She was sitting on the couch.

"Hey, there he is," said Willie. He was seated in a low wheelchair near the fireplace. Gertrude smiled but said nothing. She was standing on the other side of Willie near the window, one hand on the back of his chair. Her hair was a bit shorter, I noticed, with little waves above her ears. She wore a blazer and shirt. It looked like a man's clothing. That's what women were wearing then though. It was strange to see her dressed as if she cared about the current style.

There were two small chairs near the couch, and the walls were of a dark wood color. On my left was the hall that led to the bedrooms. I had been in this room before, although only briefly, and that had been a long time ago.

"Well, come in," said Mrs. Delgrew.

"Yes, sit down," said Jack, his hand on my shoulder.

"You two have met before, I see," Mrs. Delgrew said as I moved toward one of the chairs, keeping a frozen smile on my face. I just nodded.

"Yes, yes, we've met," said Jack, who walked through the center of the room, around the coffee table, and sat next to Mrs. Delgrew on the couch.

"I'll bet Cobb was confused to see you answer the door," chuckled Willie. "Sorry about that...he just jumped up. I would've done it, but I knew he'd beat me to the jump," he laughed some more, and his mother and sister both smiled the same smile of humility.

Willie's eyes looked a bit sunken in behind his glasses. I could make out circles of grayish shadow around each one. Aside from that, though, he looked perfectly normal, as if he was simply sitting in a chair, tired out from running around all day. I smiled back at him, ignoring the fact that he would never run again.

"I was surprised," I said, trying not to look at his legs. There was a bright orange crocheted blanket resting across his lap. I was sure that Gertrude had made it for him. I could see his ankles below the blanket, though, just between the ends of his trousers and his oxfords. They looked thin and insubstantial to me.

I wondered what it was like not to be able to feel a part of yourself. His legs were attached to him, but they had become foreign objects that he had to carry around, now. Would it be better to just cut them off? That was terrible, of course. It reminded me of Jim, in a way. It didn't matter where the injury took place.

"Well, Colbert, it certainly was nice of you to drop by today," said Mrs. Delgrew.

"I hope it's all right," I said to her.

"Of course it is. I asked you to, didn't I?"

"Yes," I said.

"We've been wondering how you're doing. How is your Aunt, the poor thing?"

"Oh, she's doing all right," I answered. "Doctor Morris comes by every few weeks now, and he says that she should be just fine as long as she doesn't strain herself." A wave of nervousness suddenly washed over me. I realized, as I spoke, that all of them were watching me intently. I was sure that I sounded foolish. I continued to talk about my Aunt, hoping that my voice didn't give away my discomfort. I had caught Gertrude's eye as I spoke, as well as Jack's. Now I looked toward Willie, and saw that he was still studying me as I spoke.

What was Jack doing here? His presence angered me, in a way. I felt close to these other people, and I'd thought that this would be almost like a little homecoming. I had imagined how happy they would be that I had finally stopped by. Jack's being there meant that things were different, somehow, but I still didn't know how. Maybe Mrs. Delgrew had run into him and asked him to stop by as well, I thought. Perhaps he'd been delivering some bolts of fabric to Gertrude or something.

"Well," Mrs. Delgrew was saying, "I hope she feels better."

"You still in the insurance business?" asked Willie.

"Yes," I said, turning to him now. "I am. It's not so bad," I glanced up at Gertrude, who was looking at her mother now.

"Oh, Colbert, would you like something to drink?" asked Mrs. Delgrew.

"No," I said. "No thank you."

"Are you sure?"

"Yes, I'm fine. Thank you, though."

There was a moment of awkward silence. I'm sure that it wasn't really that long, but for me it seemed almost intolerable. I stood up and held the book out toward Gertrude.

"Here you are," I said. "I'm sorry I held onto it for so long."

Everyone seemed confused. But then she stepped forward and took it with a little smile. She just held it. She had nowhere to put it, of course. Suddenly I felt foolish for having given it to her like that.

"Thank you," she said.

"Hey, Cobb," said Willie. "You remember that time they had us holed up in the dug-out and they were hitting us from way over on the other ridge?"

I smiled, and nodded. Willie turned toward Jack now.

"They were shooting at us...they knew we were in there, but they didn't know exactly where. So they started aiming all over the place. They moved down a line, trying to hit us. And we didn't move...we all just sat there and waited. I thought we were gonna die that day.

Didn't you?" He had turned back toward me now. Jack was leaning forward, feigning interest.

"I sure did," I said.

Mrs. Delgrew stood and walked past me.

"I'll let you boys talk," she said, going into the kitchen.

"Well, they missed us," Willie went on. "Nobody really said much, but it went right over us. From one side to the other. Whatever calculation they were using…however many feet, they were off by just a little. I don't think I've ever seen so many grown men with such terror on their faces." He laughed a little, and I did too. Gertrude walked slowly around behind me, and then moved toward the couch. Jack slid over, and she sat beside him.

"Who was that fella who we thought would never crack?" Willie asked me. "You know, he thought he was a real tough guy. Irishman."

"James O'Malley," I said.

"That's right," he laughed. "I remember. I've never seen somebody's face so white."

I laughed. Willie almost had tears in his eyes, he was laughing so hard. Just as his laughter died, though, he had a far off look.

"That guy was so crooked," Willie was saying. "He always had something going on. I don't know what old O'Malley did after the war, but I wouldn't be surprised if we found out he was leasing a part of the Teapot Dome oil field himself."

I laughed a little.

"I think that was the scariest part of all, though," Willie was saying now, wiping his eyes with the back of his sleeve and getting serious. "The bombs."

I sat back in my chair. Then I thought of something to say.

"You know what I've heard?" I asked. They all looked at me. "I've heard that so many bombs went off in some places that they churned the soil up so much that these flowers started poking up. Flowers that nobody's seen since the Middle Ages." I glanced at all of them. "Can you believe that?"

"Really?" asked Willie. I could tell he was interested.

"I doubt that," said Jack, sitting back a little himself. Still, he looked back and forth between Willie and me, smiling. I wondered what he thought about Debs and everyone being pardoned. I wondered if he ever thought about Henry at all. Maybe he never even thought about any of it. Maybe no one remembered anything. Maybe that was the only way to go on. That was the same year Fatty Arbuckle was exonerated, too, I think. Everyone was forgiven. Everyone got away.

"Well, why not?" Willie said, leaning forward. Could he lean forward, or had it been just my imagination? "If we can dig up the city of Ur and the tomb of Tutankhamen...those were thousands of years old, right? And we did that on purpose. So why not turn up a few old flowers by accident?"

He was right, I thought. They had just found both of those things, and they were ancient. Thought to be long dead, I'm sure. Things had a way of coming back around, if we let them. I was nodding.

"I guess I just never saw any of those bombs up close, boys," said Jack. "So maybe you're right. It's just an experience I didn't get to have. I know the war made some changes, though. I've seen some of its effects. You know what we're doing over at the factory now? The new women's cotton...well, *undies*, sorry, dear...they've got us dying them with surplus khaki dye. They're calling them *ivory* now. Can you believe it? Surplus khaki dye."

Gertrude was looking out the window, embarrassed at the topic.

"Really?" I said.

"Sure."

"It has been a while, hasn't it?" Willie was saying, looking at me. I wasn't sure if he'd heard Jack at all. "When was the last time I saw you, Cobb?"

"I think it was at Drake's house, actually," I said. The memory of Ralph Lockehart and our conversation that night caused my heart to leap suddenly. I was so close to Jack. My mind was racing, hoping that I wouldn't give anything away about what I knew. Would he remember that Drake had a party the night of his speech? Probably not. "It was a party that he had last summer."

"Are you sure?" Willie looked confused. He looked down at the blanket and studied it, twisting some of the fringed brown and orange yarn in his fingers. I thought I saw his face turn a little red then. He didn't remember, I could tell.

"What did you think of the book?" It was Gertrude. I turned to her. She stared at me expectantly. She looked so young to me still. The two men were looking at me now, too. I was on the spot again. In a way, I felt as if I had been since I'd walked in the house. She lifted the book up and waved it at me.

"Oh," I said. "I…I enjoyed it. I thought it was great, actually. I read it over and over." I realized that I had probably been a bit too enthusiastic.

"Really?" she asked.

"Sure," I said. I felt silly, so I decided to downplay my enthusiasm now. "Of course, I haven't given it much thought lately. I've had a lot on my mind. Charles Robertson and Jesse Barnes both pitched no hitters this year, after all."

She smiled a little, slowly, as if she wanted to laugh.

"What is this?" asked Jack, taking it from her and turning over the cover.

"It's just a book," she said.

"Hmmm," he replied, returning it. "Well, Cobb, it was certainly nice seeing you again. Unfortunately, I must be going now…I have some business." He stood. Gertrude and I stood as well, and I shook his hand as he offered it. "I'm sure I'll see you around town," he said, smiling happily. "I hope your Aunt feels better."

"Thank you," I replied. He and Gertrude went into the kitchen, and I sat back down. It was just Willie and me now.

"I didn't even shake your hand when you came in, pal," he said. I stood and leaned over, taking his hand and shaking it. We both smiled and nodded, and I sat back down. He looked at the floor now, lost in his own thoughts. I could hear Mrs. Delgrew talking to Jack and Gertrude in the kitchen.

"That sure was an interesting Christmas we had over there, wasn't it?" said Willie. I thought about that Christmas Eve night, and the soldier hanging in the barn.

I nodded. A few more moments of silence passed. I heard the front door open and close. I looked out the window, but the side of Dr. Crowe's house was unchanged.

"Mama says you helped out...a few times...around here," he said now, indicating the house.

I nodded again.

"Thanks," he said. "I'm sure you really helped her out. Crowe over there is getting a little old," he pointed his thumb at the window with a smile.

"It was my pleasure," I said.

Silence again. It was as if he wanted to say something, but couldn't.

Mrs. Delgrew and Gertrude came back into the room. I stood up until Gertrude reached the couch and sat down. Mrs. Delgrew remained standing behind me, motioning for me to sit. When I did, she looked over at Willie, an excited expression on her face. I had never seen her like this.

"Well?" she asked Willie. "Did you tell him?"

Willie looked at her.

"No," he said. "I thought Gertrude was going to."

We all turned back to Gertrude. It was odd, seeing the sister and brother so close together. Their faces were so alike.

"Well, someone tell him," Mrs. Delgrew said. "Gertrude."

Gertrude and I looked at each other. It was difficult to look at her, for some reason. She looked back to her mother, and then down again, at the floor.

"Did you wonder why he was here?" Mrs. Delgrew asked me. I turned toward her. "Jack," she clarified. "They're engaged. What do you think, Colbert?" asked Mrs. Delgrew. "I wanted to tell you...not many people know about it yet."

They were all looking at me now.

"I think...it's wonderful," I said with a smile. "Congratulations." Gertrude looked back at me, but I wouldn't really call what was on her face a smile. She was a strange girl. Very little that she did would surprise me, but this certainly did.

"The wedding is going to be in August," said Mrs. Delgrew.

"That's fantastic," I said. "Wow," I shook my head a little. "Congratulations again."

"Thank you," said Gertrude.

"You helped us out so much around here," Mrs. Delgrew was saying to me now. "It's like you're one of the family, so we wanted you to know."

"Well, thank you," I said. "I'm honored." I didn't feel like one of the family at all, though. I couldn't have felt more out of place.

There was a knock on the door then.

"Oh, that's probably Misses Poole," she said. "If she brought the girls, they'll want to congratulate us. Excuse me." She made her way back into the kitchen, and the three of us sat there.

We heard her open the door, and women's voices drifted in from the kitchen.

"Are you surprised?" asked Gertrude finally, looking at me.

"Of course," I said. "I mean...well, I had no idea."

"I think Jack's a great fella," said Willie.

"Sure," I said, looking back and forth between them. What did they want me to say? They were clearly waiting for something.

"You don't know him that well, do you?" she asked me.

"Well, no," I said.

"What do you think of him?" asked Willie.

They were both eagerly awaiting my response. I marveled at how alike they looked now. Mrs. Delgrew was in the kitchen talking to whoever it was that had come in.

Should I tell them all that I knew about Jack? About the type of man he really was, and the things he was capable of? Perhaps it was my duty. I knew things that no one else knew, after all.

There was something pathetic about her, then, as she watched me and waited. I thought about the type of wife that she would be. Part of me thought she would be exactly like her own mother, and part of me thought that she would be nothing like that. I'm sure she had been enjoying herself immensely lately. The Nineteenth Amendment had been officially declared constitutional earlier that year. I could imagine how happy she would have been at that. They would be very happy together. It was a world for them, it seemed. More and more.

I remembered something I had just read a few weeks before in one of my Mother's magazines. I had been paging through it out of boredom one evening, and it said something about the new woman that stuck with me. It was something about how she would never knit you a necktie, but she would go skiing along with you. I imagined Gertrude and Jack skiing somewhere together, happily. They were the same age, I thought. I'm sure they felt the same about a lot of things that I didn't even think about. Perhaps it wasn't such a big surprise, after all.

I looked at the book, which was now lying face down on the little table beside the couch, and I thought about all the books she had given me to read. That seemed so long ago, now. That was another person, not me. I remembered the first time I met her, sitting at the table in the kitchen, when she asked for my help in finding her brother.

Maybe Jack had changed. Maybe she had changed him. I had no idea. But in a way, it didn't really matter.

Gertrude was smarter than I was, of course. Willie was too. And yet, I knew what they didn't know. If Gertrude was so smart, she should have seen through him, I thought. She should have been able to tell, by herself, who Jack really was. And look what had happened to poor Willie. Maybe I was as smart as they were, after all.

Mrs. Delgrew laughed loudly in the kitchen. The whole house was happy now. I thought back to a few days ago when I had run into her in the drugstore. She had seemed strangely happy even then. I had assumed it was because Willie was home, but I knew now that it was really because of this. This was a change in their family. This was a move forward. They had been stagnant for a long time. This was a positive change, the type of thing my own family might be jealous over.

Jack was intelligent, and handsome, and I'm sure that he had some money. So, in the end, it would be a cruel thing, I decided, to tell them the truth. I didn't really know what Gertrude thought of me, or if she even thought of me at all. But there was a poetic justice, it seemed, in my withholding the truth from her, at last.

I looked at Willie, sitting there in the chair with wheels. He would never leave that chair again. I simply couldn't burst the bubble of happiness that this family was now floating on. I couldn't take that away from them. I had no reason to, really. Another secret to keep to myself.

"I've heard he's a good guy," I said with a smile. They both smiled as well, truly sincere smiles. They were like children in that moment. I wondered why my approval meant so much to them.

And just like that, I considered any debt I might have had to the Delgrew family to be paid. I had declined to take away their happiness. My life and my fate had been intertwined with theirs ever since that Christmas Eve night just after the end of the war. The rest of the guys that had been there had all gotten out of it. But not me. I had put in my time, and done what I could to make things better. And now, when I had a real choice, I chose to allow them to be happy. And I felt a palpable release. Debs, Fatty Arbuckle, Henry, and now me. All released at last.

Mrs. Delgrew entered with two women, and introduced me to them. They started to talk almost at once, crowding toward Gertrude with congratulations. I said my goodbyes to both of them, shaking Willie's hand and congratulating Gertrude once again, who smiled and nodded in return. Mrs. Delgrew let me out the front door. I could tell she wanted to get back to the parlor.

I stepped outside. I heard music floating on the wind, coming from somewhere. Either a phonograph or a radio. I listened for the buzz of the telephone in Dr. Crowe's house, but I didn't hear anything. What a world.

I turned and strained my neck, trying to get a glimpse between the houses and into the Delgrews' back yard. I was wondering if anything had ever taken root there. I couldn't really see though, from where I was, so I started home.

I took my time walking across town. I thought about all of the connections I had to everyone here. And I could feel, somehow, the presence of my father, too. Not through some silly seance, but through something real, stretching across time and circumstance proudly, each of us claiming one another.

I thought about all the people I saw in Europe, and then never saw again. I thought about all the guys from my squad. I carried a piece of each of them with me now. Sure, they might have changed a lot since then, but the good part was that they would always be the same to me.

The same was true of my brother Henry, of course. I wondered if he ever thought of me, wherever he was. And I realized that he himself was different things to different people. He was an angel to his Mother, just like her other son who had passed away as an infant. He was a struggling spirit to my Aunt, one which she expected to join soon. He was a strange, deceitful man to my cousin Ambrose. He was an enemy to Jack Wolfe, perhaps never forgiven.

To me, though, he was always a boy, the other part of me, the presence often at my side. And he would remain that way for the rest of my life. In the aftermath of everything, the memory of the child is what grew back in my mind, and pushed all of the others aside.

It was like the Medieval flowers returning to the bombed out fields in France. The same fields that my father had worked as a boy. He knew, somehow, wherever he was, that they had returned. I imagined them as the most beautiful things on Earth, just waiting for the right time to resurface. Their roots must have gone so deep that they had never really died.

About the Author

Joseph Kerwin graduated Phi Beta Kappa from the University of Tulsa with a Bachelor of Arts degree in English, With Honors. He earned his Master of Arts in Literature, With Distinction, from DeP-aul University. He is the winner of the Satin and English Scholar Awards and a member of American Mensa. He currently lives and works in the San Diego area with his wife Regan.

0-595-25248-(